Love ♡ at ♡ Fourteen

Fuka Mizutani

4

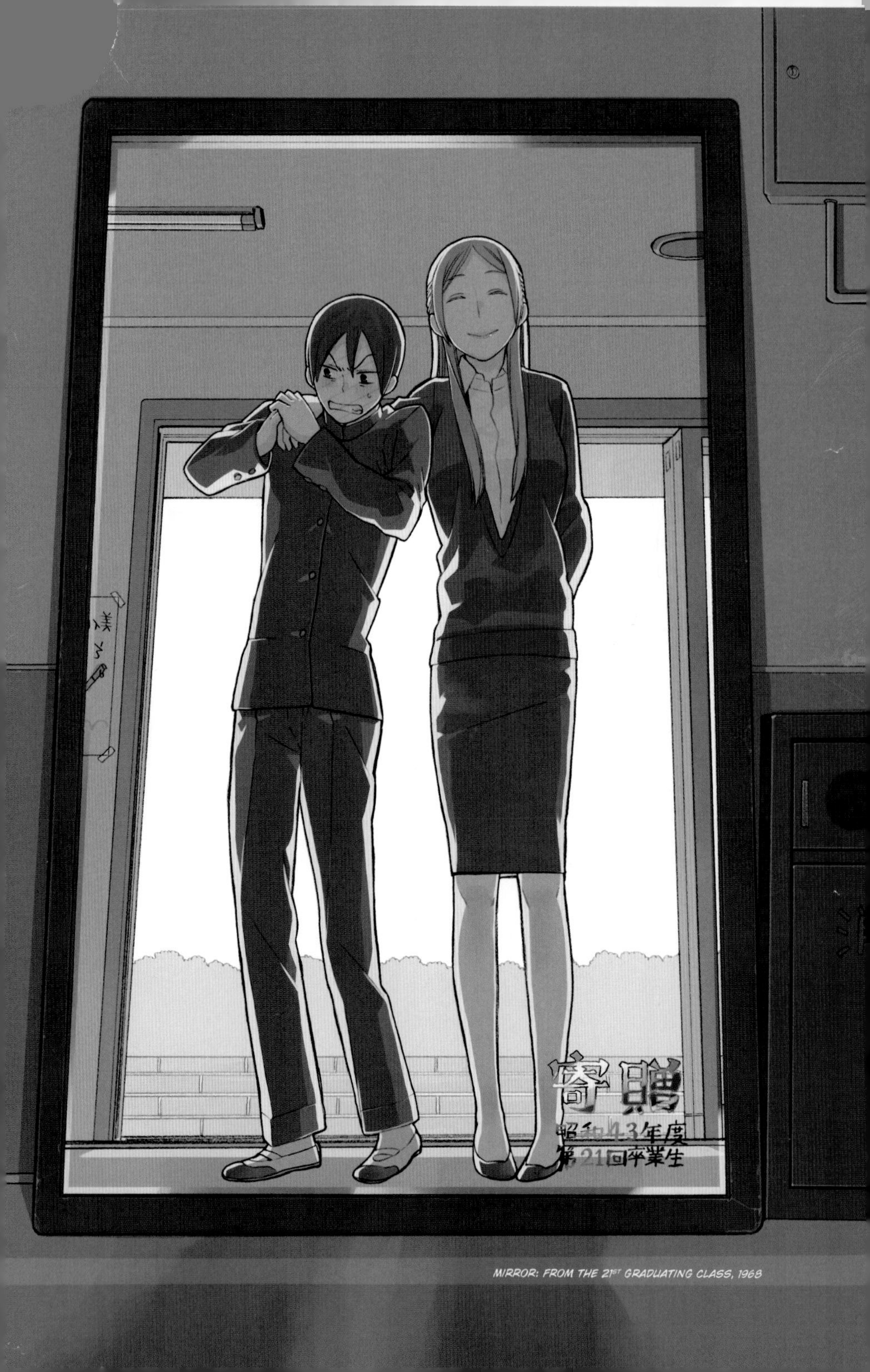
寄贈
昭和43年度
第21回卒業生
MIRROR: FROM THE 21ST GRADUATING CLASS, 1968

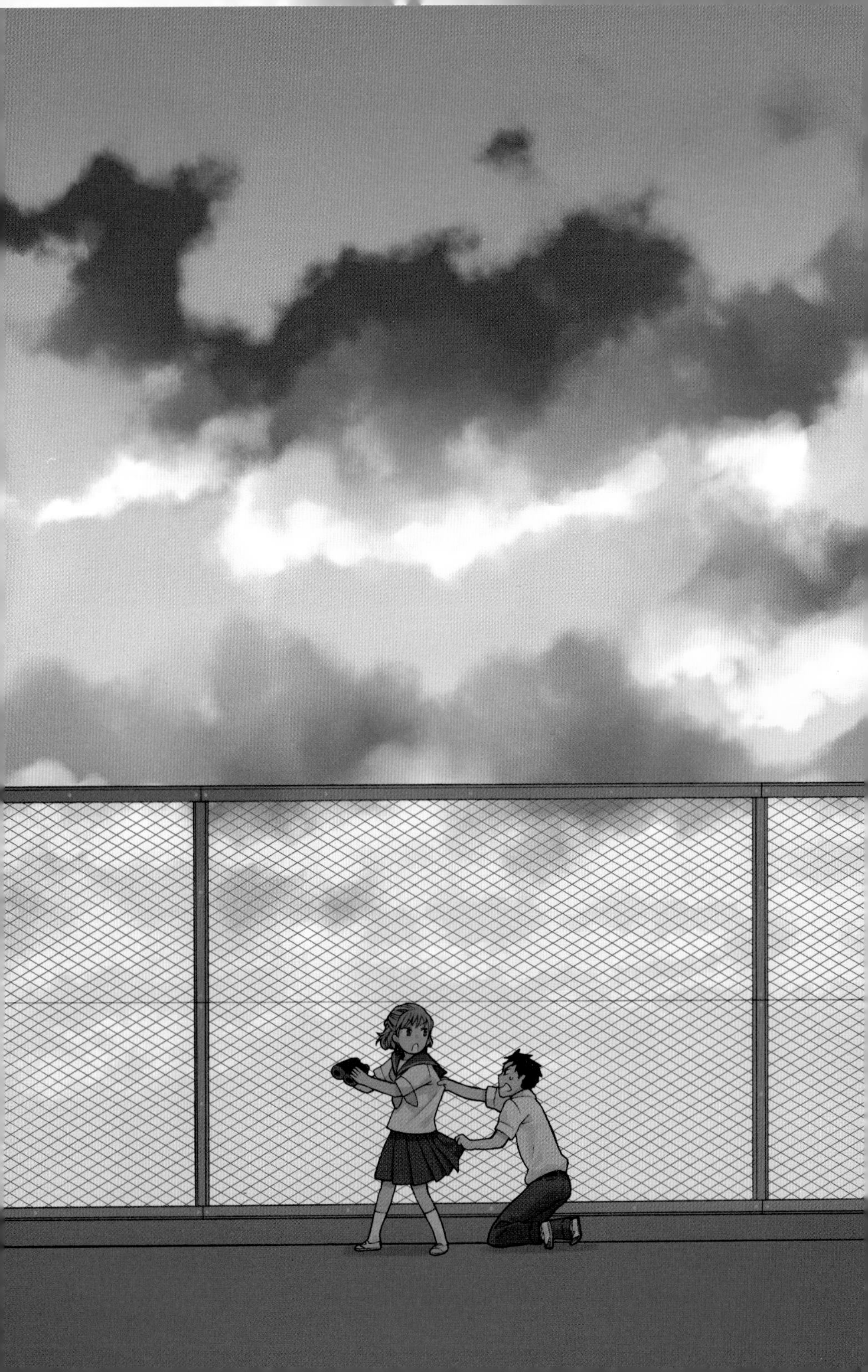

Contents

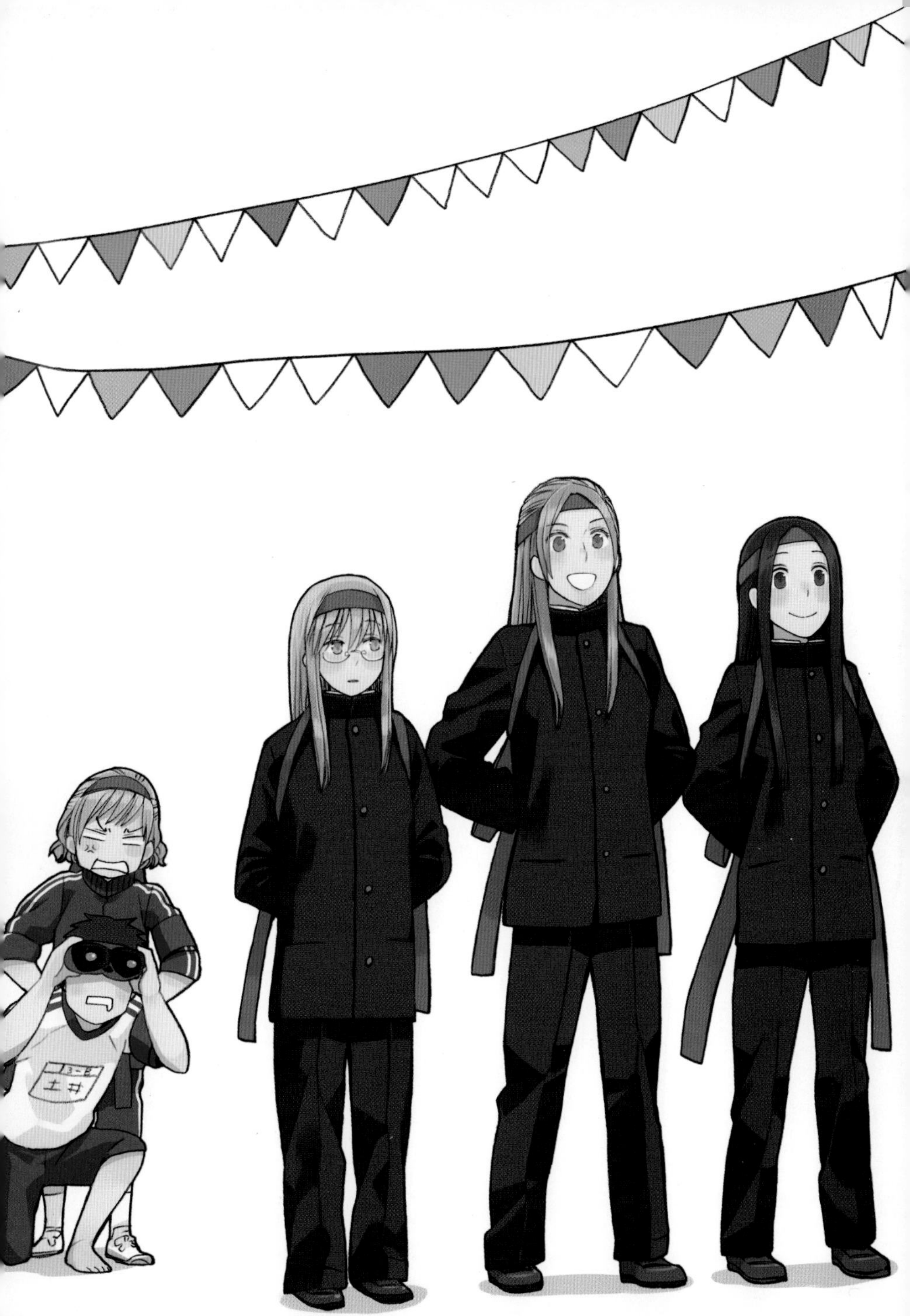

SHIRT: DOI

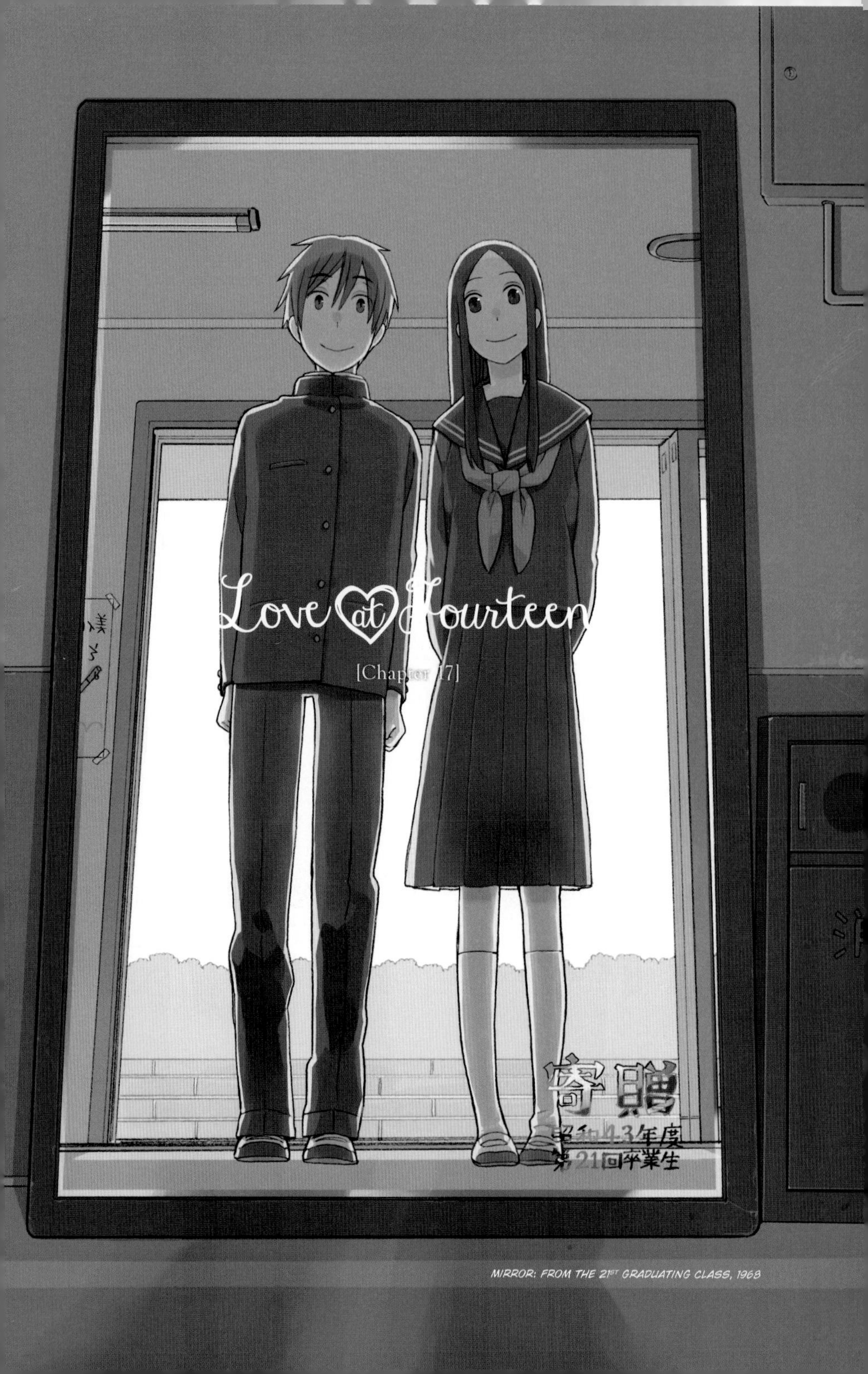
Love at Fourteen
[Chapter 17]
寄贈
昭和43年度
第21回卒業生
MIRROR: FROM THE 21ST GRADUATING CLASS, 1968

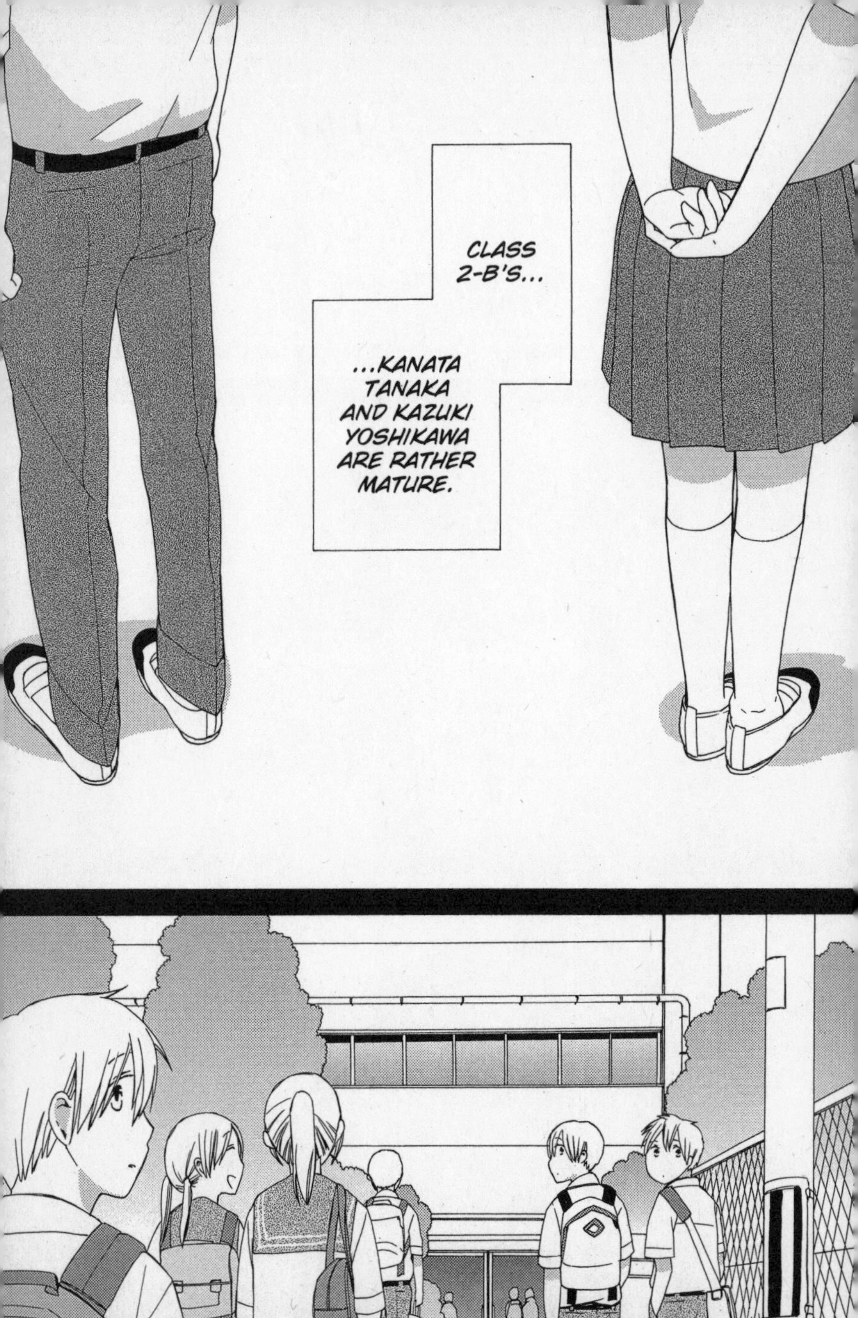
CLASS 2-B'S...
...KANATA TANAKA AND KAZUKI YOSHIKAWA ARE RATHER MATURE.

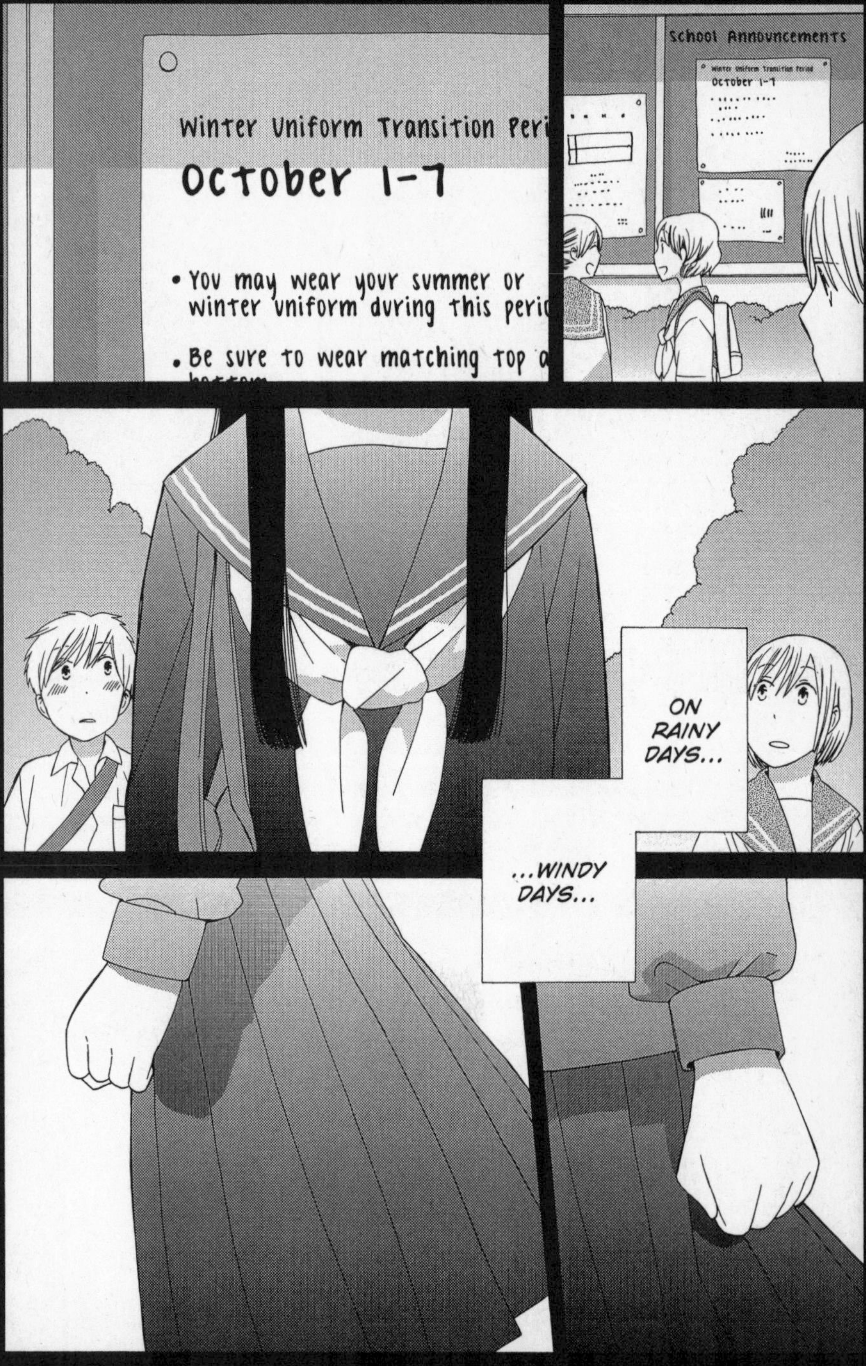
School Announcements
Winter Uniform Transition Period
October 1-7
Winter Uniform Transition Peri
October 1-7
• You may wear your summer or winter uniform during this peri
• Be sure to wear matching top a
ON RAINY DAYS...
...WINDY DAYS...

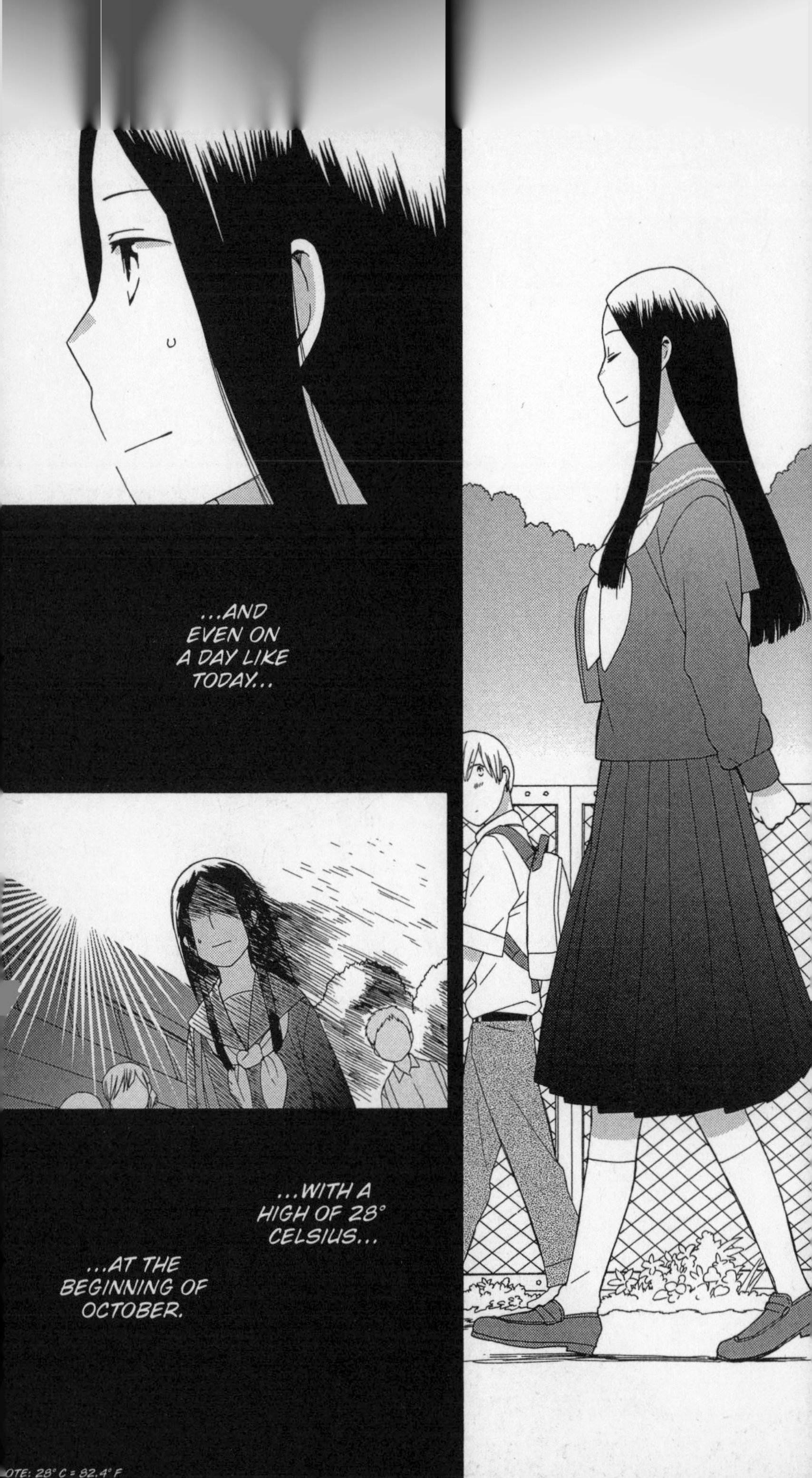
...AND EVEN ON A DAY LIKE TODAY...
...WITH A HIGH OF 28° CELSIUS...
...AT THE BEGINNING OF OCTOBER.

OTE: 28° C = 82.4° F

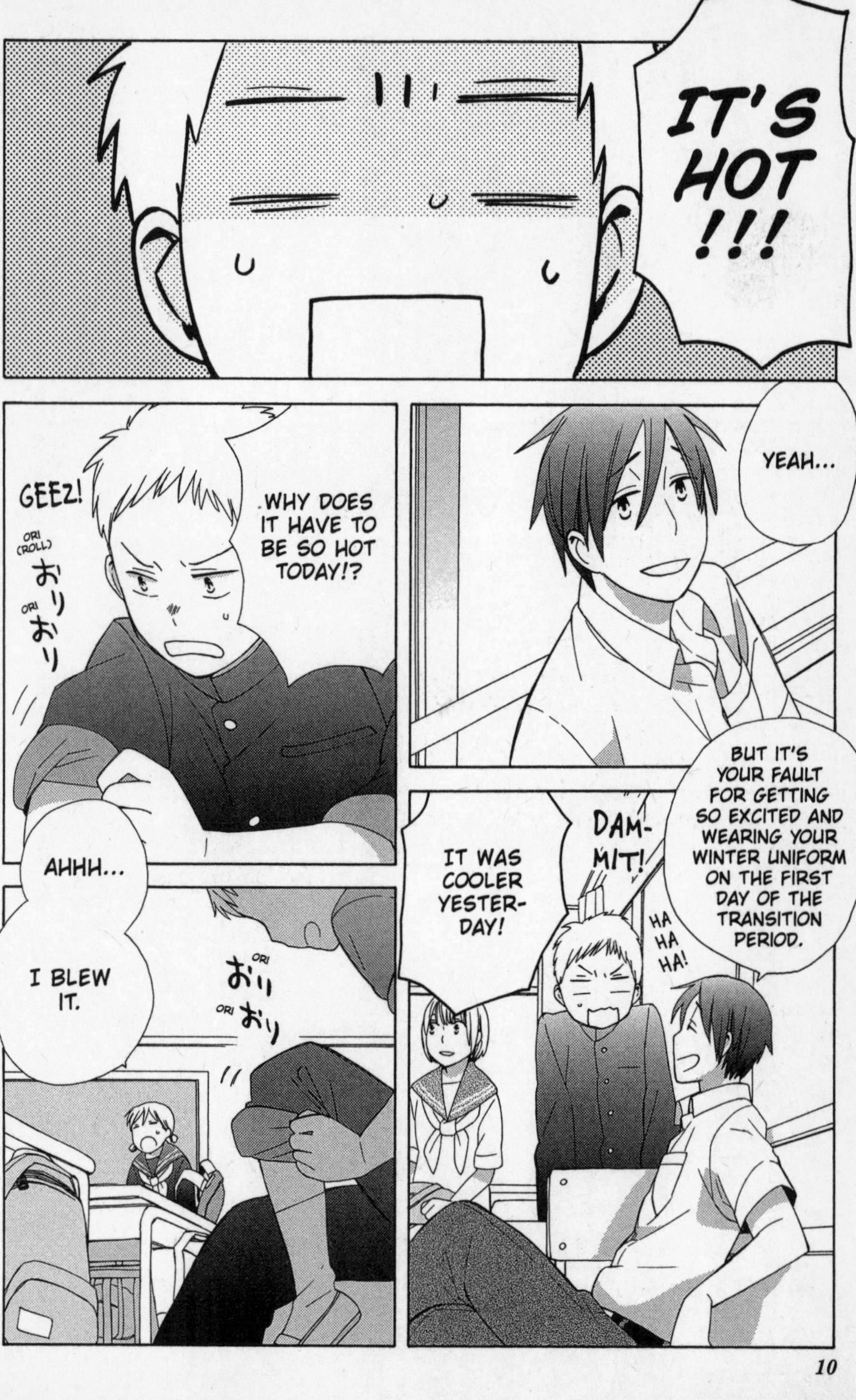
IT'S HOT!!!
YEAH...
GEEZ!
WHY DOES IT HAVE TO BE SO HOT TODAY!?
ORI (ROLL) おり ORI おり
BUT IT'S YOUR FAULT FOR GETTING SO EXCITED AND WEARING YOUR WINTER UNIFORM ON THE FIRST DAY OF THE TRANSITION PERIOD.
HA HA HA!
DAM-MIT!
IT WAS COOLER YESTER-DAY!
AHHH...
I BLEW IT.
ORI おり ORI おり

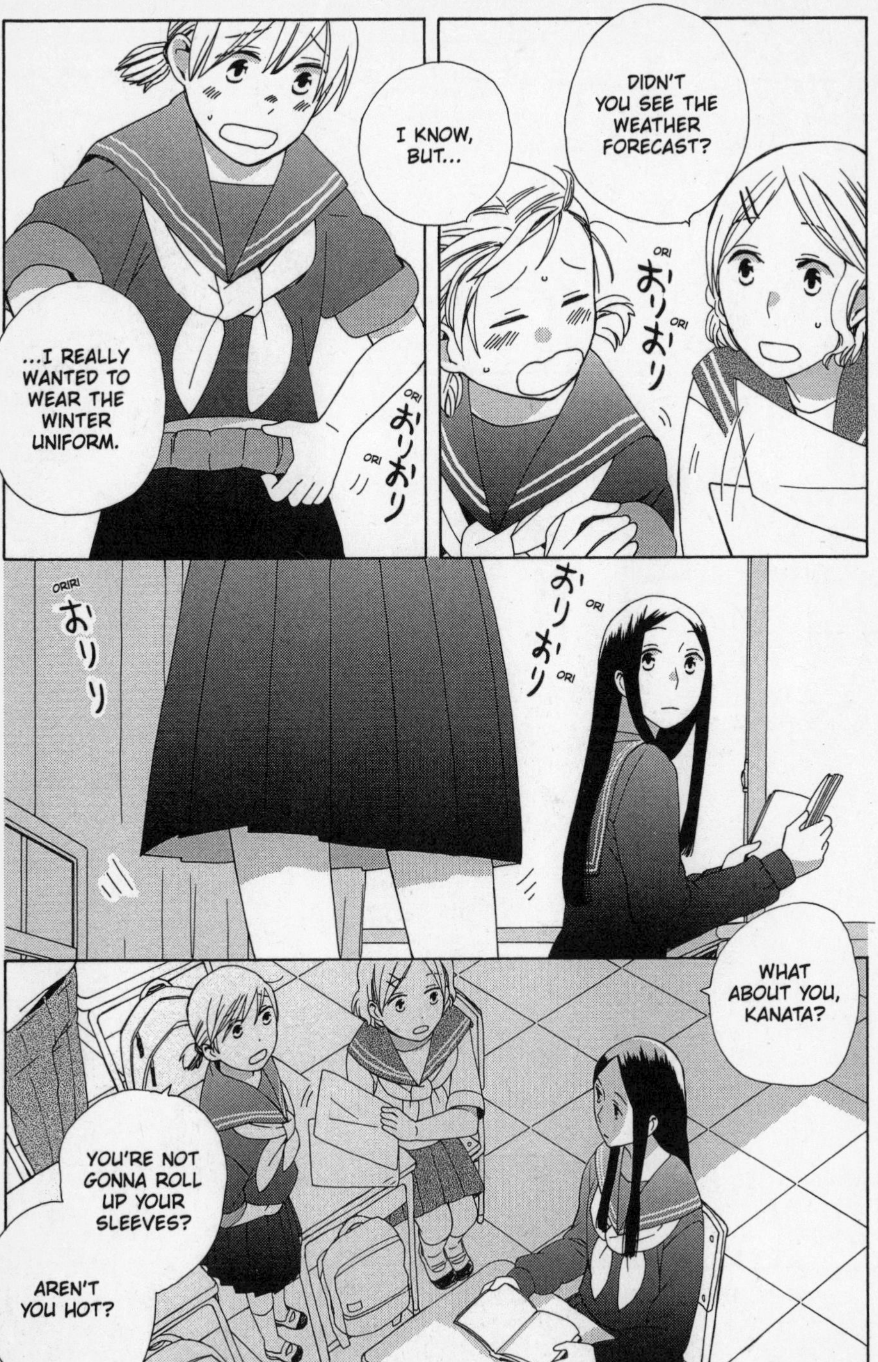
DIDN'T YOU SEE THE WEATHER FORECAST?
I KNOW, BUT...
ORI おりおり ORI
...I REALLY WANTED TO WEAR THE WINTER UNIFORM.
ORI おりおり ORI
おりおり ORI ORI
ORIRI おりり
WHAT ABOUT YOU, KANATA?
YOU'RE NOT GONNA ROLL UP YOUR SLEEVES?
AREN'T YOU HOT?

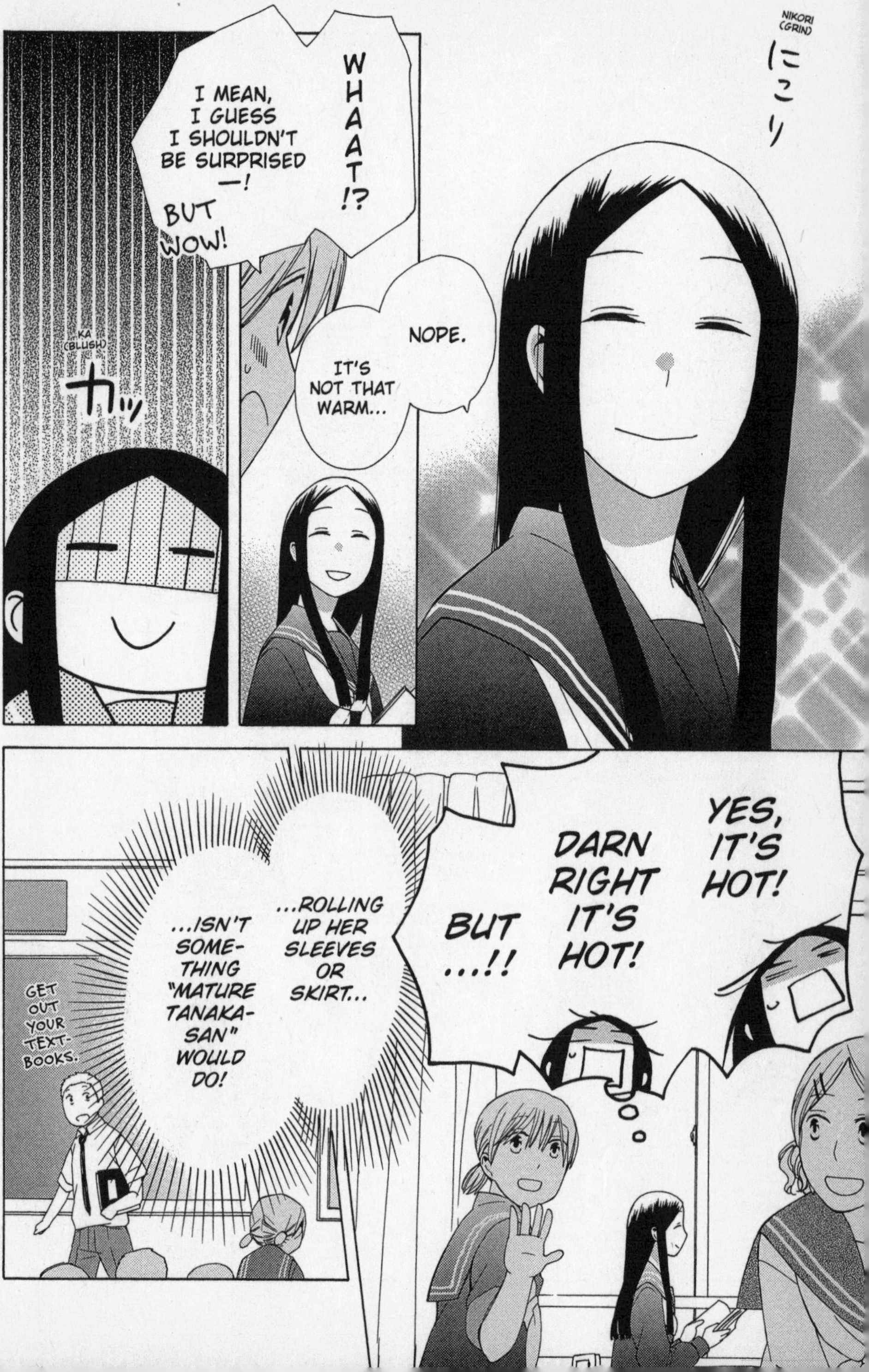
NIKORI (GRIN)
にこり
WHAAT!?
NOPE.
IT'S NOT THAT WARM...
I MEAN, I GUESS I SHOULDN'T BE SURPRISED—!
BUT WOW!
KA (BLUSH)
カッ
YES, IT'S HOT!
DARN RIGHT IT'S HOT!
BUT...!!
...ROLLING UP HER SLEEVES OR SKIRT...
...ISN'T SOMETHING "MATURE TANAKA-SAN" WOULD DO!
GET OUT YOUR TEXT-BOOKS.

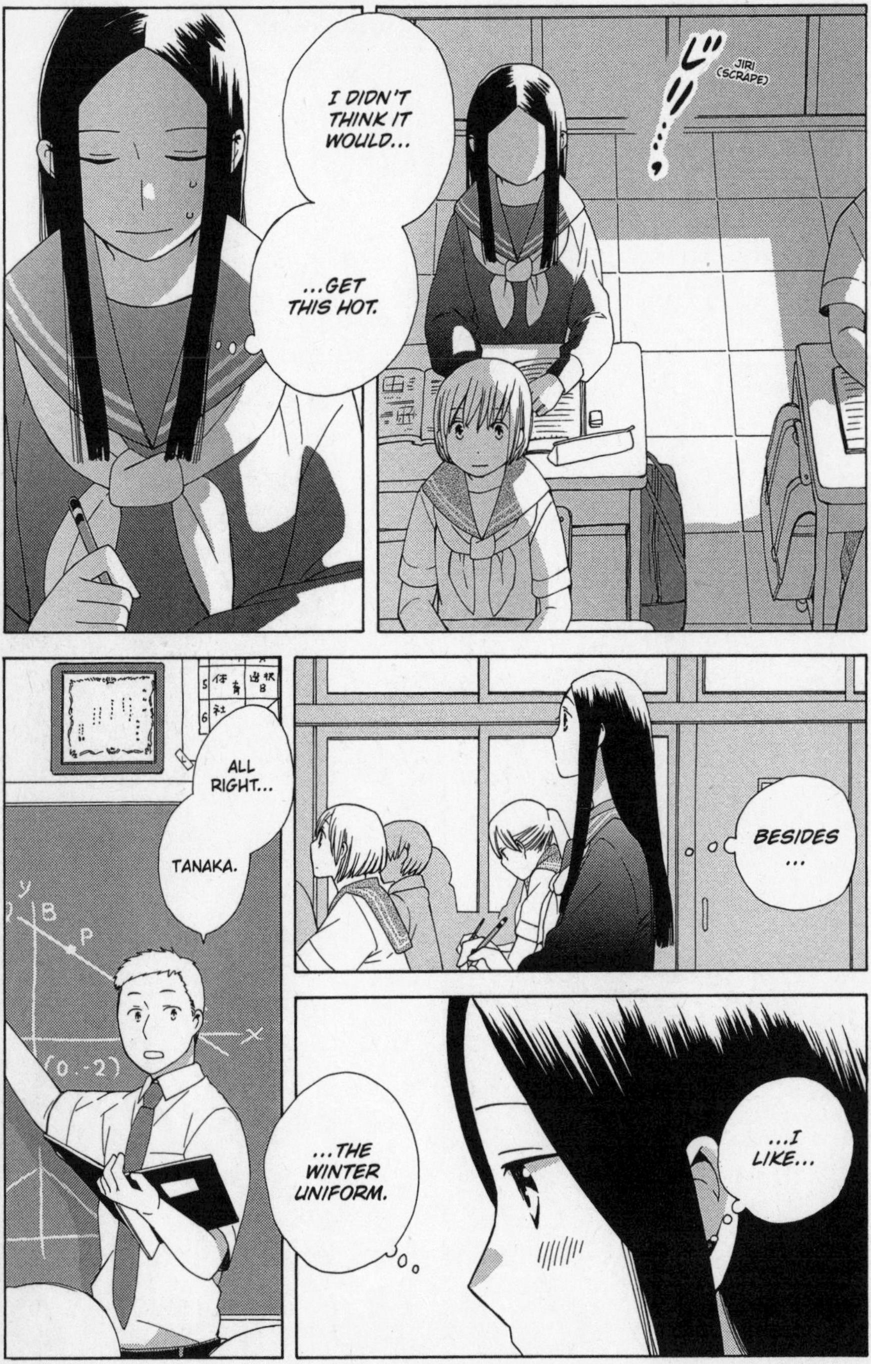
JIRI (SCRAPE)
I DIDN'T THINK IT WOULD...
...GET THIS HOT.
BESIDES...
...I LIKE...
...THE WINTER UNIFORM.
ALL RIGHT...
TANAKA.

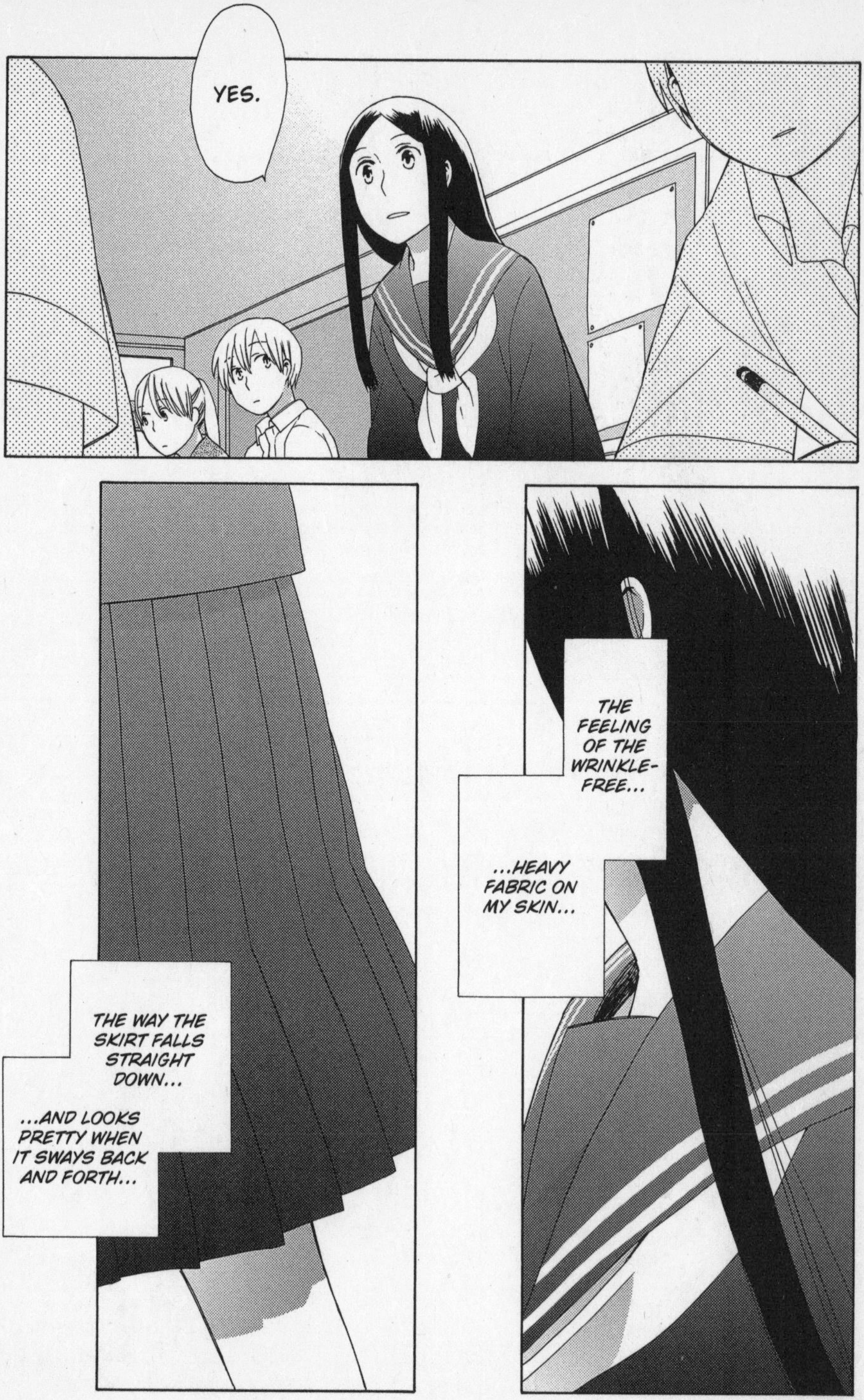
YES.
THE FEELING OF THE WRINKLE-FREE...
...HEAVY FABRIC ON MY SKIN...
THE WAY THE SKIRT FALLS STRAIGHT DOWN...
...AND LOOKS PRETTY WHEN IT SWAYS BACK AND FORTH...

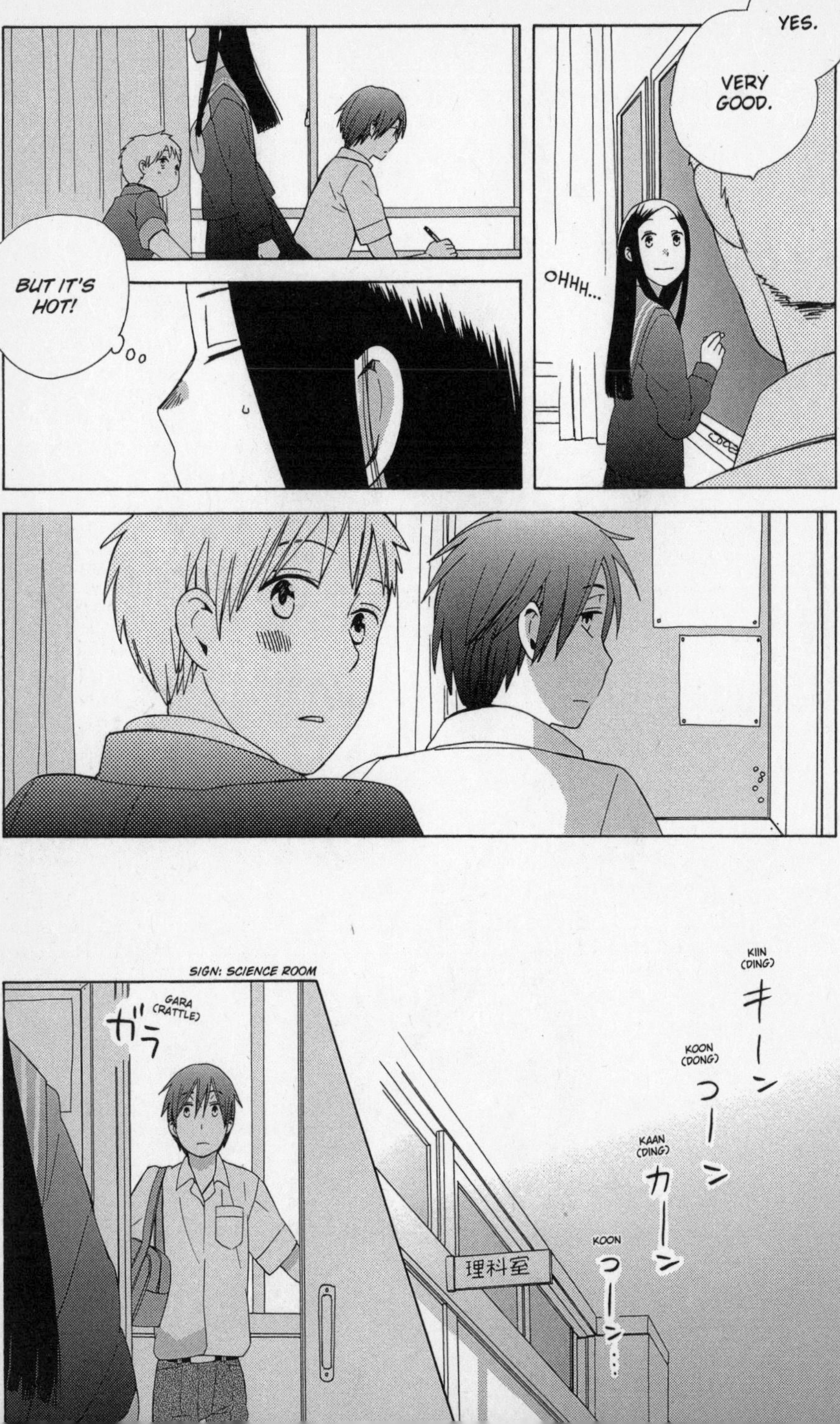
YES.
VERY GOOD.
OHHH...
BUT IT'S HOT!
SIGN: SCIENCE ROOM
KIIN (DING)
キーン
KOON (DONG)
コーン
KAAN (DING)
カーン
KOON
コーン…
GARA (RATTLE)
ガラ
理科室

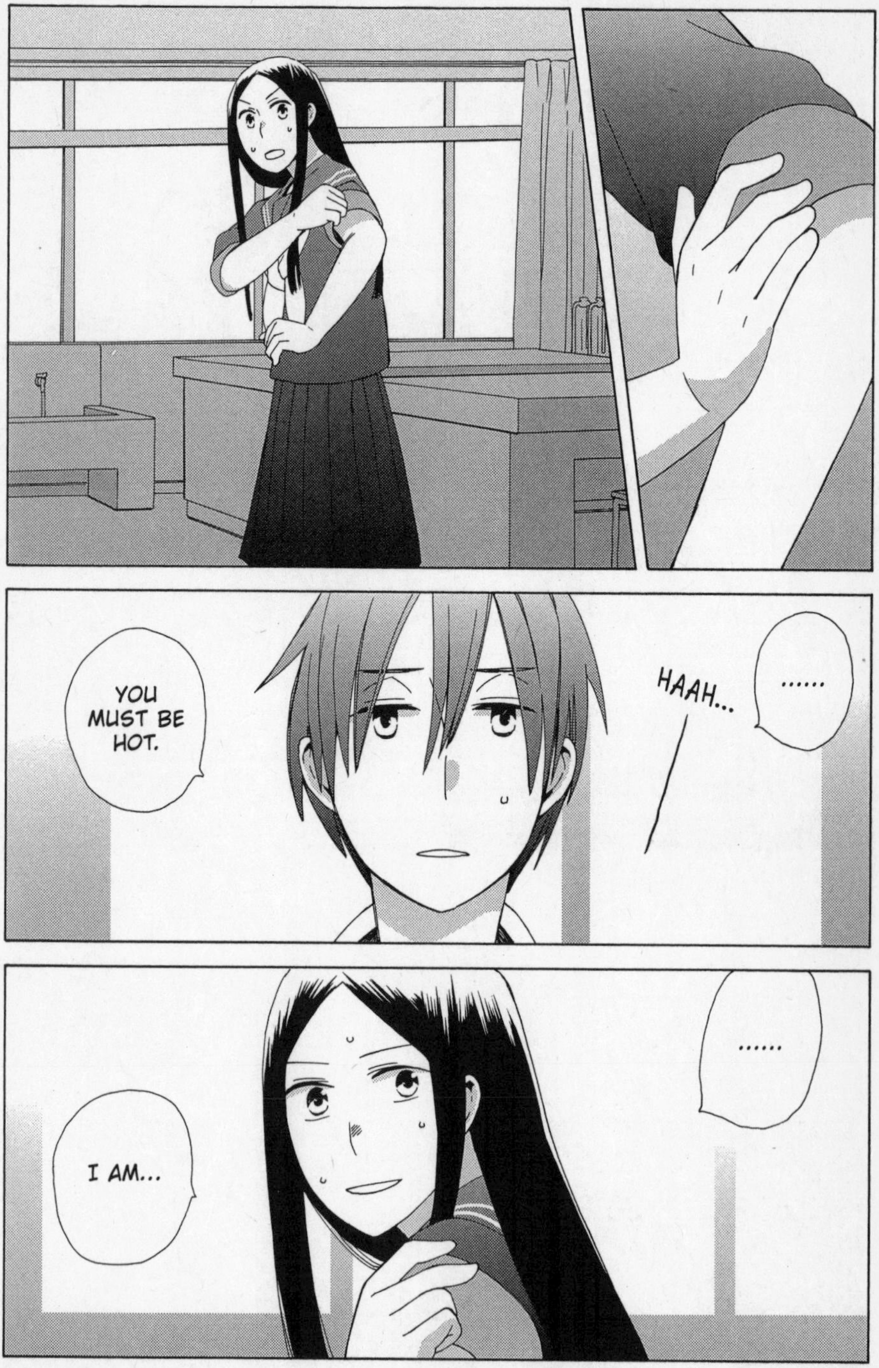
......
HAAH...
YOU MUST BE HOT.
......
I AM...

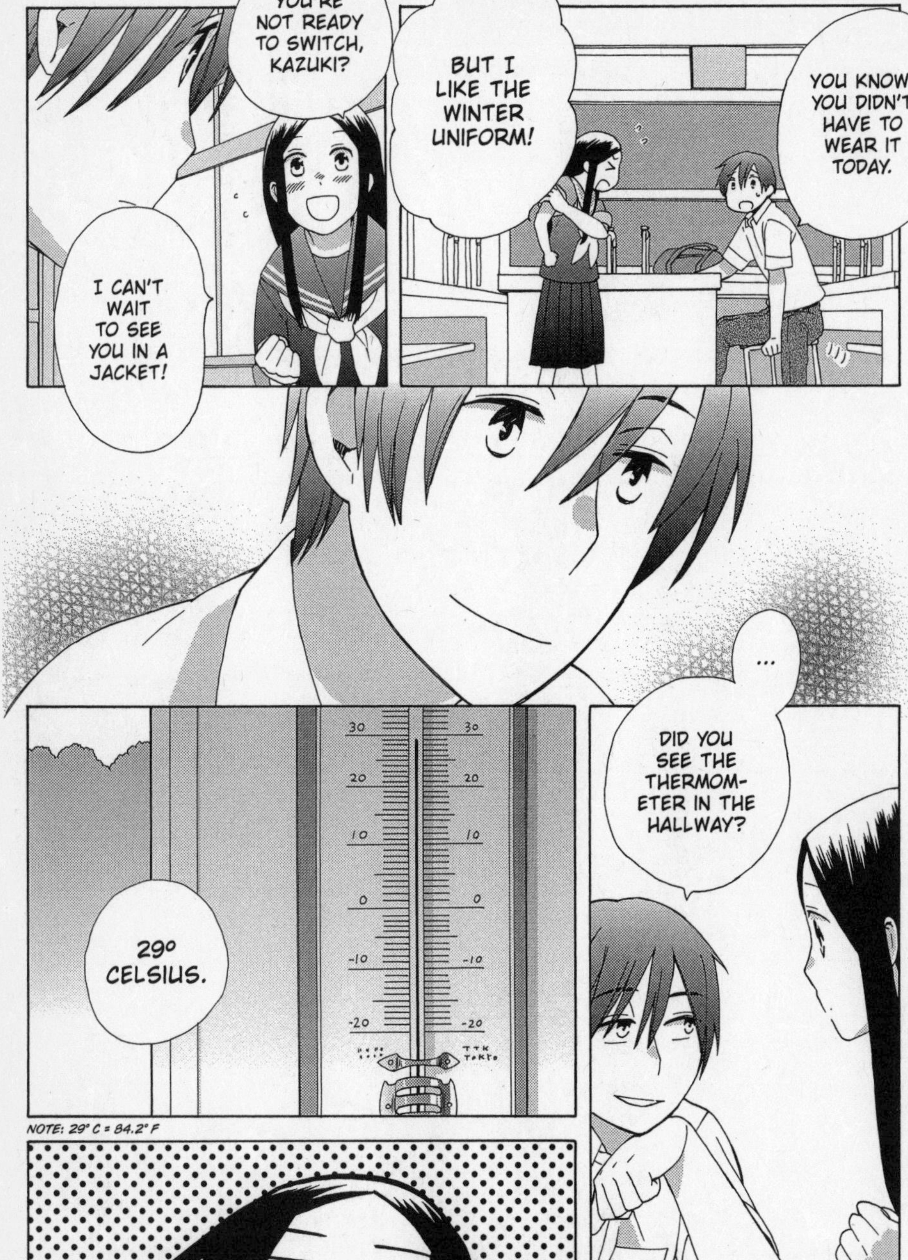
YOU KNOW, YOU DIDN'T HAVE TO WEAR IT TODAY.
BUT I LIKE THE WINTER UNIFORM!
YOU'RE NOT READY TO SWITCH, KAZUKI?
I CAN'T WAIT TO SEE YOU IN A JACKET!
...
DID YOU SEE THE THERMOMETER IN THE HALLWAY?
29° CELSIUS.

NOTE: 29° C = 84.2° F

THAT'S TOO HIGH!

ORI
ORIORIORI
ORI
ORIORIORI
ORI

ORI (ROLL)
おり...

WHAT LENGTH...

...DO YOU LIKE, KAZUKI?

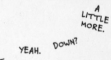

A LITTLE MORE.

YEAH. DOWN?

JUST A BIT MORE.

ABOUT THERE...

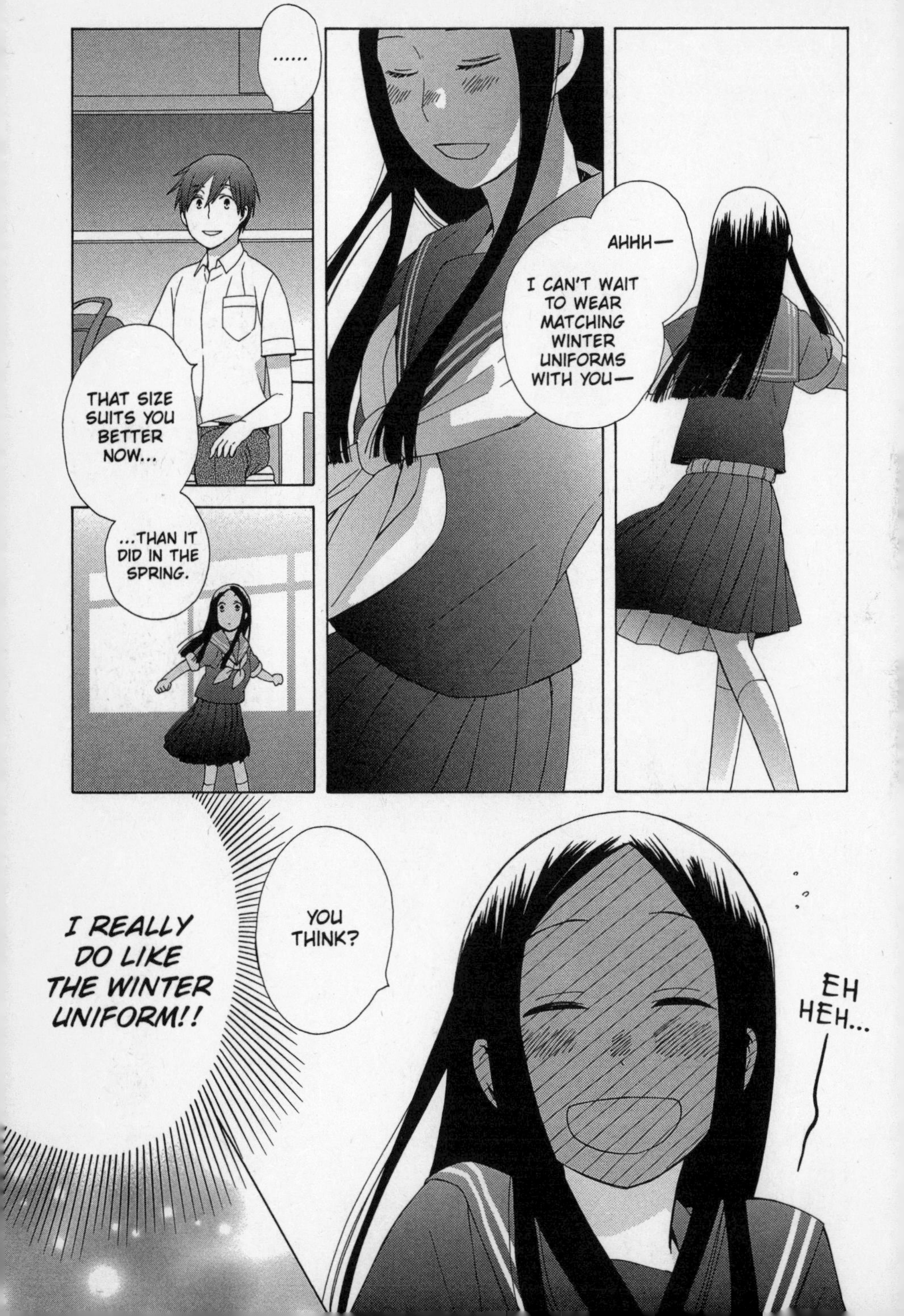
AHHH—
I CAN'T WAIT TO WEAR MATCHING WINTER UNIFORMS WITH YOU—
......
THAT SIZE SUITS YOU BETTER NOW...
...THAN IT DID IN THE SPRING.
EH HEH...
YOU THINK?
I REALLY DO LIKE THE WINTER UNIFORM!!

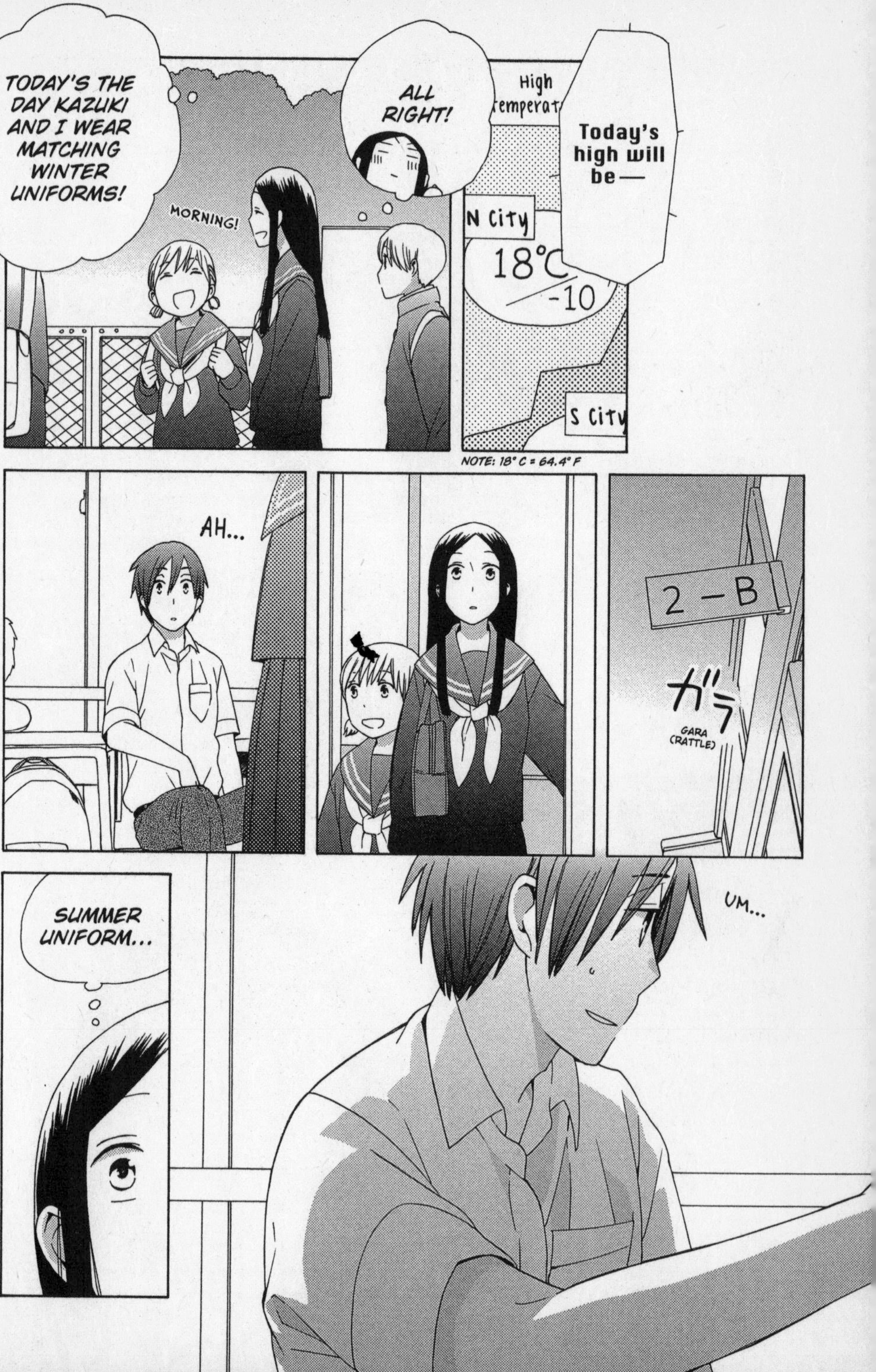

High temperat
Today's high will be—
N City
18°C
-10
S City
NOTE: 18° C = 64.4° F
TODAY'S THE DAY KAZUKI AND I WEAR MATCHING WINTER UNIFORMS!
ALL RIGHT!
MORNING!
2 — B
ガラ
GARA (RATTLE)
AH...
UM...
SUMMER UNIFORM...

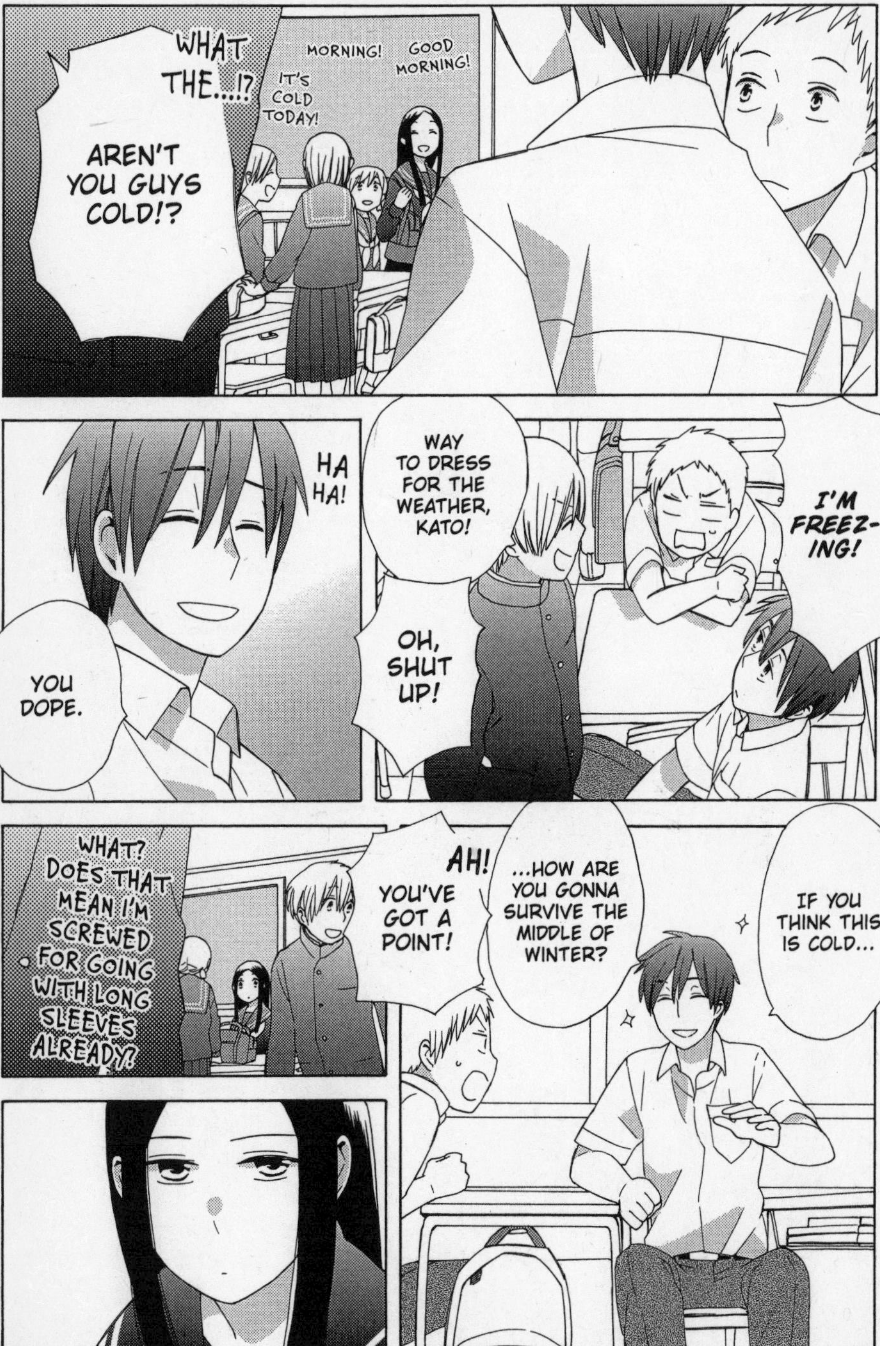
GOOD MORNING!
MORNING!
IT'S COLD TODAY!
WHAT THE...!?
AREN'T YOU GUYS COLD!?
I'M FREEZ-ING!
WAY TO DRESS FOR THE WEATHER, KATO!
OH, SHUT UP!
HA HA!
YOU DOPE.
IF YOU THINK THIS IS COLD...
...HOW ARE YOU GONNA SURVIVE THE MIDDLE OF WINTER?
AH!
YOU'VE GOT A POINT!
WHAT? DOES THAT MEAN I'M SCREWED FOR GOING WITH LONG SLEEVES ALREADY?

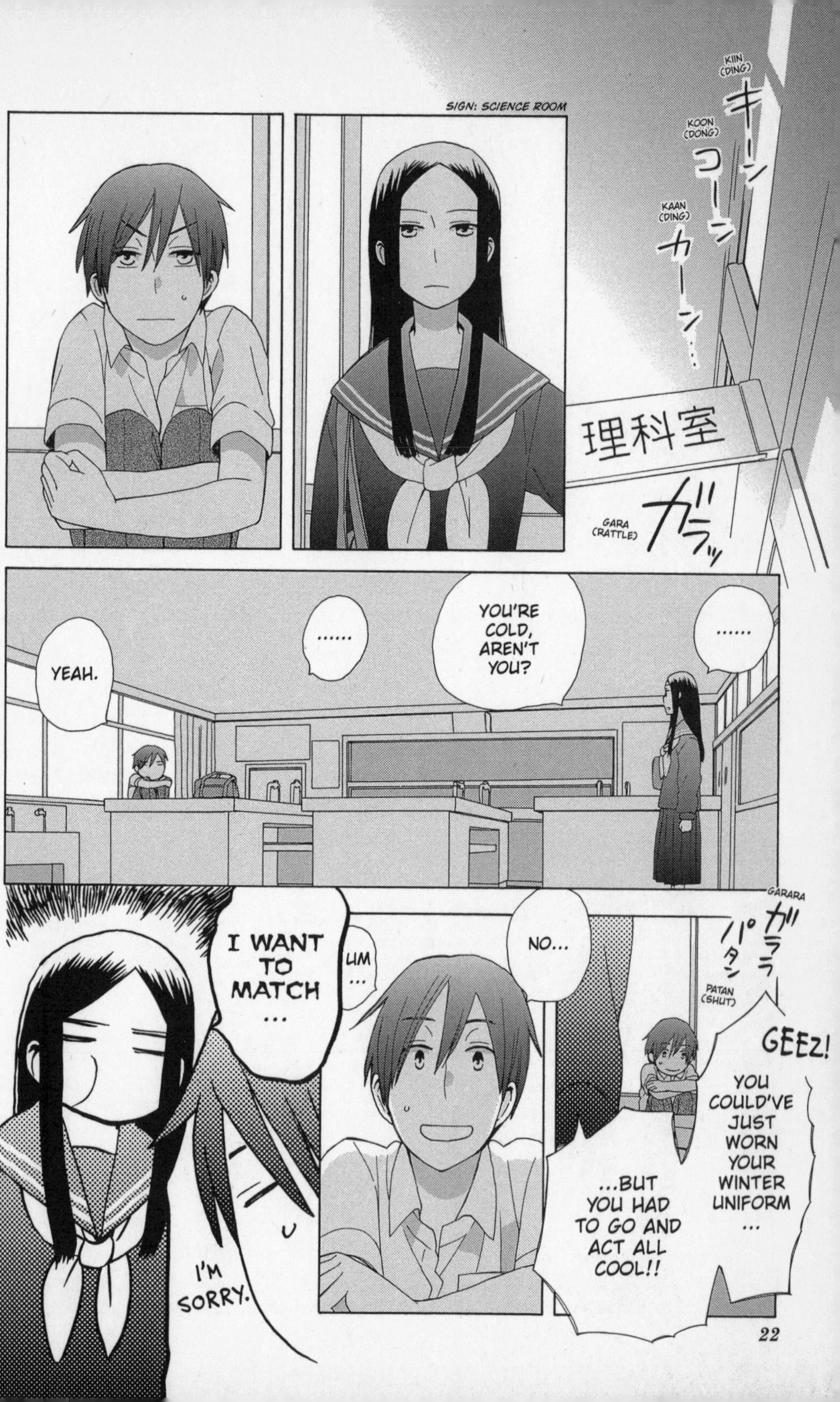
KIIN (DING)
キーン
KOON (DONG)
コーン
KAAN (DING)
カーン…
理科室
GARA (RATTLE)
ガラッ
SIGN: SCIENCE ROOM
......
YOU'RE COLD, AREN'T YOU?
......
YEAH.
GARARA
ガララ
PATAN (SHUT)
パタン
GEEZ!
YOU COULD'VE JUST WORN YOUR WINTER UNIFORM...
...BUT YOU HAD TO GO AND ACT ALL COOL!!
NO...
UM...
I WANT TO MATCH...
I'M SORRY.

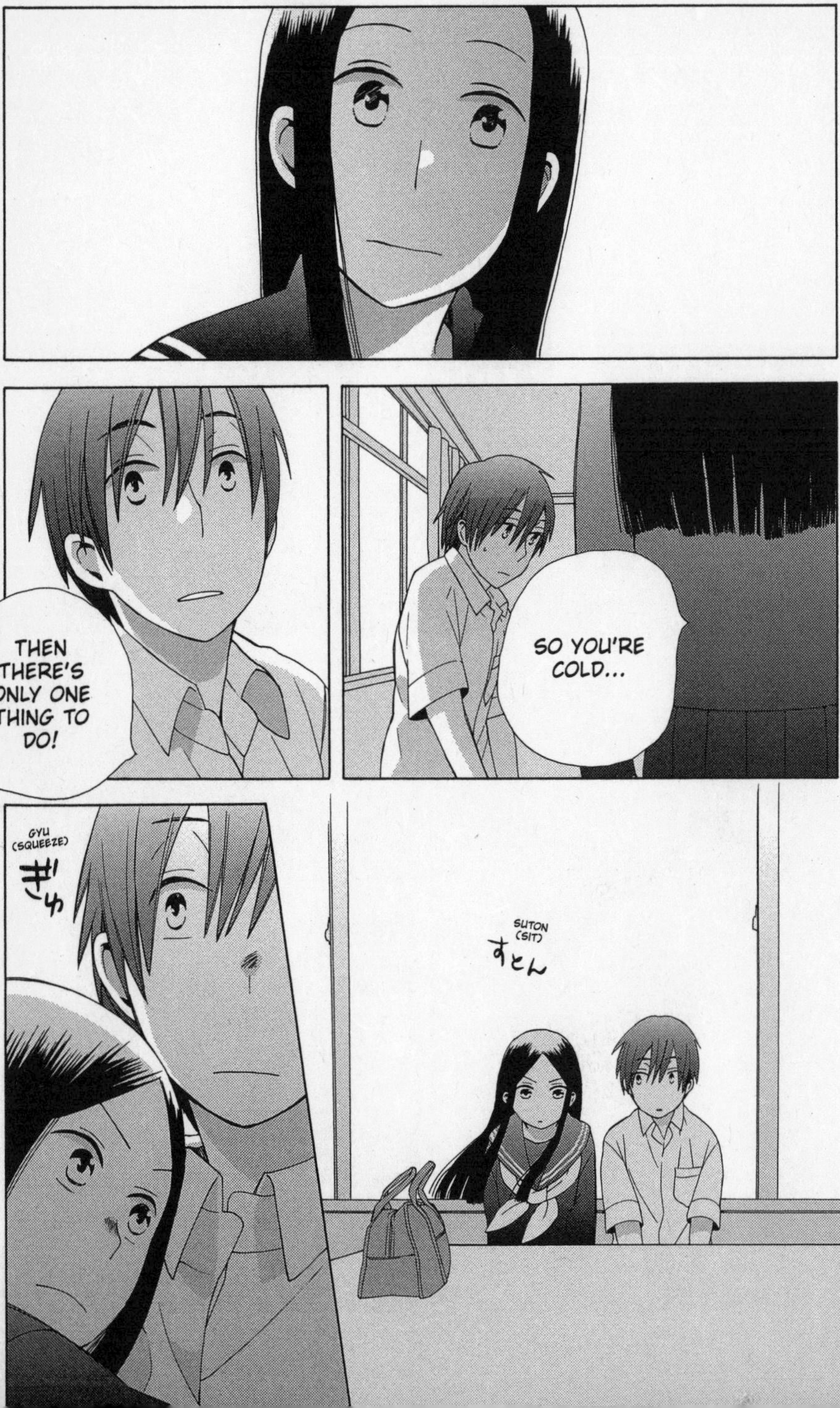
SO YOU'RE COLD...
THEN THERE'S ONLY ONE THING TO DO!
SUTON (SIT)
すとん
GYU (SQUEEZE)
ぎゅ

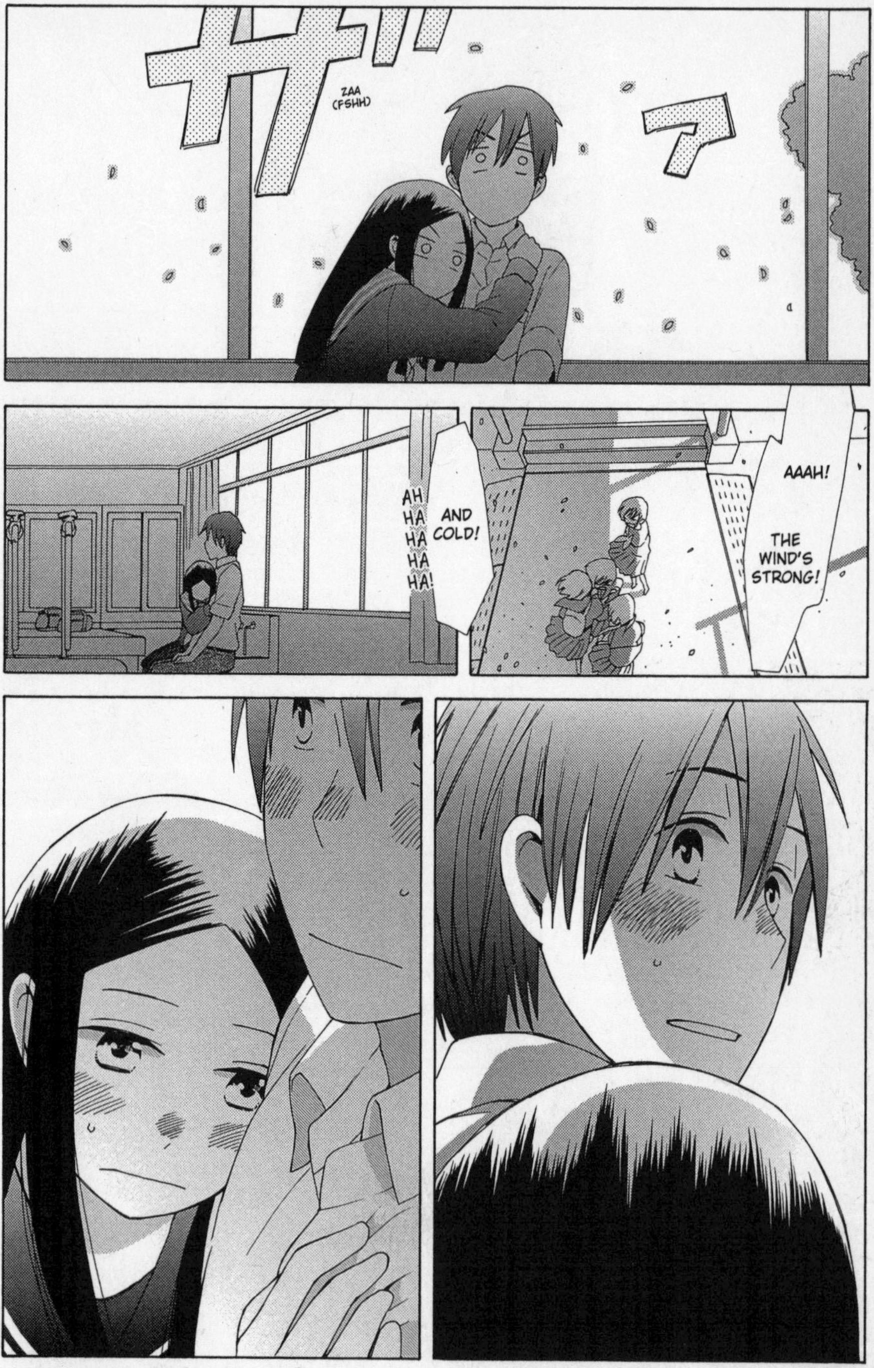
ZAA (FSHH)
AAAH!
THE WIND'S STRONG!
AND COLD!
AH HA HA HA HA!

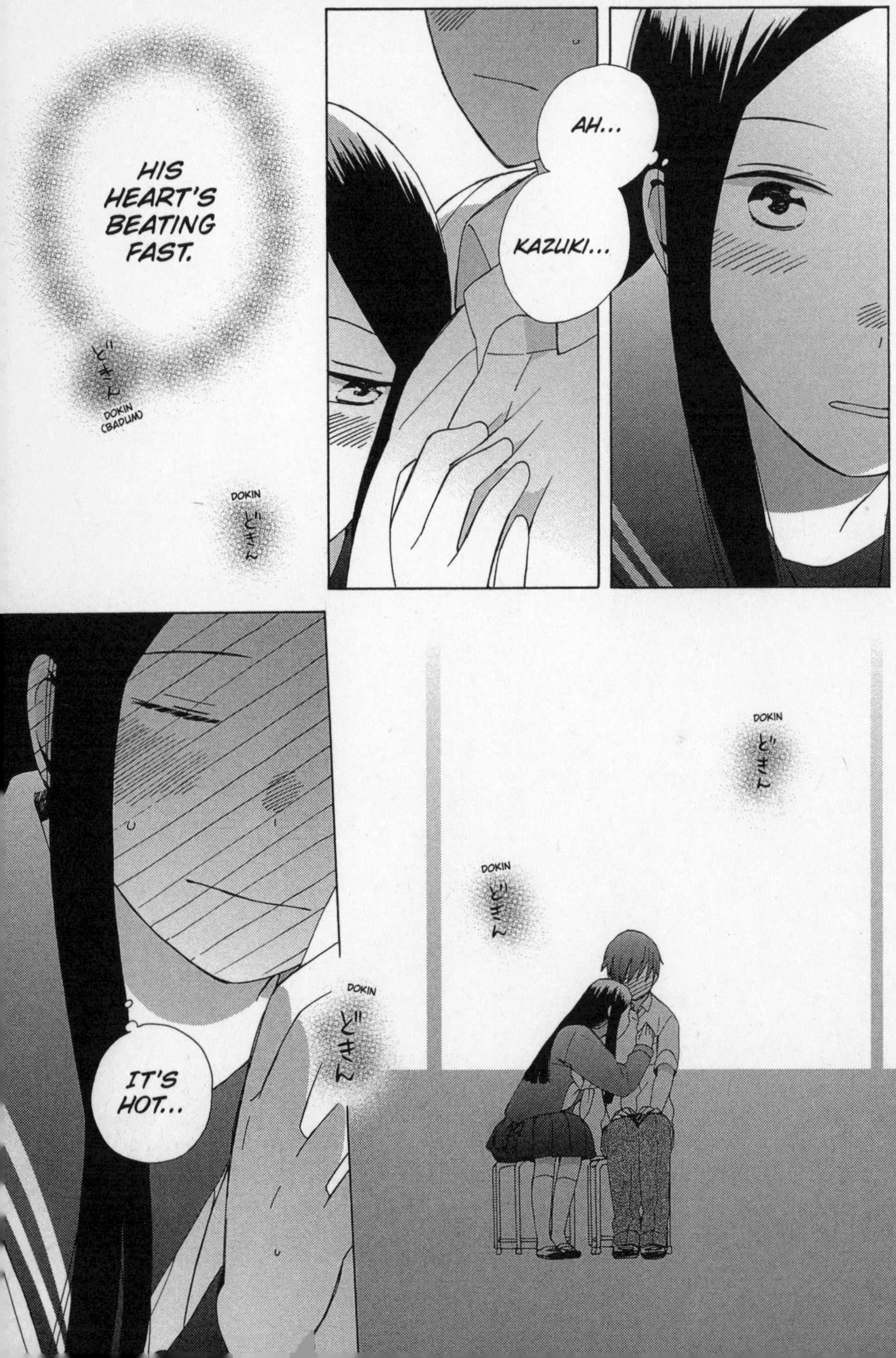
AH...
KAZUKI...
HIS HEART'S BEATING FAST.
どきん
DOKIN (BADUM)
DOKIN
どきん
DOKIN
どきん
DOKIN
どきん
DOKIN
どきん
IT'S HOT...

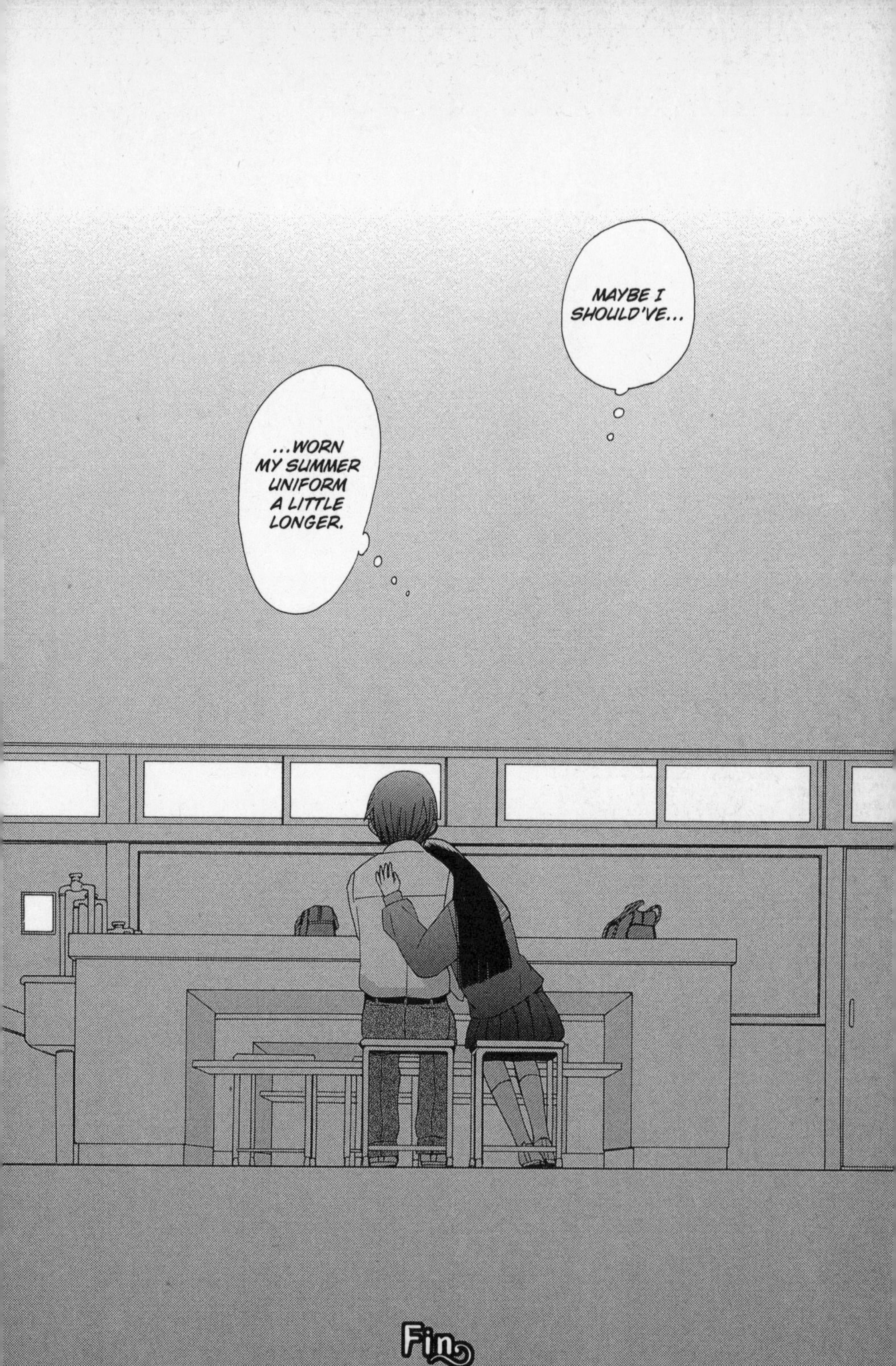
MAYBE I SHOULD'VE...
...WORN MY SUMMER UNIFORM A LITTLE LONGER.
Fin

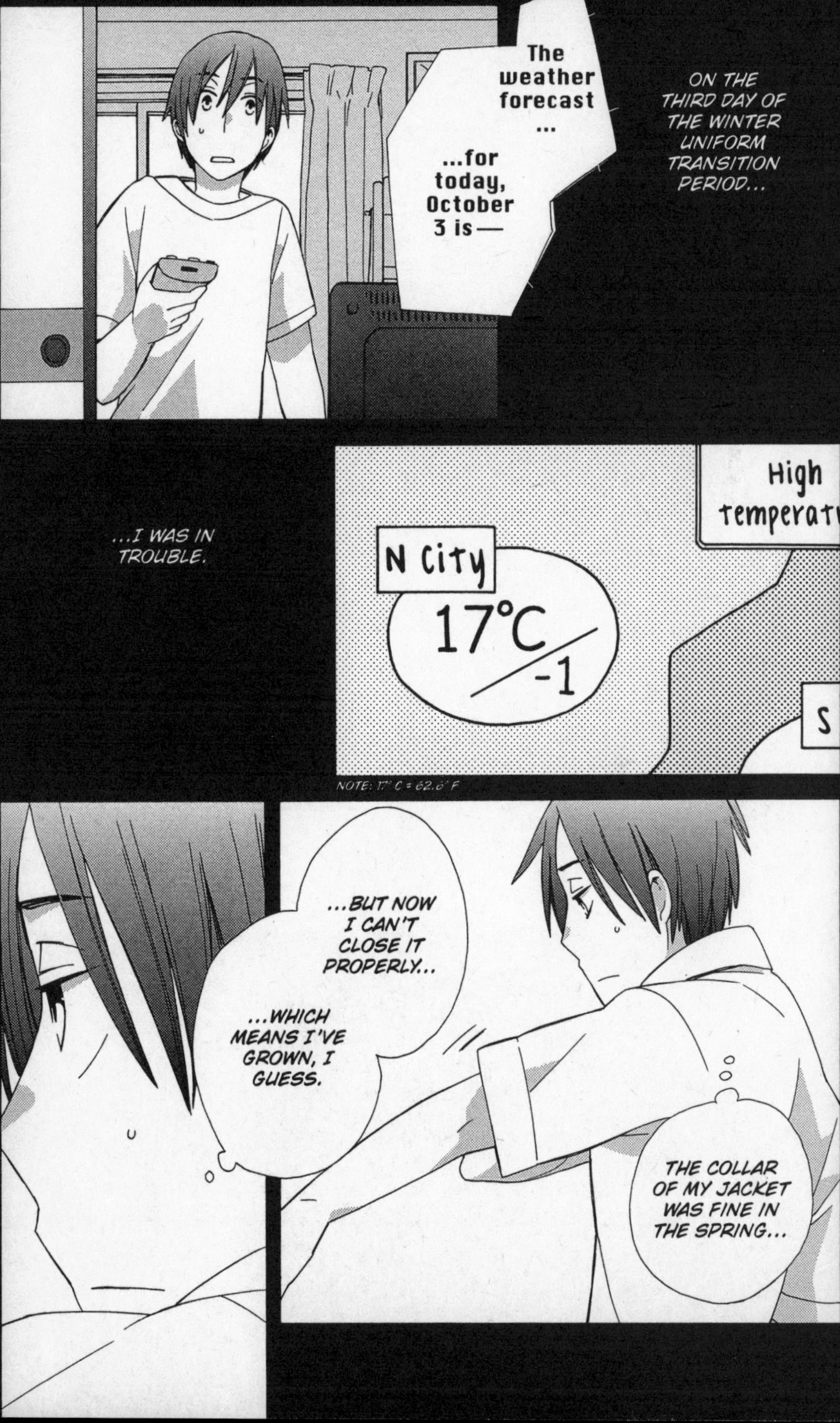
ON THE THIRD DAY OF THE WINTER UNIFORM TRANSITION PERIOD...
The weather forecast...
...for today, October 3 is—
High temperat
N City
17°C
-1
S
...I WAS IN TROUBLE.
NOTE: 17° C = 62.6° F
THE COLLAR OF MY JACKET WAS FINE IN THE SPRING...
...BUT NOW I CAN'T CLOSE IT PROPERLY...
...WHICH MEANS I'VE GROWN, I GUESS.

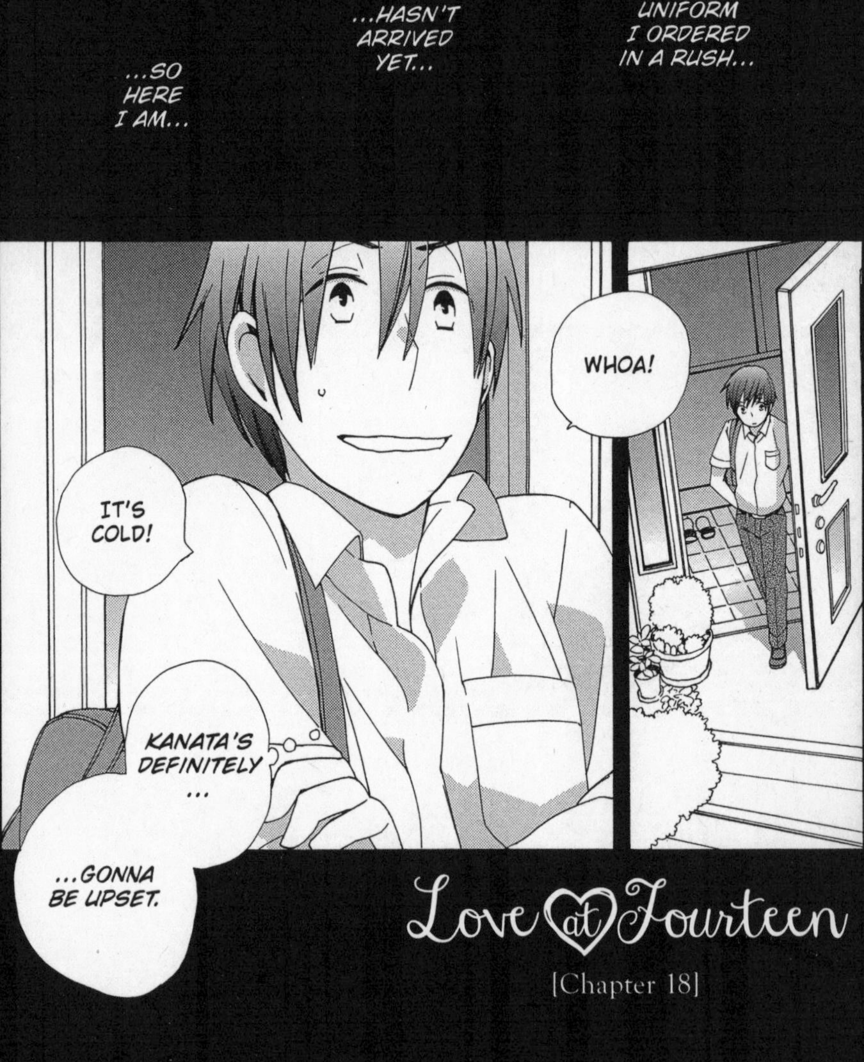
UNIFORM I ORDERED IN A RUSH...
...HASN'T ARRIVED YET...
...SO HERE I AM...
WHOA!
IT'S COLD!
KANATA'S DEFINITELY ...
...GONNA BE UPSET.

Love at Fourteen

[Chapter 18]

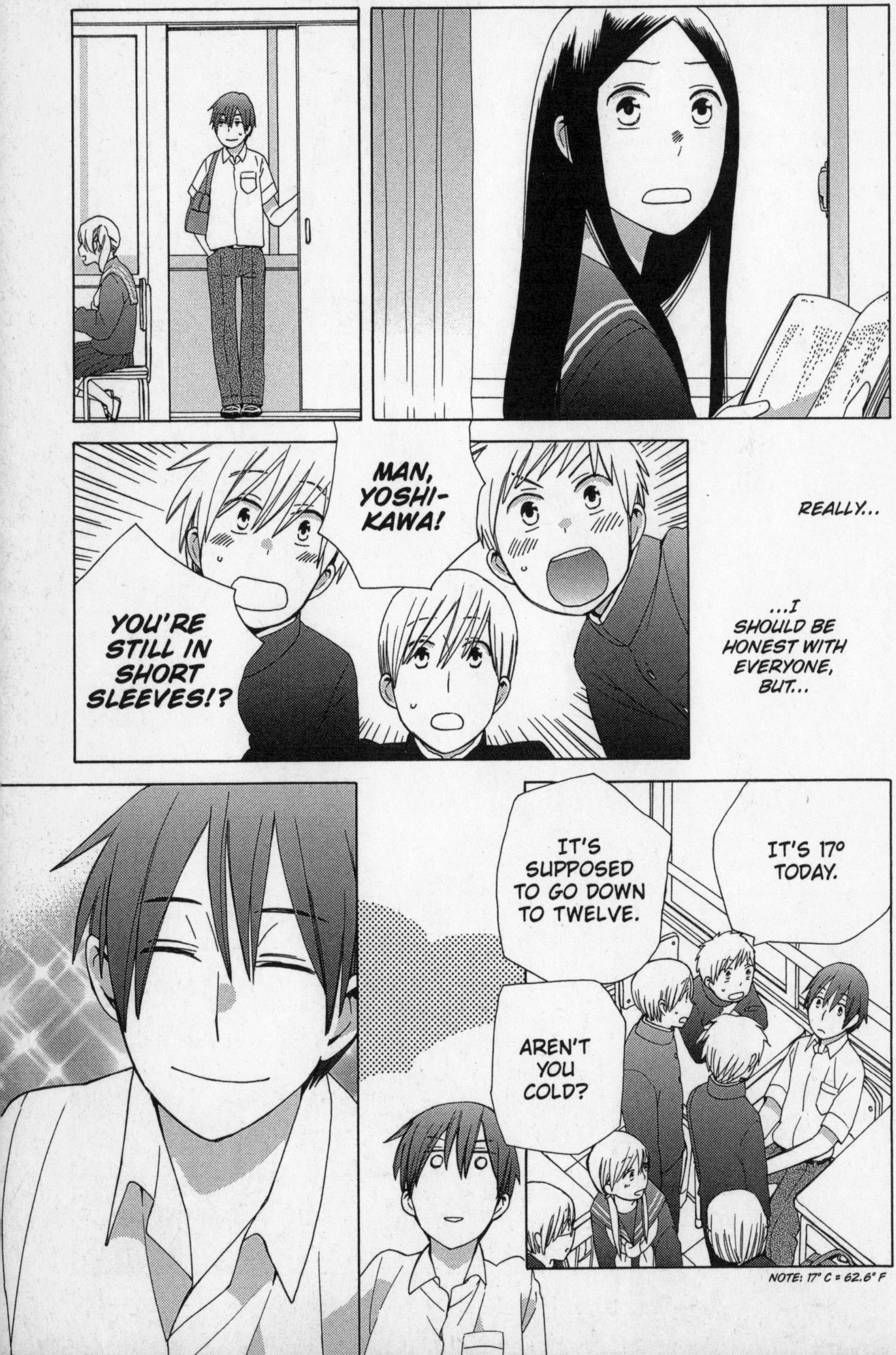
REALLY...
...I SHOULD BE HONEST WITH EVERYONE, BUT...
MAN, YOSHI-KAWA!
YOU'RE STILL IN SHORT SLEEVES!?
IT'S 17° TODAY.
IT'S SUPPOSED TO GO DOWN TO TWELVE.
AREN'T YOU COLD?

NOTE: 17° C = 62.6° F

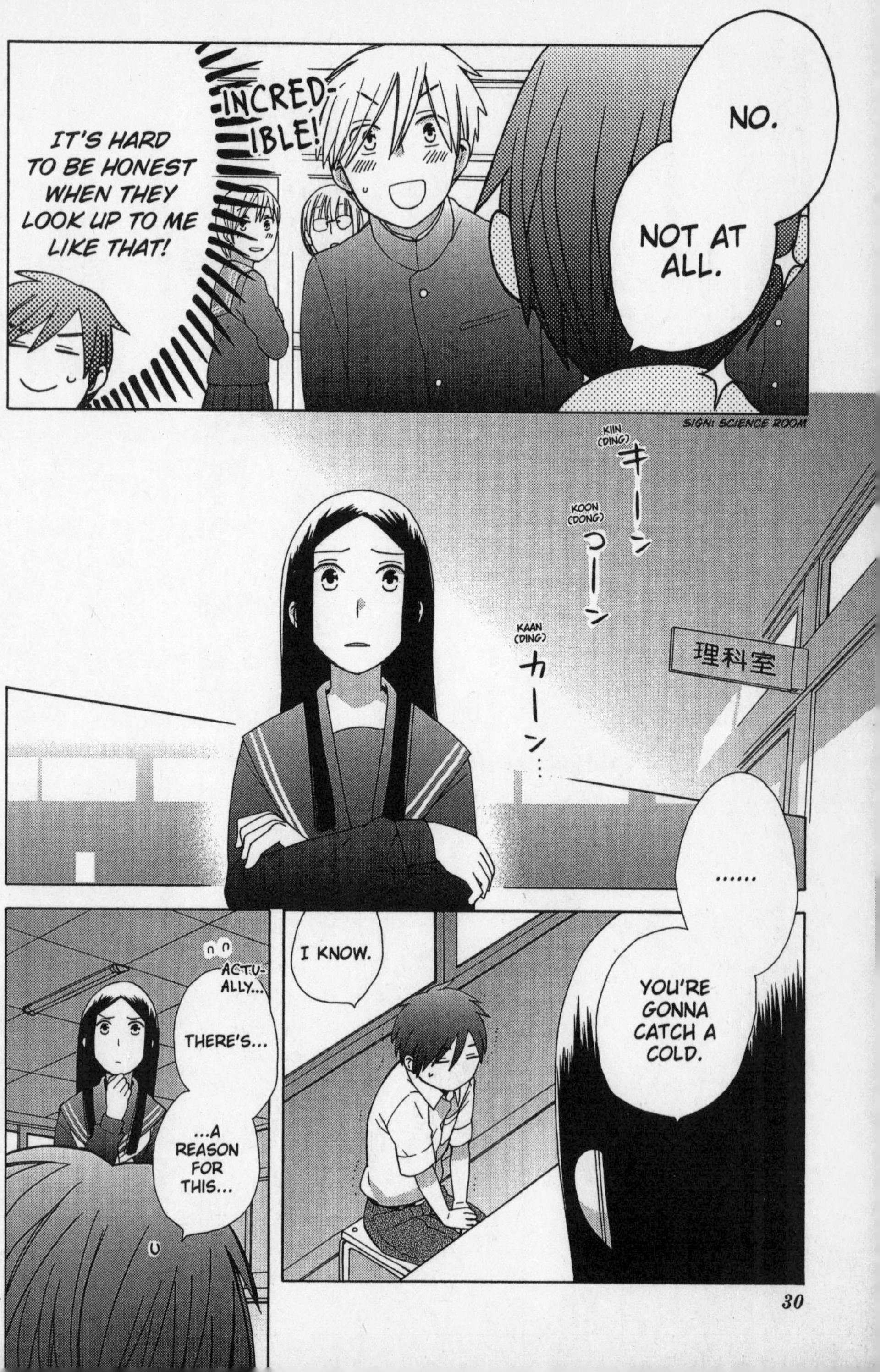
NO.
NOT AT ALL.
INCRED-IBLE!
IT'S HARD TO BE HONEST WHEN THEY LOOK UP TO ME LIKE THAT!
SIGN: SCIENCE ROOM
KIIN (DING) キーン
KOON (DONG) コーン
KAAN (DING) カーン…
理科室
......
YOU'RE GONNA CATCH A COLD.
I KNOW.
ACTU-ALLY...
THERE'S...
...A REASON FOR THIS...

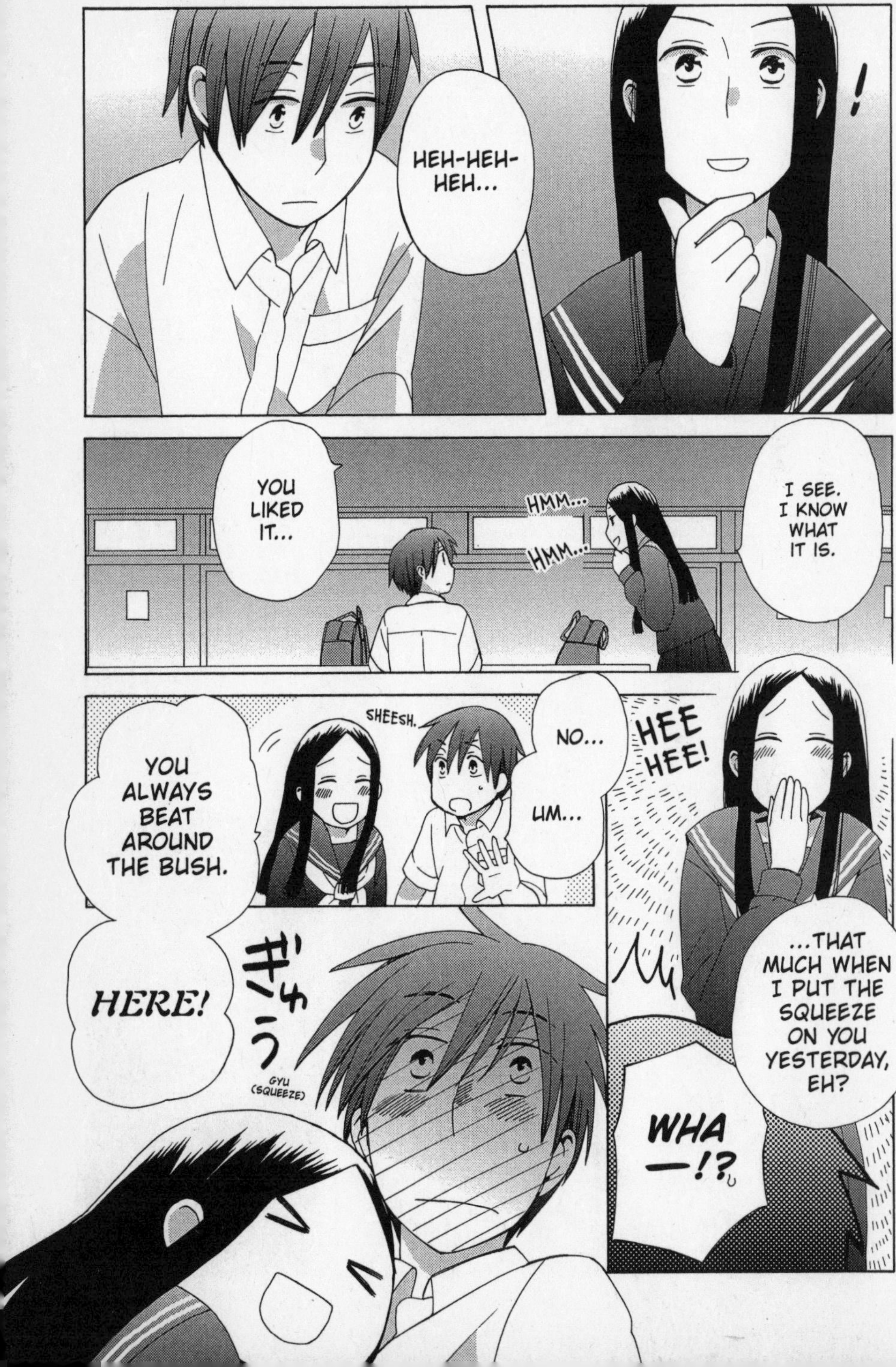
!
HEH-HEH-HEH...
I SEE. I KNOW WHAT IT IS.
HMM... HMM...
YOU LIKED IT...
HEE HEE!
...THAT MUCH WHEN I PUT THE SQUEEZE ON YOU YESTERDAY, EH?
WHA—!?
NO...
UM...
SHEESH.
YOU ALWAYS BEAT AROUND THE BUSH.
HERE!
ぎゅう
GYU (SQUEEZE)

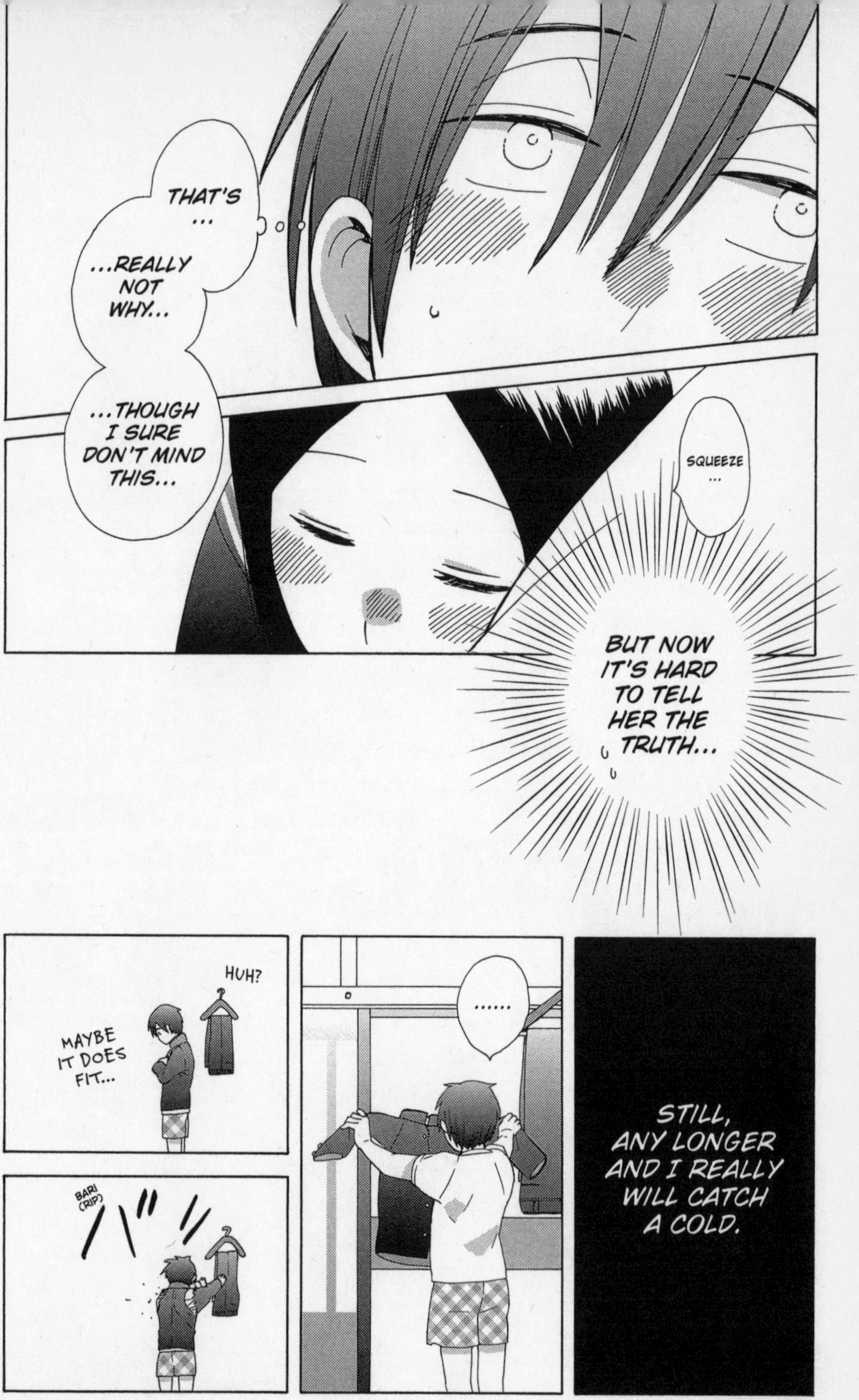
THAT'S ...
...REALLY NOT WHY...
...THOUGH I SURE DON'T MIND THIS...
SQUEEZE ...
BUT NOW IT'S HARD TO TELL HER THE TRUTH...
STILL, ANY LONGER AND I REALLY WILL CATCH A COLD.
......
HUH?
MAYBE IT DOES FIT...
BARI (RIP)
バリ

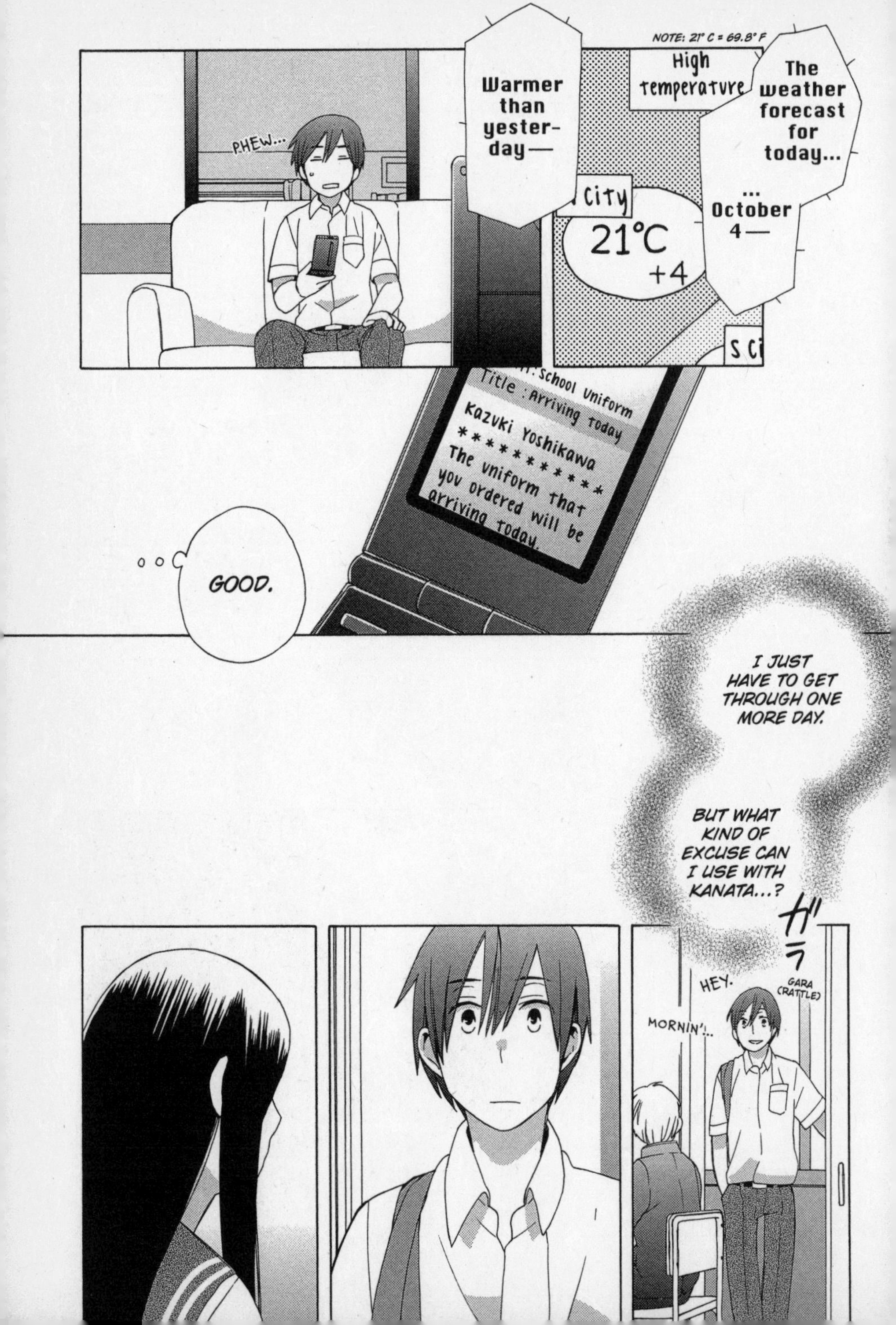
The weather forecast for today...
...October 4—
NOTE: 21° C = 69.8° F
High temperature
City
21°C
+4
S Ci
Warmer than yester-day—
PHEW...
School Uniform
Title : Arriving today
Kazuki Yoshikawa
****
The uniform that you ordered will be arriving today.
GOOD.
I JUST HAVE TO GET THROUGH ONE MORE DAY.
BUT WHAT KIND OF EXCUSE CAN I USE WITH KANATA...?
ガラ
GARA (RATTLE)
HEY.
MORNIN'...

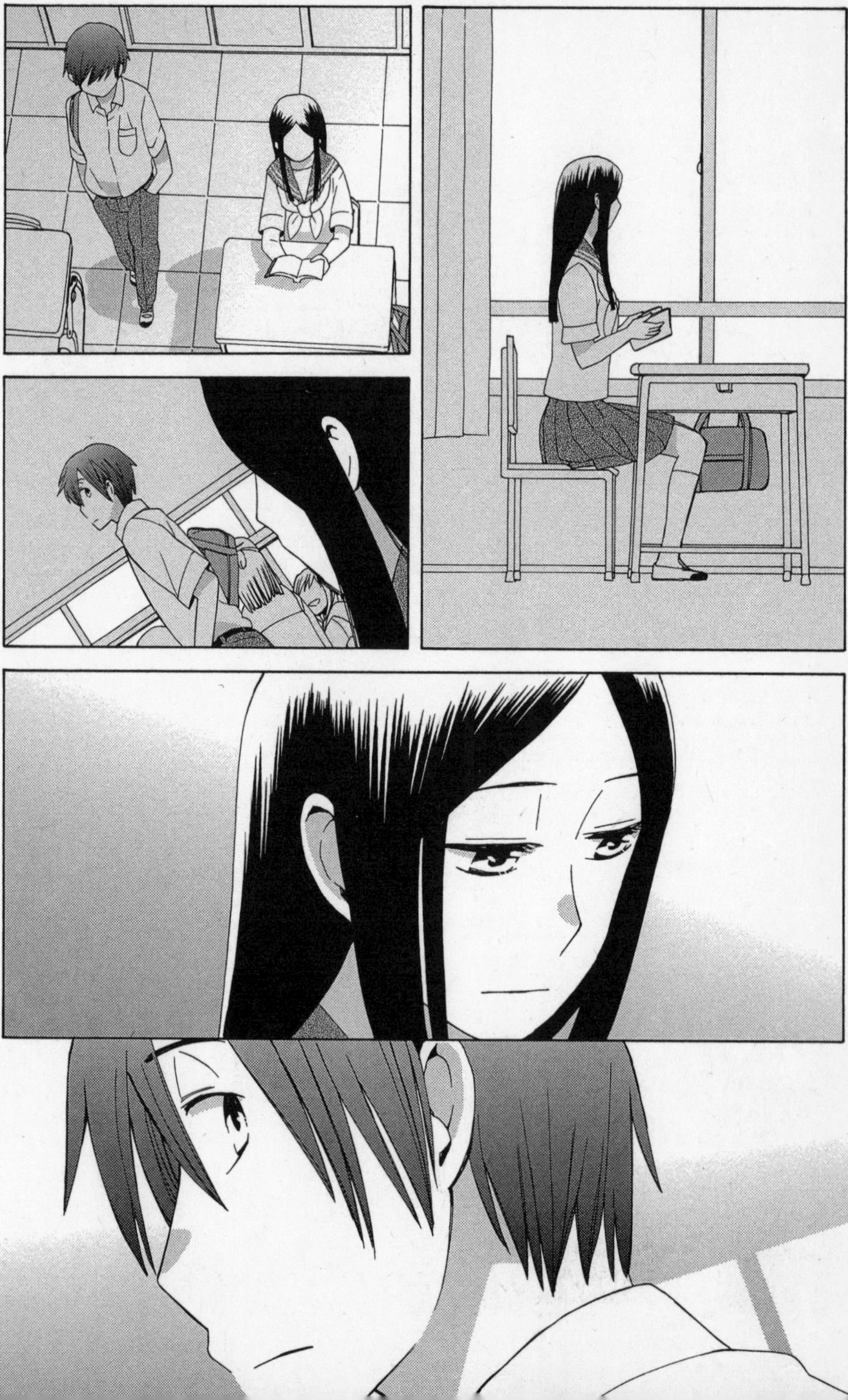

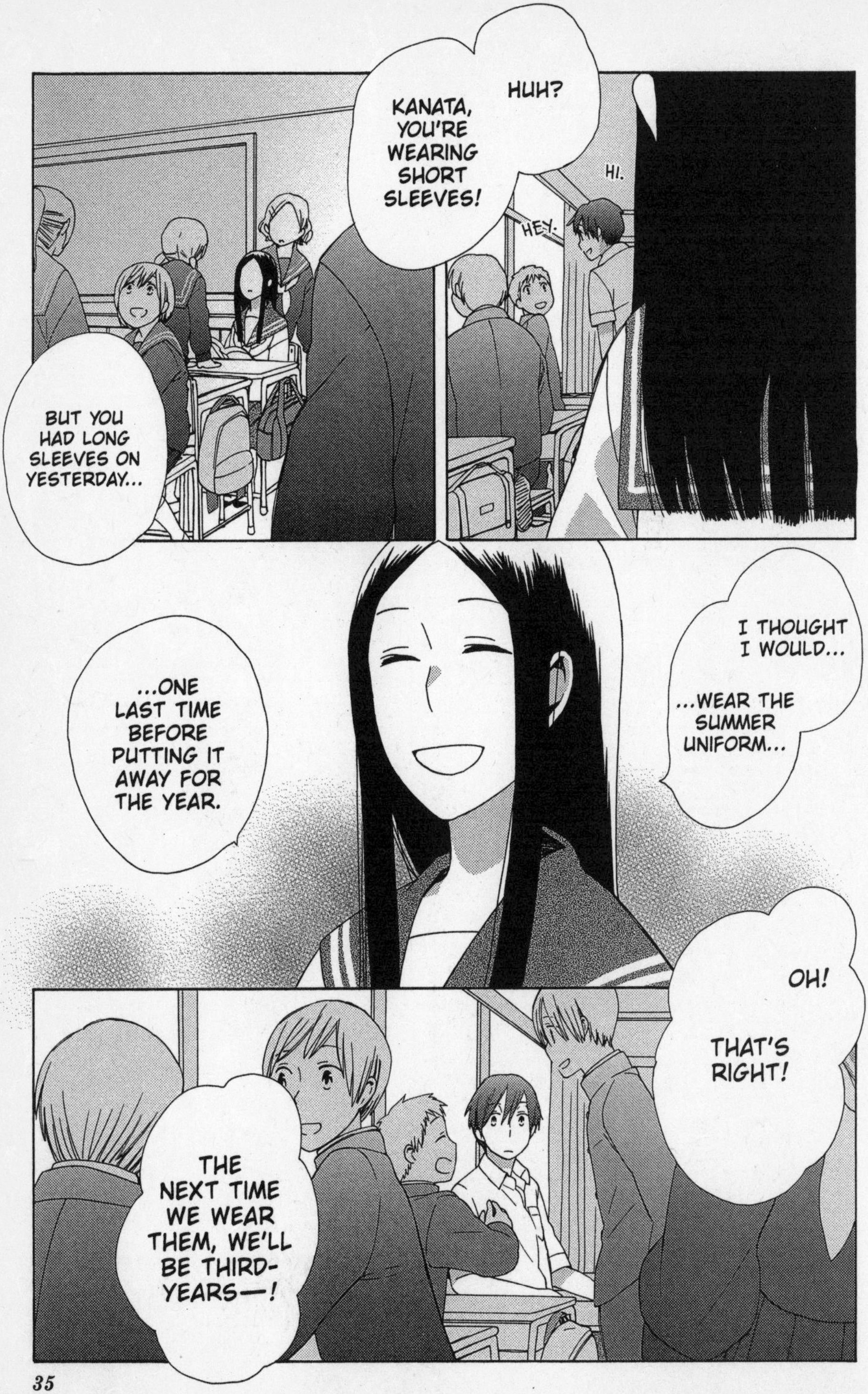
HI.
HEY.
HUH? KANATA, YOU'RE WEARING SHORT SLEEVES!
BUT YOU HAD LONG SLEEVES ON YESTERDAY...
I THOUGHT I WOULD... ...WEAR THE SUMMER UNIFORM...
...ONE LAST TIME BEFORE PUTTING IT AWAY FOR THE YEAR.
OH! THAT'S RIGHT!
THE NEXT TIME WE WEAR THEM, WE'LL BE THIRD-YEARS—!

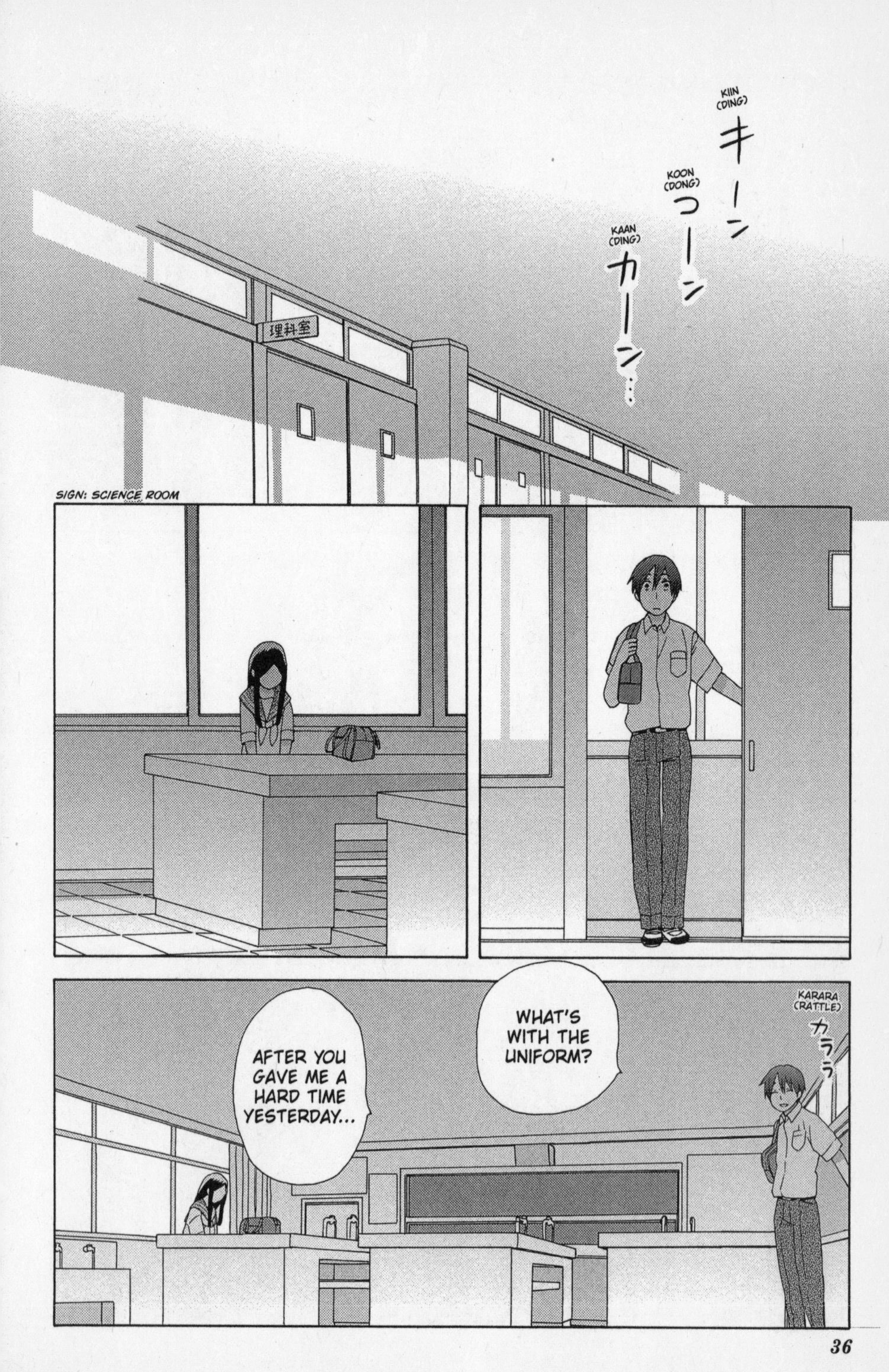
KIIN (DING)
キーン
KOON (DONG)
コーン
KAAN (DING)
カーン…
SIGN: SCIENCE ROOM
理科室
KARARA (RATTLE)
カララ
WHAT'S WITH THE UNIFORM?
AFTER YOU GAVE ME A HARD TIME YESTERDAY...

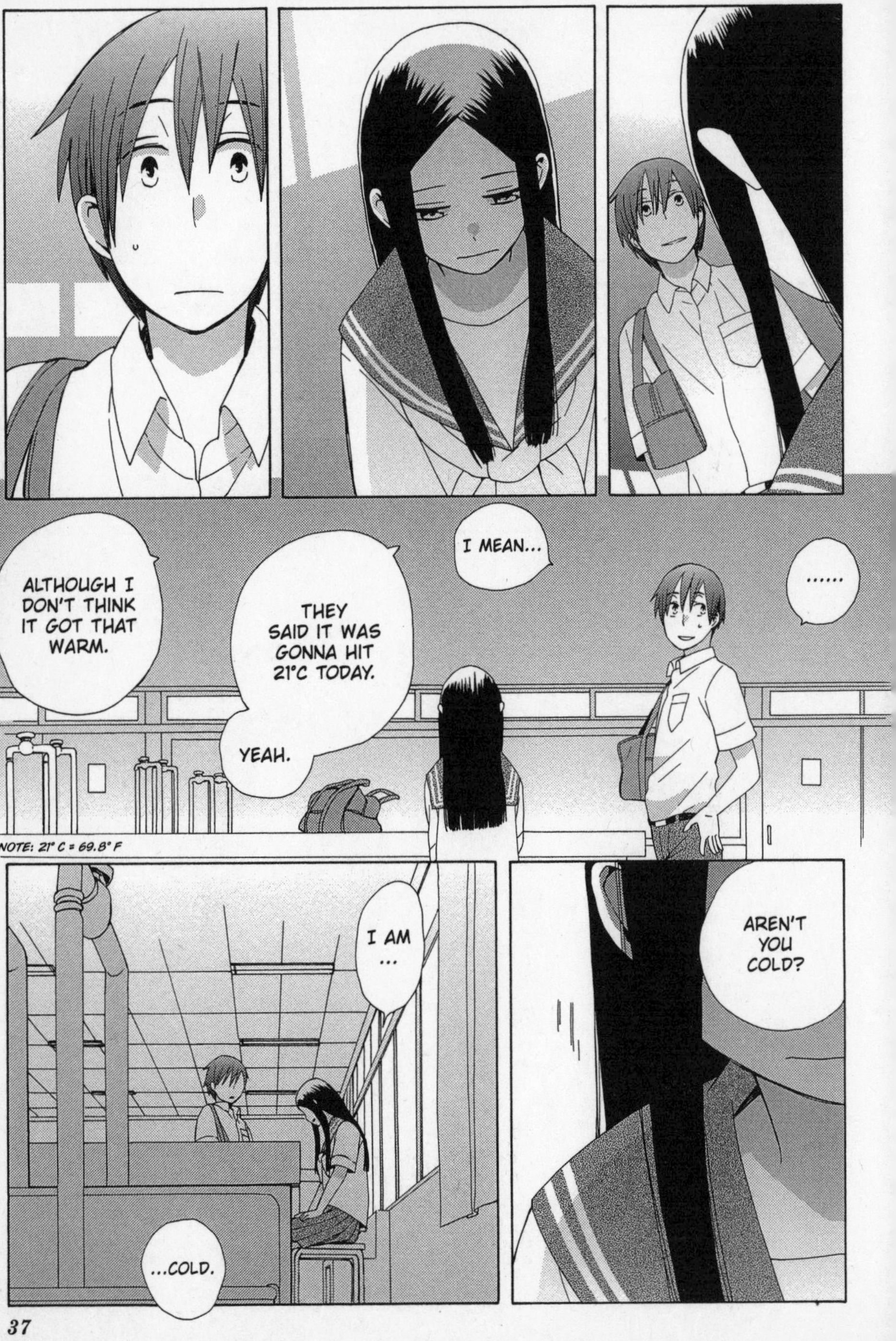
......
I MEAN...
THEY SAID IT WAS GONNA HIT 21°C TODAY.
YEAH.
ALTHOUGH I DON'T THINK IT GOT THAT WARM.
NOTE: 21° C = 69.8° F
AREN'T YOU COLD?
I AM ...
...COLD.

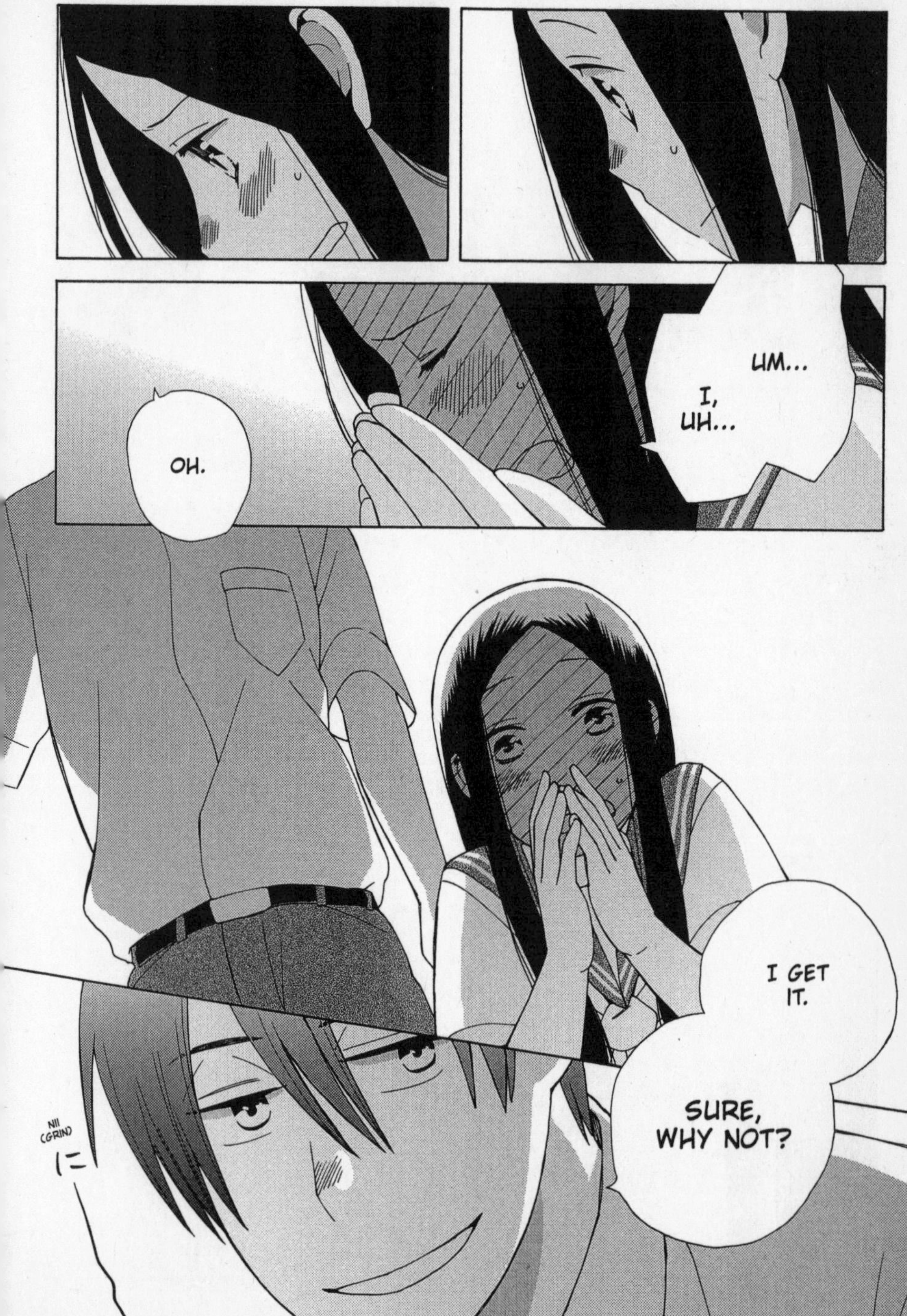
UM...
I, UH...
OH.
I GET IT.
SURE, WHY NOT?
NII (GRIN)
に

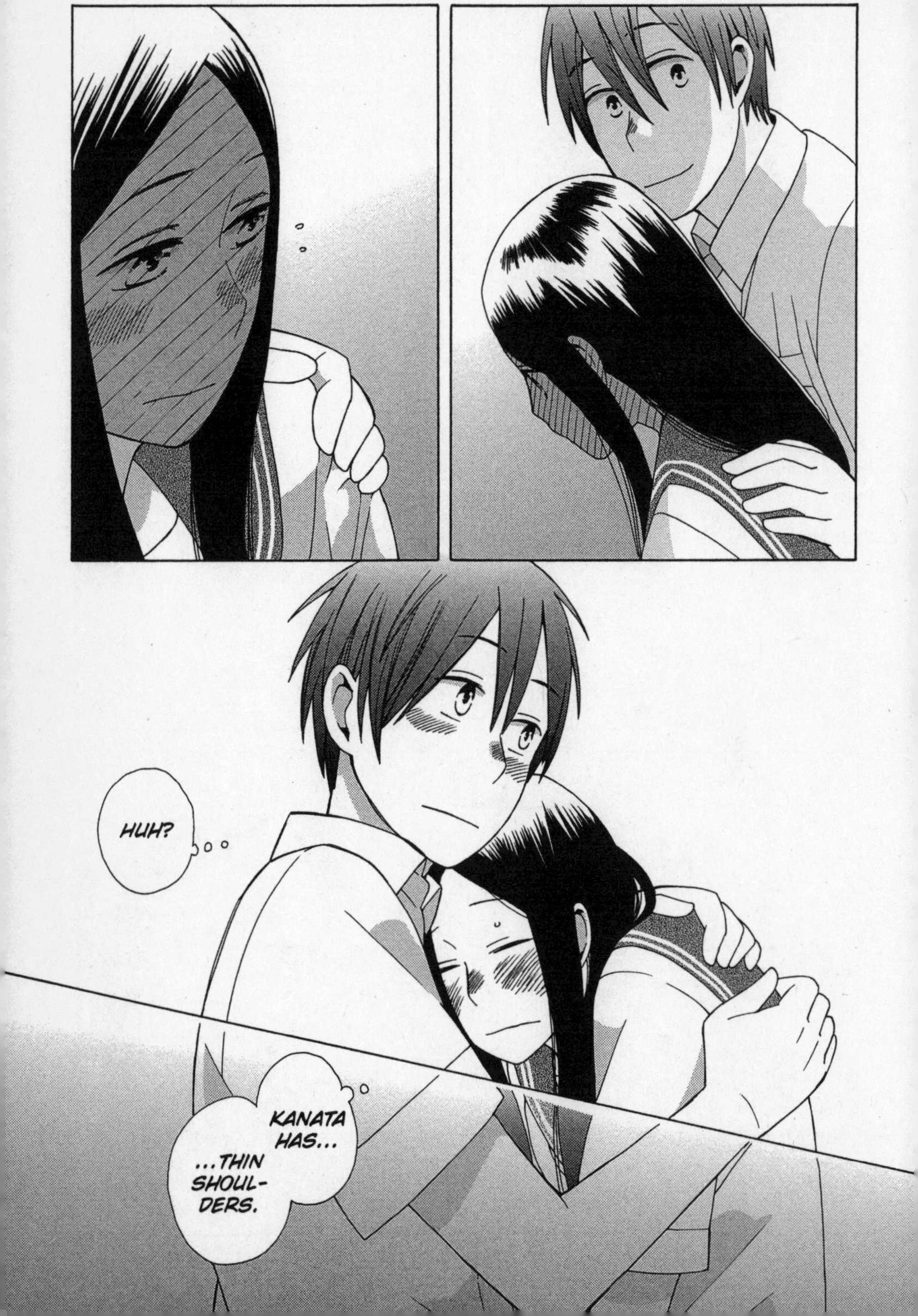
HUH?
KANATA HAS...
...THIN SHOULDERS.

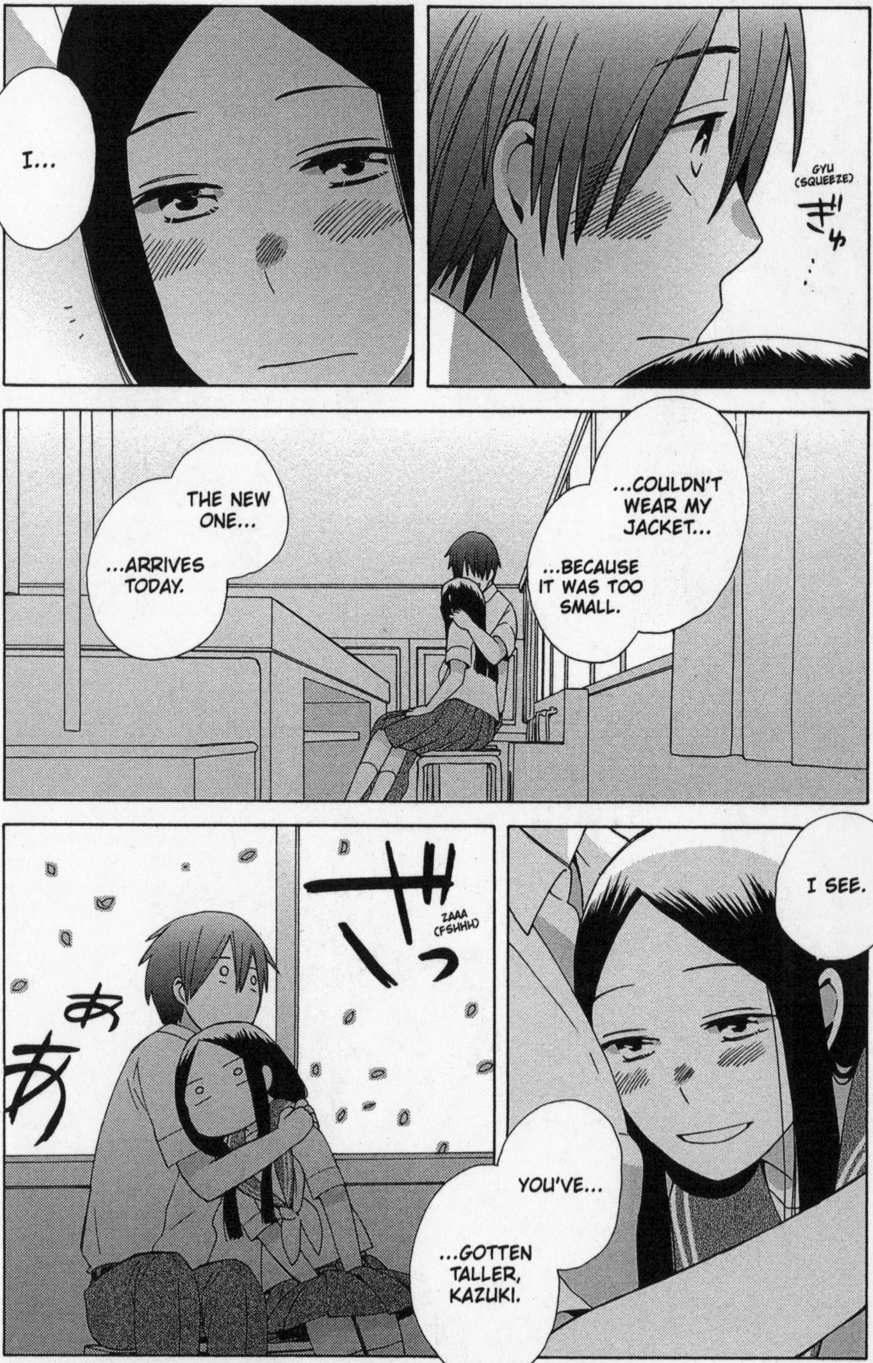
GYU (SQUEEZE)
ぎゅ…
I...
...COULDN'T WEAR MY JACKET...
...BECAUSE IT WAS TOO SMALL.
THE NEW ONE...
...ARRIVES TODAY.
I SEE.
YOU'VE...
...GOTTEN TALLER, KAZUKI.
ざっ
ZAAA (FSHHH)
ああ

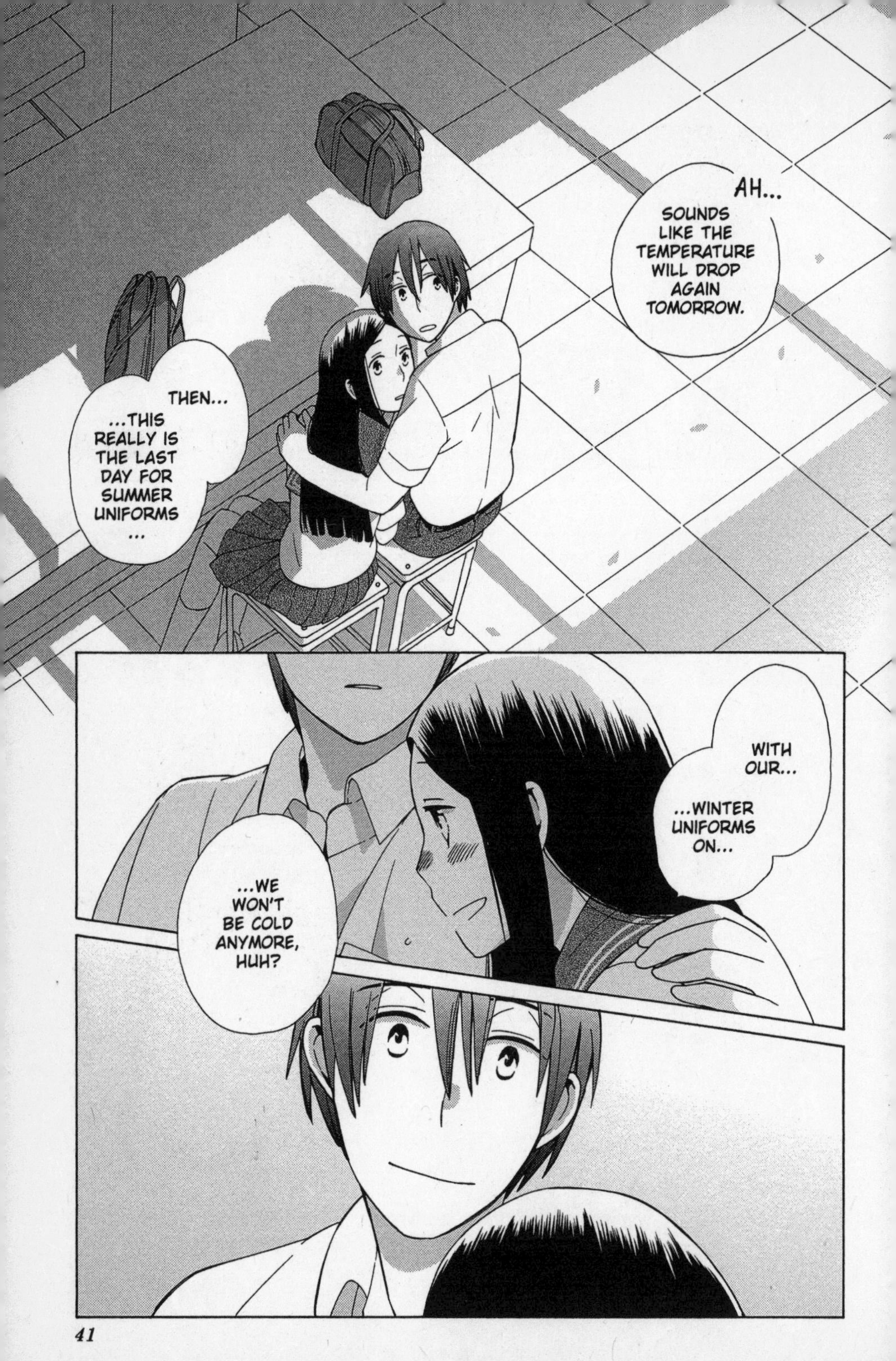
AH... SOUNDS LIKE THE TEMPERATURE WILL DROP AGAIN TOMORROW.
THEN... ...THIS REALLY IS THE LAST DAY FOR SUMMER UNIFORMS ...
WITH OUR... ...WINTER UNIFORMS ON...
...WE WON'T BE COLD ANYMORE, HUH?

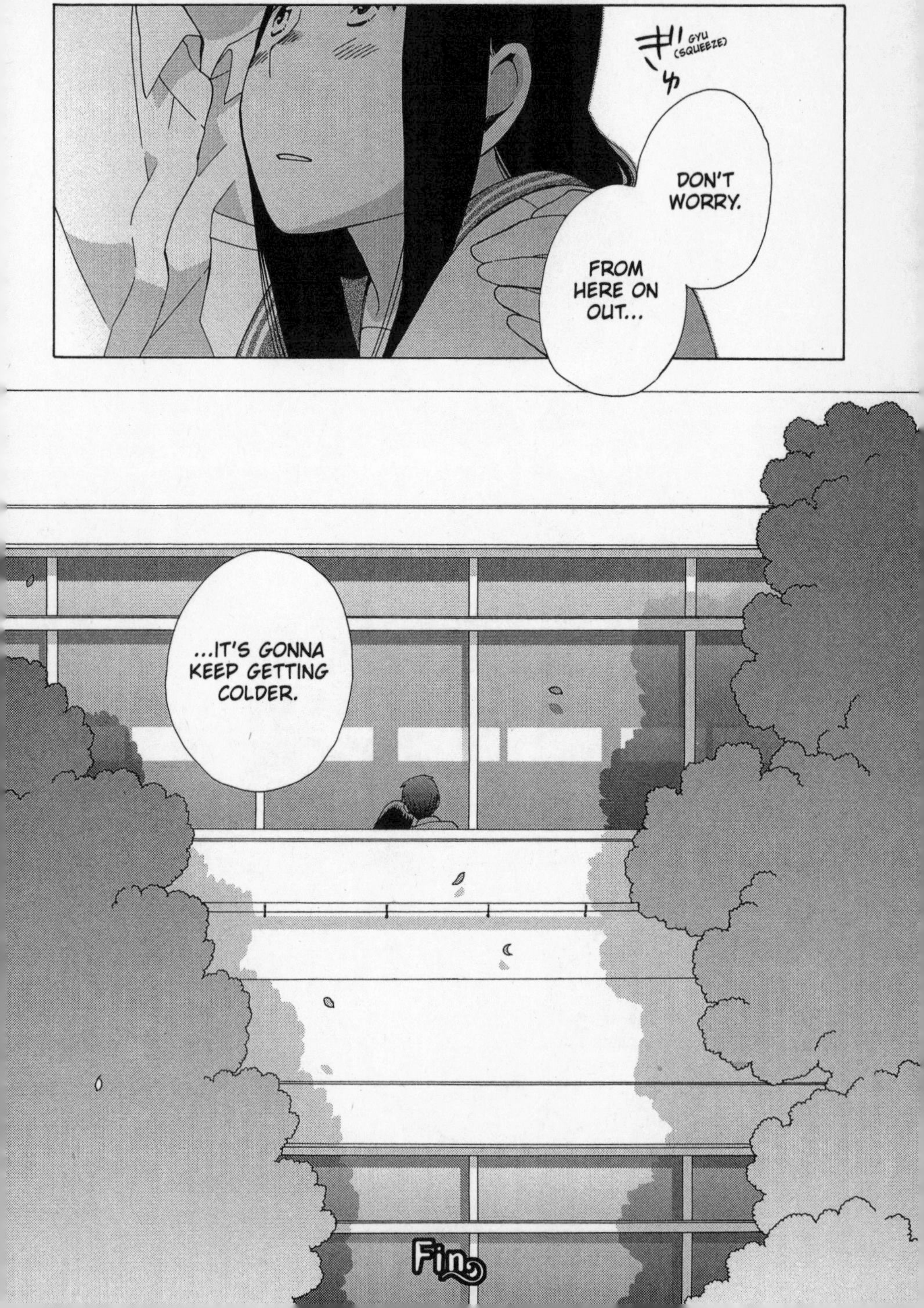
ぎゅ GYU (SQUEEZE)
DON'T WORRY.
FROM HERE ON OUT...
...IT'S GONNA KEEP GETTING COLDER.
Fin

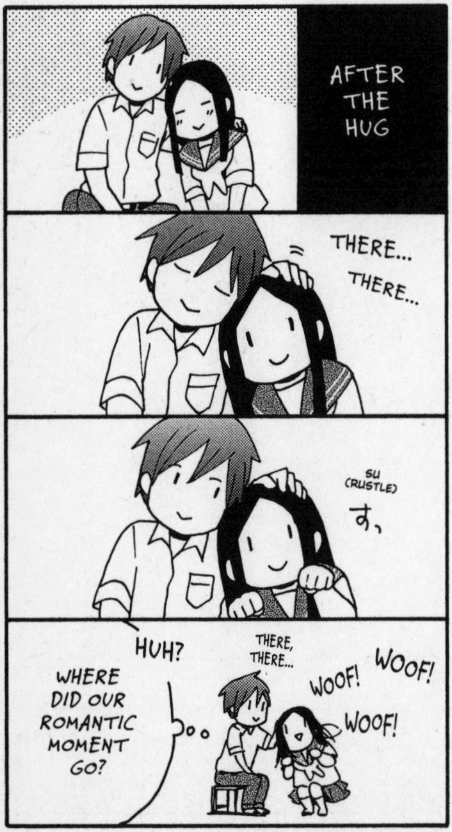

AFTER THE HUG
THERE... THERE...
SU (RUSTLE)
す、
WOOF!
WOOF!
WOOF!
THERE, THERE...
HUH?
WHERE DID OUR ROMANTIC MOMENT GO?

Love at Fourteen

Fuka Mizutani

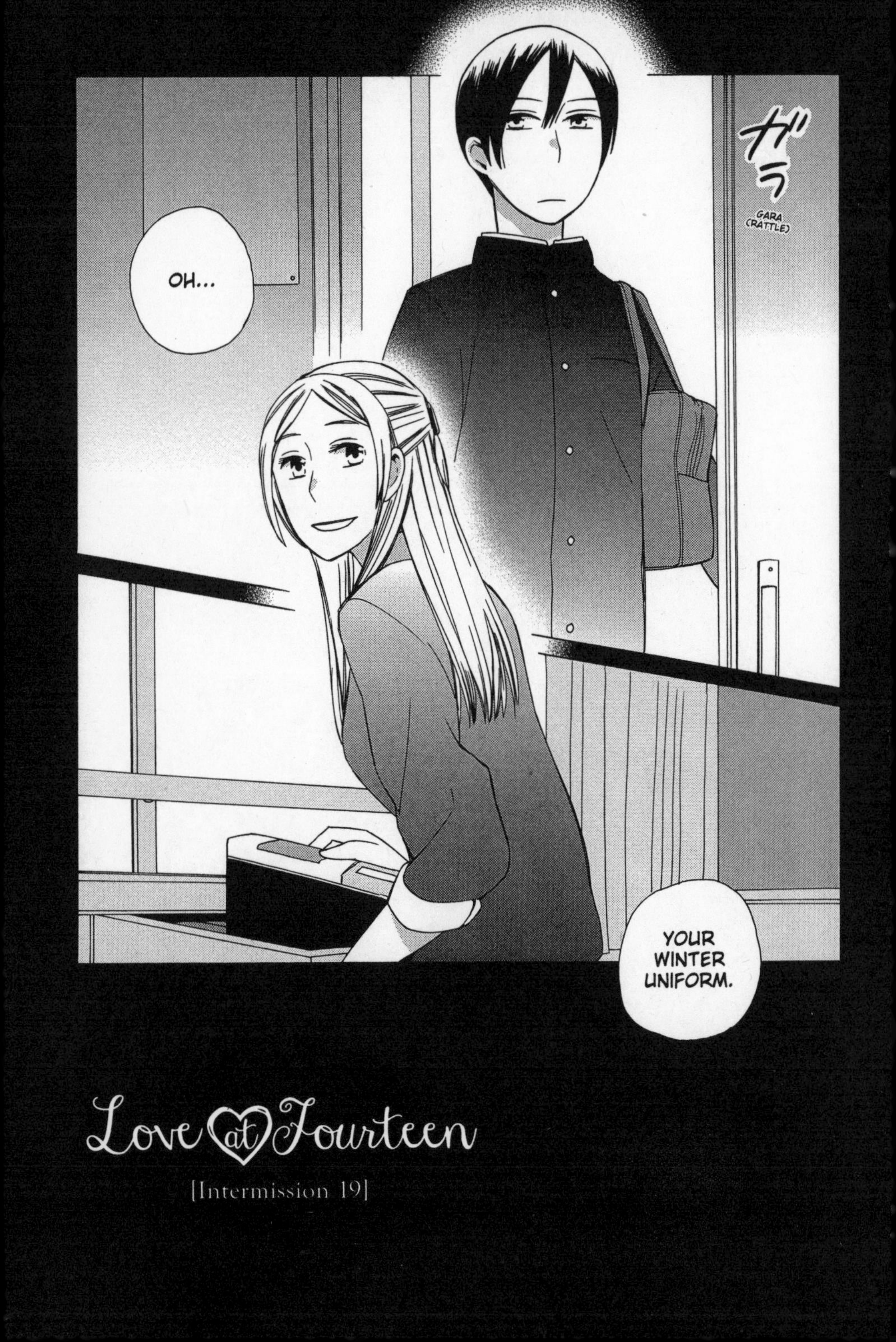
ガラ
GARA (RATTLE)
OH...
YOUR WINTER UNIFORM.

Love at Fourteen

[Intermission 19]

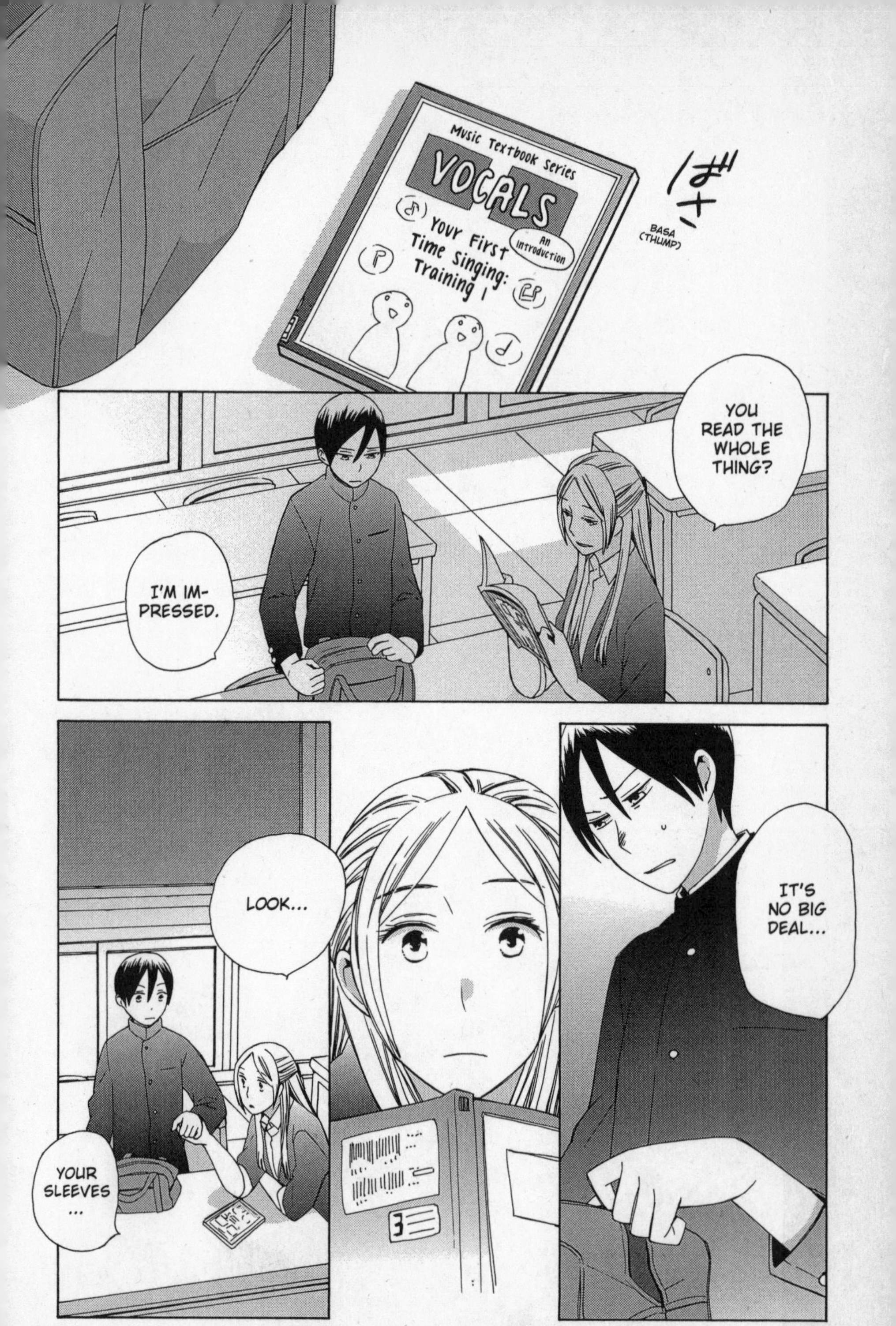
Music Textbook Series
VOCALS
An Introduction
Your First Time Singing: Training 1
ばさ
BASA (THUMP)
YOU READ THE WHOLE THING?
I'M IM-PRESSED.
IT'S NO BIG DEAL...
LOOK...
YOUR SLEEVES ...

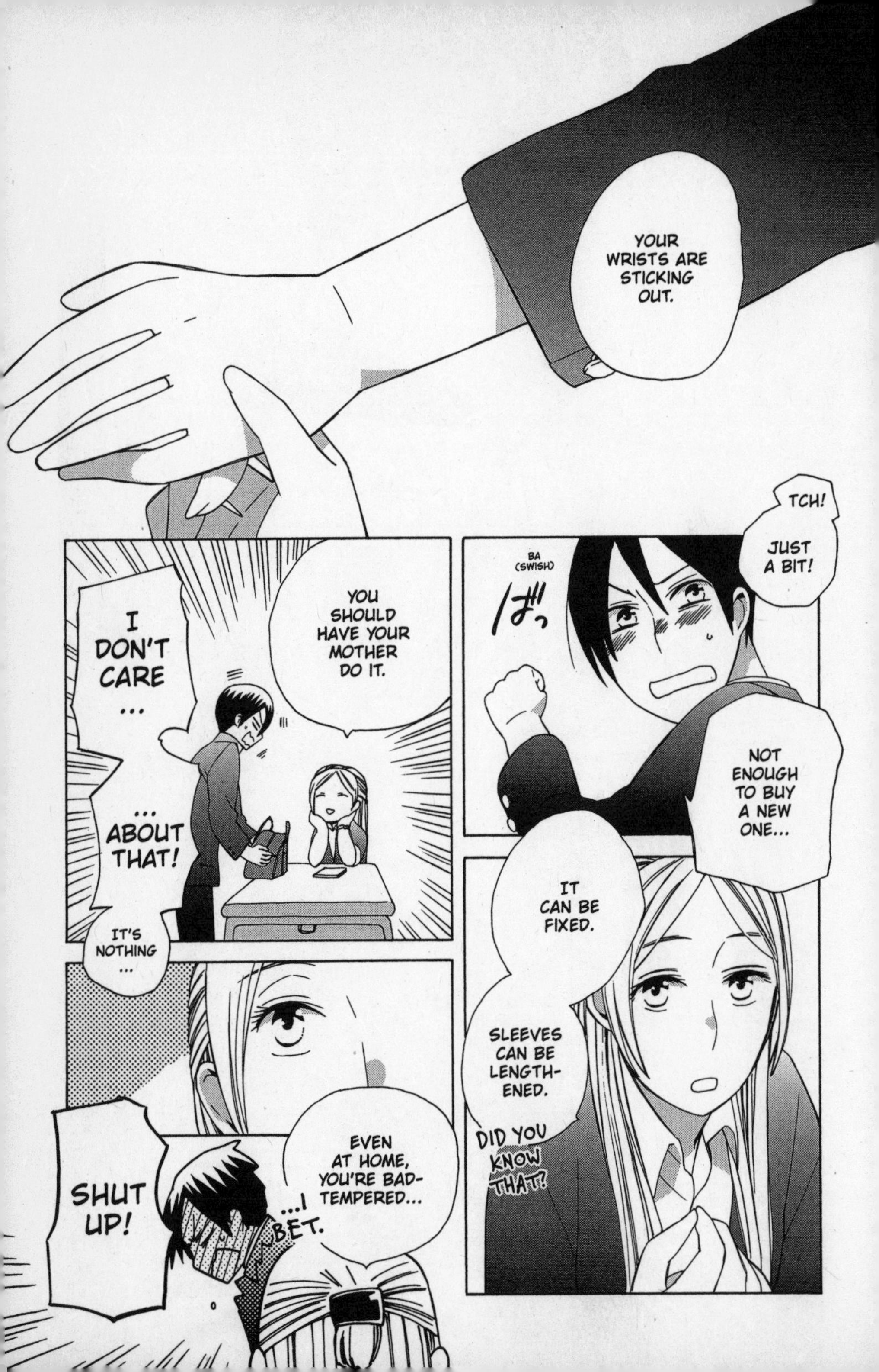
YOUR WRISTS ARE STICKING OUT.
TCH! JUST A BIT!
BA (SWISH)
ばっ
NOT ENOUGH TO BUY A NEW ONE...
YOU SHOULD HAVE YOUR MOTHER DO IT.
I DON'T CARE...
...ABOUT THAT!
IT'S NOTHING...
IT CAN BE FIXED.
SLEEVES CAN BE LENGTH-ENED.
DID YOU KNOW THAT?
EVEN AT HOME, YOU'RE BAD-TEMPERED...
...I BET.
SHUT UP!

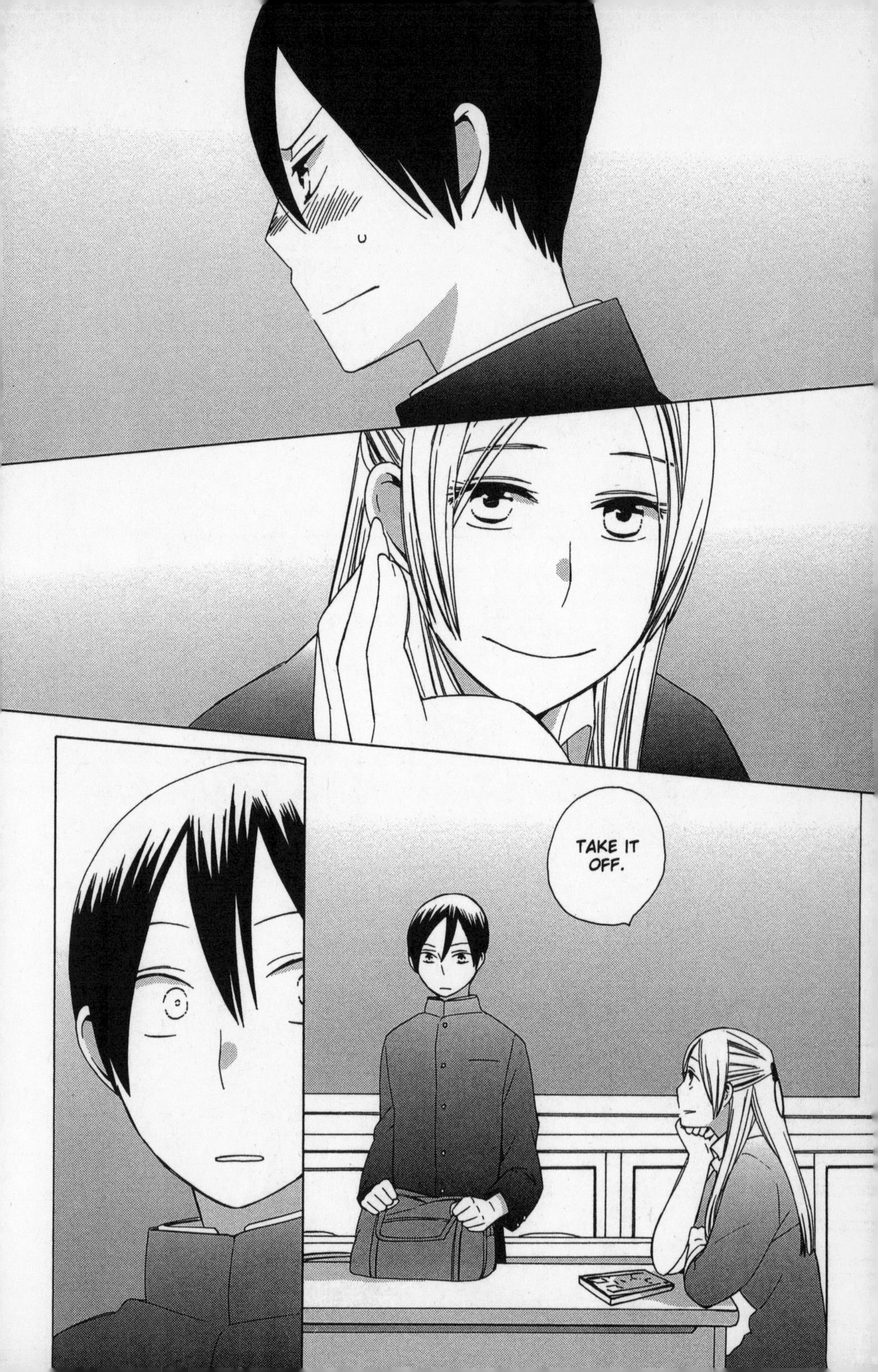
TAKE IT OFF.

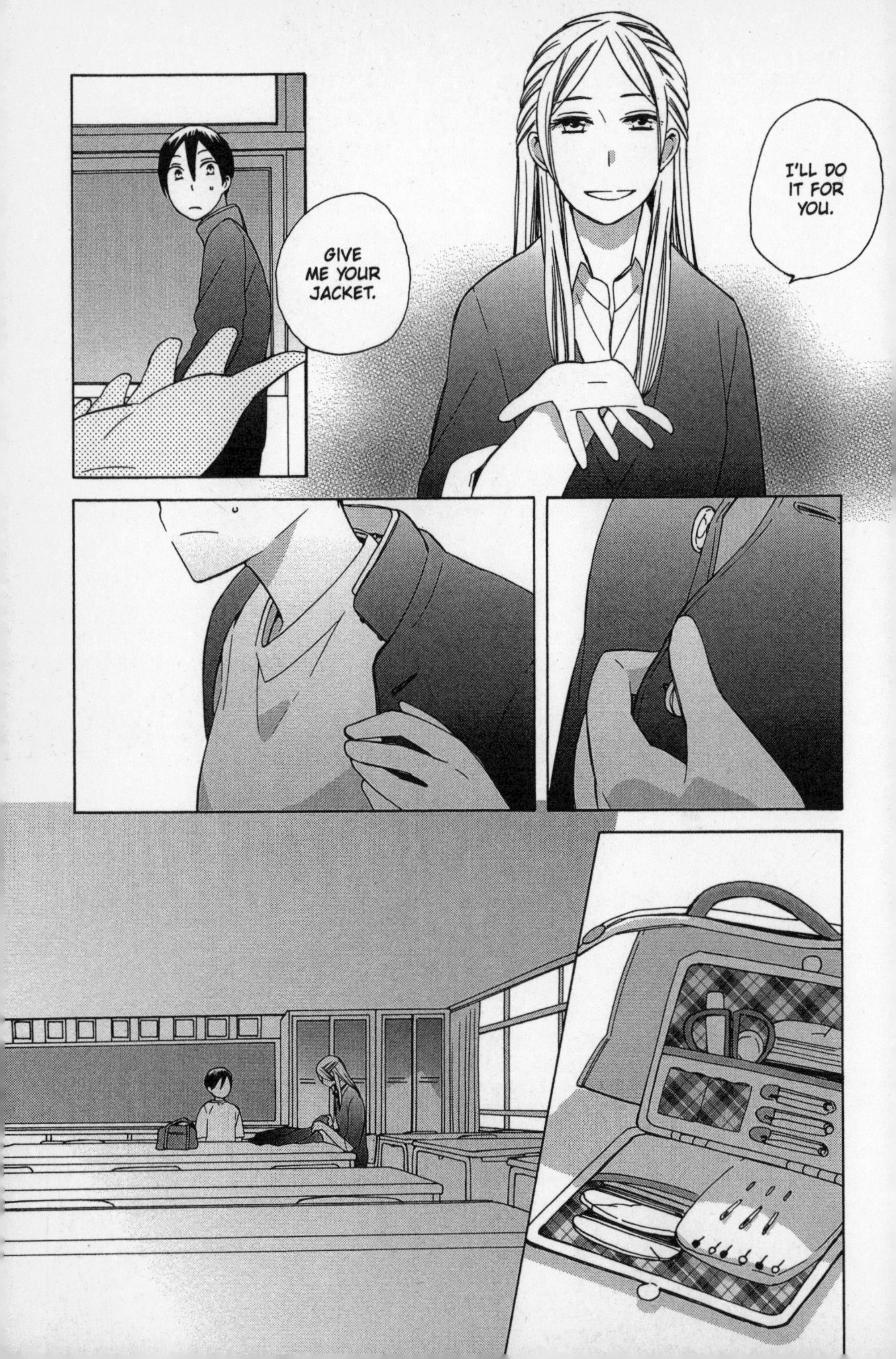
I'LL DO IT FOR YOU.
GIVE ME YOUR JACKET.

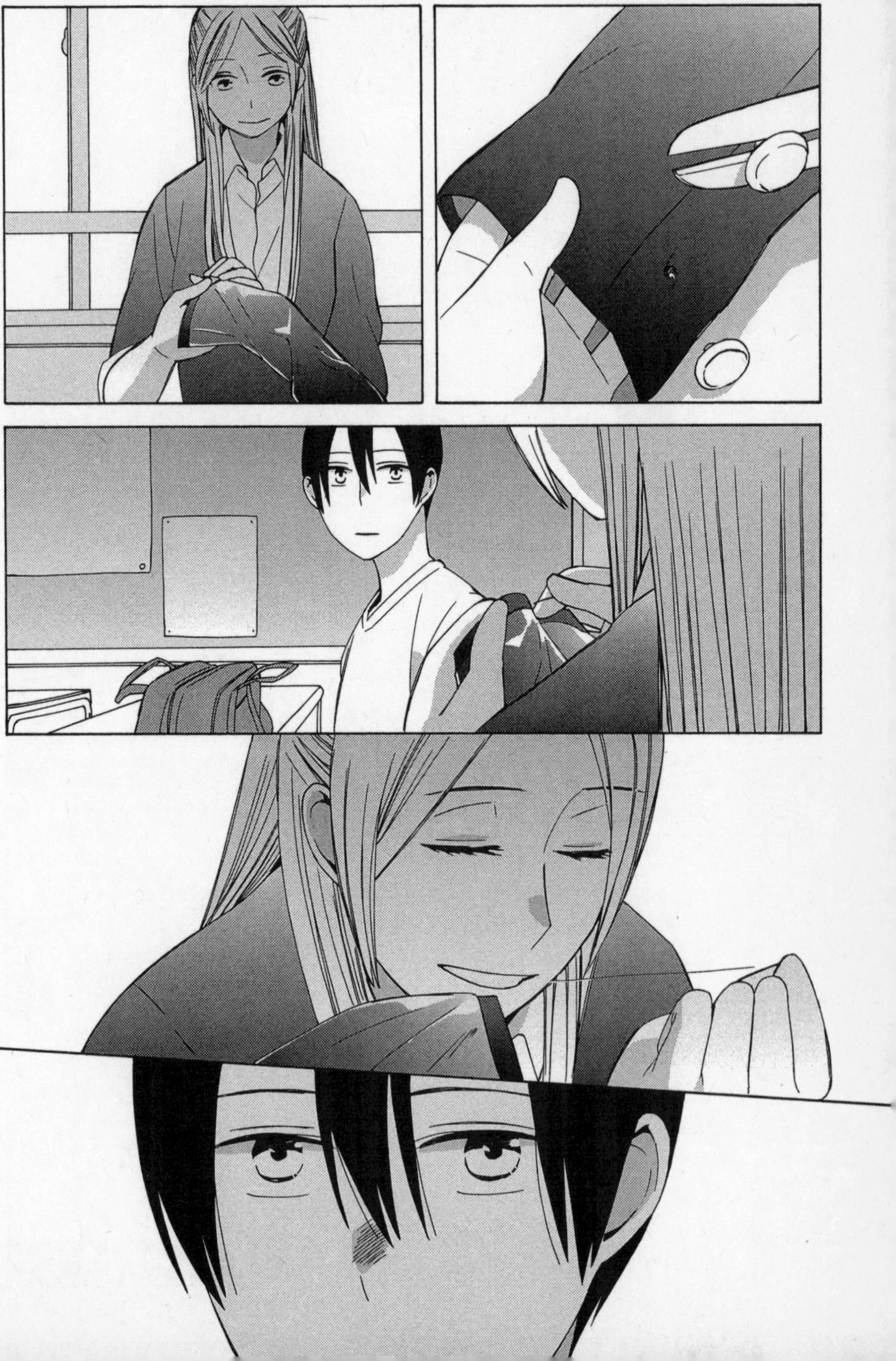

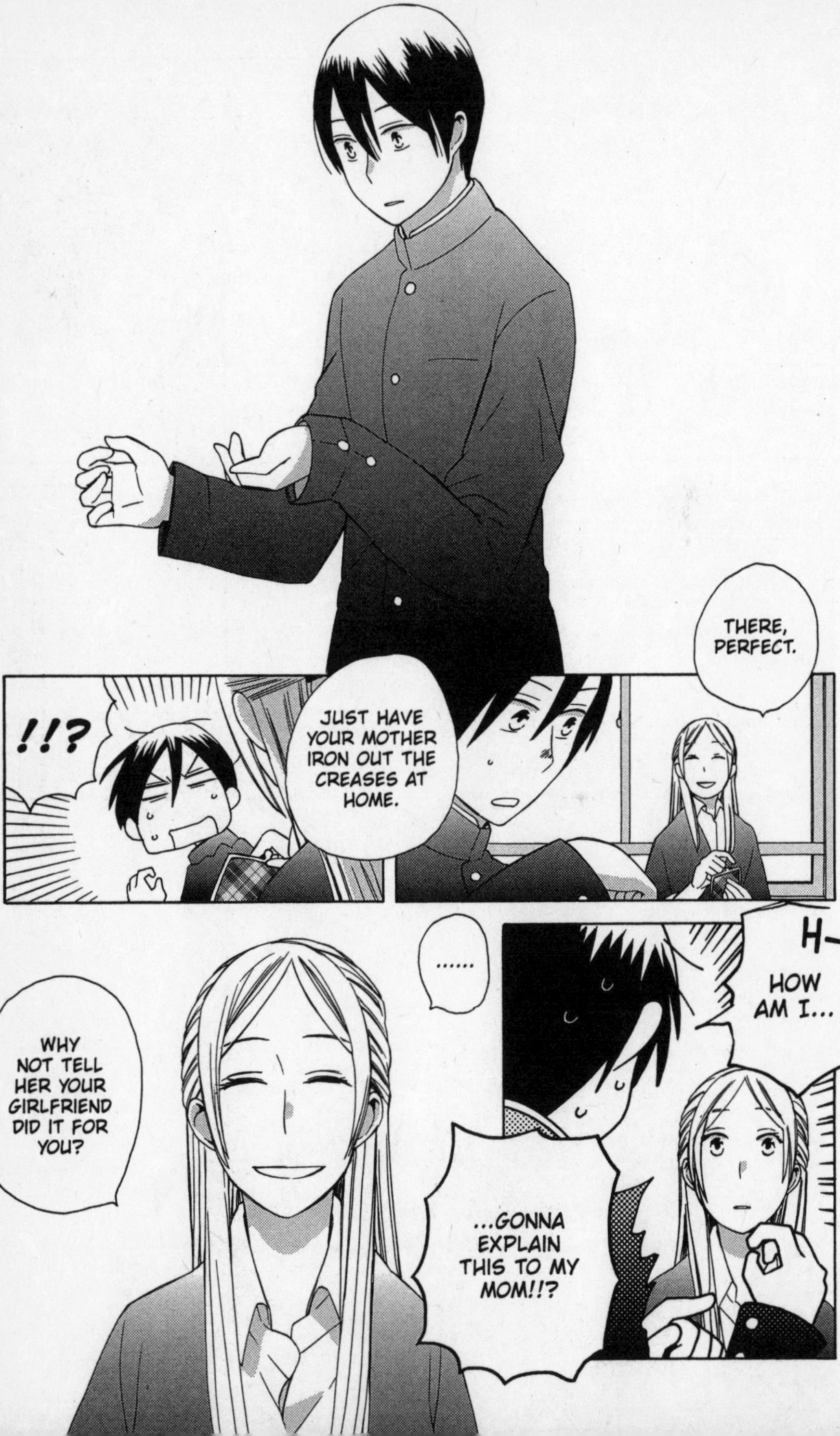
THERE, PERFECT.
JUST HAVE YOUR MOTHER IRON OUT THE CREASES AT HOME.
!!?
H—
HOW AM I...
...GONNA EXPLAIN THIS TO MY MOM!!?
......
WHY NOT TELL HER YOUR GIRLFRIEND DID IT FOR YOU?

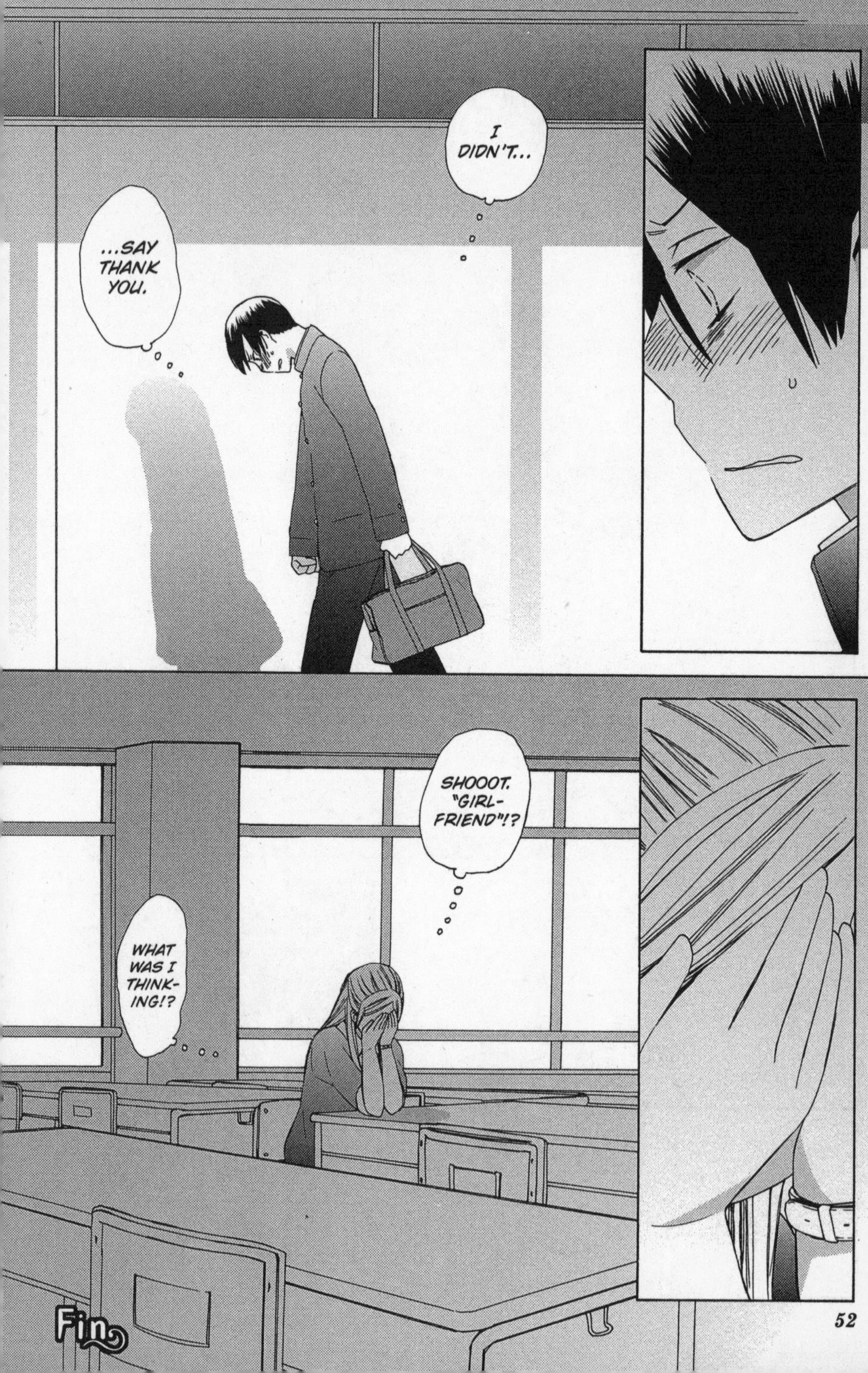
I DIDN'T...
...SAY THANK YOU.
SHOOOT. "GIRL-FRIEND"!?
WHAT WAS I THINKING!?
Fin

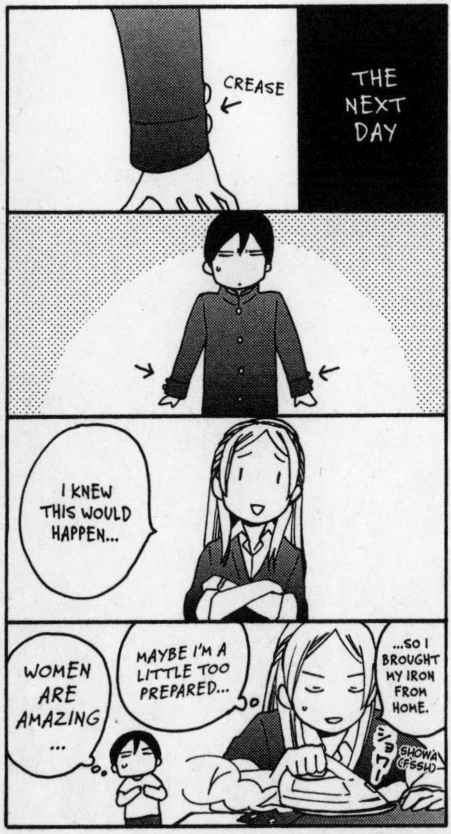
THE NEXT DAY
CREASE
I KNEW THIS WOULD HAPPEN...
...SO I BROUGHT MY IRON FROM HOME.
SHOWA (FSSH)
MAYBE I'M A LITTLE TOO PREPARED...
WOMEN ARE AMAZING ...

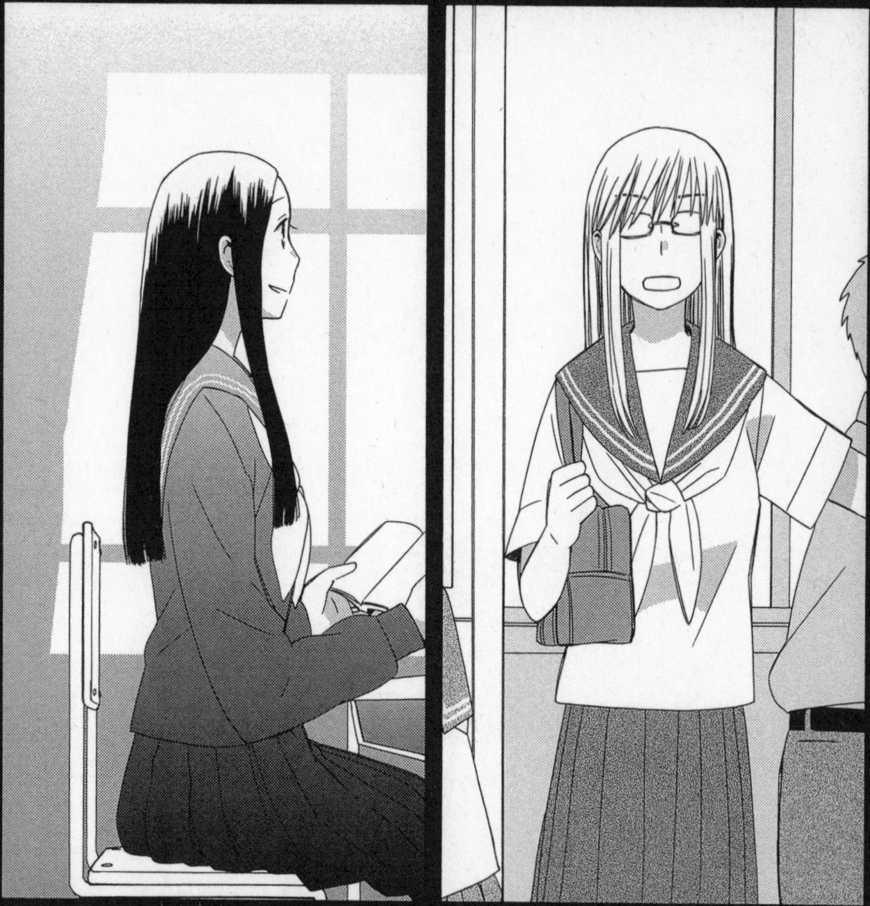

Love at Fourteen

[Intermission 20]

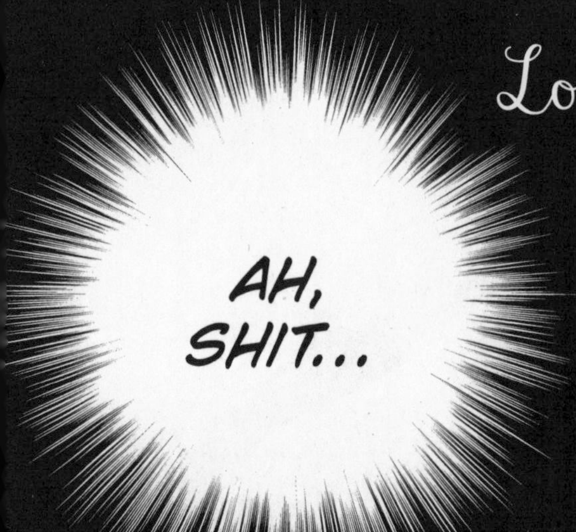
AH, SHIT...

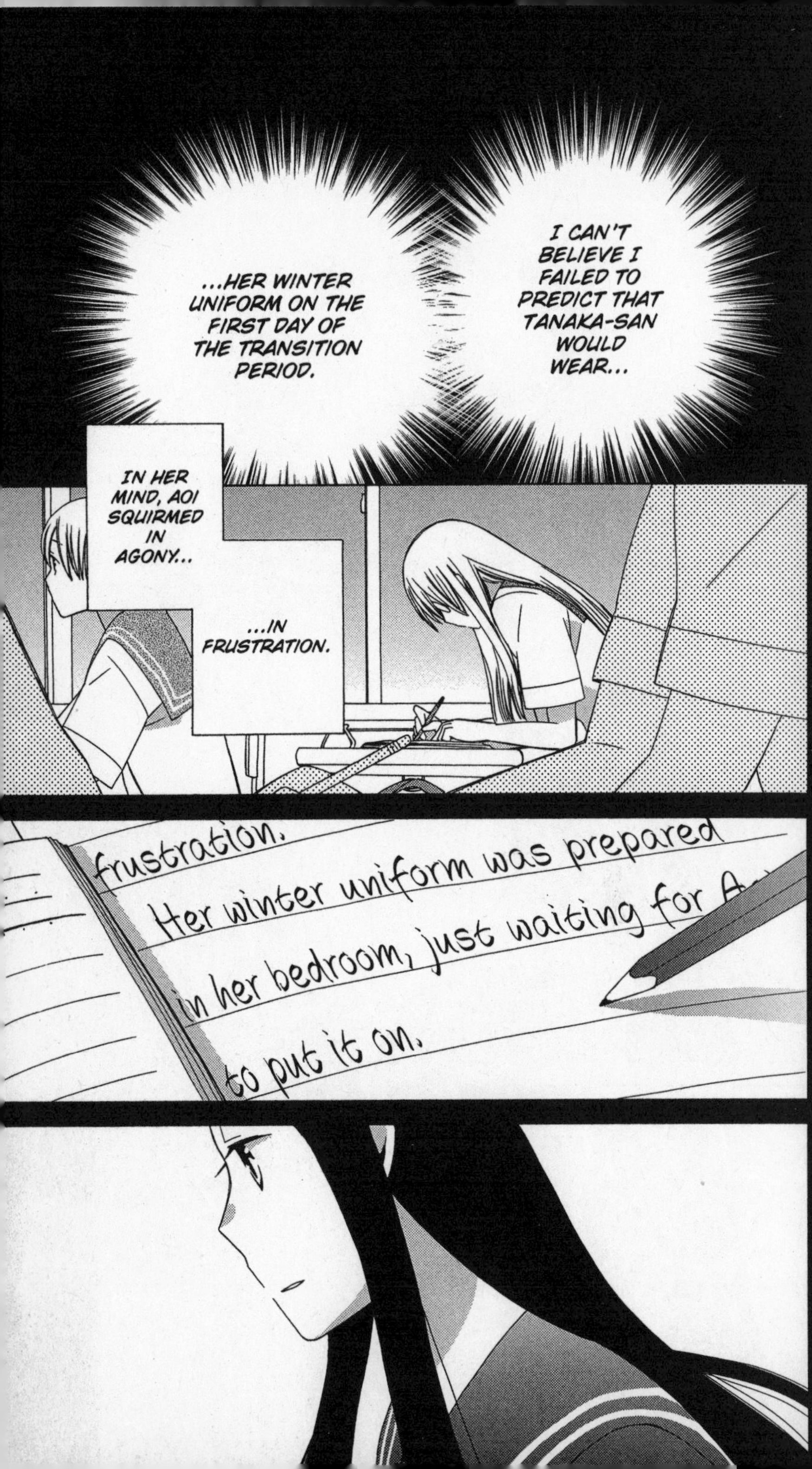
I CAN'T BELIEVE I FAILED TO PREDICT THAT TANAKA-SAN WOULD WEAR...
...HER WINTER UNIFORM ON THE FIRST DAY OF THE TRANSITION PERIOD.
IN HER MIND, AOI SQUIRMED IN AGONY...
...IN FRUSTRATION.
frustration.
Her winter uniform was prepared
in her bedroom, just waiting for A
to put it on.

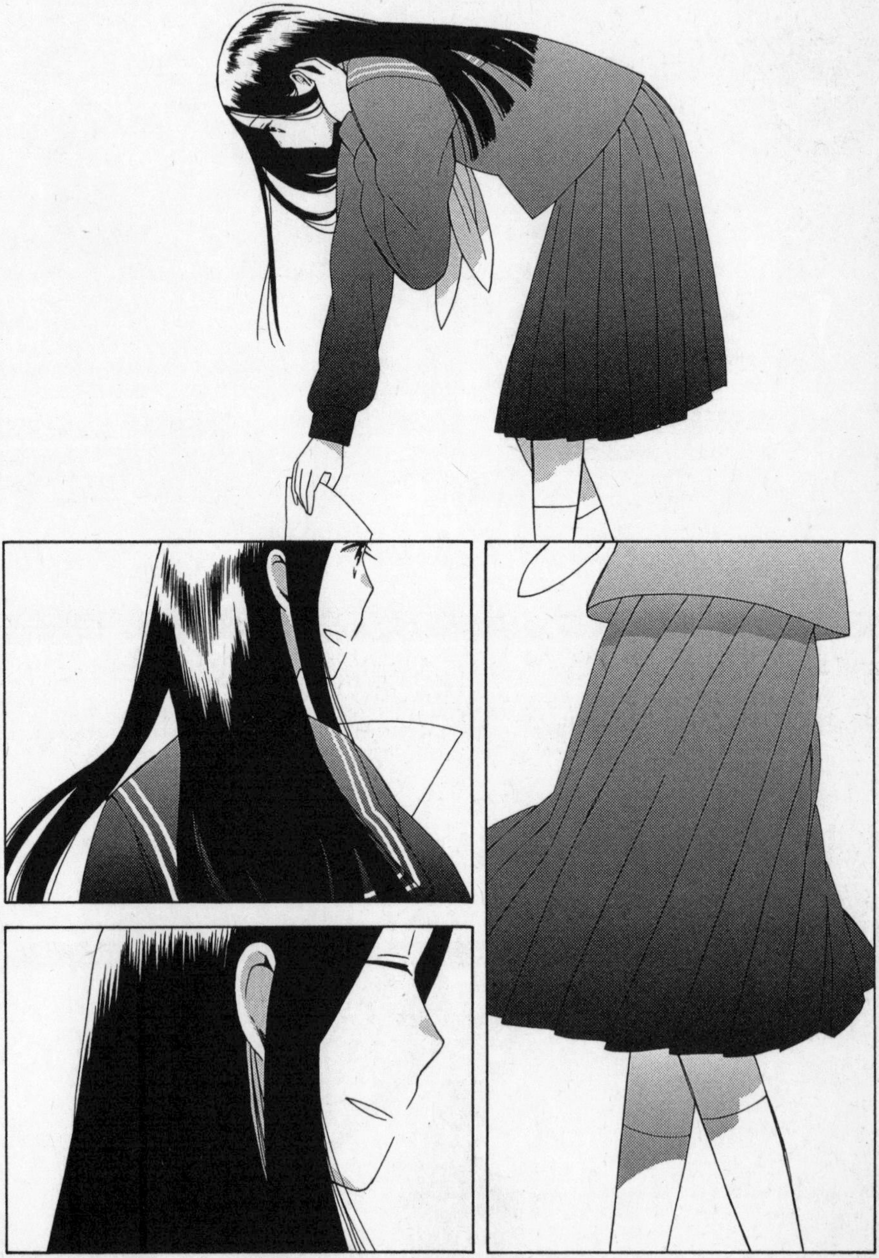

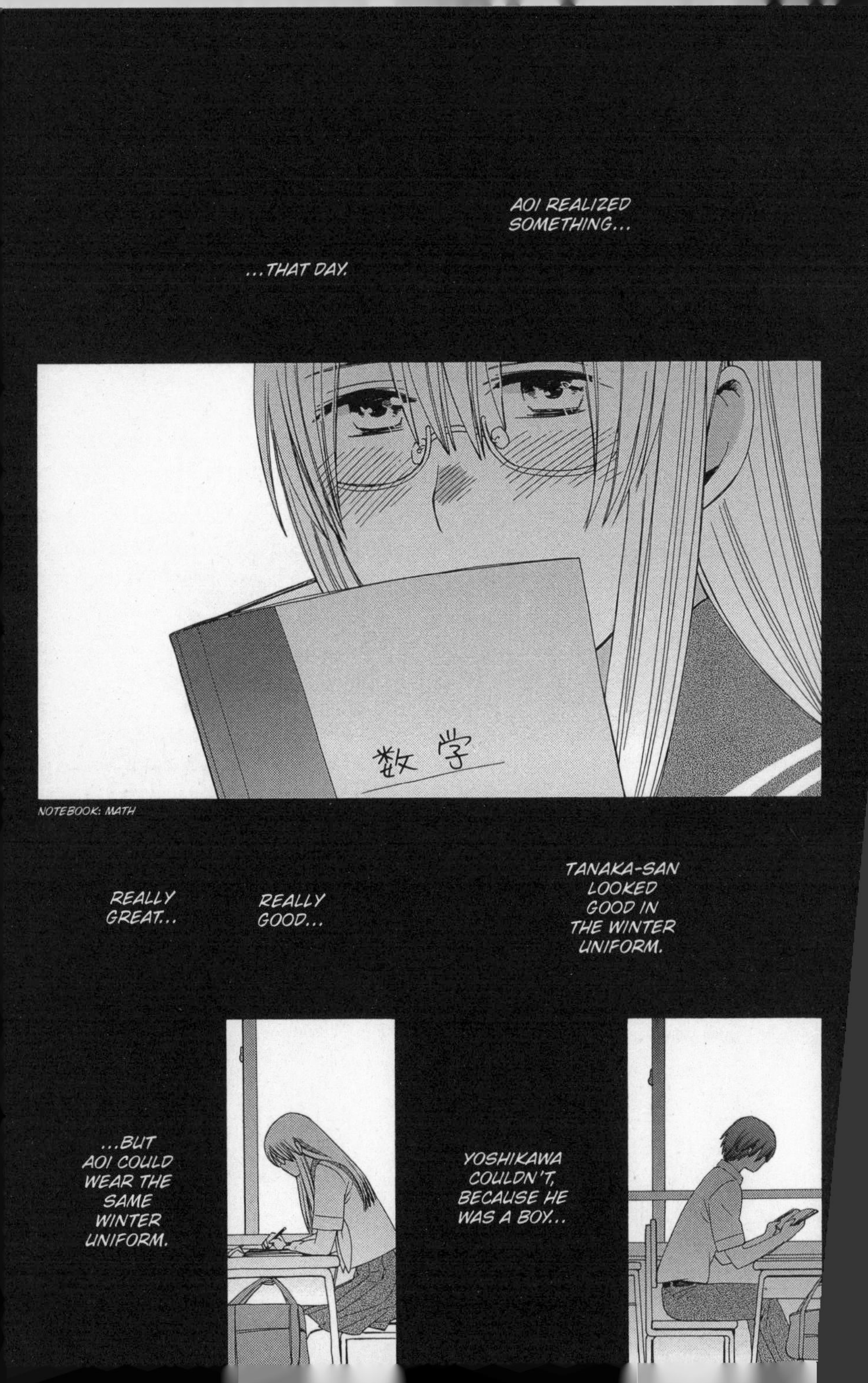
AOI REALIZED SOMETHING...
...THAT DAY.
数学
NOTEBOOK: MATH
TANAKA-SAN LOOKED GOOD IN THE WINTER UNIFORM.
REALLY GOOD...
REALLY GREAT...
YOSHIKAWA COULDN'T, BECAUSE HE WAS A BOY...
...BUT AOI COULD WEAR THE SAME WINTER UNIFORM.

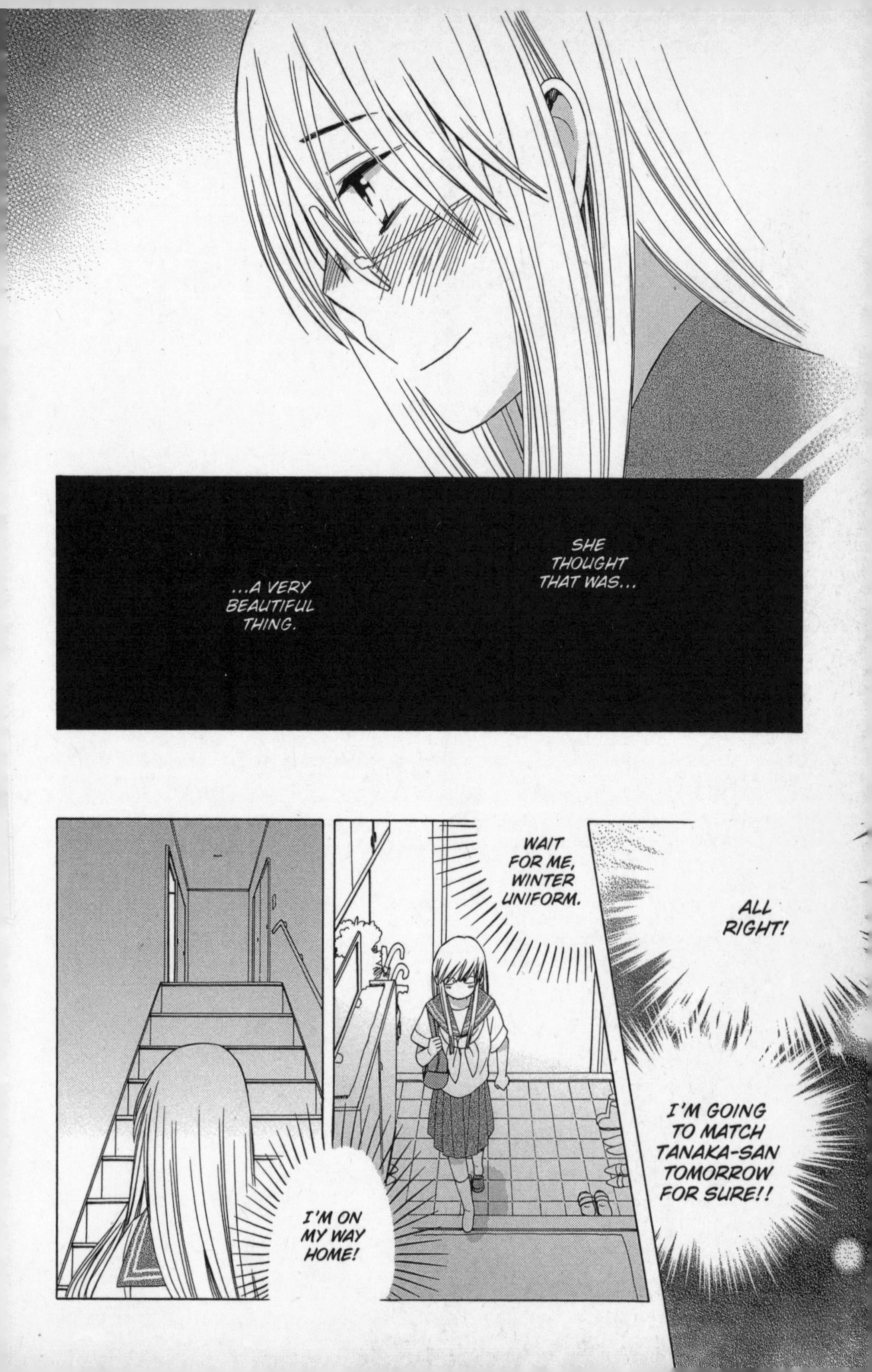
SHE THOUGHT THAT WAS...
...A VERY BEAUTIFUL THING.
ALL RIGHT!
I'M GOING TO MATCH TANAKA-SAN TOMORROW FOR SURE!!
WAIT FOR ME, WINTER UNIFORM.
I'M ON MY WAY HOME!

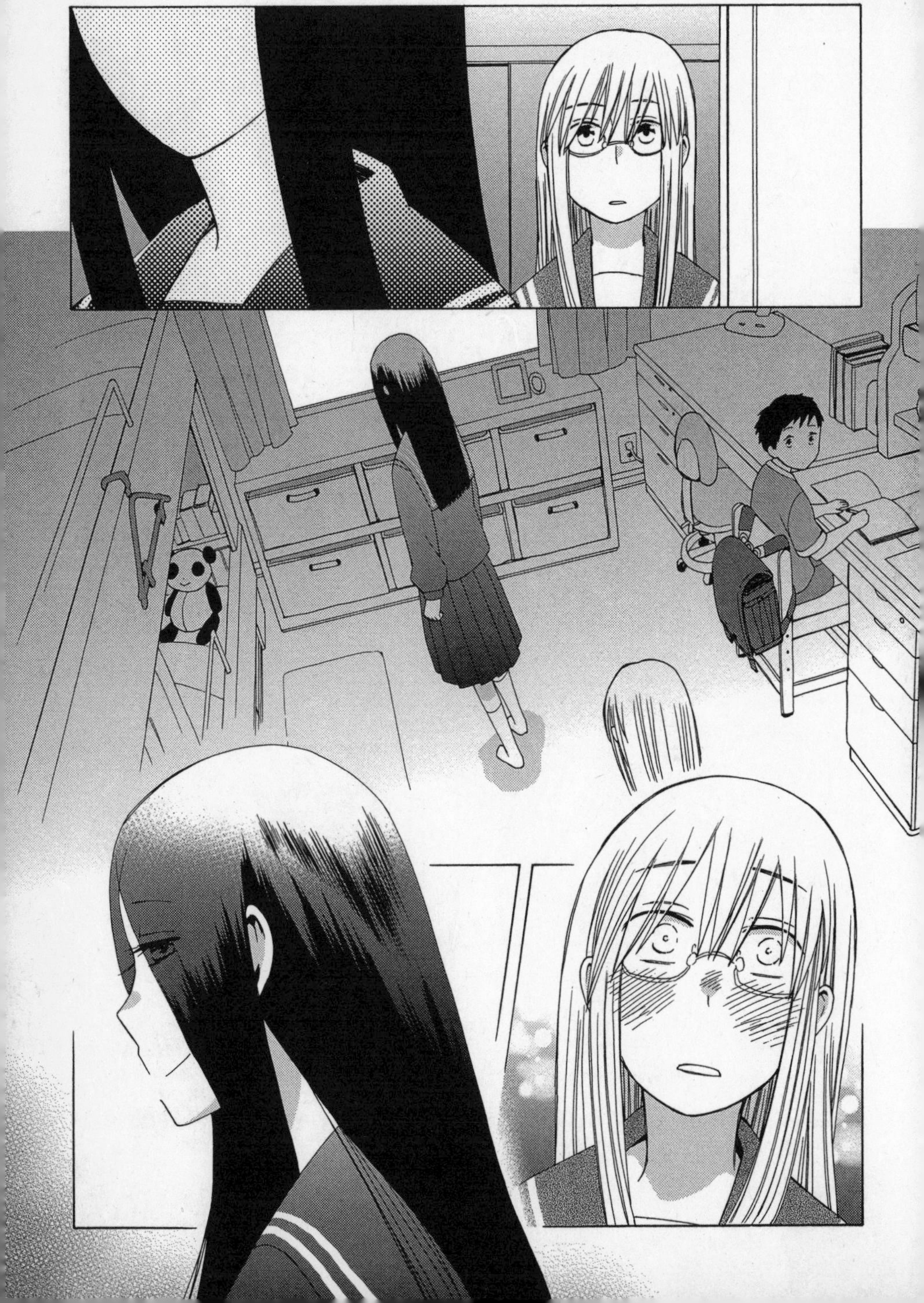

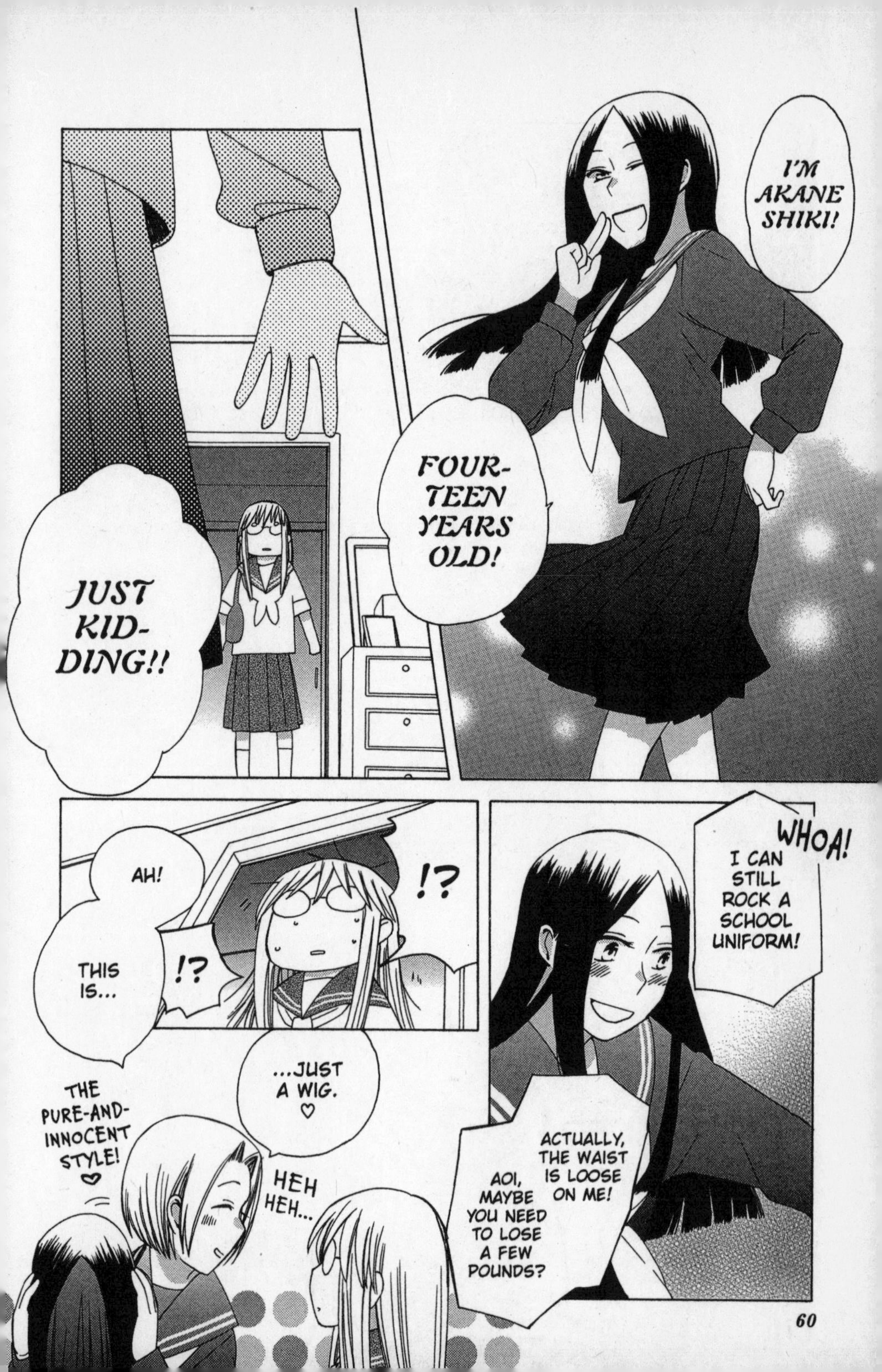
I'M AKANE SHIKI!
FOUR-TEEN YEARS OLD!
JUST KID-DING!!
WHOA!
I CAN STILL ROCK A SCHOOL UNIFORM!
ACTUALLY, THE WAIST IS LOOSE ON ME!
AOI, MAYBE YOU NEED TO LOSE A FEW POUNDS?
!?
!?
AH!
THIS IS...
...JUST A WIG. ♡
THE PURE-AND-INNOCENT STYLE! ♡
HEH HEH...

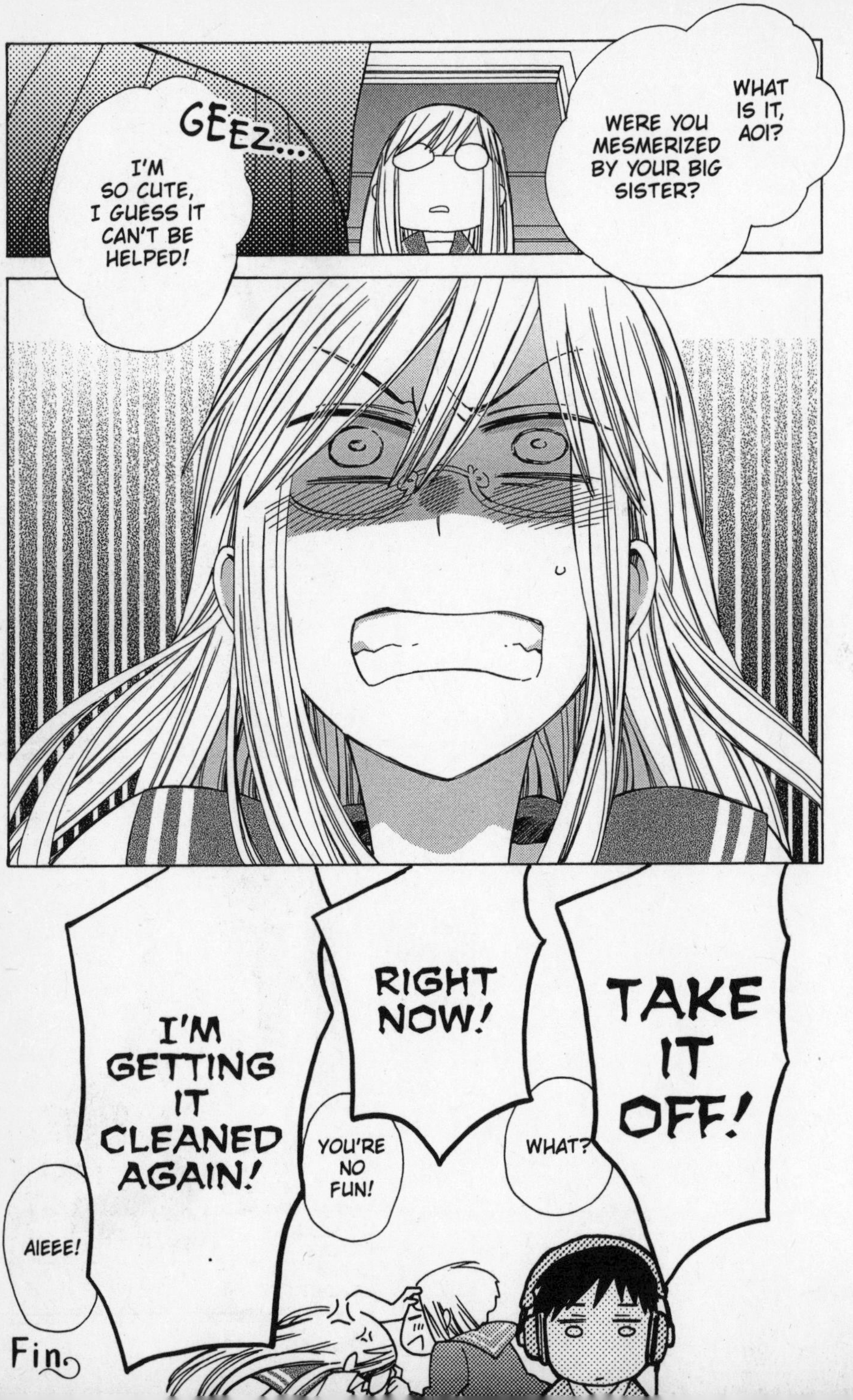
WHAT IS IT, AOI?
WERE YOU MESMERIZED BY YOUR BIG SISTER?
GEEZ...
I'M SO CUTE, I GUESS IT CAN'T BE HELPED!
TAKE IT OFF!
RIGHT NOW!
I'M GETTING IT CLEANED AGAIN!
WHAT?
YOU'RE NO FUN!
AIEEE!
Fin

Love at Fourteen

Fuka Mizutani

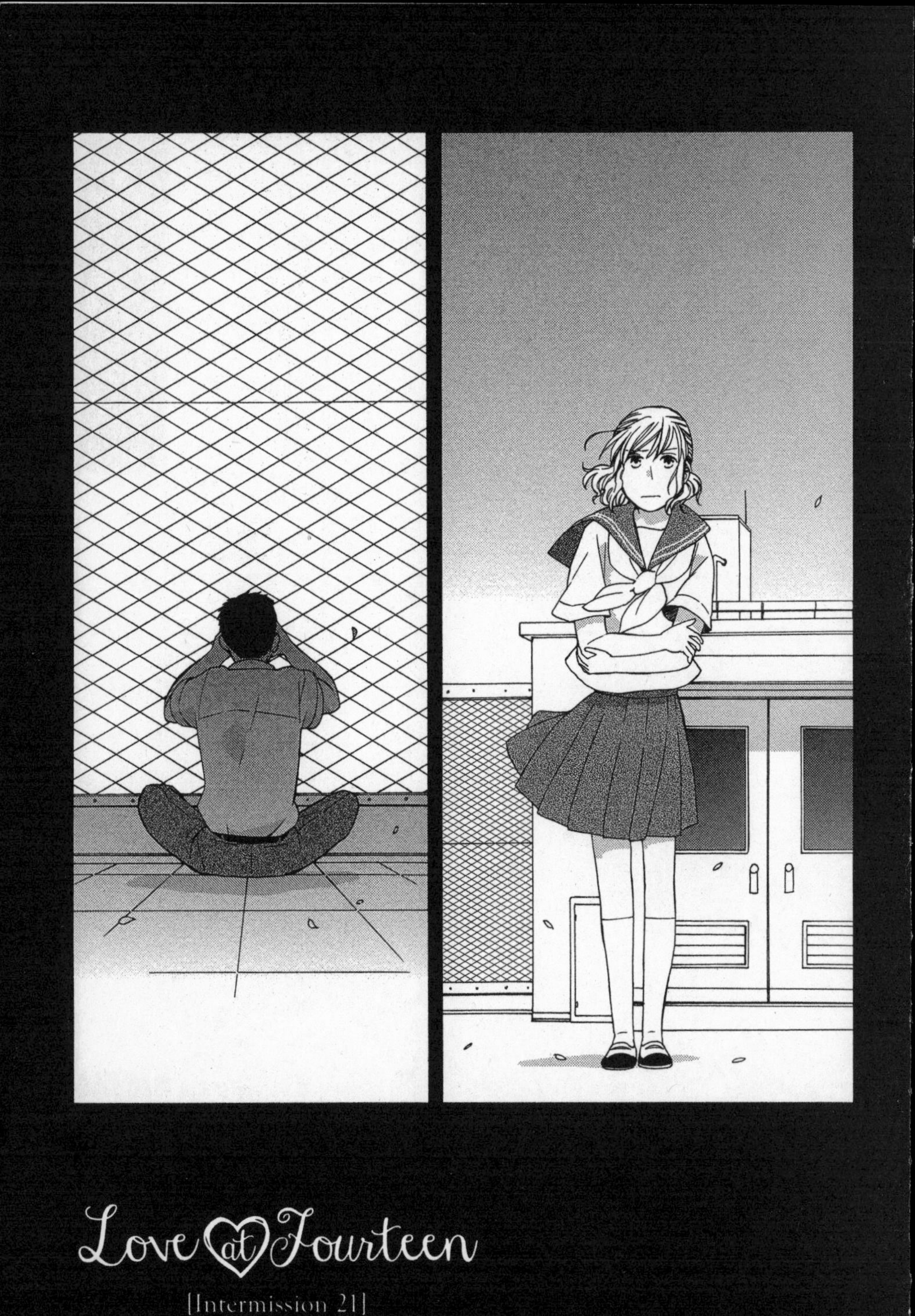

Love at Fourteen

[Intermission 21]

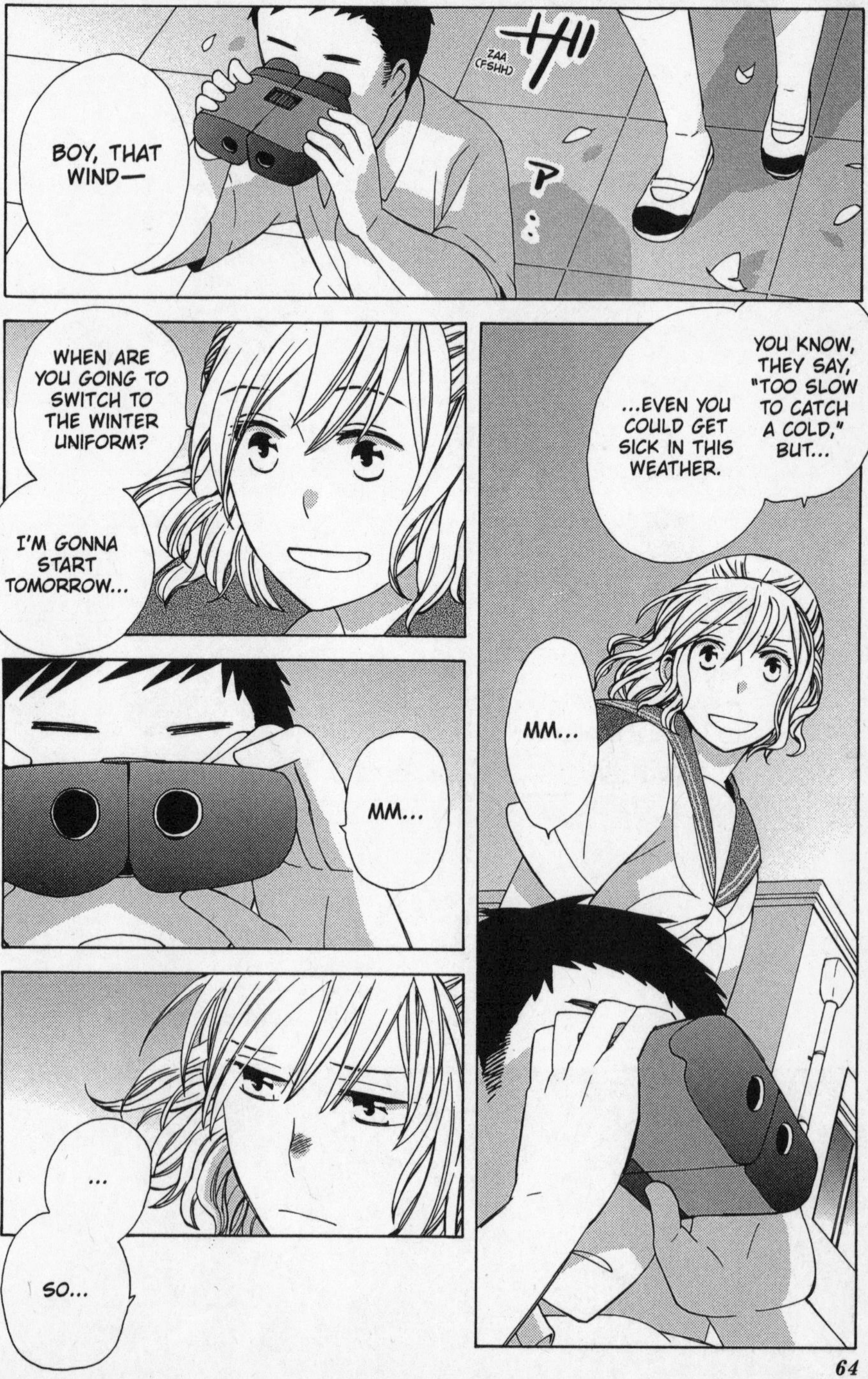
ZAA (FSHH)
BOY, THAT WIND—
YOU KNOW, THEY SAY, "TOO SLOW TO CATCH A COLD," BUT...
...EVEN YOU COULD GET SICK IN THIS WEATHER.
MM...
WHEN ARE YOU GOING TO SWITCH TO THE WINTER UNIFORM?
I'M GONNA START TOMORROW...
MM...
...
SO...

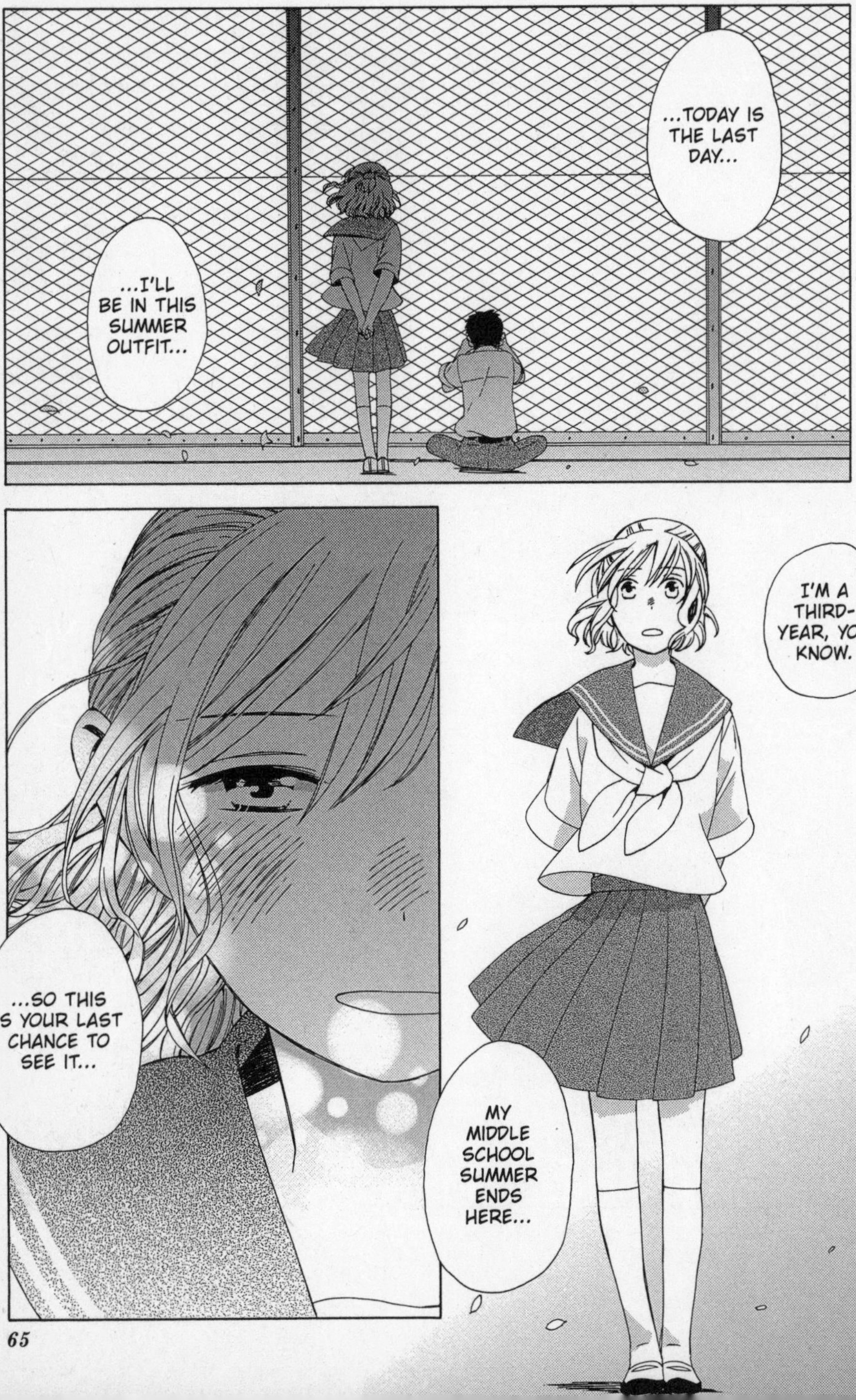
...TODAY IS THE LAST DAY...
...I'LL BE IN THIS SUMMER OUTFIT...
I'M A THIRD-YEAR, YOU KNOW.
MY MIDDLE SCHOOL SUMMER ENDS HERE...
...SO THIS IS YOUR LAST CHANCE TO SEE IT...

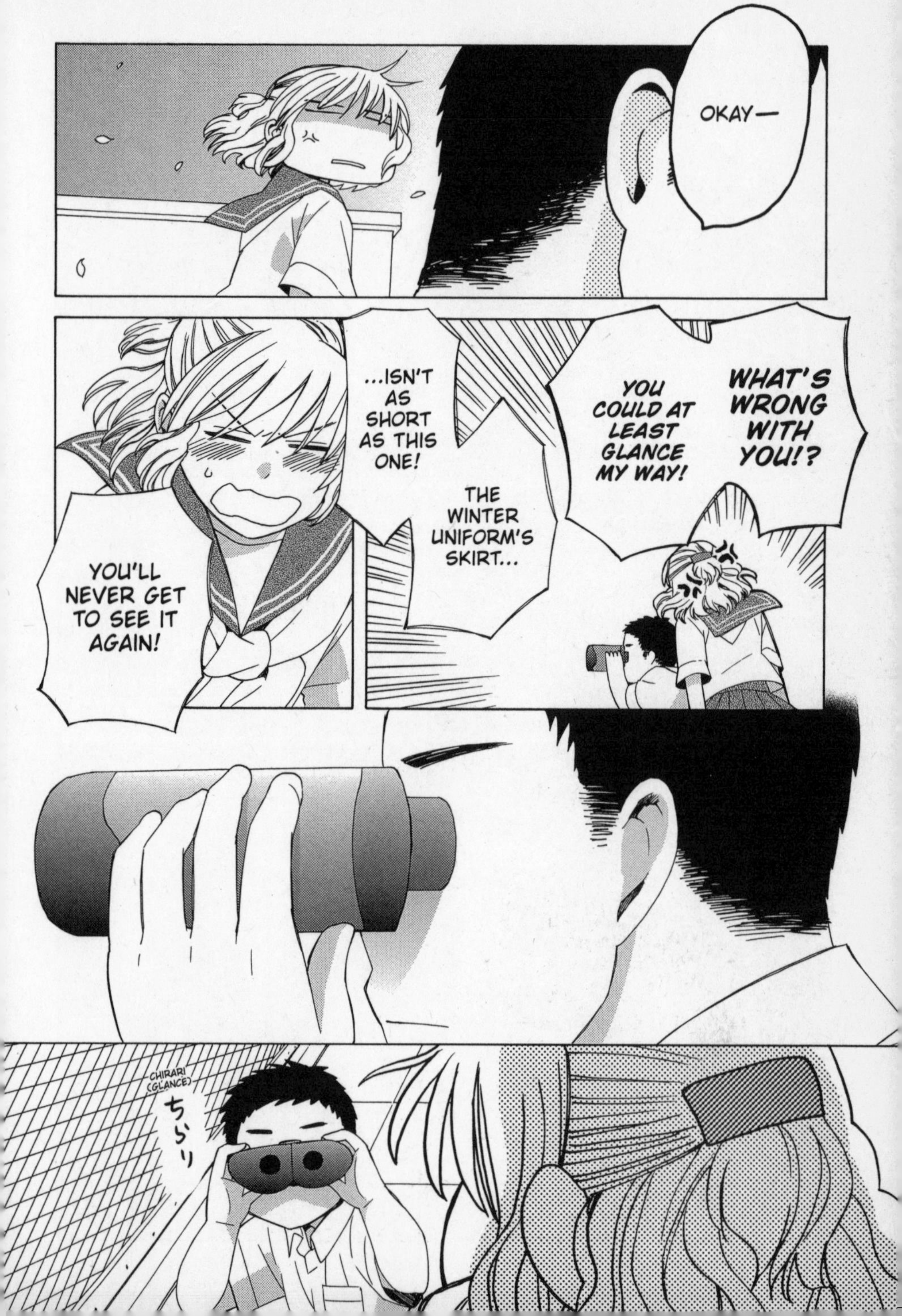
OKAY—
WHAT'S WRONG WITH YOU!?
YOU COULD AT LEAST GLANCE MY WAY!
THE WINTER UNIFORM'S SKIRT...
...ISN'T AS SHORT AS THIS ONE!
YOU'LL NEVER GET TO SEE IT AGAIN!
ちらり
CHIRARI (GLANCE)

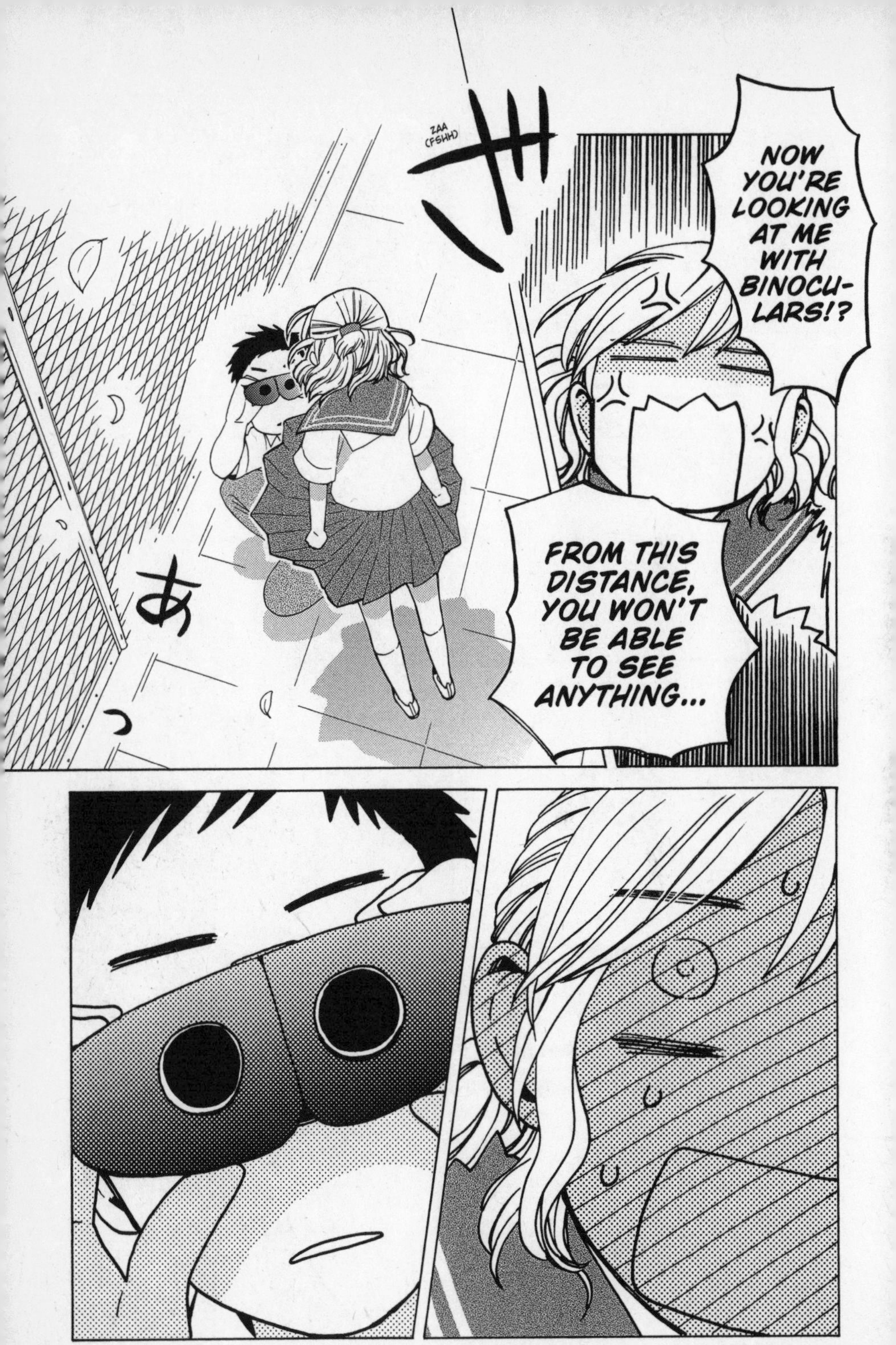
NOW YOU'RE LOOKING AT ME WITH BINOCU-LARS!?
FROM THIS DISTANCE, YOU WON'T BE ABLE TO SEE ANYTHING...
ZAA (FSHH)
あっ

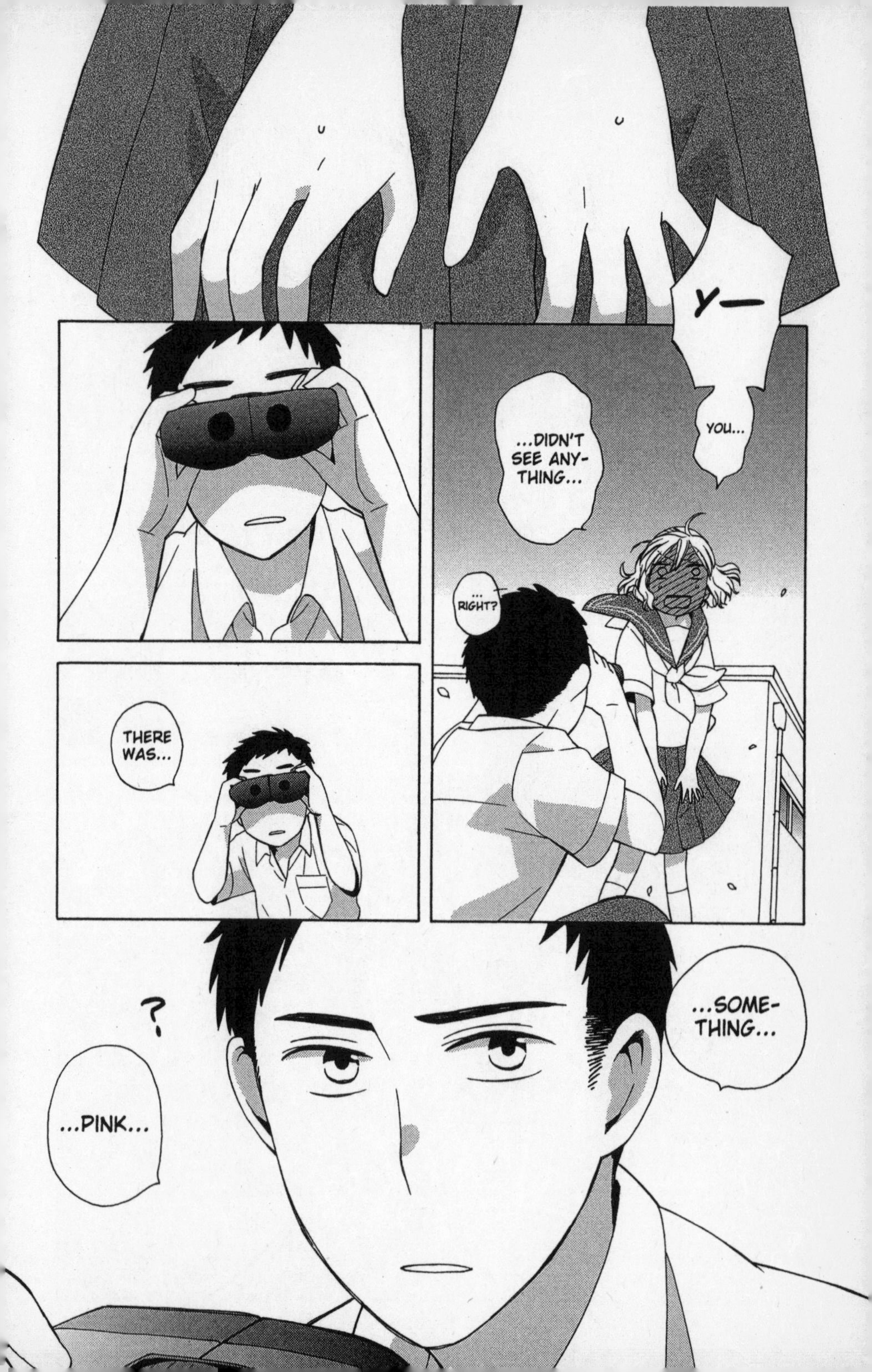
Y—
YOU...
...DIDN'T SEE ANY-THING...
...RIGHT?
THERE WAS...
...SOME-THING...
?
...PINK...

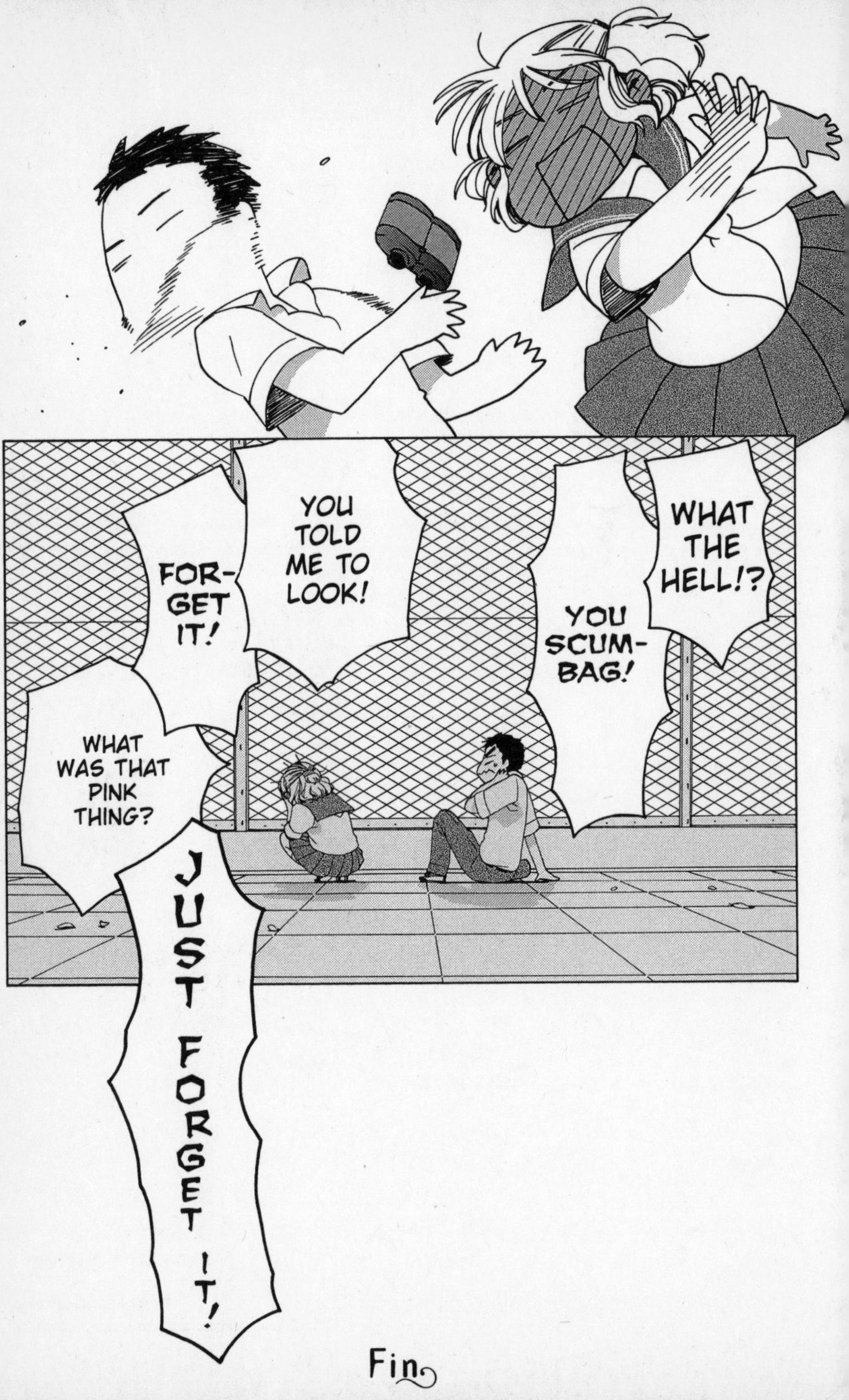
WHAT THE HELL!?
YOU SCUM-BAG!
YOU TOLD ME TO LOOK!
FOR-GET IT!
WHAT WAS THAT PINK THING?
JUST FORGET IT!
Fin

Love at Fourteen

Fuka Mizutani

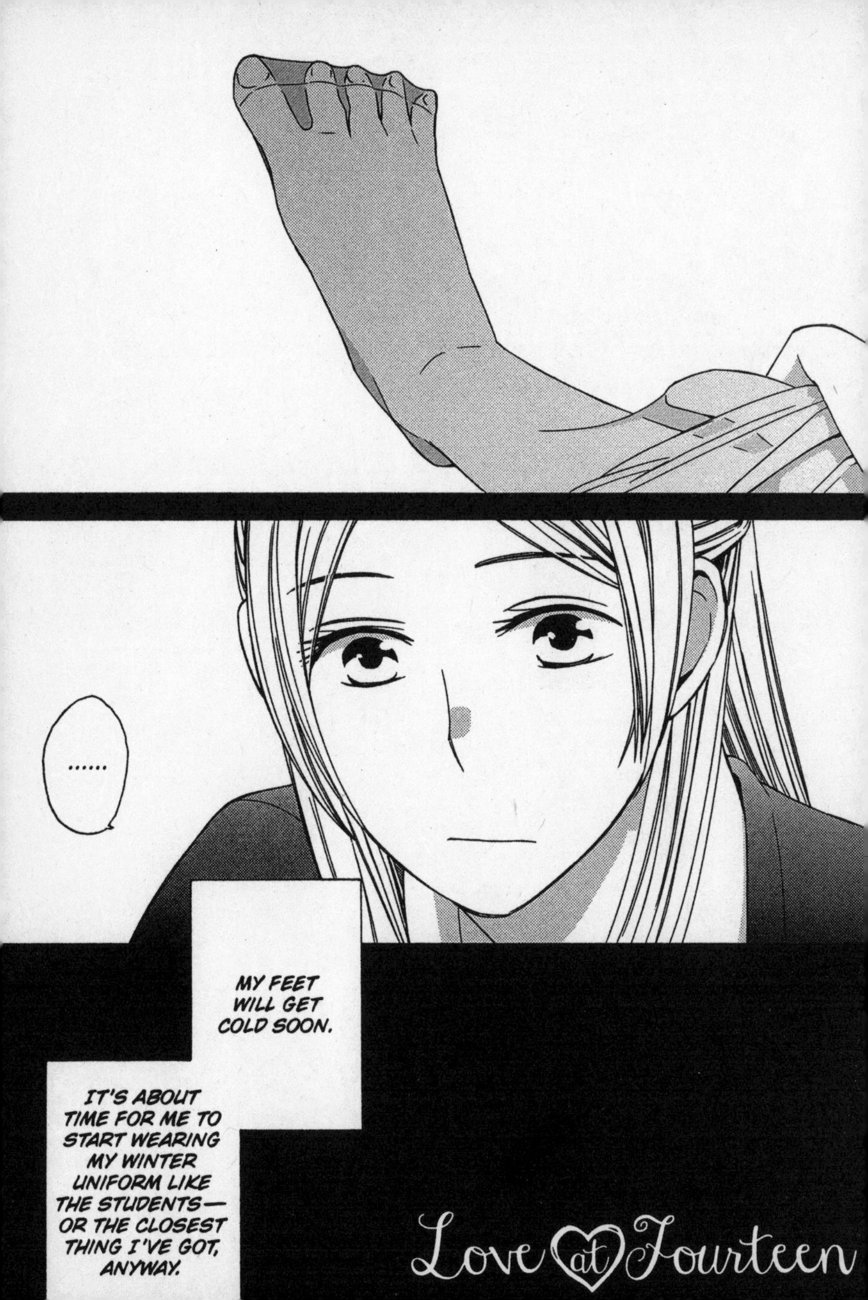
......
MY FEET WILL GET COLD SOON.
IT'S ABOUT TIME FOR ME TO START WEARING MY WINTER UNIFORM LIKE THE STUDENTS— OR THE CLOSEST THING I'VE GOT, ANYWAY.
Love at Fourteen

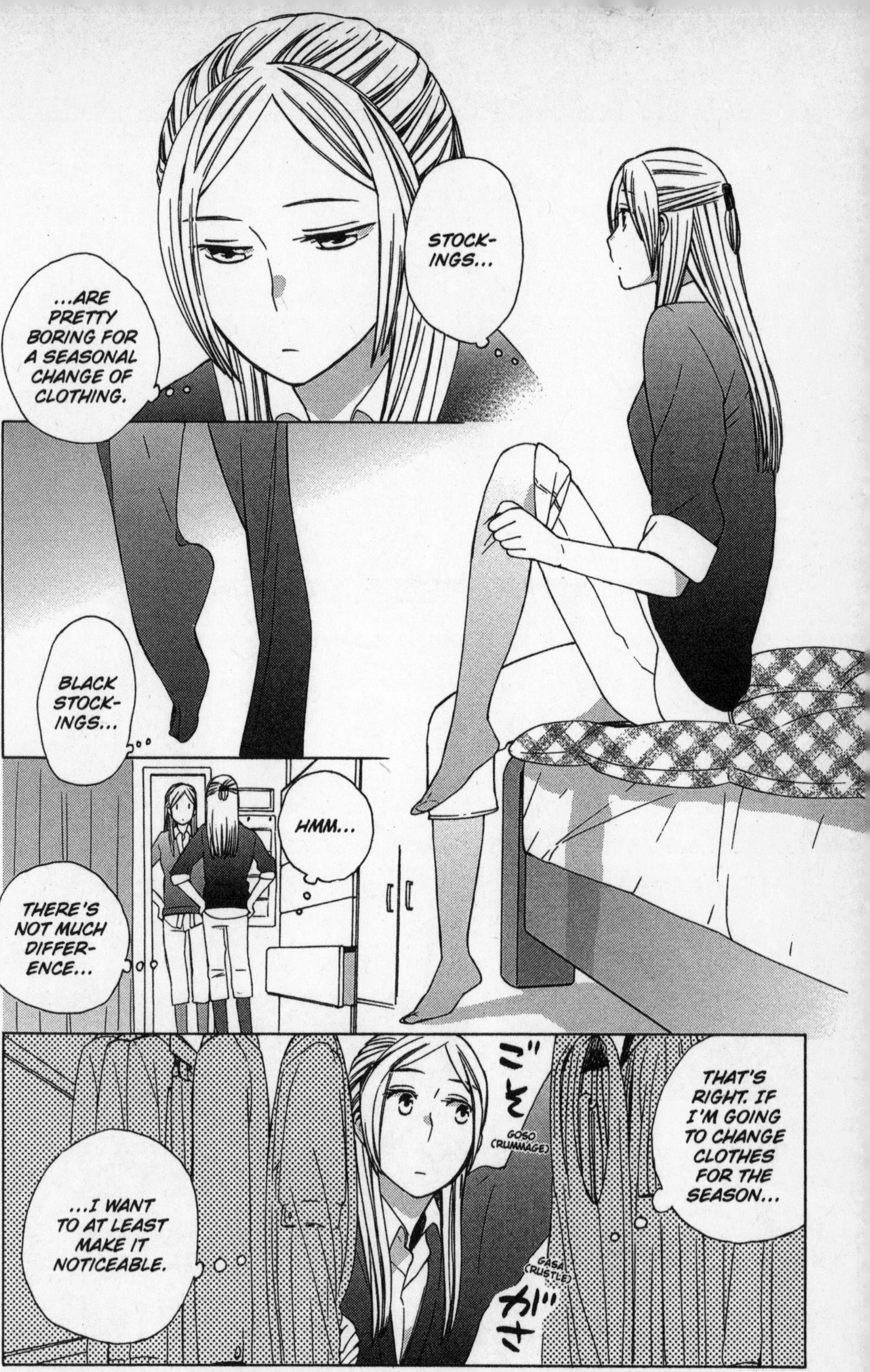
STOCKINGS...
...ARE PRETTY BORING FOR A SEASONAL CHANGE OF CLOTHING.
BLACK STOCKINGS...
HMM...
THERE'S NOT MUCH DIFFERENCE...
THAT'S RIGHT. IF I'M GOING TO CHANGE CLOTHES FOR THE SEASON...
ごそ
GOSO (RUMMAGE)
がさ
GASA (RUSTLE)
...I WANT TO AT LEAST MAKE IT NOTICEABLE.

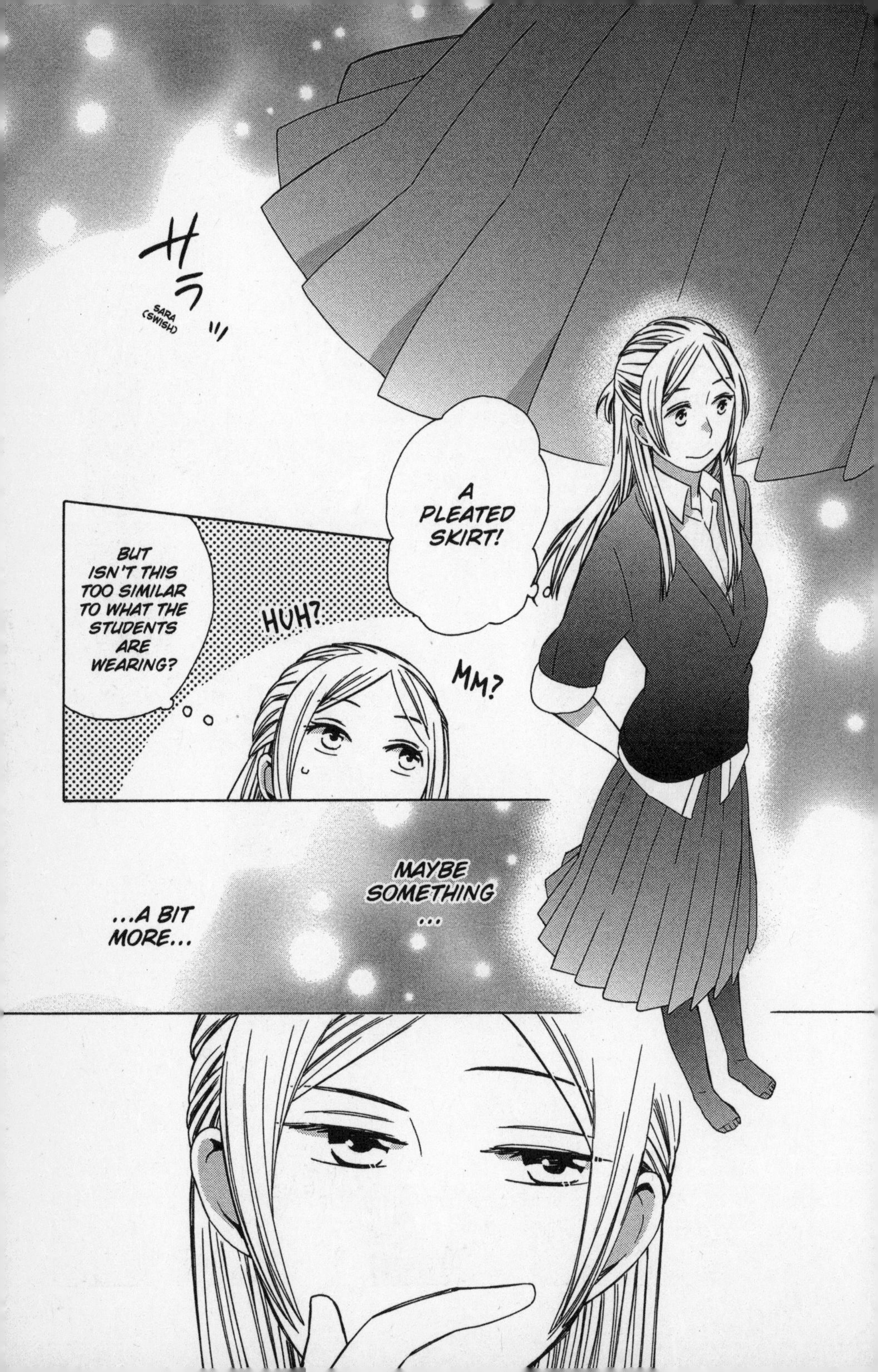
サラッ
SARA (SWISH)
A PLEATED SKIRT!
MM?
HUH?
BUT ISN'T THIS TOO SIMILAR TO WHAT THE STUDENTS ARE WEARING?
MAYBE SOMETHING ...
...A BIT MORE...

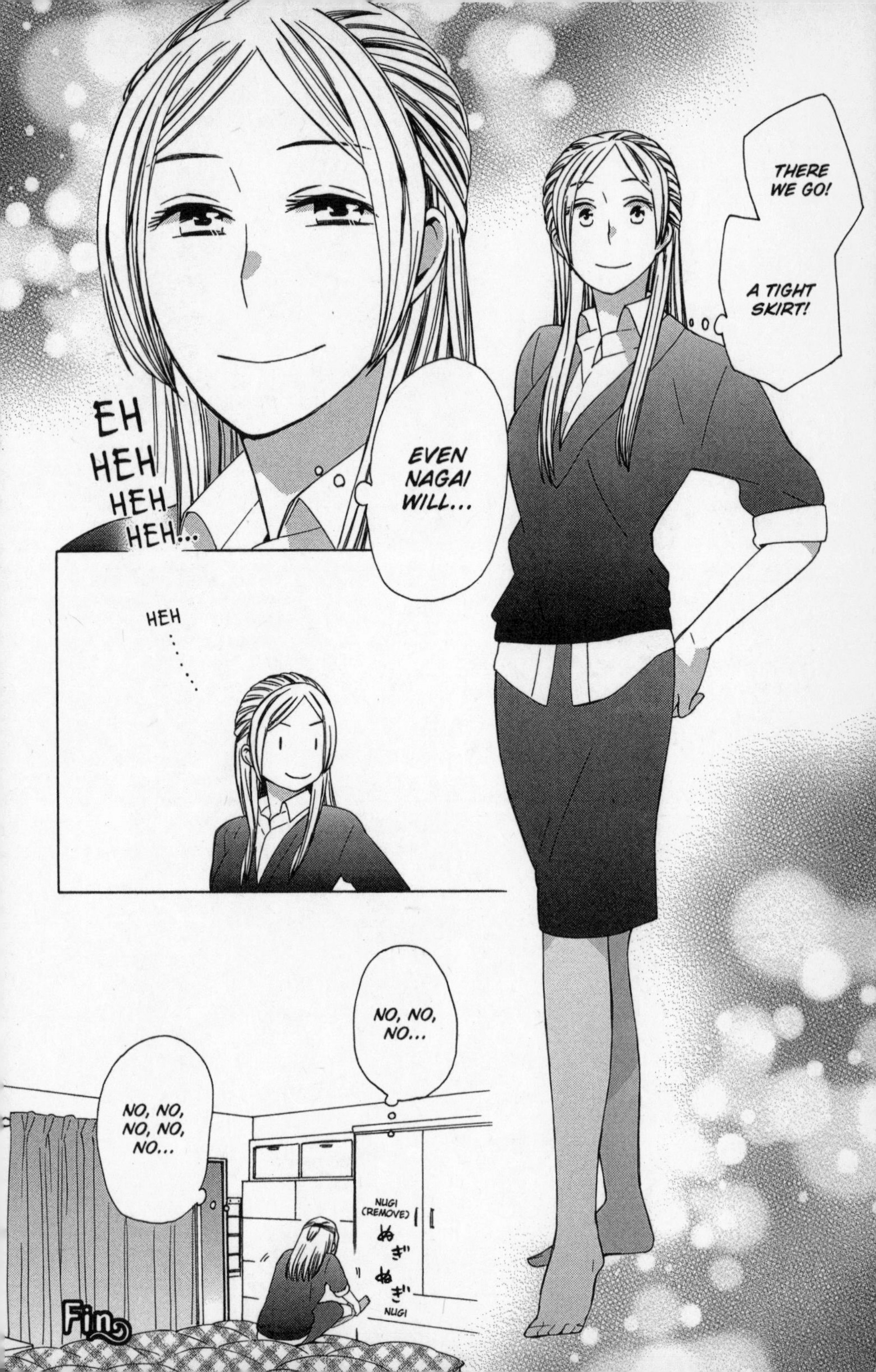
THERE WE GO!
A TIGHT SKIRT!
EVEN NAGAI WILL...
EH HEH HEH HEH...
HEH...
NO, NO, NO...
NO, NO, NO, NO, NO...
NUGI (REMOVE) ぬぎ
ぬぎ NUGI
Fin

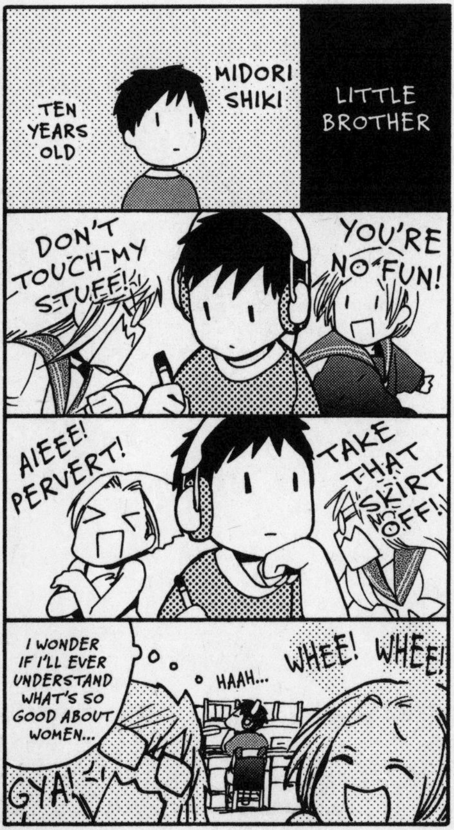
LITTLE BROTHER
MIDORI SHIKI
TEN YEARS OLD
YOU'RE NO FUN!
DON'T TOUCH MY STUFF!!
TAKE THAT SKIRT OFF!!
AIEEE! PERVERT!
WHEE! WHEE!
HAAH...
I WONDER IF I'LL EVER UNDERSTAND WHAT'S SO GOOD ABOUT WOMEN...
GYA!

Love at Fourteen

Fuka Mizutani

Love at Fourteen

[Chapter 19]

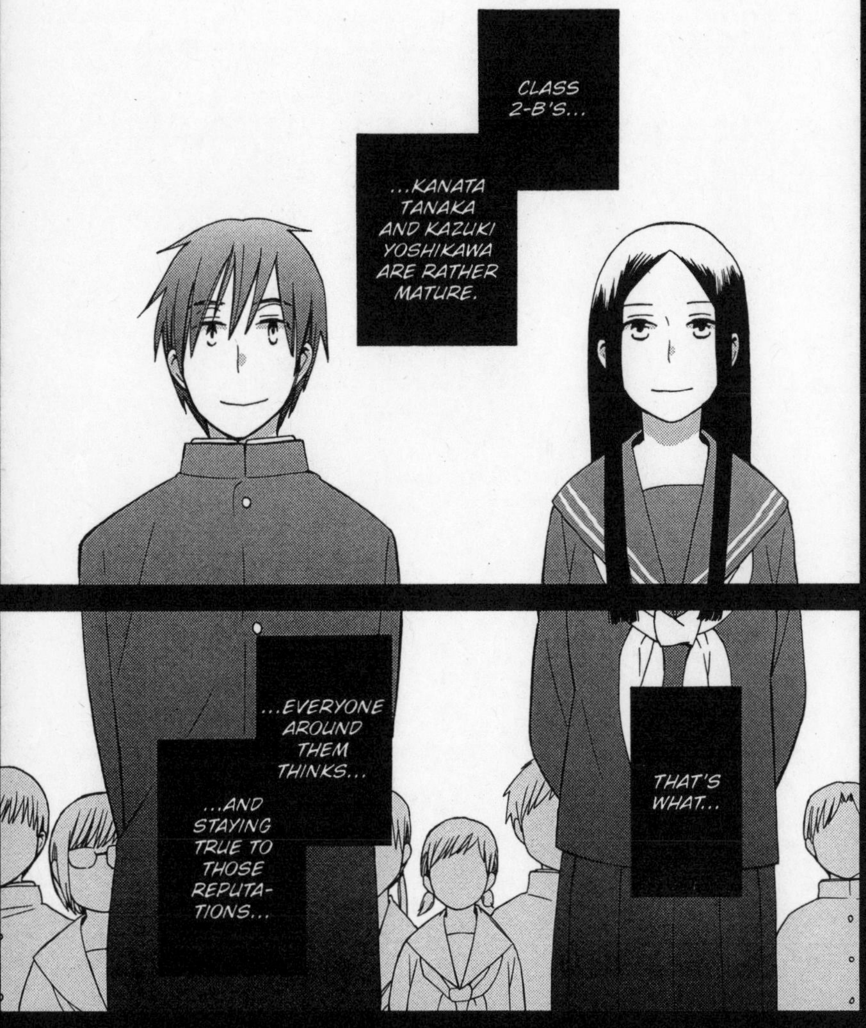
CLASS 2-B'S...
...KANATA TANAKA AND KAZUKI YOSHIKAWA ARE RATHER MATURE.
THAT'S WHAT...
...EVERYONE AROUND THEM THINKS...
...AND STAYING TRUE TO THOSE REPUTATIONS...

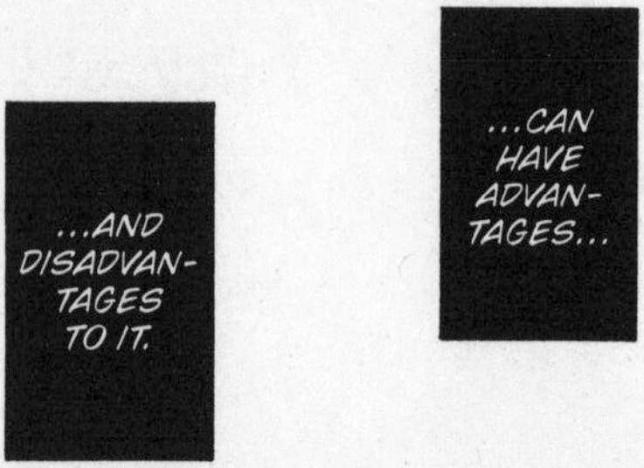
...CAN HAVE ADVANTAGES...
...AND DISADVANTAGES TO IT.

BOARD: 2-B'S SLOGAN FOR THE SPORTS FESTIVAL: LET'S WORK TOGETHER!!

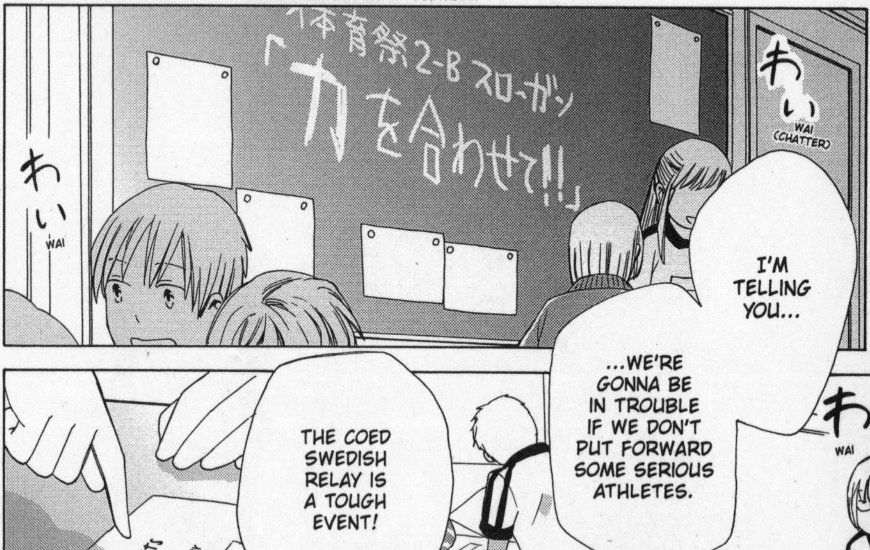
わい
WAI (CHATTER)
体育祭2-B スローガン
「力を合わせて!!」
わい
WAI
I'M TELLING YOU...

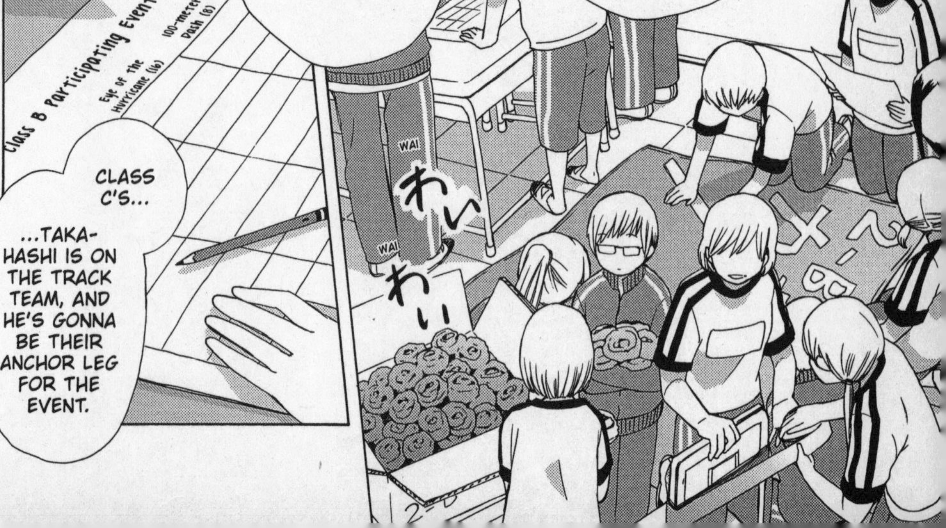
わい
WAI
...WE'RE GONNA BE IN TROUBLE IF WE DON'T PUT FORWARD SOME SERIOUS ATHLETES.
THE COED SWEDISH RELAY IS A TOUGH EVENT!
Class B Participating Events
Eye of the Hurricane (16)
100-meter Dash (8)
WAI
わい
WAI
わい
CLASS C'S...
...TAKAHASHI IS ON THE TRACK TEAM, AND HE'S GONNA BE THEIR ANCHOR LEG FOR THE EVENT.

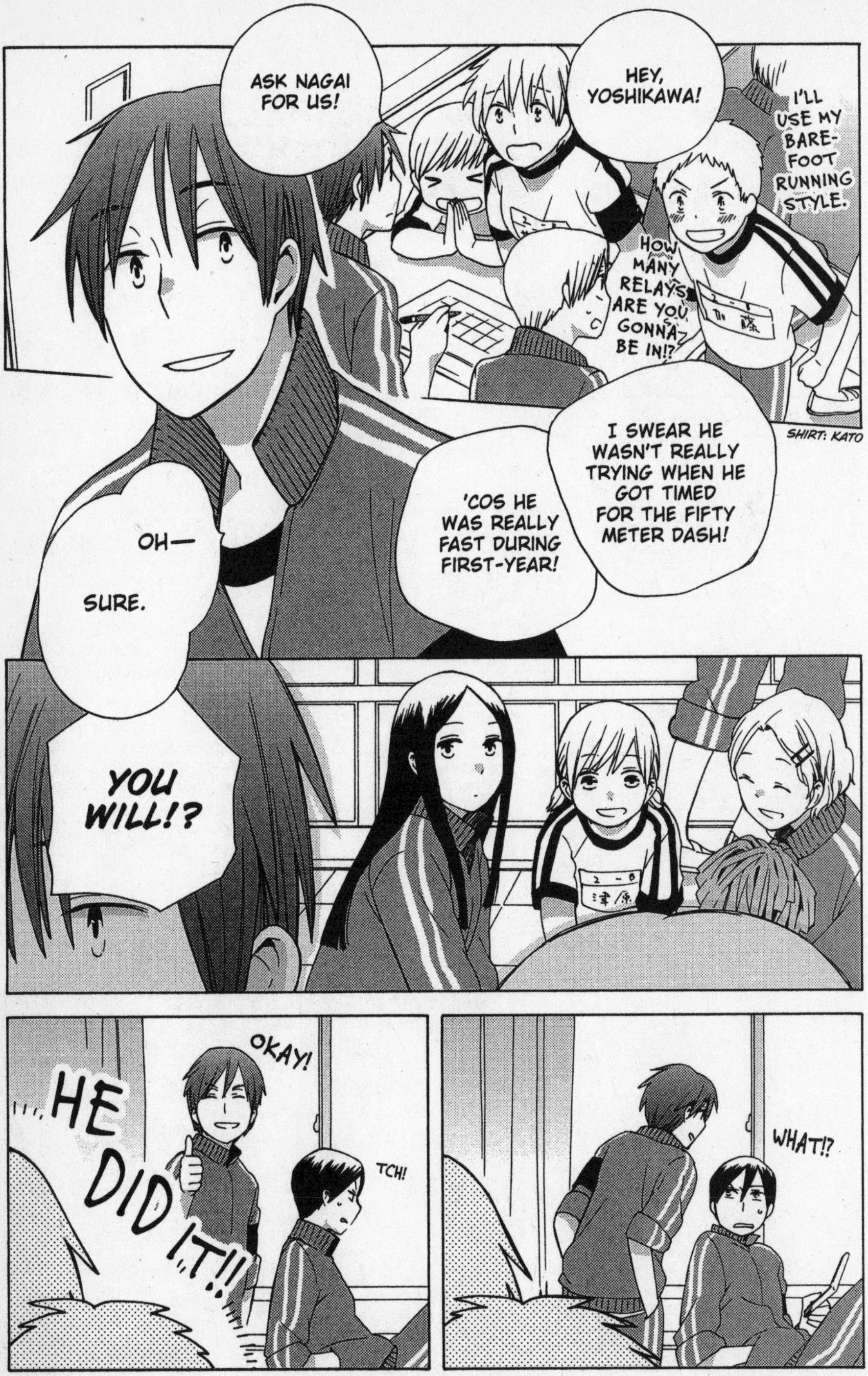
I'LL USE MY BARE-FOOT RUNNING STYLE.
HEY, YOSHIKAWA!
ASK NAGAI FOR US!
HOW MANY RELAYS ARE YOU GONNA BE IN!?
I SWEAR HE WASN'T REALLY TRYING WHEN HE GOT TIMED FOR THE FIFTY METER DASH!
'COS HE WAS REALLY FAST DURING FIRST-YEAR!
OH— SURE.
SHIRT: KATO
YOU WILL!?
WHAT!?
OKAY!
TCH!
HE DID IT!!

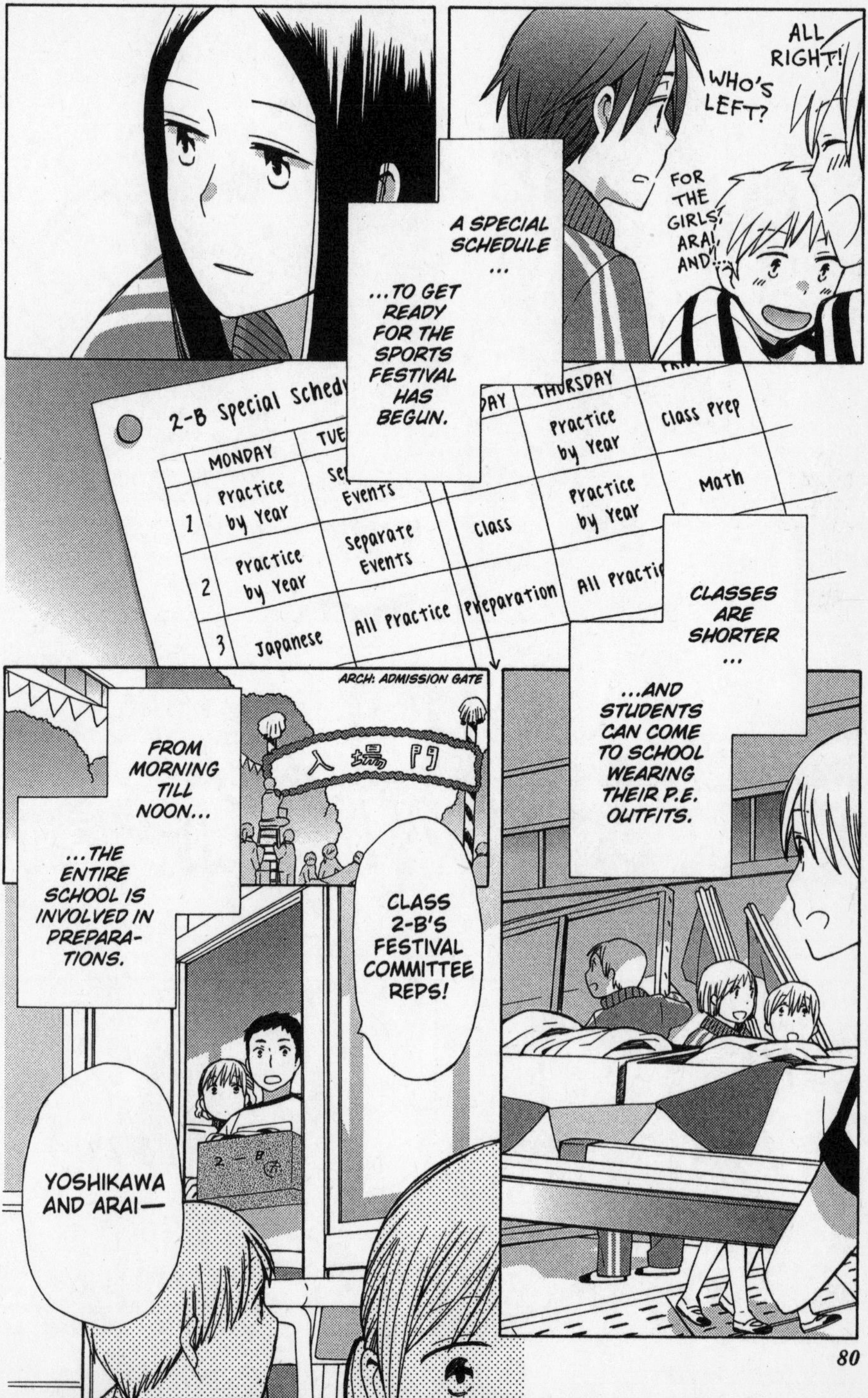
ALL RIGHT!
WHO'S LEFT?
FOR THE GIRLS, ARAI, AND...
A SPECIAL SCHEDULE ...
...TO GET READY FOR THE SPORTS FESTIVAL HAS BEGUN.
2-B Special Schedu
MONDAY
TUE
DAY
THURSDAY
1
Practice by Year
Separate Events
Class
Practice by Year
Practice by Year
Class Prep
Math
2
Practice by Year
Separate Events
Preparation
All Practic
3
Japanese
All Practice
CLASSES ARE SHORTER ...
...AND STUDENTS CAN COME TO SCHOOL WEARING THEIR P.E. OUTFITS.
ARCH: ADMISSION GATE
入場門
FROM MORNING TILL NOON...
...THE ENTIRE SCHOOL IS INVOLVED IN PREPARATIONS.
CLASS 2-B'S FESTIVAL COMMITTEE REPS!
YOSHIKAWA AND ARAI—

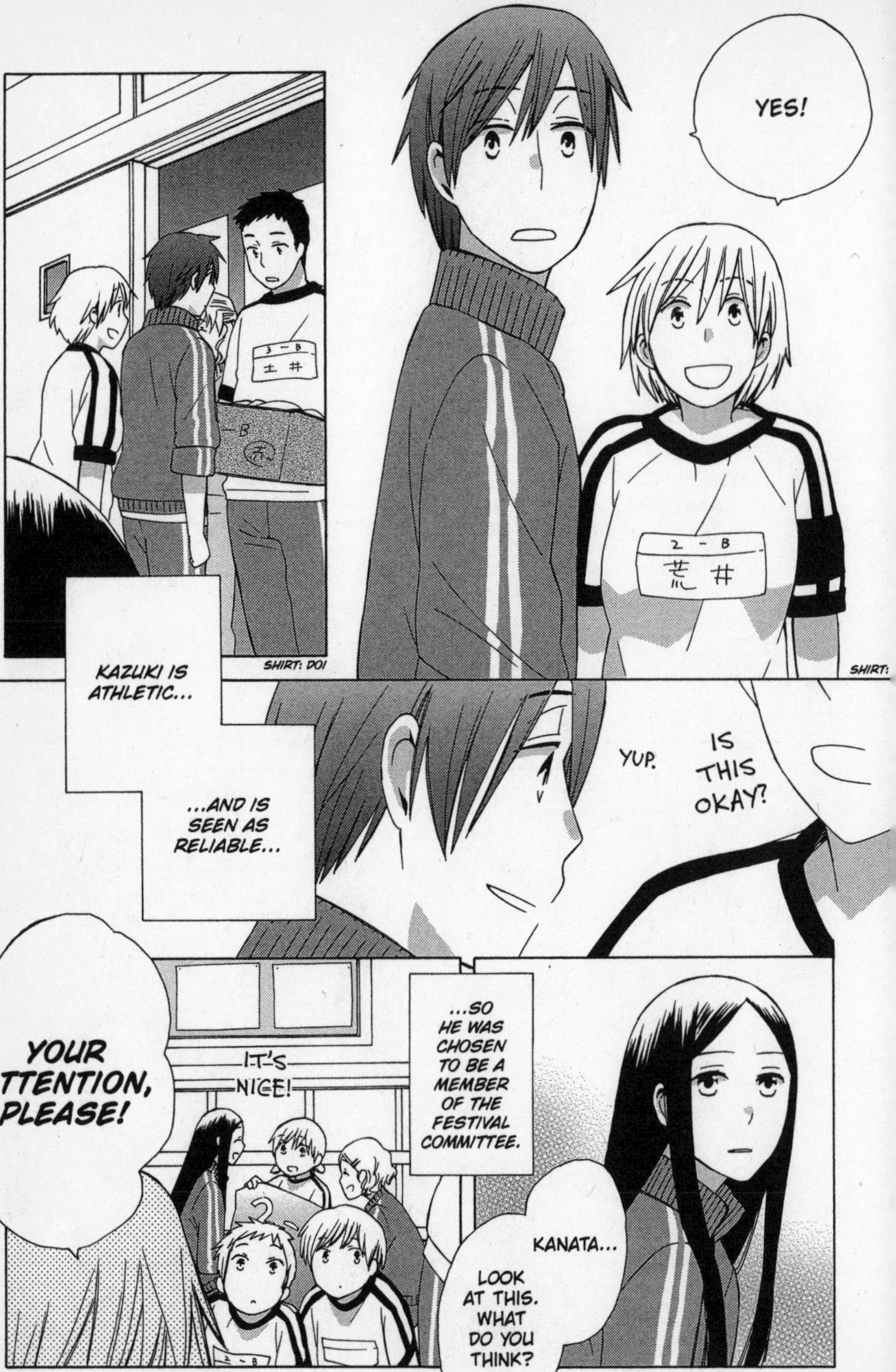
YES!
2-B 荒井
SHIRT:
3-B 土井
SHIRT: DOI
IS THIS OKAY?
YUP.
KAZUKI IS ATHLETIC...
...AND IS SEEN AS RELIABLE...
...SO HE WAS CHOSEN TO BE A MEMBER OF THE FESTIVAL COMMITTEE.
KANATA...
LOOK AT THIS. WHAT DO YOU THINK?
IT'S NICE!
YOUR ATTENTION, PLEASE!

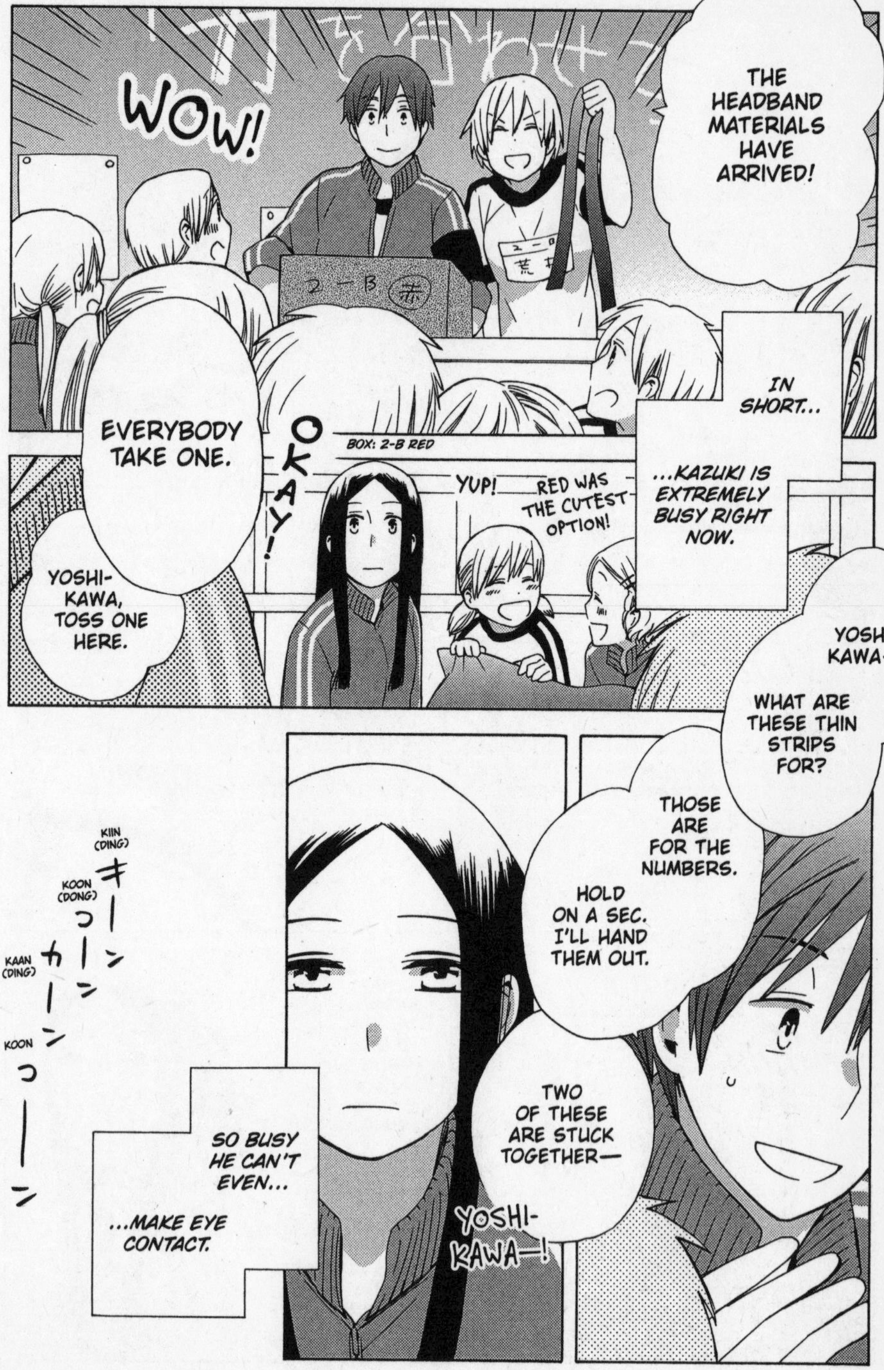
THE HEADBAND MATERIALS HAVE ARRIVED!
WOW!
EVERYBODY TAKE ONE.
IN SHORT...
...KAZUKI IS EXTREMELY BUSY RIGHT NOW.
BOX: 2-B RED
RED WAS THE CUTEST OPTION!
YUP!
OKAY!
YOSHI-KAWA, TOSS ONE HERE.
YOSHI-KAWA—
WHAT ARE THESE THIN STRIPS FOR?
THOSE ARE FOR THE NUMBERS.
HOLD ON A SEC. I'LL HAND THEM OUT.
TWO OF THESE ARE STUCK TOGETHER—
YOSHI-KAWA—!
SO BUSY HE CAN'T EVEN...
...MAKE EYE CONTACT.
KIIN (DING) キーン
KOON (DONG) コーン
KAAN (DING) カーン
KOON コーン

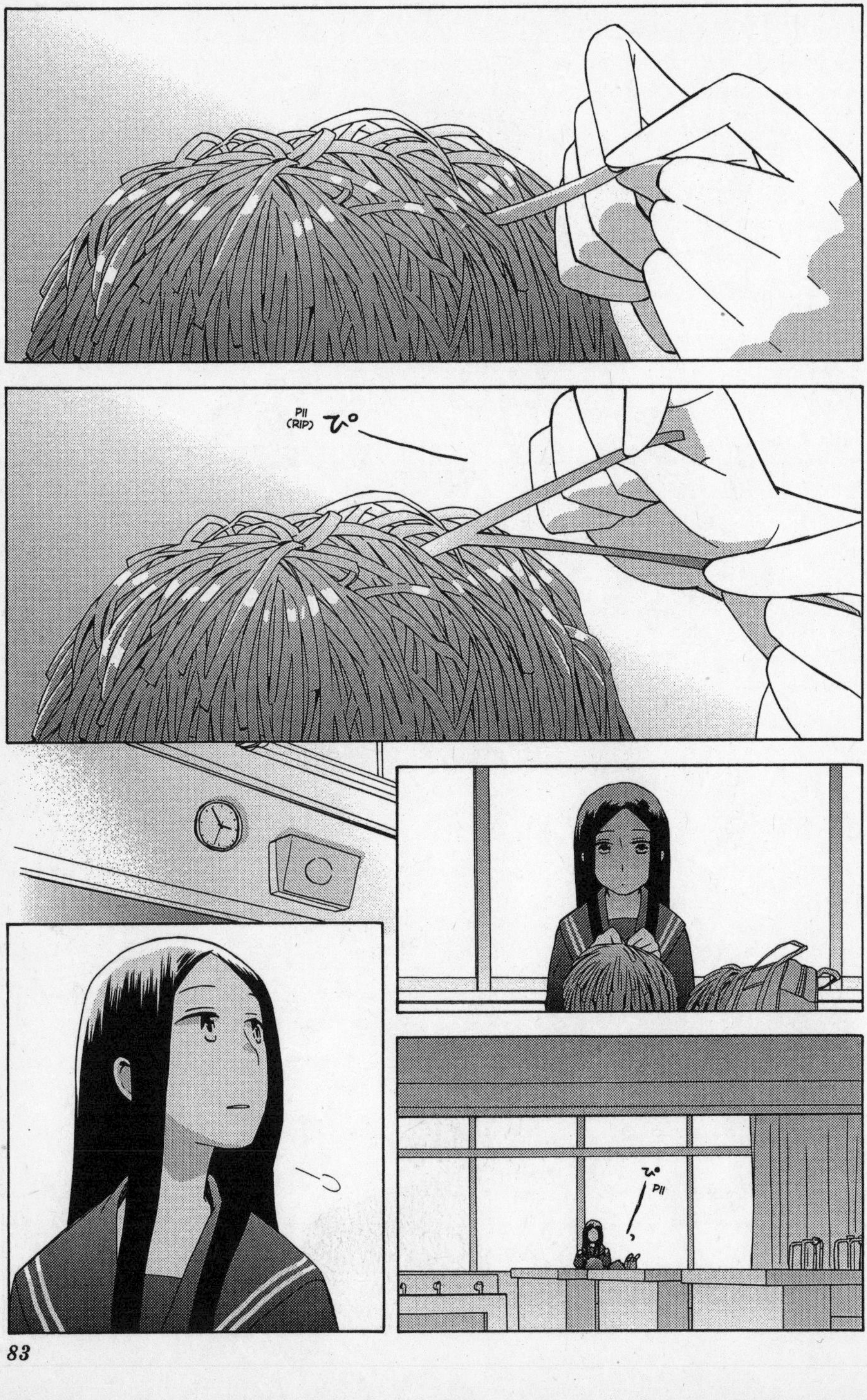
PII (RIP) ぴ
ぴ PII

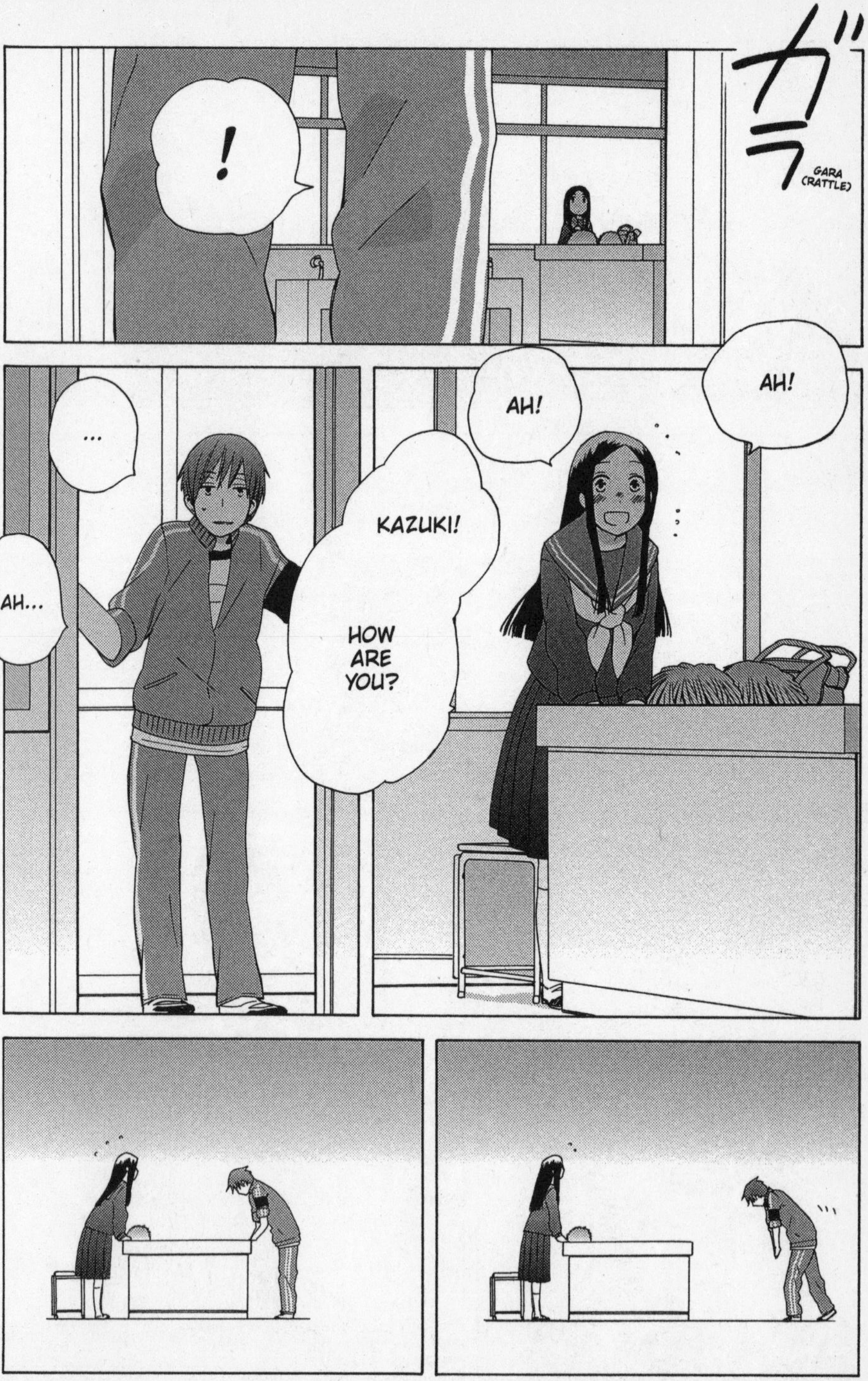
ガラ
GARA (RATTLE)
!
AH!
AH!
KAZUKI! HOW ARE YOU?
...
AH...

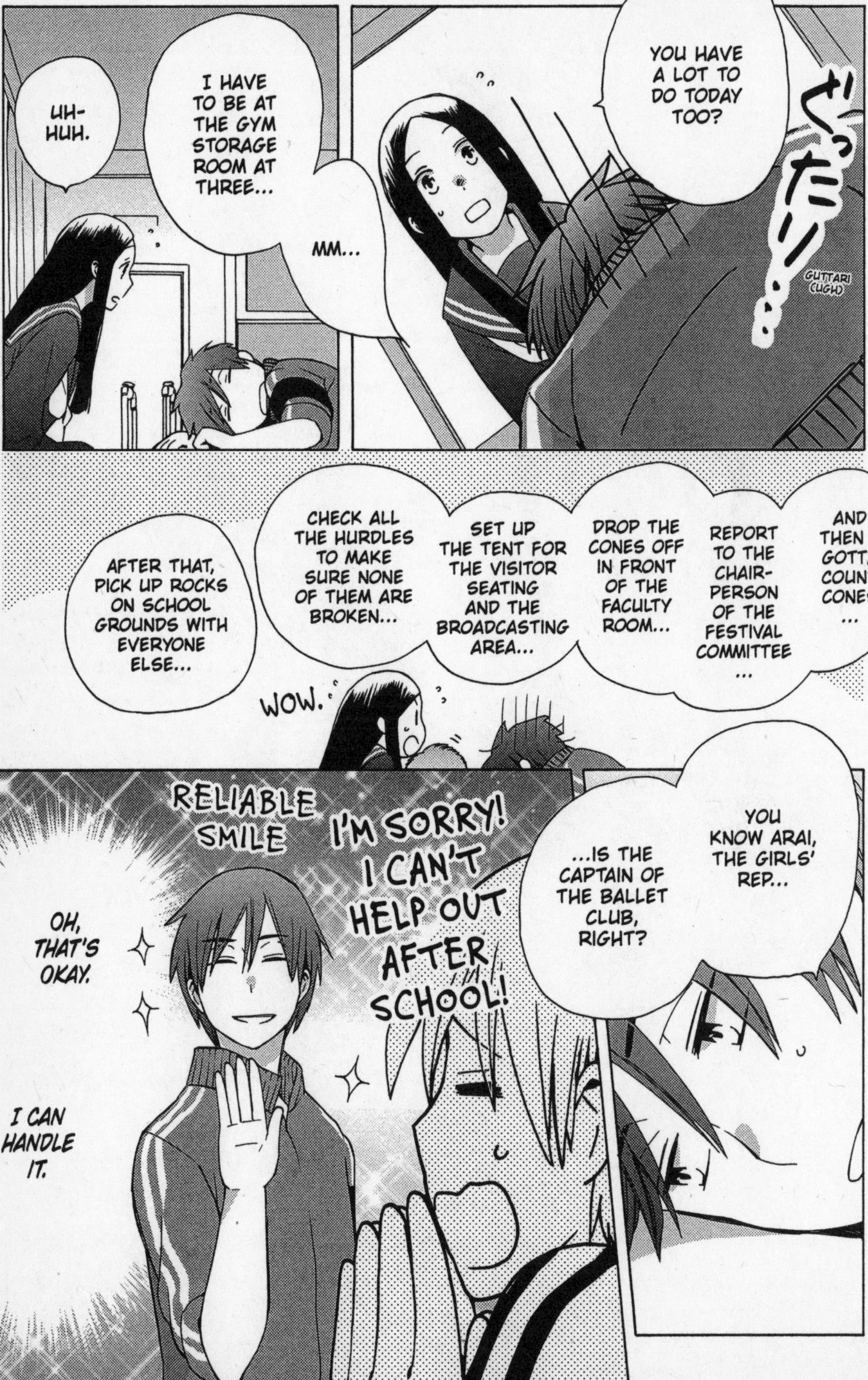
YOU HAVE A LOT TO DO TODAY TOO?
ぐったりー…
GUTTARI (UGH)
MM...
I HAVE TO BE AT THE GYM STORAGE ROOM AT THREE...
UH-HUH.
AND THEN I GOTTA COUNT CONES...
REPORT TO THE CHAIRPERSON OF THE FESTIVAL COMMITTEE...
DROP THE CONES OFF IN FRONT OF THE FACULTY ROOM...
SET UP THE TENT FOR THE VISITOR SEATING AND THE BROADCASTING AREA...
CHECK ALL THE HURDLES TO MAKE SURE NONE OF THEM ARE BROKEN...
AFTER THAT, PICK UP ROCKS ON SCHOOL GROUNDS WITH EVERYONE ELSE...
WOW.
YOU KNOW ARAI, THE GIRLS' REP...
...IS THE CAPTAIN OF THE BALLET CLUB, RIGHT?
I'M SORRY! I CAN'T HELP OUT AFTER SCHOOL!
RELIABLE SMILE
OH, THAT'S OKAY.
I CAN HANDLE IT.

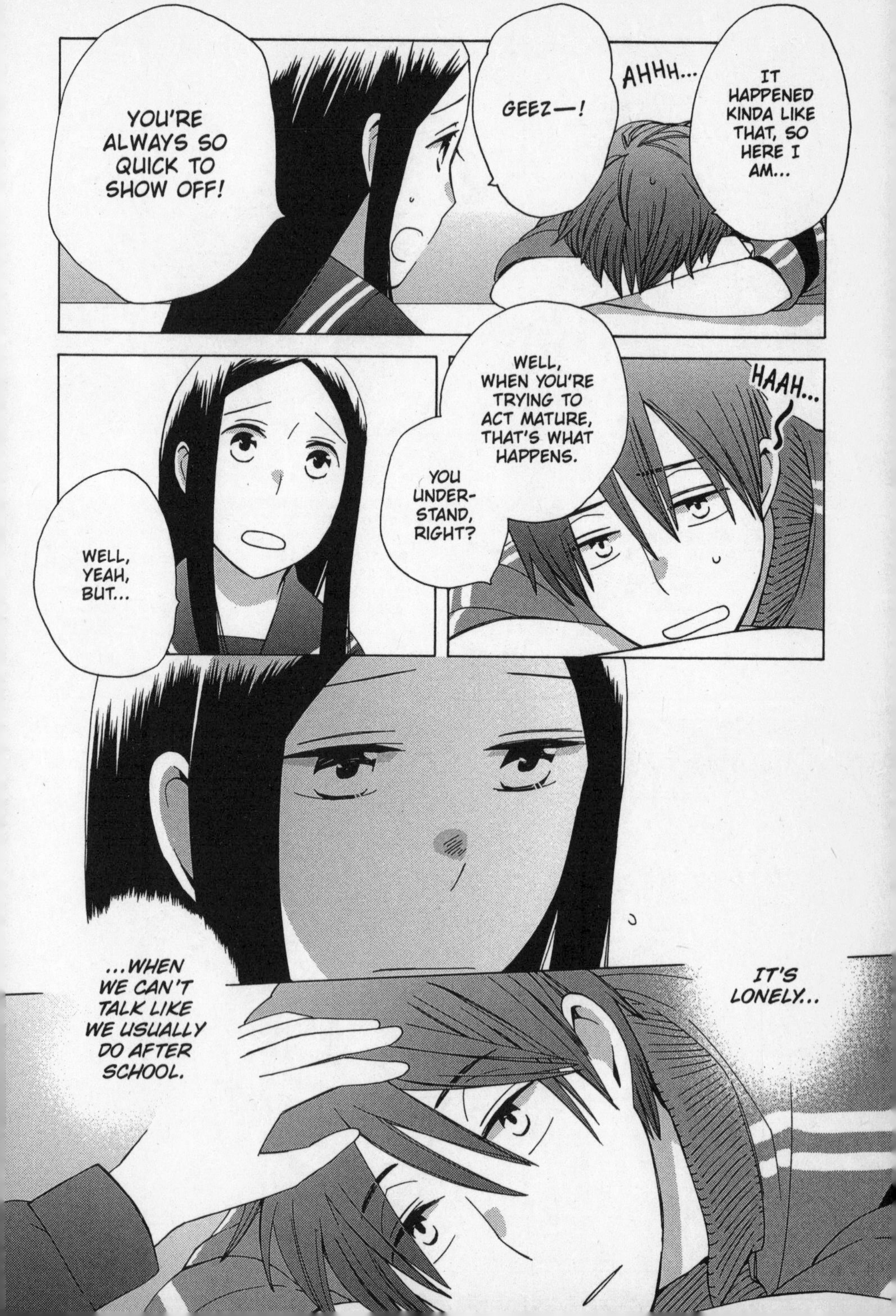
IT HAPPENED KINDA LIKE THAT, SO HERE I AM...
AHHH...
GEEZ—!
YOU'RE ALWAYS SO QUICK TO SHOW OFF!
HAAH...
WELL, WHEN YOU'RE TRYING TO ACT MATURE, THAT'S WHAT HAPPENS.
YOU UNDERSTAND, RIGHT?
WELL, YEAH, BUT...
IT'S LONELY...
...WHEN WE CAN'T TALK LIKE WE USUALLY DO AFTER SCHOOL.

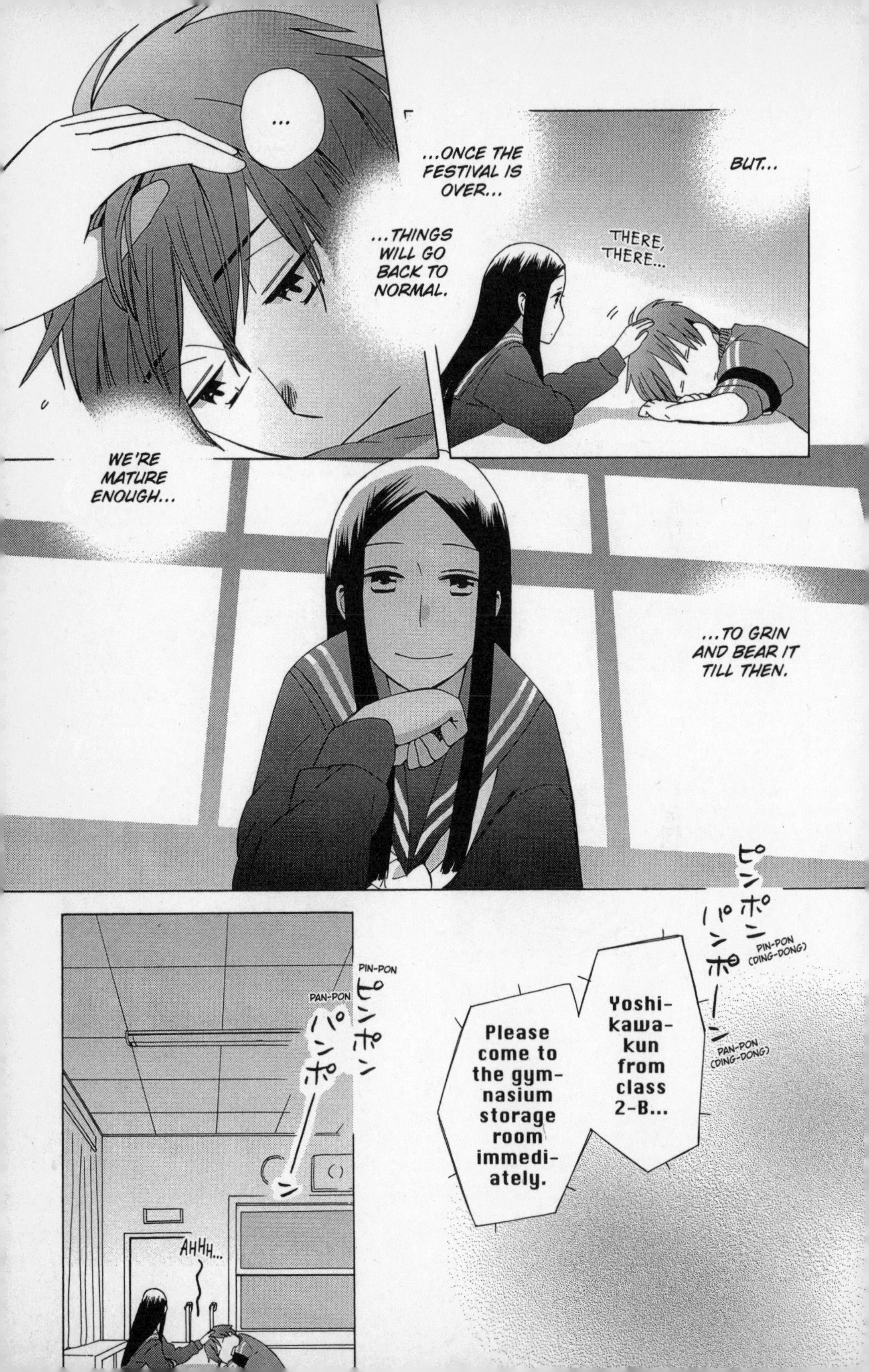
BUT...
THERE, THERE...
...ONCE THE FESTIVAL IS OVER...
...THINGS WILL GO BACK TO NORMAL.
...
WE'RE MATURE ENOUGH...
...TO GRIN AND BEAR IT TILL THEN.
ピンポンパンポーン
PIN-PON (DING-DONG)
PAN-PON (DING-DONG)
Yoshi-kawa-kun from class 2-B...
Please come to the gym-nasium storage room immedi-ately.
PIN-PON
PAN-PON
ピンポンパンポーン
AHHH...

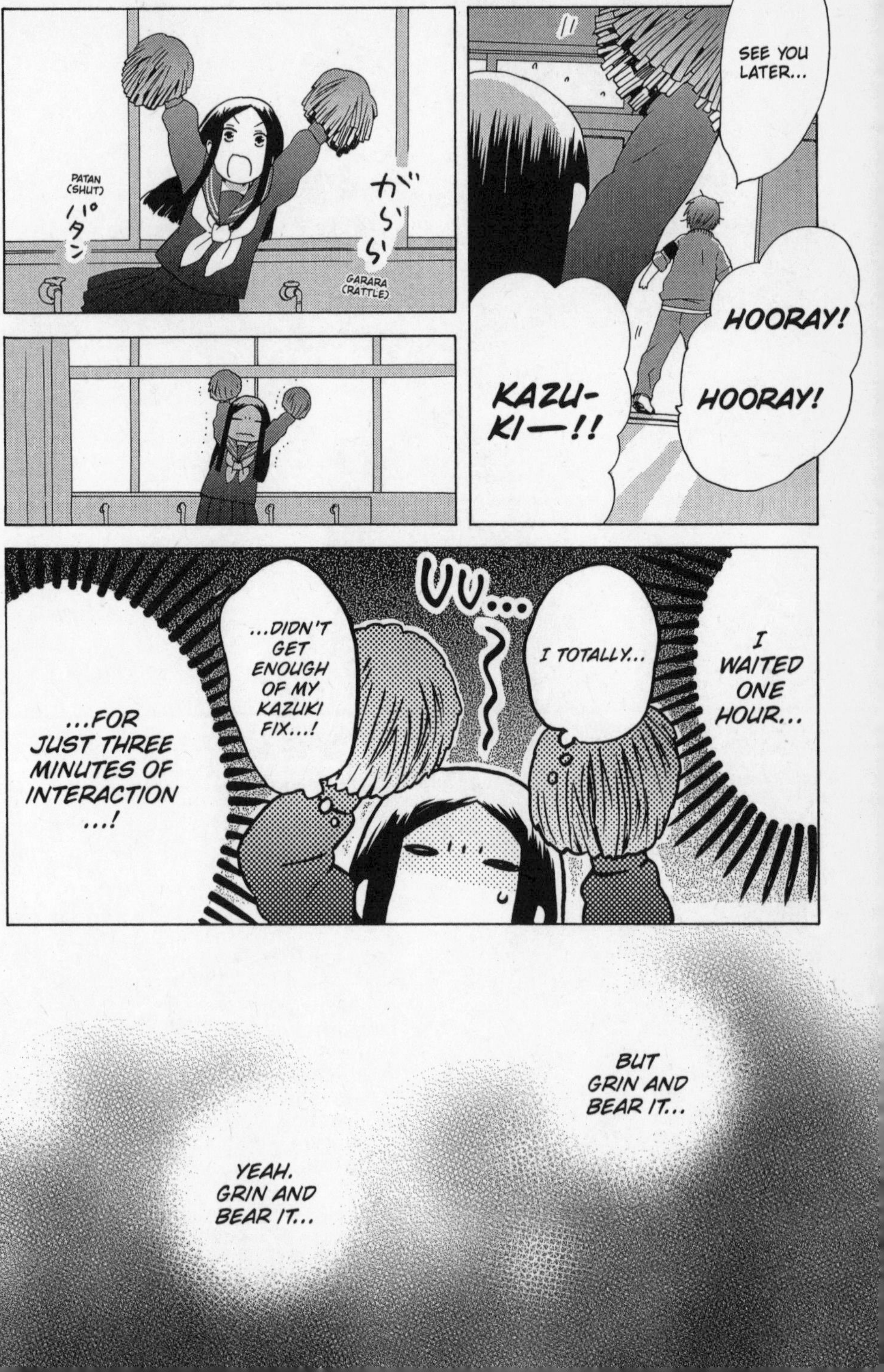
SEE YOU LATER...
HOORAY!
HOORAY!
KAZU-KI—!!
がらら
GARARA (RATTLE)
パタン
PATAN (SHUT)
I WAITED ONE HOUR...
I TOTALLY...
UU...
...DIDN'T GET ENOUGH OF MY KAZUKI FIX...!
...FOR JUST THREE MINUTES OF INTERACTION...!
BUT GRIN AND BEAR IT...
YEAH. GRIN AND BEAR IT...

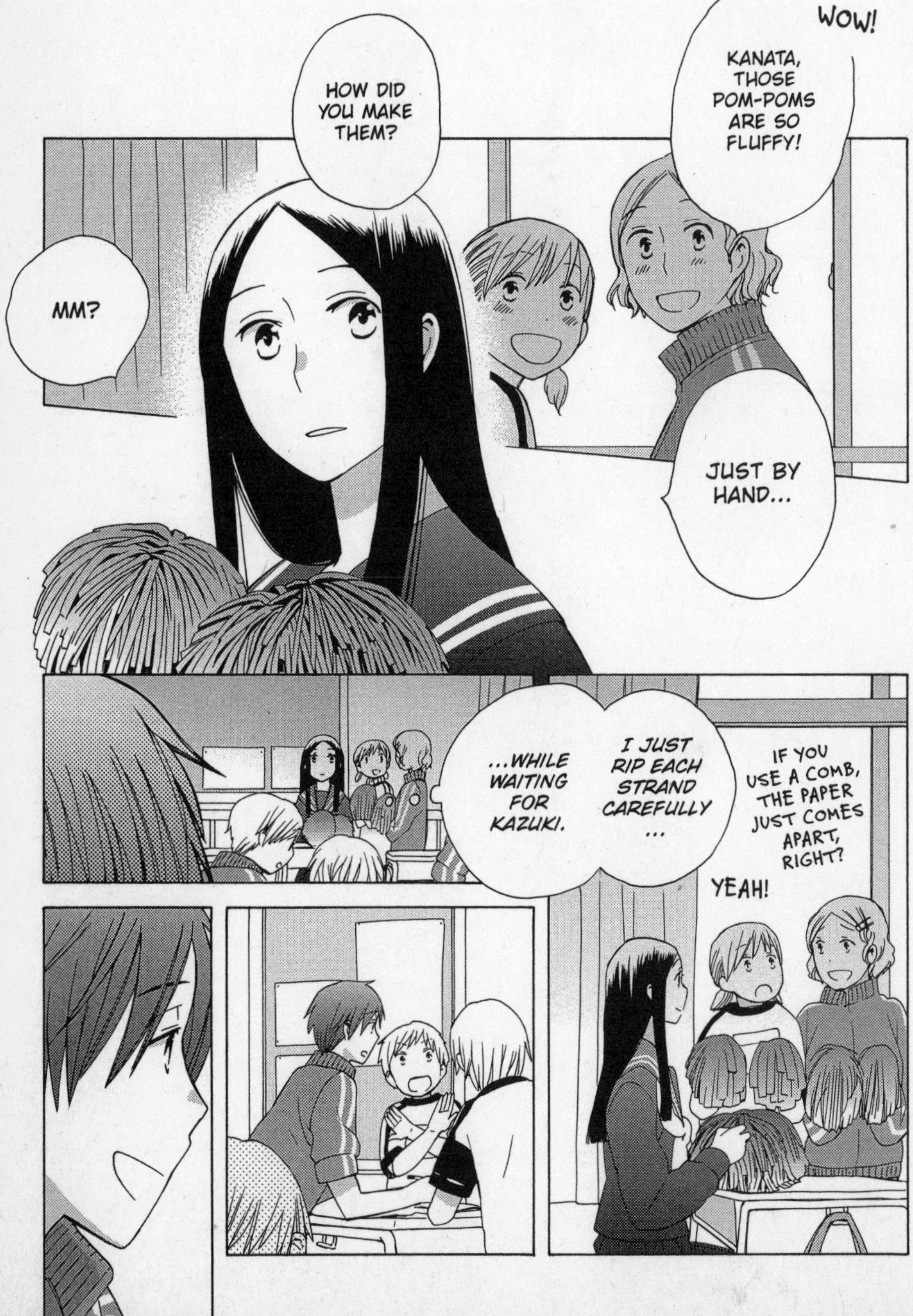
WOW!
KANATA, THOSE POM-POMS ARE SO FLUFFY!
HOW DID YOU MAKE THEM?
MM?
JUST BY HAND...
IF YOU USE A COMB, THE PAPER JUST COMES APART, RIGHT?
YEAH!
I JUST RIP EACH STRAND CAREFULLY...
...WHILE WAITING FOR KAZUKI.

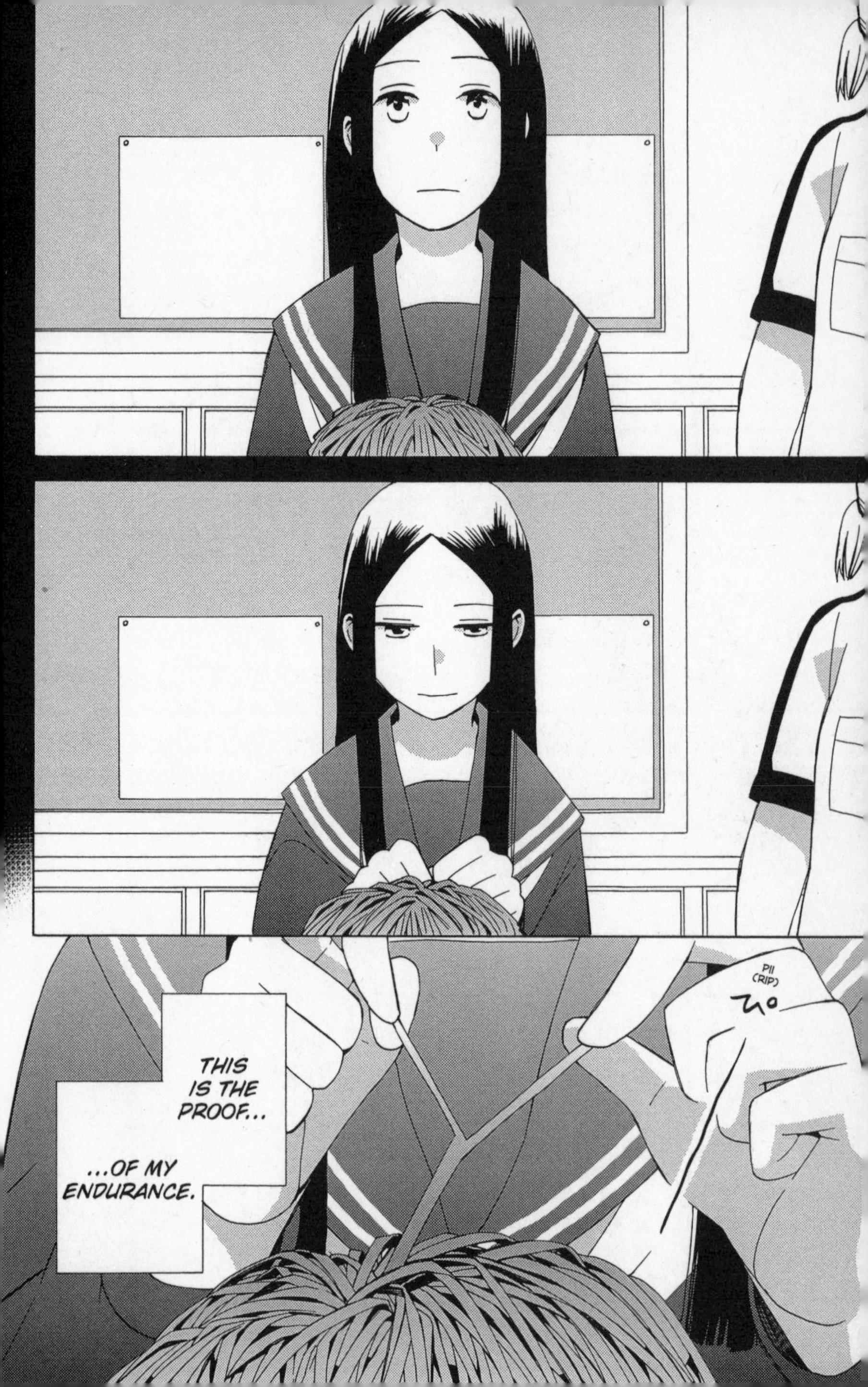
PII (RIP)
THIS IS THE PROOF...
...OF MY ENDURANCE.

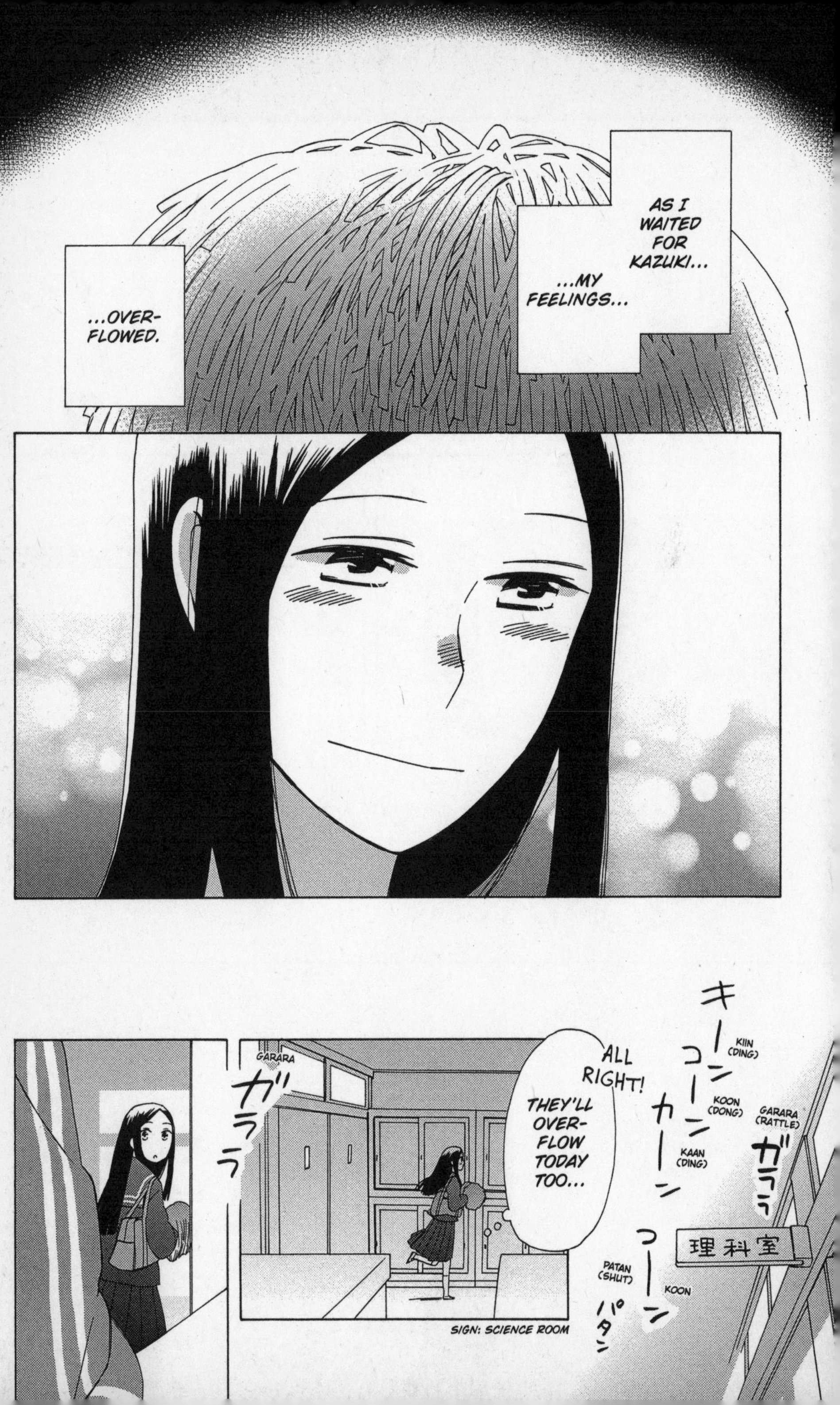
AS I WAITED FOR KAZUKI...
...MY FEELINGS...
...OVER-FLOWED.
キーンコーンカーンコーン
KIIN (DING)
KOON (DONG)
KAAN (DING)
KOON
ガララ
GARARA (RATTLE)
パタン
PATAN (SHUT)
理科室
SIGN: SCIENCE ROOM
ALL RIGHT! THEY'LL OVER-FLOW TODAY TOO...
ガララ
GARARA

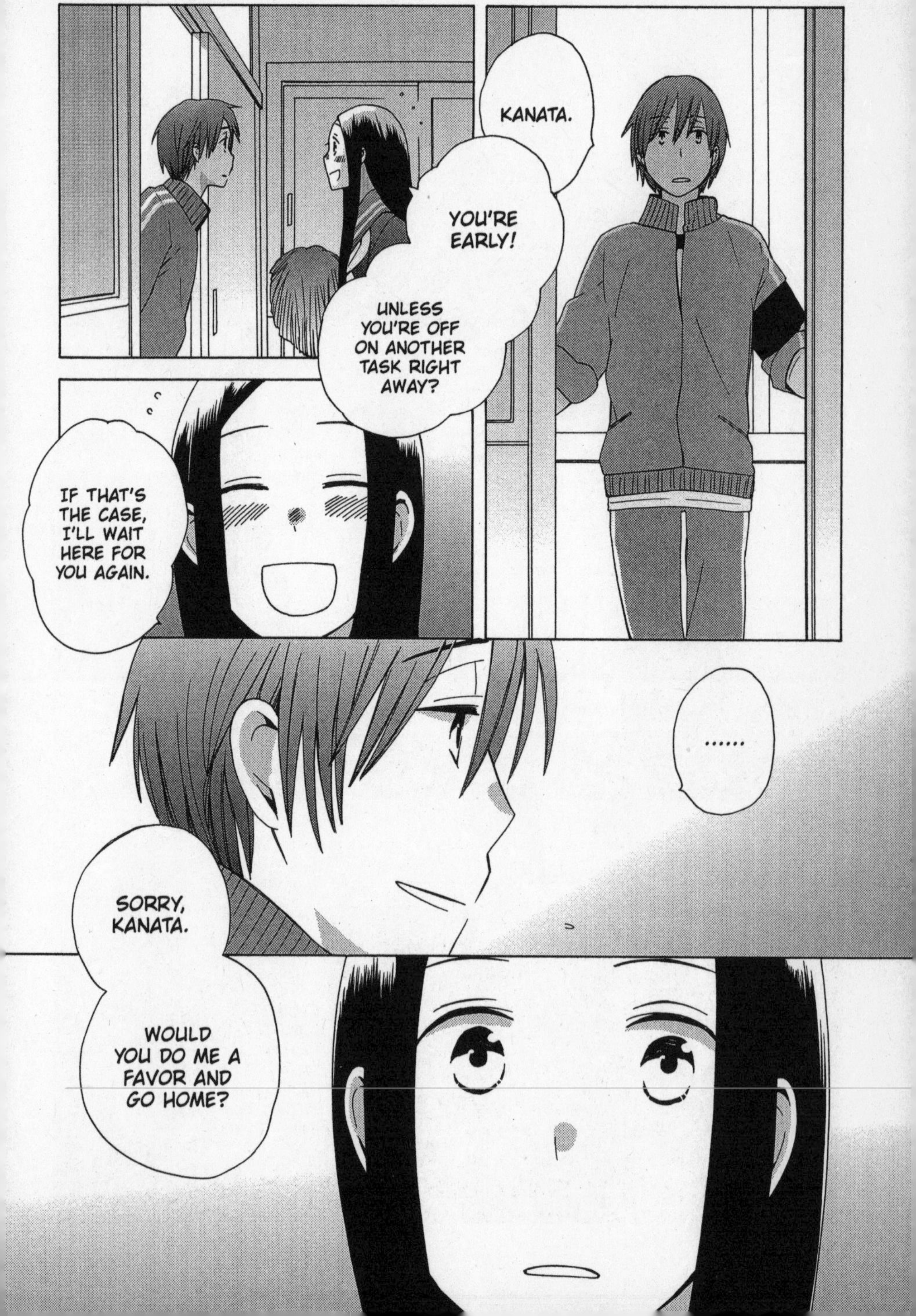
KANATA.
YOU'RE EARLY!
UNLESS YOU'RE OFF ON ANOTHER TASK RIGHT AWAY?
IF THAT'S THE CASE, I'LL WAIT HERE FOR YOU AGAIN.
......
SORRY, KANATA.
WOULD YOU DO ME A FAVOR AND GO HOME?

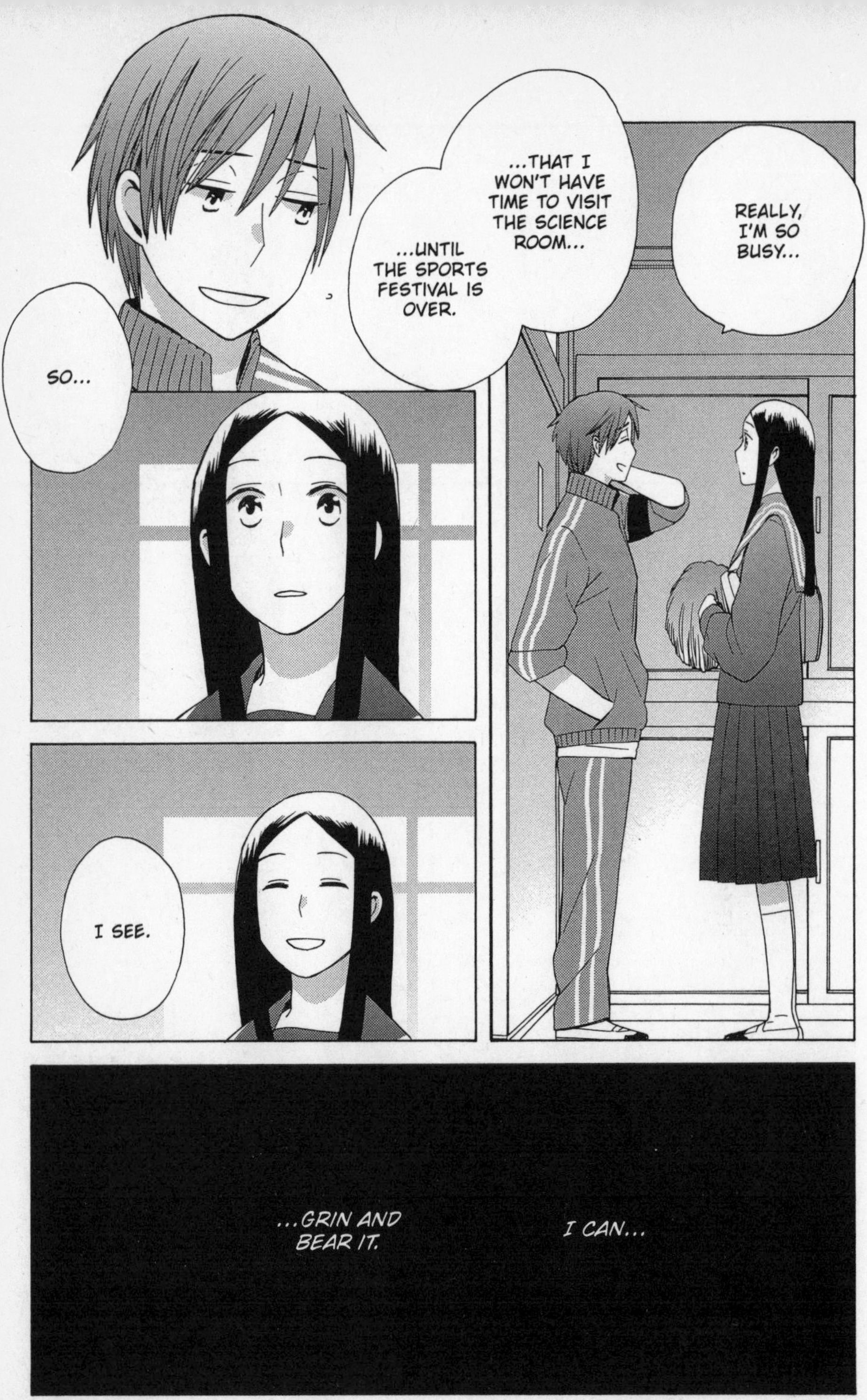
REALLY, I'M SO BUSY...
...THAT I WON'T HAVE TIME TO VISIT THE SCIENCE ROOM...
...UNTIL THE SPORTS FESTIVAL IS OVER.
SO...
I SEE.
I CAN...
...GRIN AND BEAR IT.

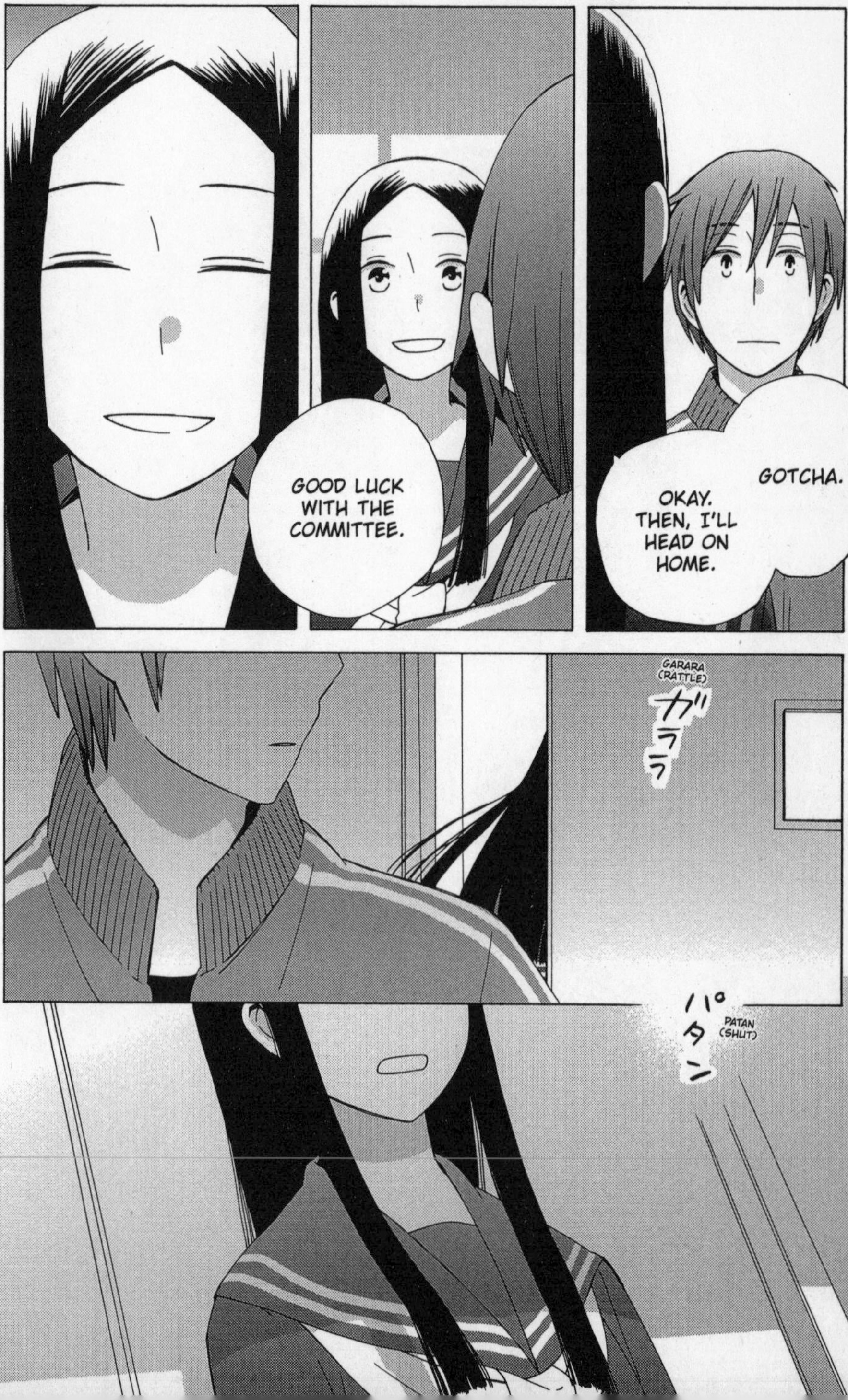
GOTCHA.
OKAY. THEN, I'LL HEAD ON HOME.
GOOD LUCK WITH THE COMMITTEE.
GARARA (RATTLE)
ガラララ
パタン
PATAN (SHUT)

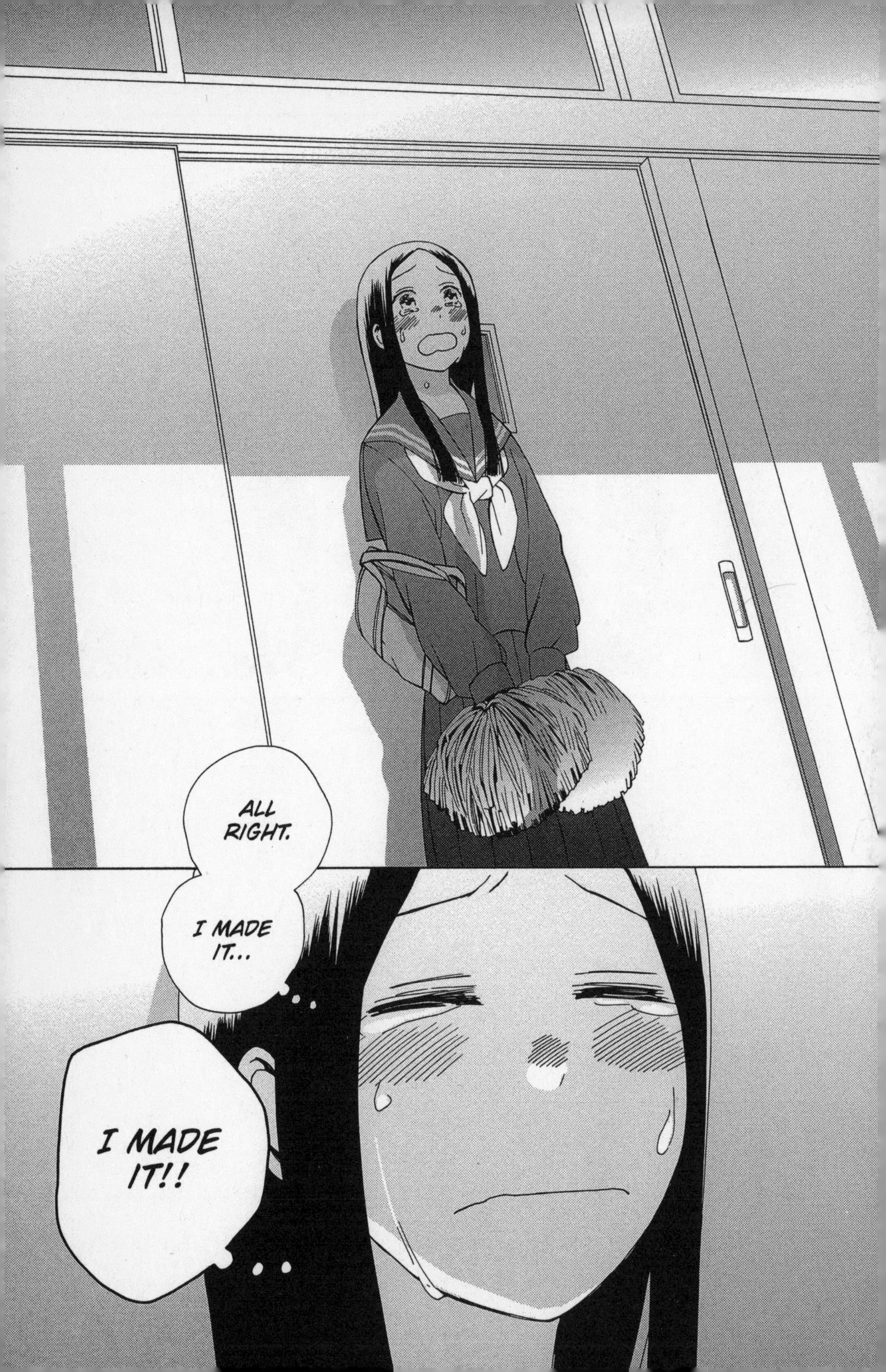
ALL RIGHT.
I MADE IT...
I MADE IT!!

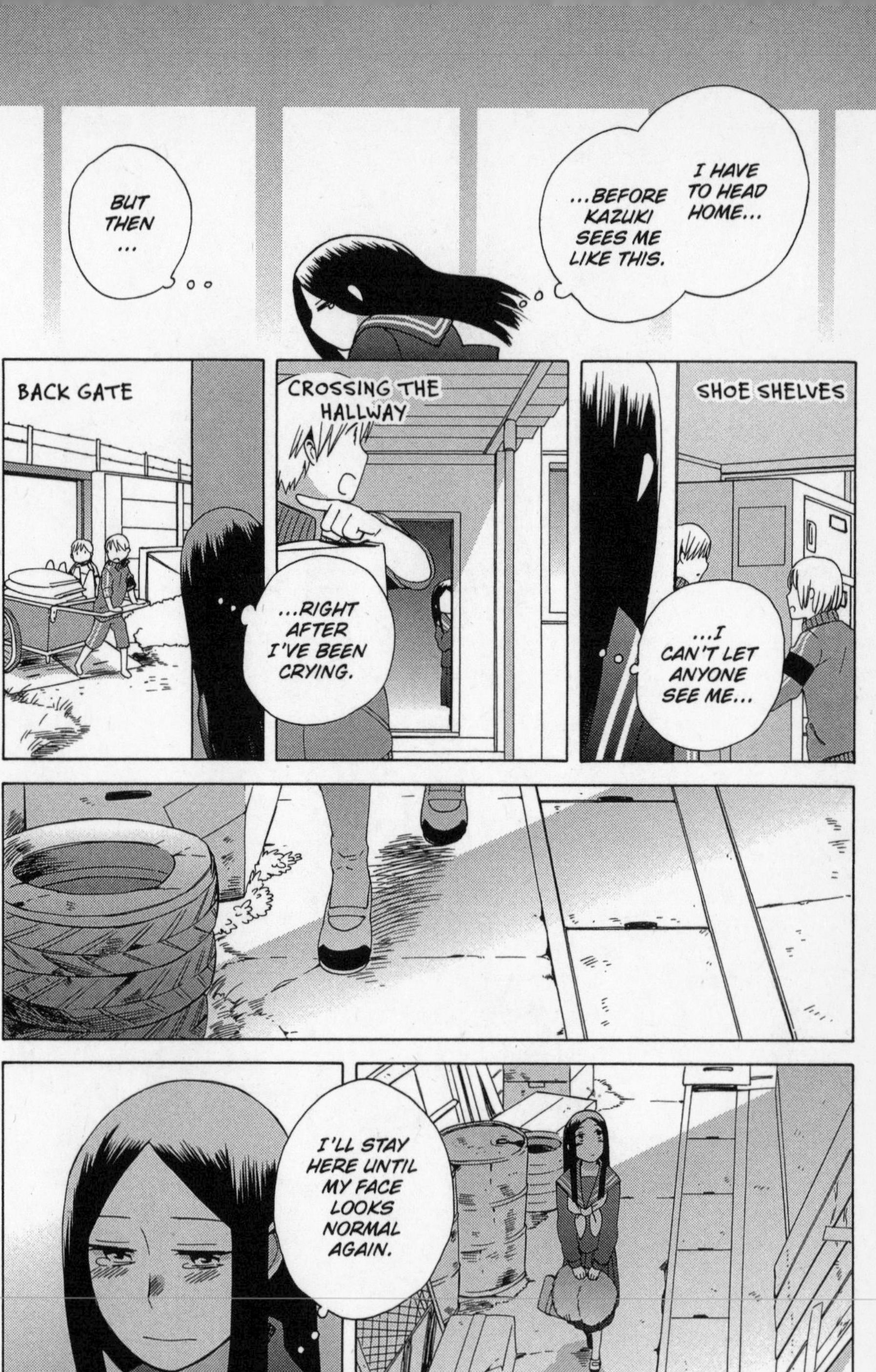
I HAVE TO HEAD HOME...
...BEFORE KAZUKI SEES ME LIKE THIS.
BUT THEN ...
SHOE SHELVES
...I CAN'T LET ANYONE SEE ME...
CROSSING THE HALLWAY
...RIGHT AFTER I'VE BEEN CRYING.
BACK GATE
I'LL STAY HERE UNTIL MY FACE LOOKS NORMAL AGAIN.

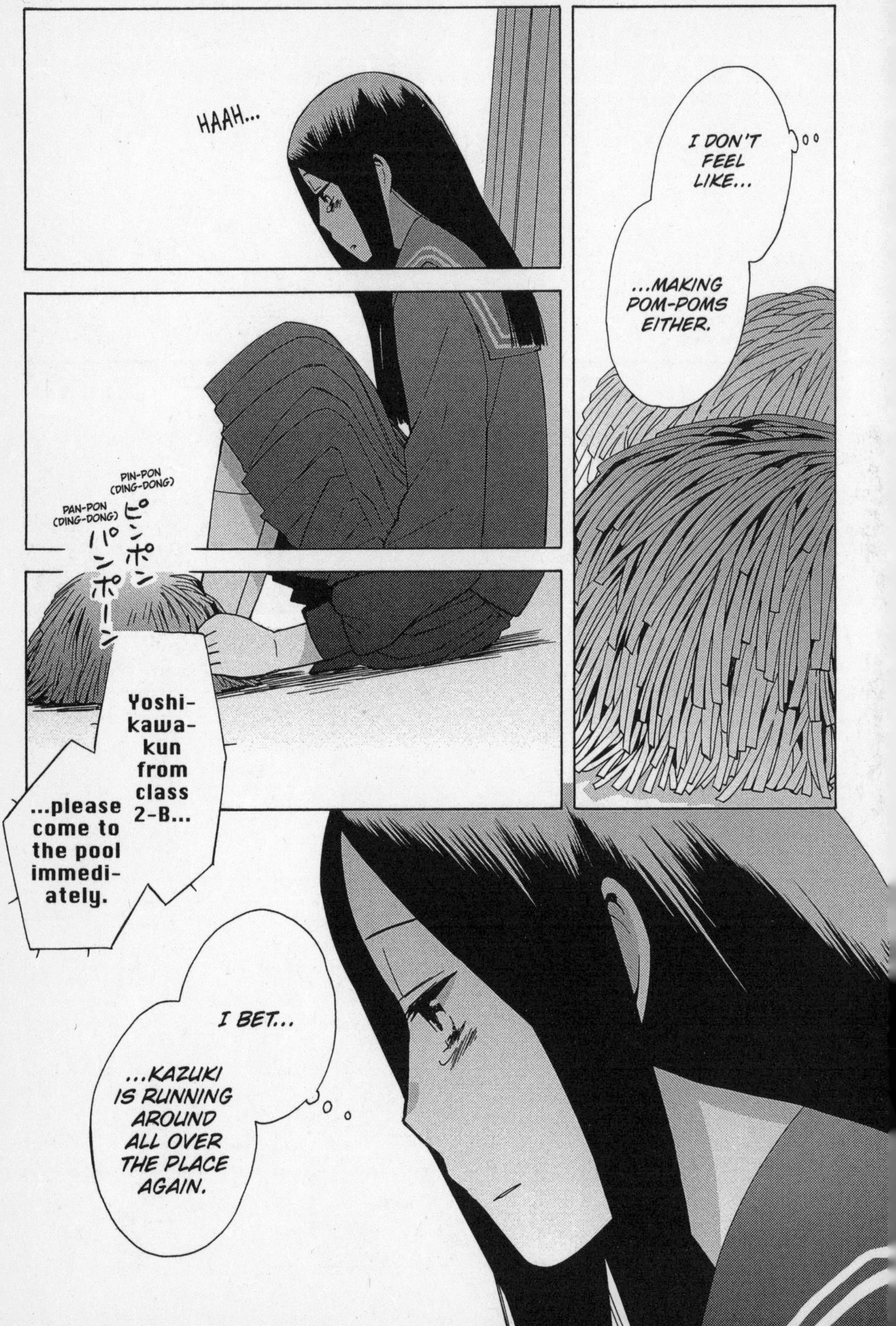
I DON'T FEEL LIKE...
...MAKING POM-POMS EITHER.
HAAH...
ピンポン
PIN-PON (DING-DONG)
パンポーン
PAN-PON (DING-DONG)
Yoshi-kawa-kun from class 2-B...
...please come to the pool immedi-ately.
I BET...
...KAZUKI IS RUNNING AROUND ALL OVER THE PLACE AGAIN.

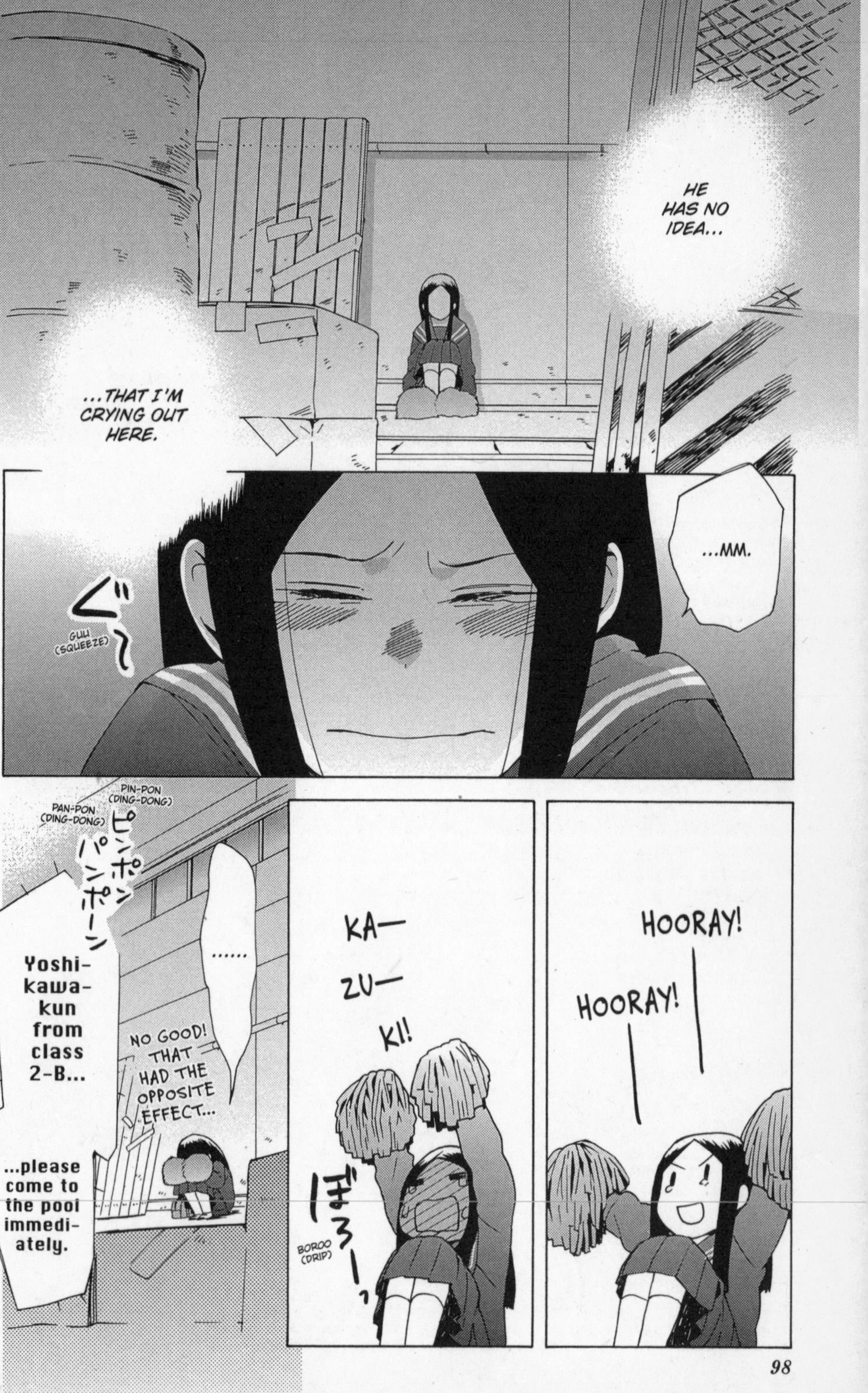
HE HAS NO IDEA...
...THAT I'M CRYING OUT HERE.
...MM.
ぐ〜
GUU (SQUEEZE)
HOORAY!
HOORAY!
KA— ZU— KI!
ぼろーっ
BOROO (DRIP)
ピンポン パンポーン
PIN-PON (DING-DONG)
PAN-PON (DING-DONG)
......
NO GOOD! THAT HAD THE OPPOSITE EFFECT...
Yoshi-kawa-kun from class 2-B...
...please come to the pool immedi-ately.

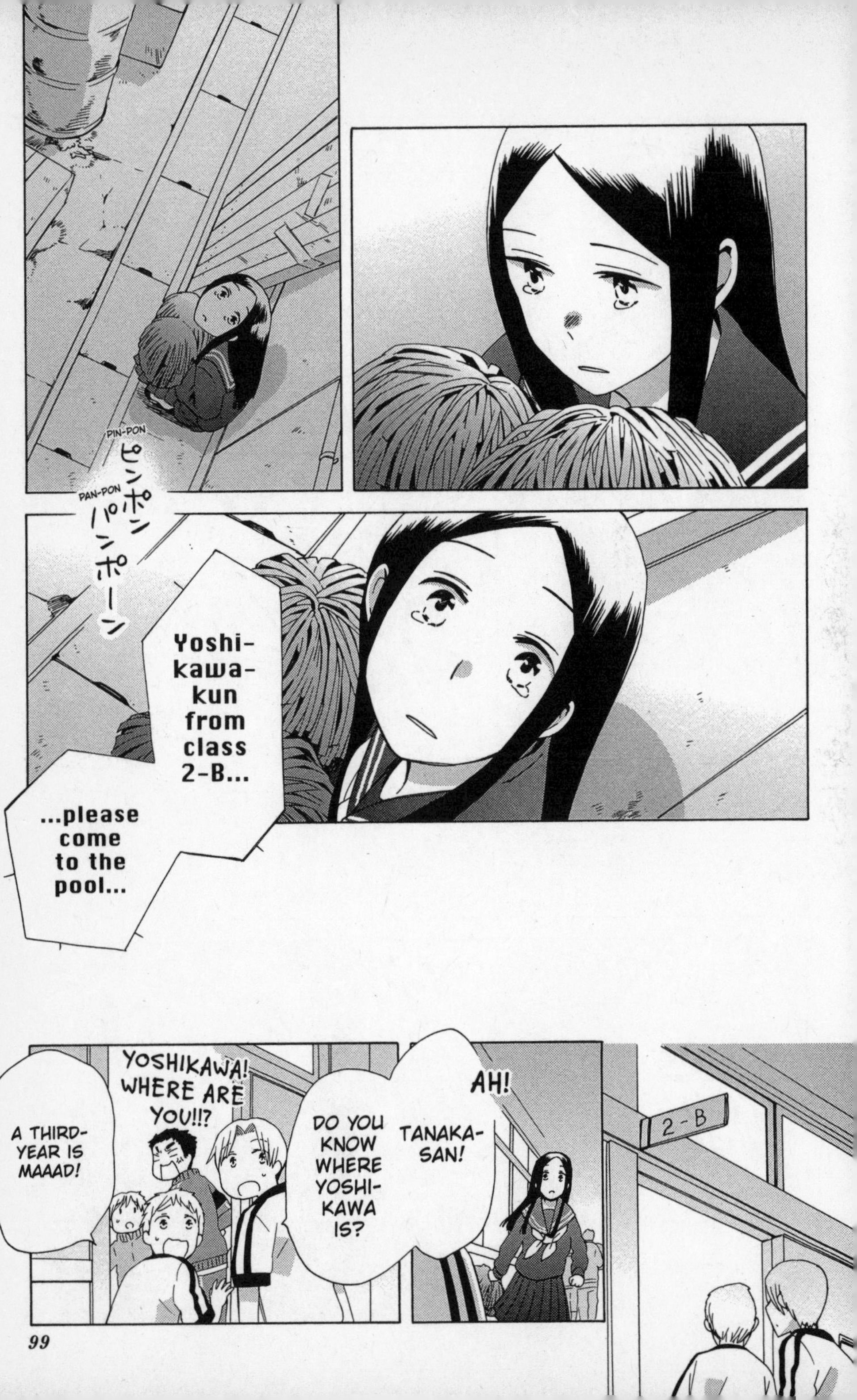

PIN-PON
PAN-PON
ピンポンパンポーン
Yoshi-kawa-kun from class 2-B...
...please come to the pool...
2-B
AH!
TANAKA-SAN!
DO YOU KNOW WHERE YOSHI-KAWA IS?
YOSHIKAWA! WHERE ARE YOU!!?
A THIRD-YEAR IS MAAAD!

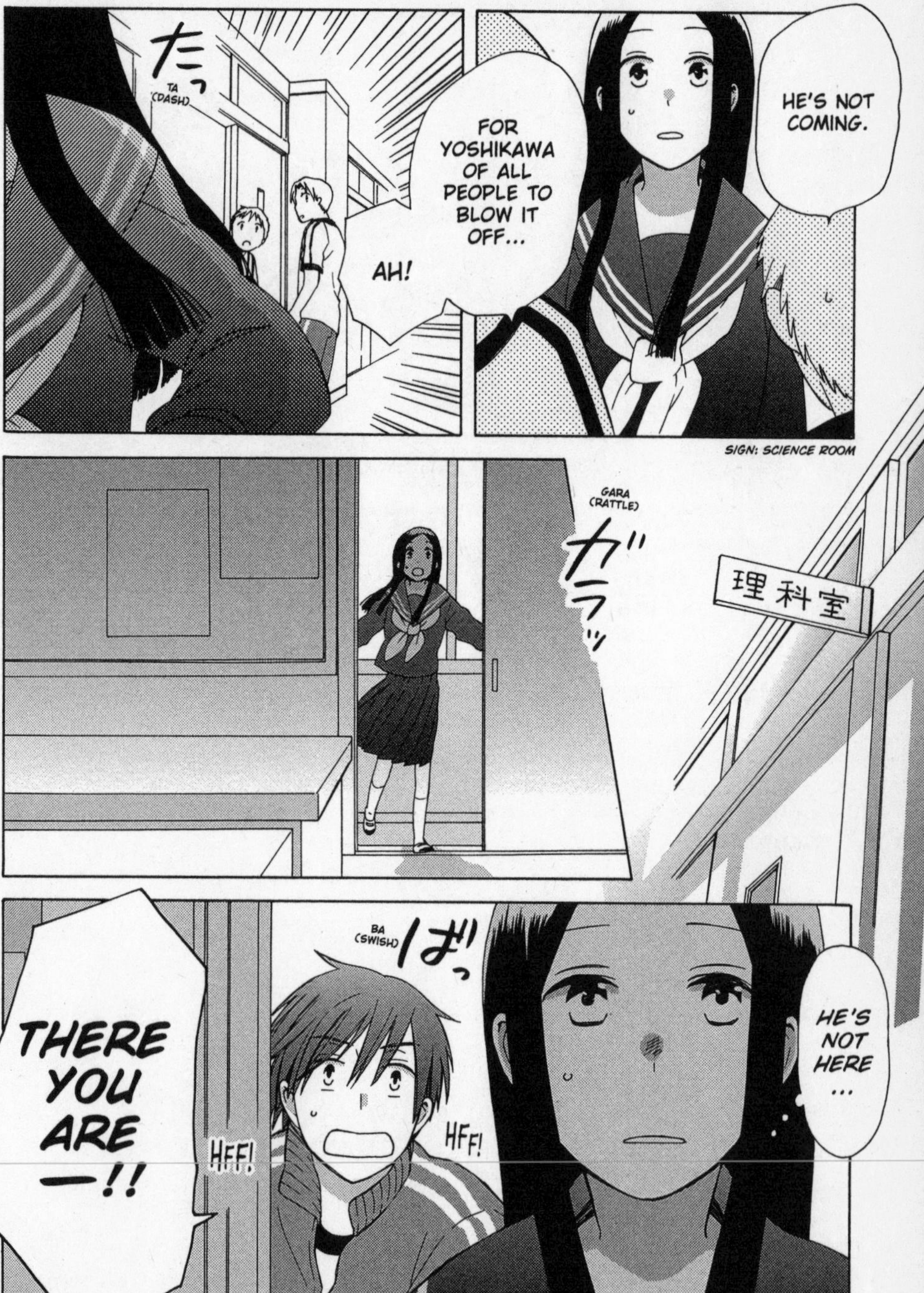
HE'S NOT COMING.
FOR YOSHIKAWA OF ALL PEOPLE TO BLOW IT OFF...
AH!
たっ
TA (DASH)
SIGN: SCIENCE ROOM
理科室
ガラッ
GARA (RATTLE)
HE'S NOT HERE ...
ばっ
BA (SWISH)
HFF!
HFF!
THERE YOU ARE—!!

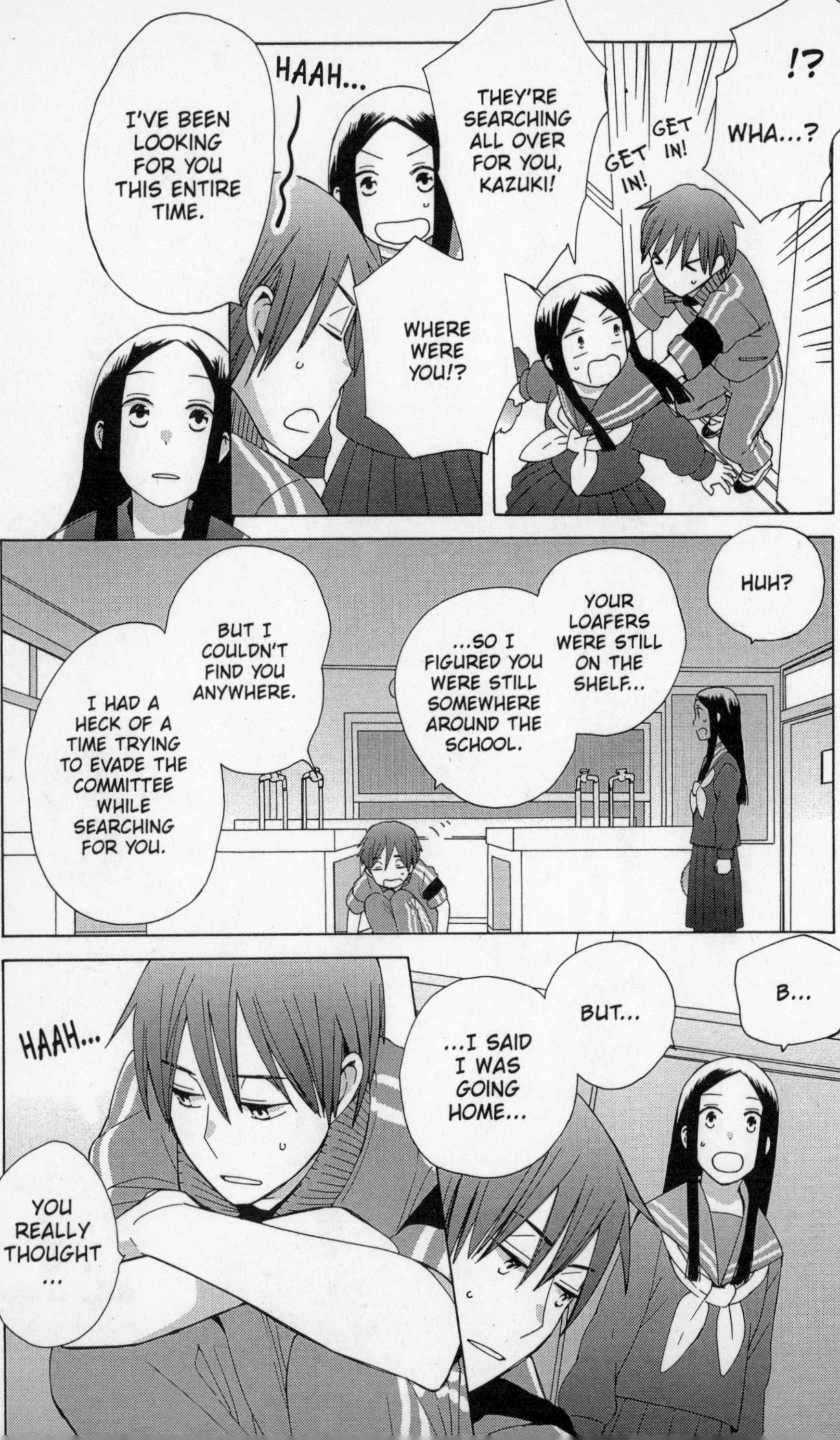
!?
WHA...?
GET IN! GET IN!
THEY'RE SEARCHING ALL OVER FOR YOU, KAZUKI!
WHERE WERE YOU!?
HAAH...
I'VE BEEN LOOKING FOR YOU THIS ENTIRE TIME.
HUH?
YOUR LOAFERS WERE STILL ON THE SHELF...
...SO I FIGURED YOU WERE STILL SOMEWHERE AROUND THE SCHOOL.
BUT I COULDN'T FIND YOU ANYWHERE.
I HAD A HECK OF A TIME TRYING TO EVADE THE COMMITTEE WHILE SEARCHING FOR YOU.
B...
BUT...
...I SAID I WAS GOING HOME...
HAAH...
YOU REALLY THOUGHT ...

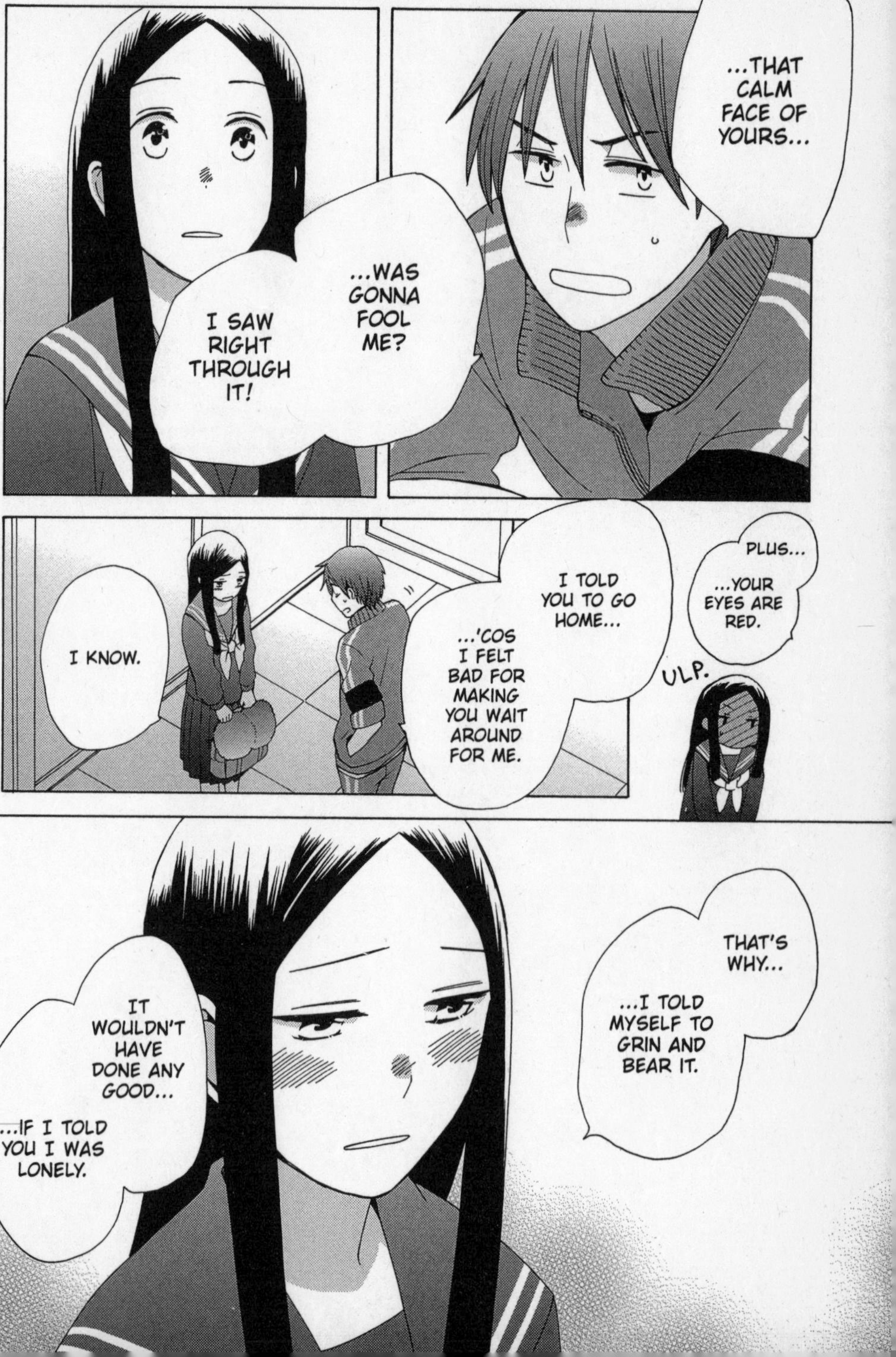
...THAT CALM FACE OF YOURS...
...WAS GONNA FOOL ME?
I SAW RIGHT THROUGH IT!
PLUS...
...YOUR EYES ARE RED.
ULP.
I TOLD YOU TO GO HOME...
...'COS I FELT BAD FOR MAKING YOU WAIT AROUND FOR ME.
I KNOW.
THAT'S WHY...
...I TOLD MYSELF TO GRIN AND BEAR IT.
IT WOULDN'T HAVE DONE ANY GOOD...
...IF I TOLD YOU I WAS LONELY.

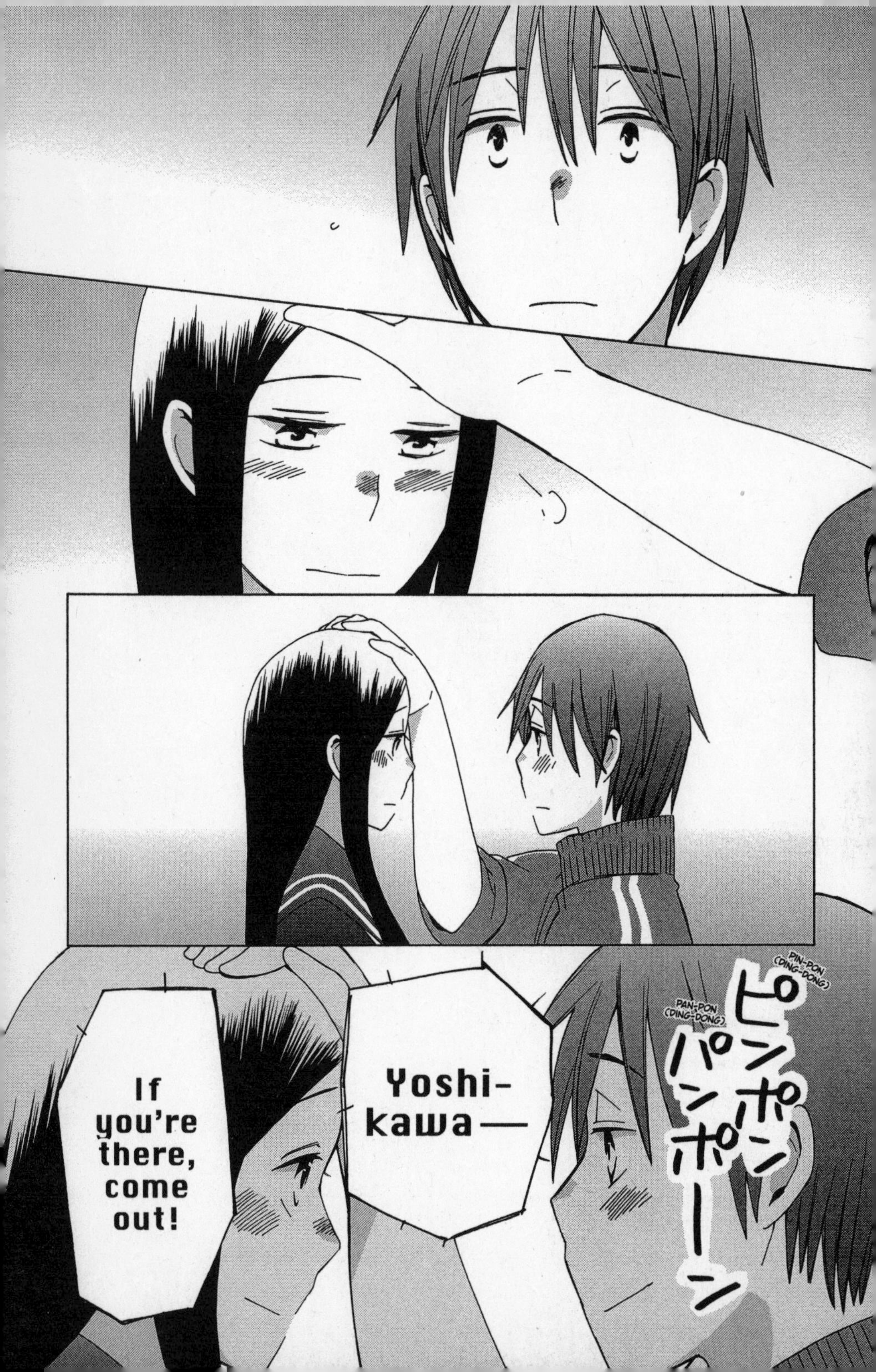
ピンポーン
PIN-PON (DING-DONG)
パンポーン
PAN-PON (DING-DONG)
Yoshi-kawa—
If you're there, come out!

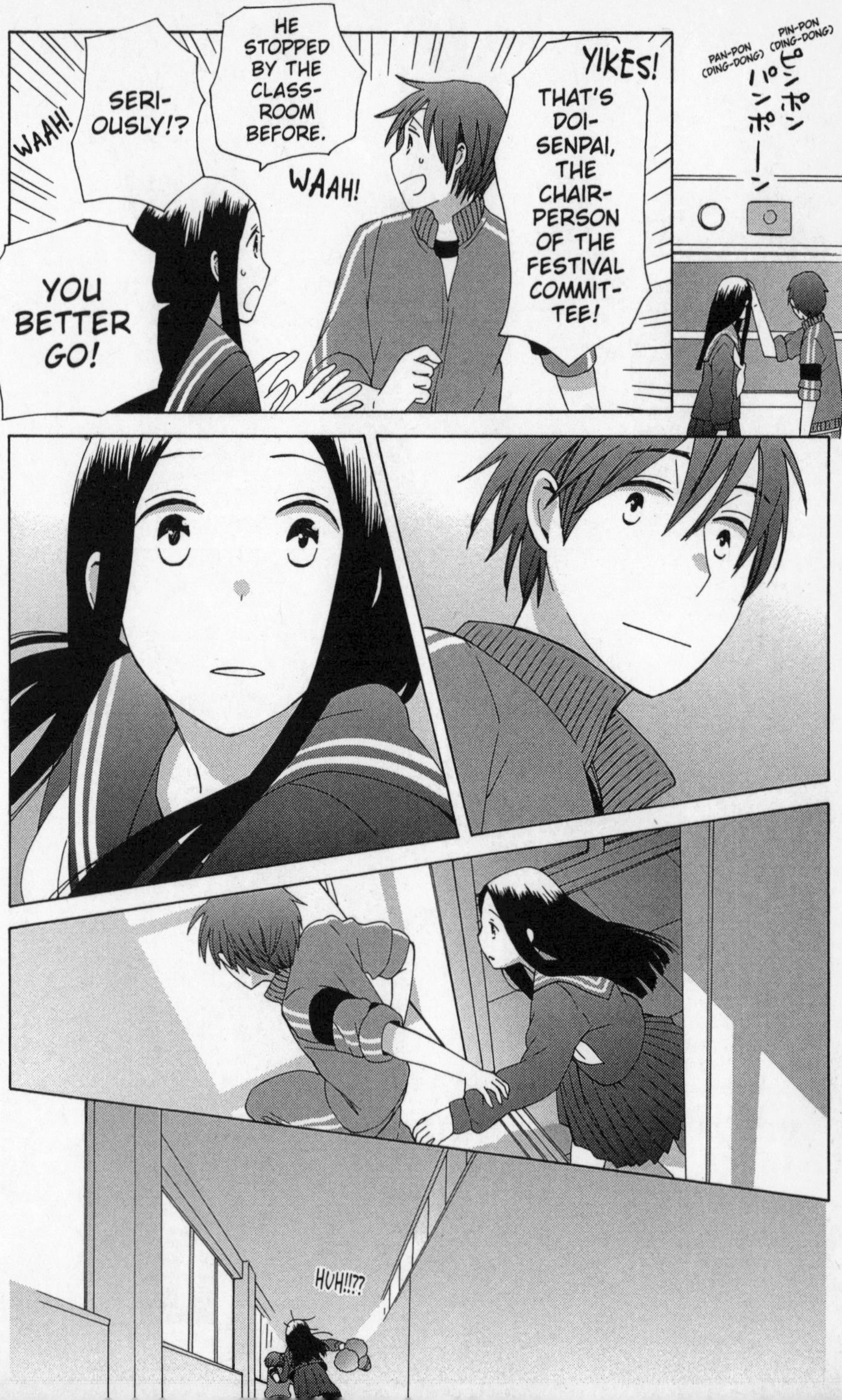
ピンポン
PIN-PON (DING-DONG)
パンポーン
PAN-PON (DING-DONG)
YIKES!
THAT'S DOI-SENPAI, THE CHAIRPERSON OF THE FESTIVAL COMMITTEE!
HE STOPPED BY THE CLASSROOM BEFORE.
WAAH!
SERIOUSLY!?
WAAH!
YOU BETTER GO!
HUH!!??

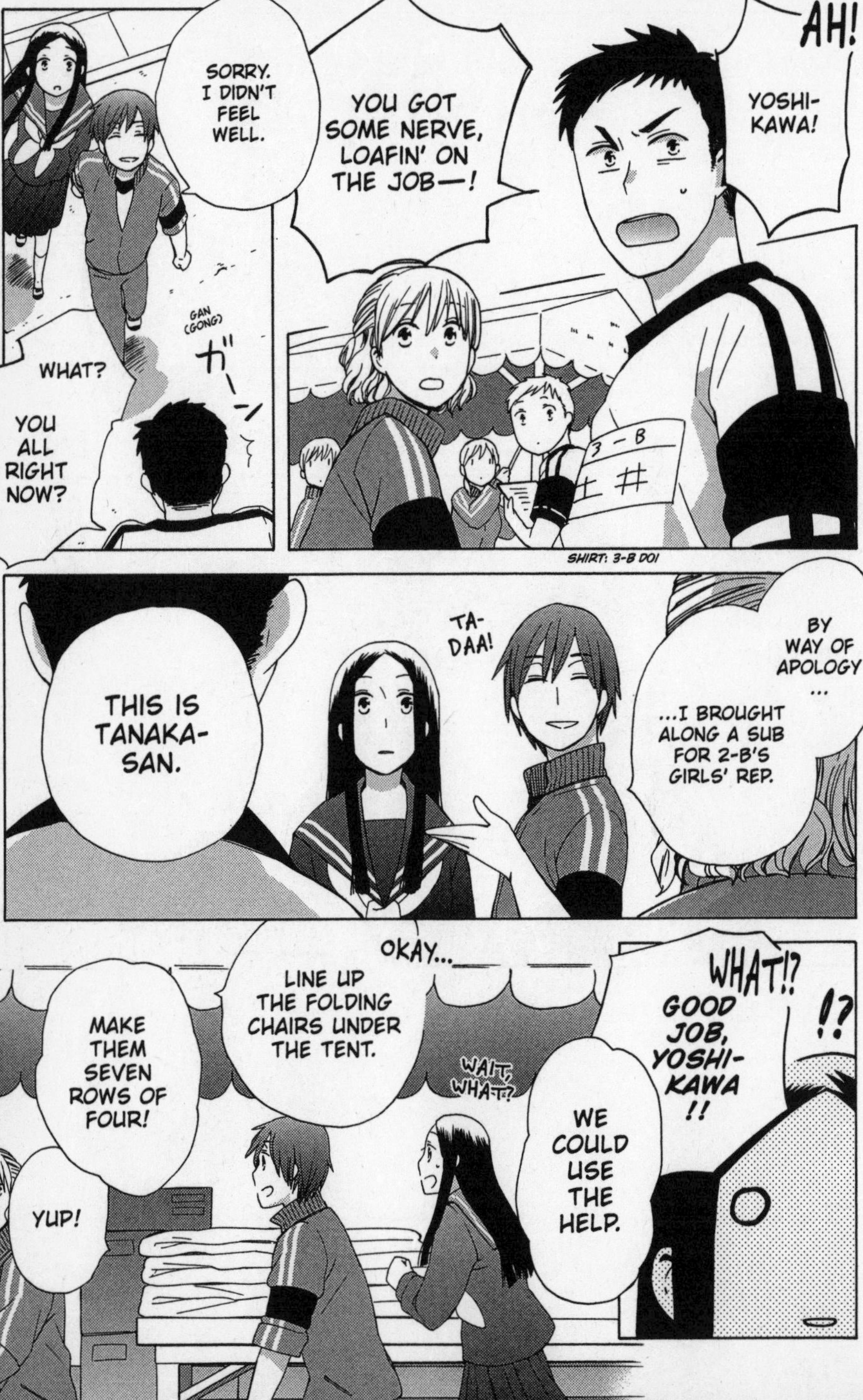
AH!
YOSHI-KAWA!
YOU GOT SOME NERVE, LOAFIN' ON THE JOB—!
SHIRT: 3-B DOI
SORRY. I DIDN'T FEEL WELL.
GAN (GONG)
ガーン
WHAT?
YOU ALL RIGHT NOW?
BY WAY OF APOLOGY ...
...I BROUGHT ALONG A SUB FOR 2-B'S GIRLS' REP.
TA-DAA!
THIS IS TANAKA-SAN.
WHAT!?
!?
GOOD JOB, YOSHI-KAWA!!
WE COULD USE THE HELP.
WAIT, WHAT!?
OKAY...
LINE UP THE FOLDING CHAIRS UNDER THE TENT.
MAKE THEM SEVEN ROWS OF FOUR!
YUP!

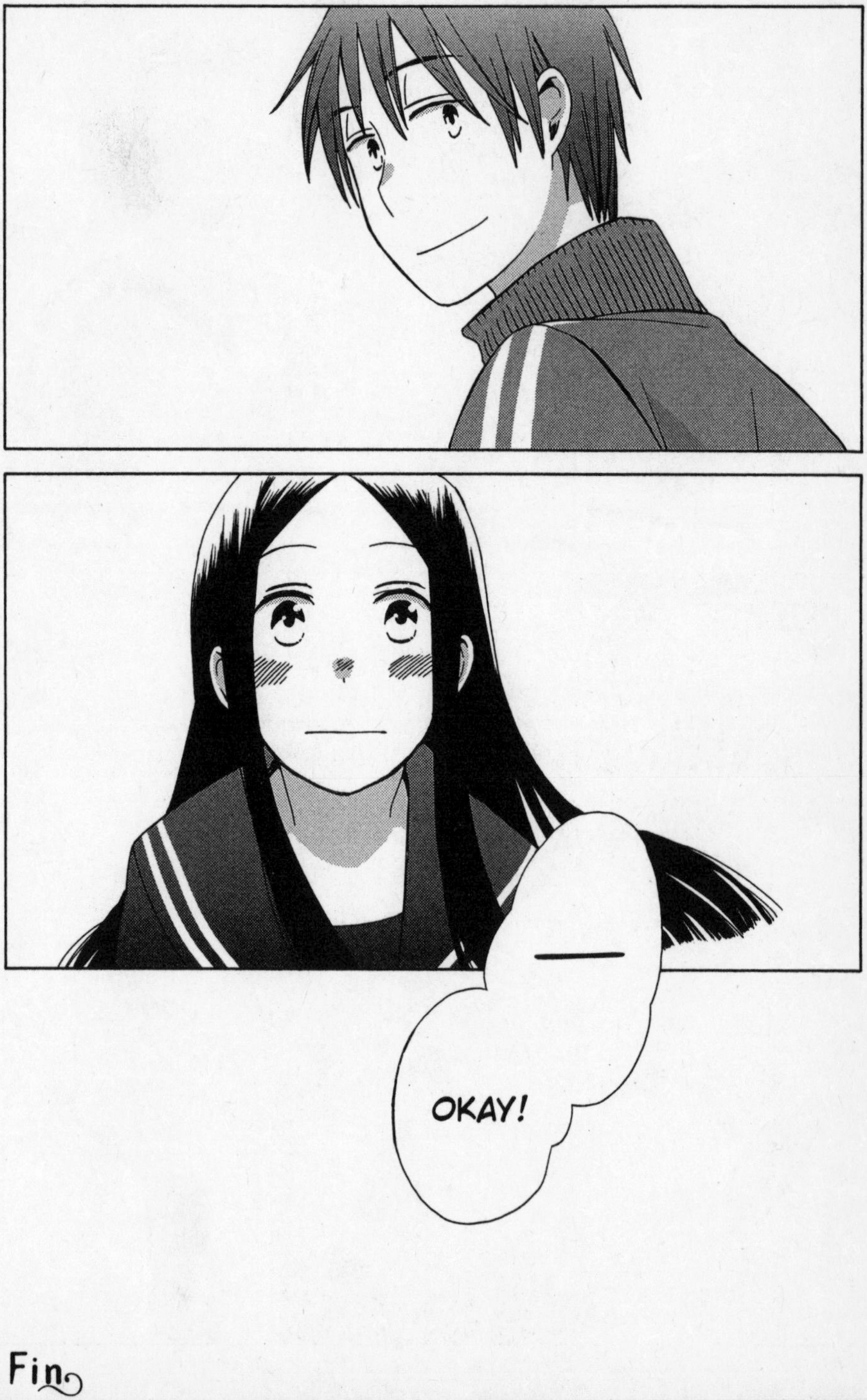
—— OKAY!
Fin

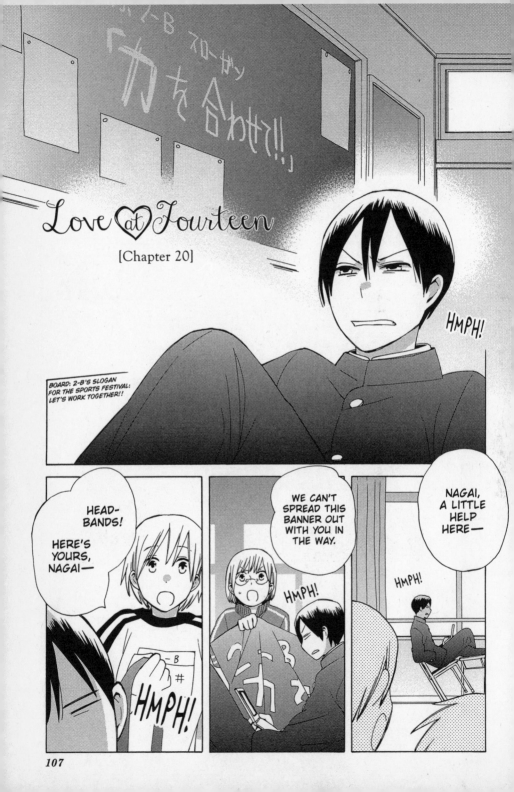

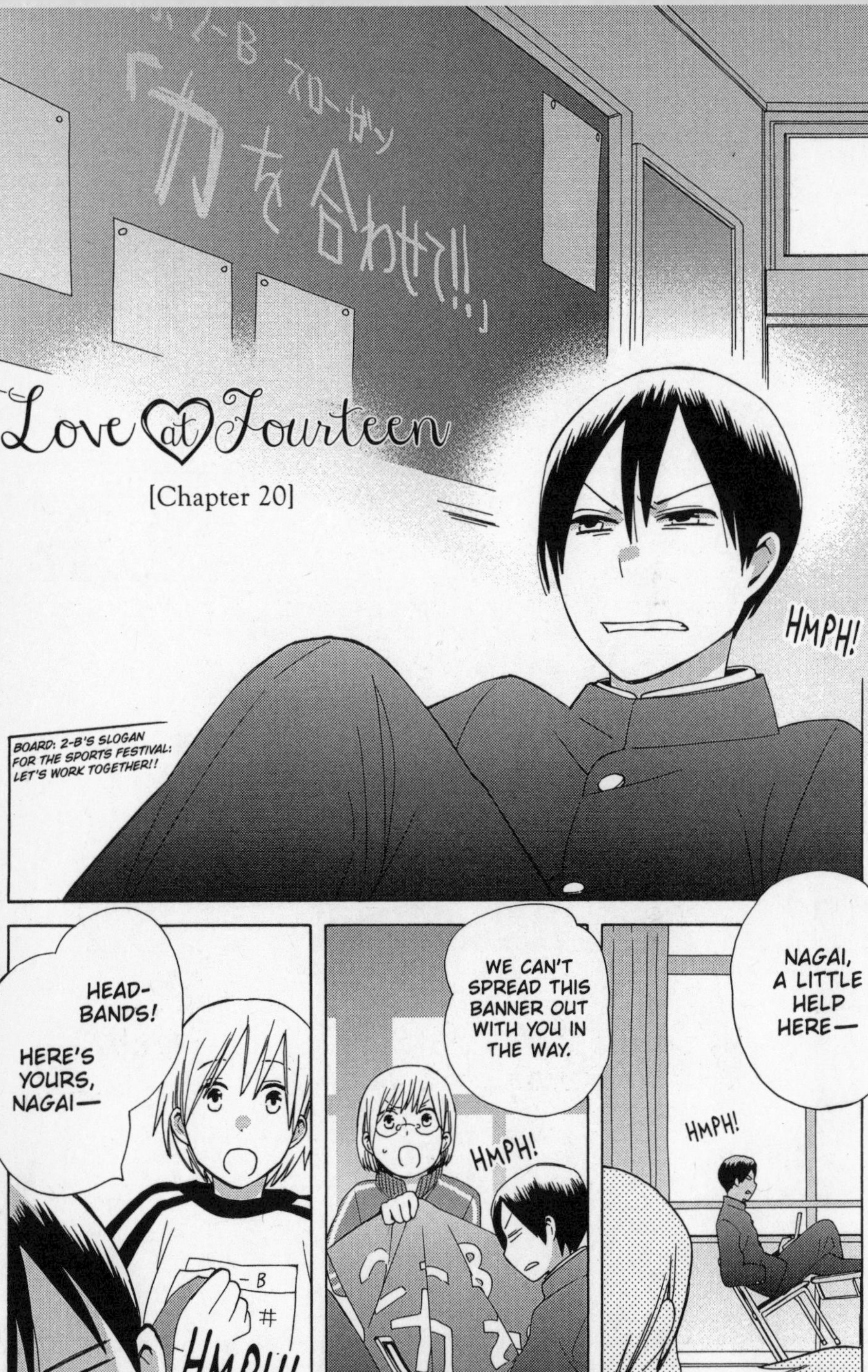
スローガン
「力を合わせて!!」
Love at Fourteen
[Chapter 20]
HMPH!
BOARD: 2-B'S SLOGAN FOR THE SPORTS FESTIVAL: LET'S WORK TOGETHER!!
NAGAI, A LITTLE HELP HERE—
HMPH!
WE CAN'T SPREAD THIS BANNER OUT WITH YOU IN THE WAY.
HMPH!
HEAD-BANDS!
HERE'S YOURS, NAGAI—
HMPH!

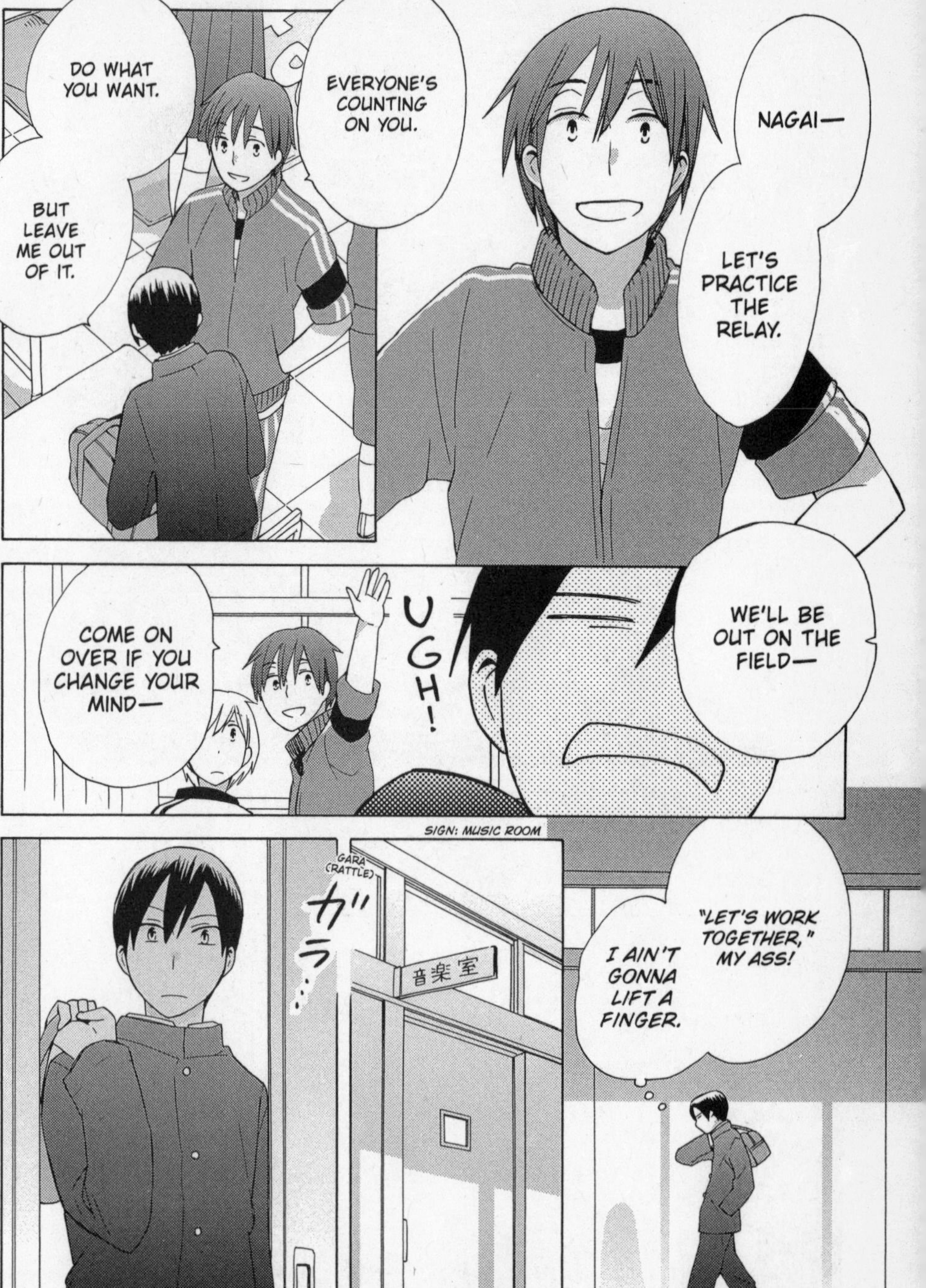
NAGAI—
LET'S PRACTICE THE RELAY.
EVERYONE'S COUNTING ON YOU.
DO WHAT YOU WANT.
BUT LEAVE ME OUT OF IT.
WE'LL BE OUT ON THE FIELD—
UGH!
COME ON OVER IF YOU CHANGE YOUR MIND—
"LET'S WORK TOGETHER," MY ASS!
I AIN'T GONNA LIFT A FINGER.
SIGN: MUSIC ROOM
音楽室
GARA (RATTLE)
ガラ...

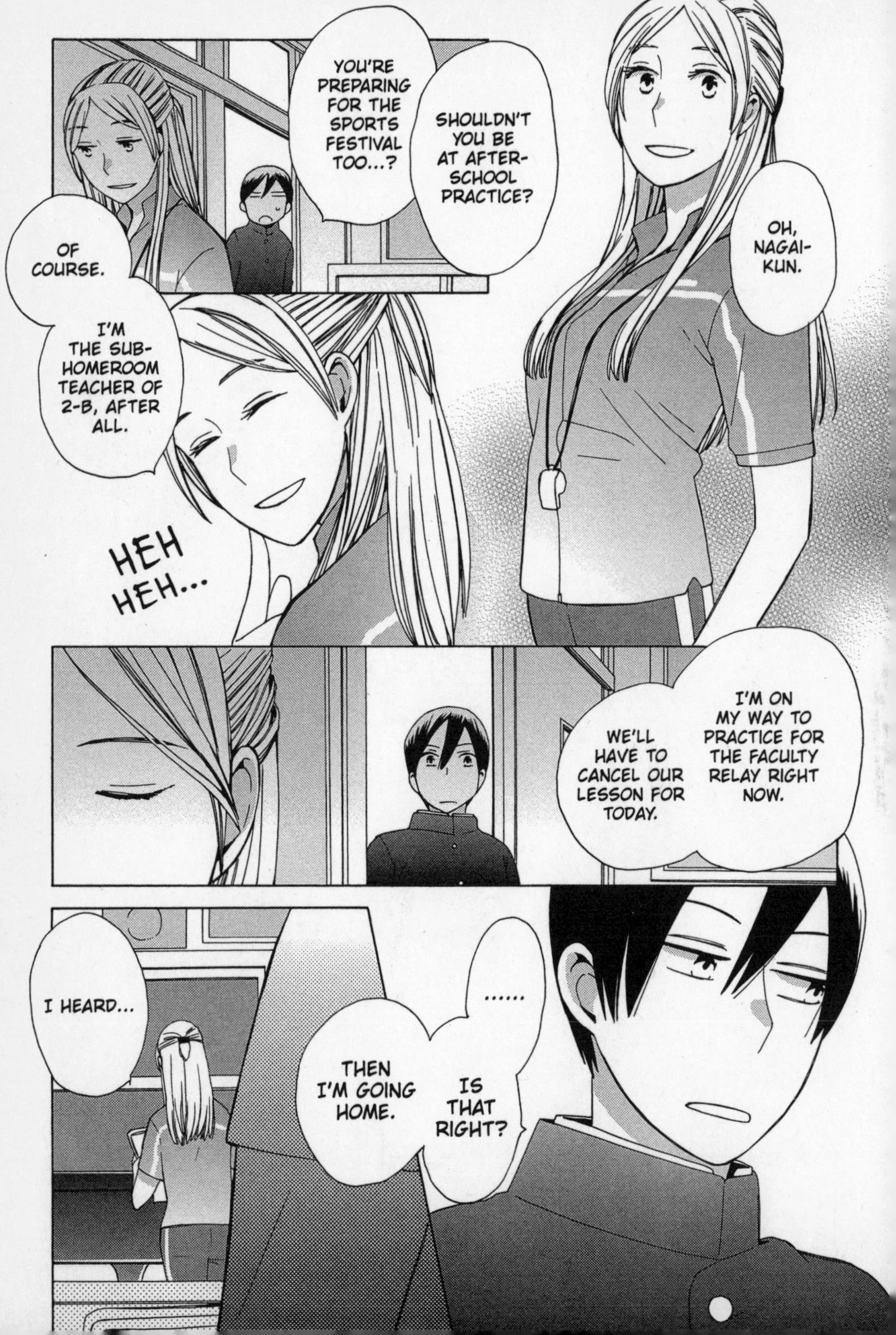
OH, NAGAI-KUN.
SHOULDN'T YOU BE AT AFTER-SCHOOL PRACTICE?
YOU'RE PREPARING FOR THE SPORTS FESTIVAL TOO...?
OF COURSE.
I'M THE SUB-HOMEROOM TEACHER OF 2-B, AFTER ALL.
HEH HEH...
I'M ON MY WAY TO PRACTICE FOR THE FACULTY RELAY RIGHT NOW.
WE'LL HAVE TO CANCEL OUR LESSON FOR TODAY.
......
IS THAT RIGHT?
THEN I'M GOING HOME.
I HEARD...

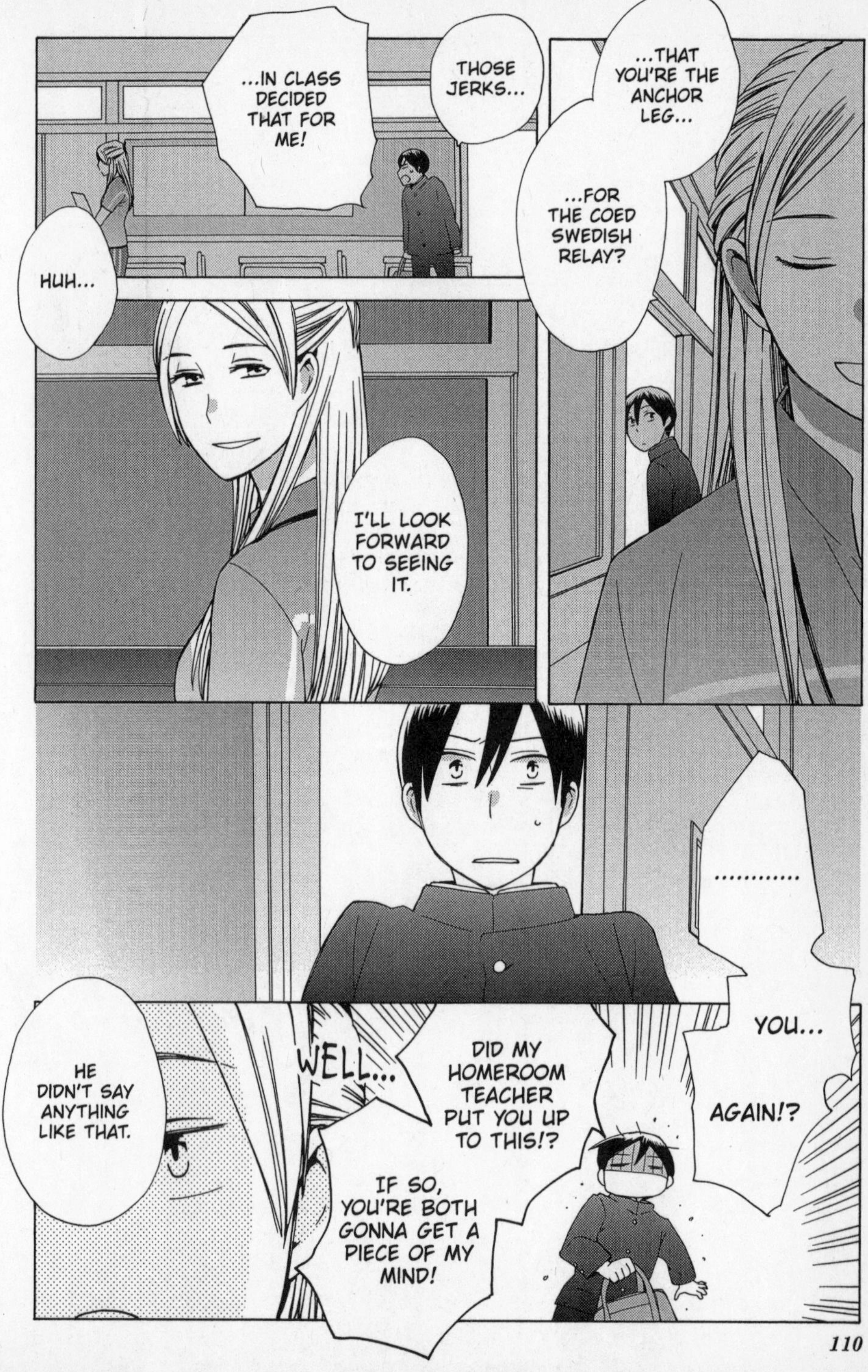
...THAT YOU'RE THE ANCHOR LEG...
...FOR THE COED SWEDISH RELAY?
THOSE JERKS...
...IN CLASS DECIDED THAT FOR ME!
HUH...
I'LL LOOK FORWARD TO SEEING IT.
....
YOU...
AGAIN!?
DID MY HOMEROOM TEACHER PUT YOU UP TO THIS!?
IF SO, YOU'RE BOTH GONNA GET A PIECE OF MY MIND!
WELL...
HE DIDN'T SAY ANYTHING LIKE THAT.

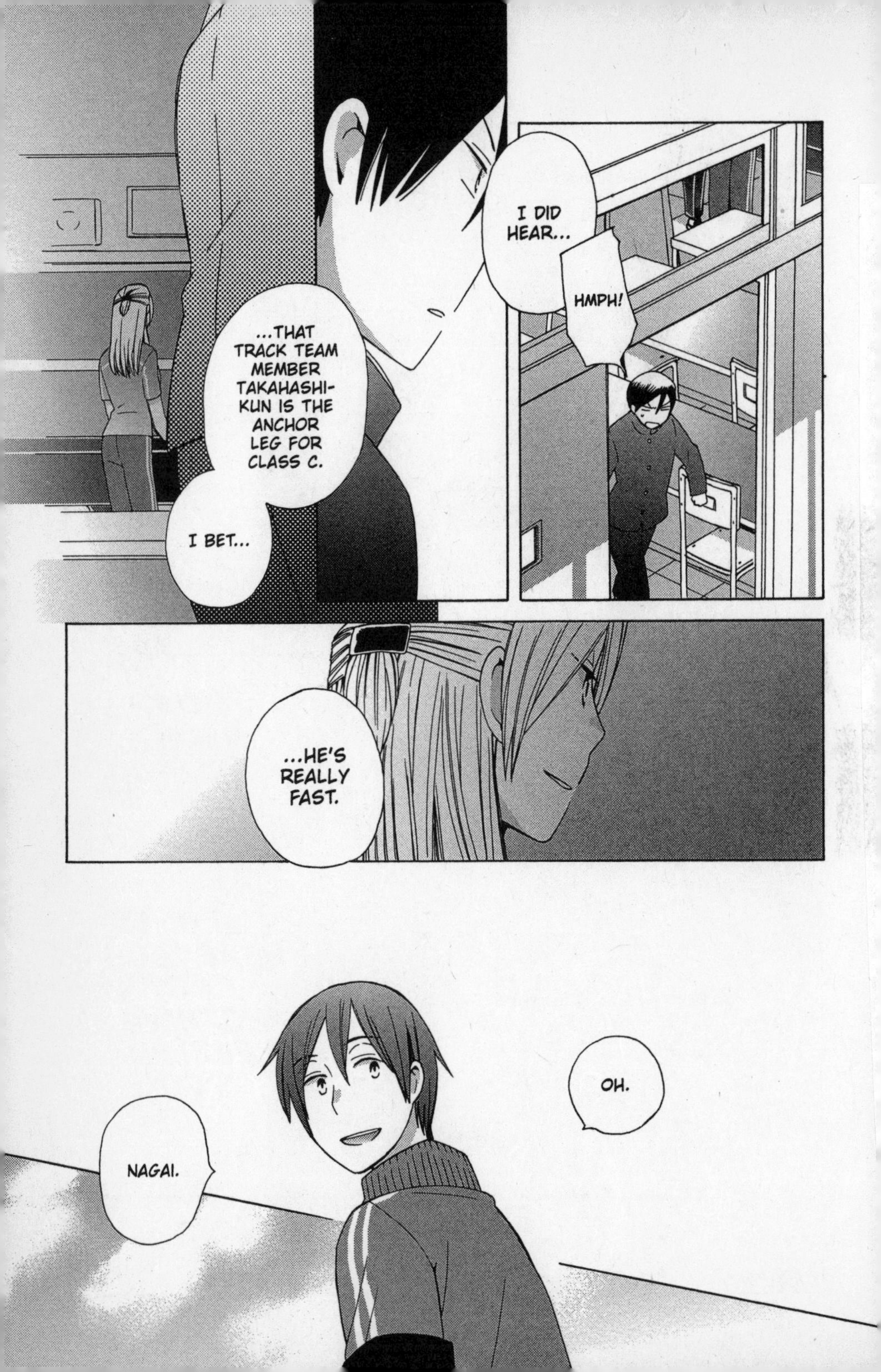
I DID HEAR...
HMPH!
...THAT TRACK TEAM MEMBER TAKAHASHI-KUN IS THE ANCHOR LEG FOR CLASS C.
I BET...
...HE'S REALLY FAST.
OH.
NAGAI.

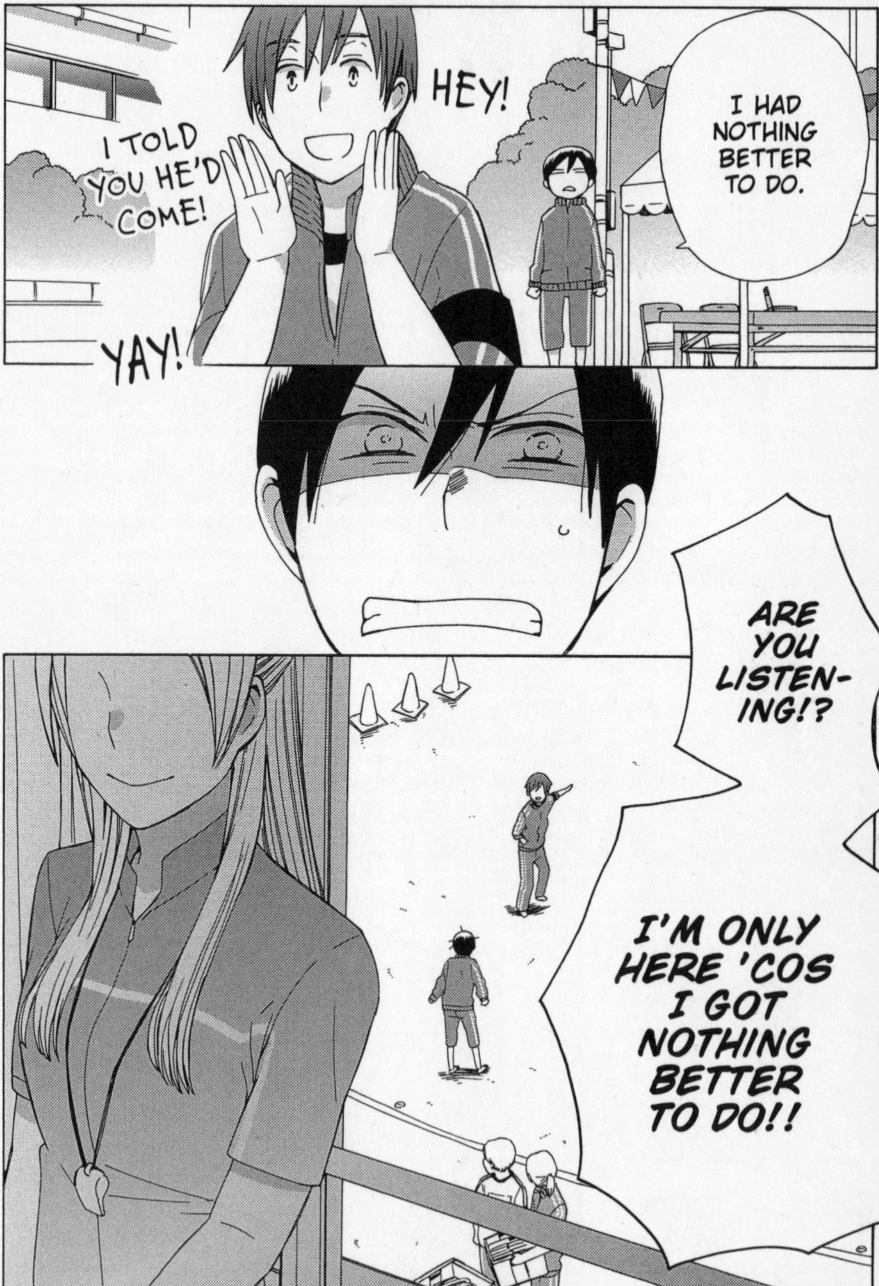
I HAD NOTHING BETTER TO DO.
HEY!
I TOLD YOU HE'D COME!
YAY!
ARE YOU LISTENING!?
I'M ONLY HERE 'COS I GOT NOTHING BETTER TO DO!!

Fin

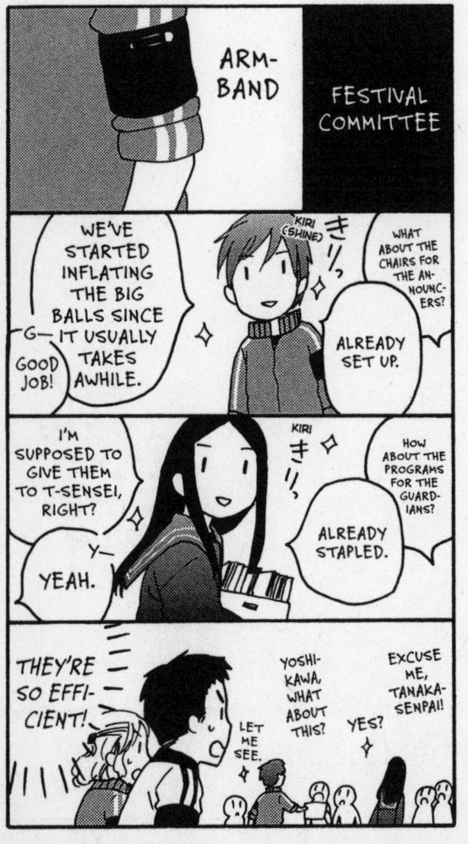
FESTIVAL COMMITTEE
ARMBAND
WHAT ABOUT THE CHAIRS FOR THE ANNOUNCERS?
KIRI (SHINE)
ALREADY SET UP.
WE'VE STARTED INFLATING THE BIG BALLS SINCE IT USUALLY TAKES AWHILE.
G— GOOD JOB!
HOW ABOUT THE PROGRAMS FOR THE GUARDIANS?
KIRI
ALREADY STAPLED.
I'M SUPPOSED TO GIVE THEM TO T-SENSEI, RIGHT?
Y— YEAH.
EXCUSE ME, TANAKA-SENPAI!
YES?
YOSHIKAWA, WHAT ABOUT THIS?
LET ME SEE.
THEY'RE SO EFFICIENT!

Love at Fourteen

Fuka Mizutani

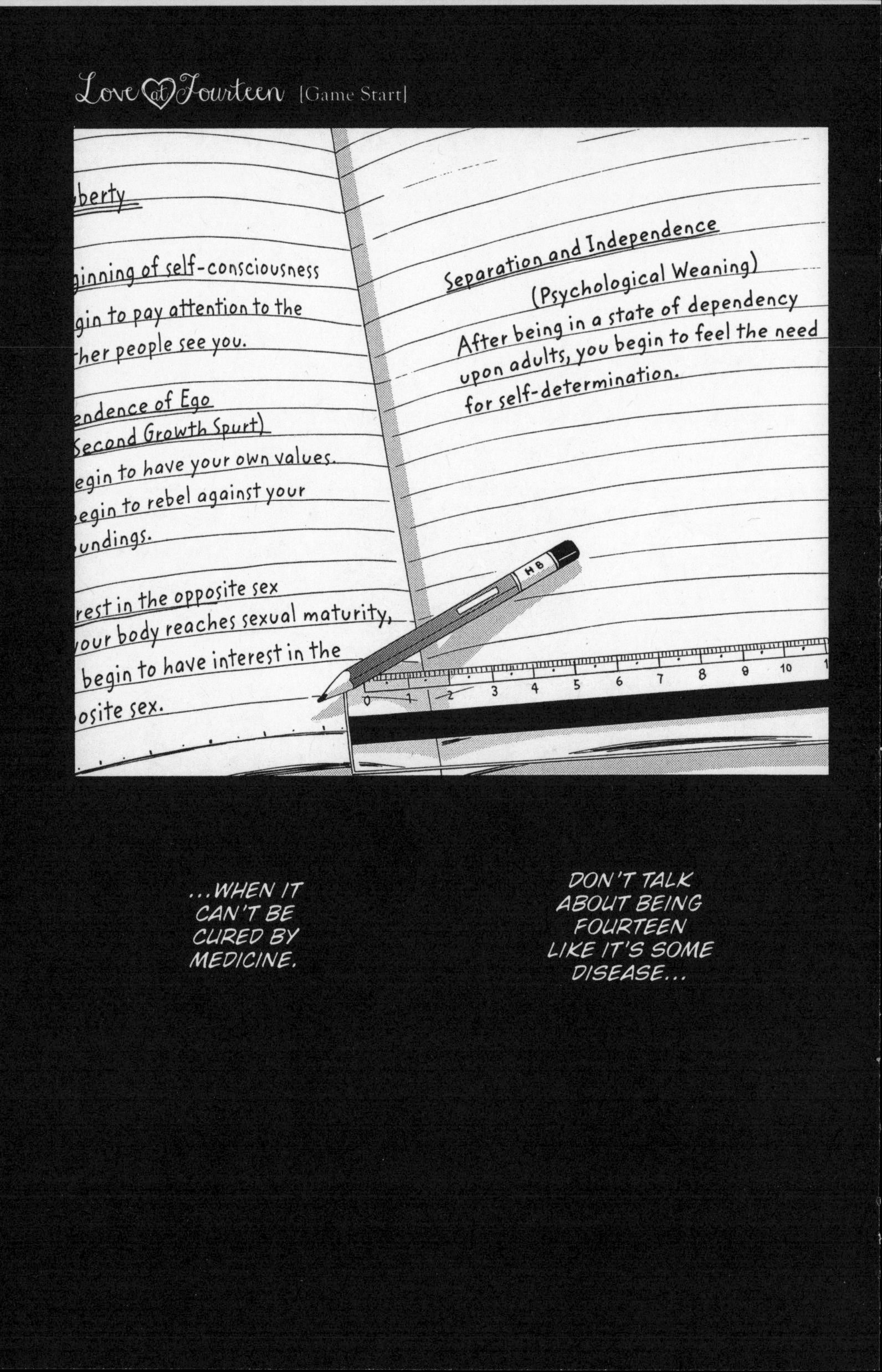
berty
ginning of self-consciousness
gin to pay attention to the
her people see you.
endence of Ego
Second Growth Spurt)
egin to have your own values.
egin to rebel against your
undings.
rest in the opposite sex
our body reaches sexual maturity,
begin to have interest in the
osite sex.
Separation and Independence
(Psychological Weaning)
After being in a state of dependency
upon adults, you begin to feel the need
for self-determination.
HB
0 1 2 3 4 5 6 7 8 9 10
DON'T TALK ABOUT BEING FOURTEEN LIKE IT'S SOME DISEASE...
...WHEN IT CAN'T BE CURED BY MEDICINE.

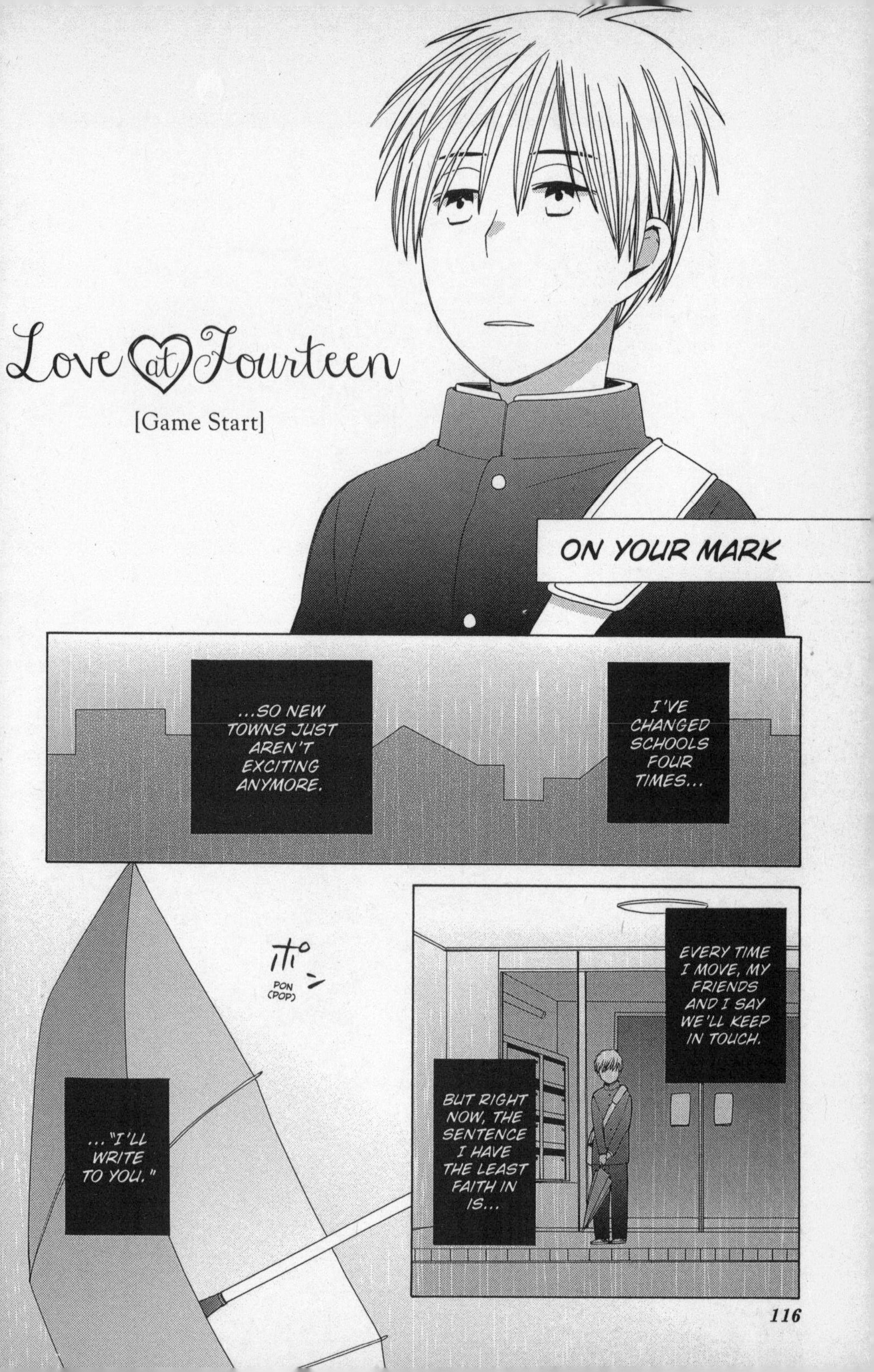
Love at Fourteen
[Game Start]
ON YOUR MARK
I'VE CHANGED SCHOOLS FOUR TIMES...
...SO NEW TOWNS JUST AREN'T EXCITING ANYMORE.
EVERY TIME I MOVE, MY FRIENDS AND I SAY WE'LL KEEP IN TOUCH.
BUT RIGHT NOW, THE SENTENCE I HAVE THE LEAST FAITH IN IS...
PON (POP)
..."I'LL WRITE TO YOU."

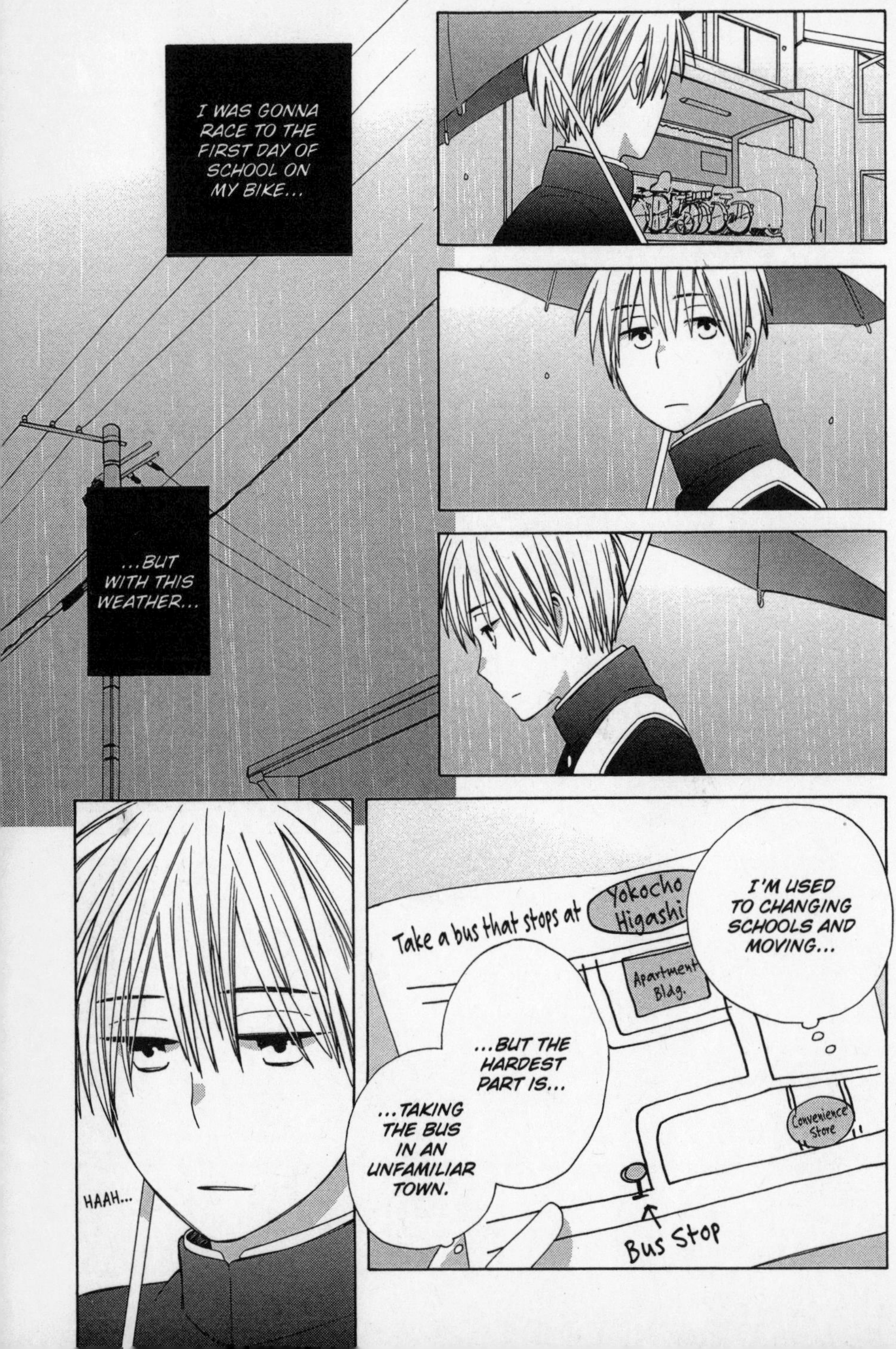
I WAS GONNA RACE TO THE FIRST DAY OF SCHOOL ON MY BIKE...
...BUT WITH THIS WEATHER...
I'M USED TO CHANGING SCHOOLS AND MOVING...
Take a bus that stops at
Yokocho Higashi
Apartment Bldg.
Convenience Store
Bus Stop
...BUT THE HARDEST PART IS...
...TAKING THE BUS IN AN UNFAMILIAR TOWN.
HAAH...

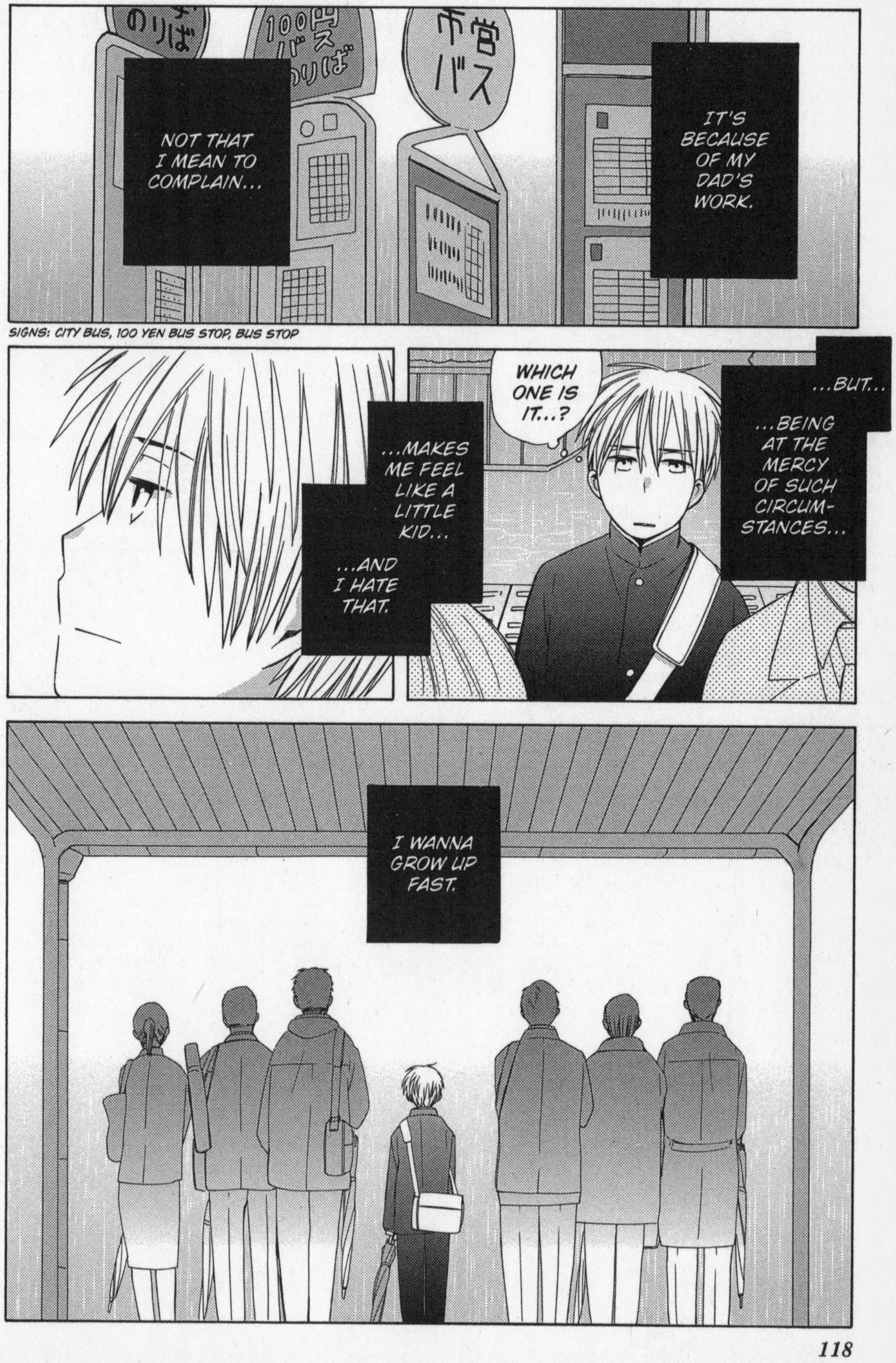
IT'S BECAUSE OF MY DAD'S WORK.
市営バス
100円バスのりば
のりば
NOT THAT I MEAN TO COMPLAIN...
SIGNS: CITY BUS, 100 YEN BUS STOP, BUS STOP
...BUT...
...BEING AT THE MERCY OF SUCH CIRCUMSTANCES...
WHICH ONE IS IT...?
...MAKES ME FEEL LIKE A LITTLE KID...
...AND I HATE THAT.
I WANNA GROW UP FAST.

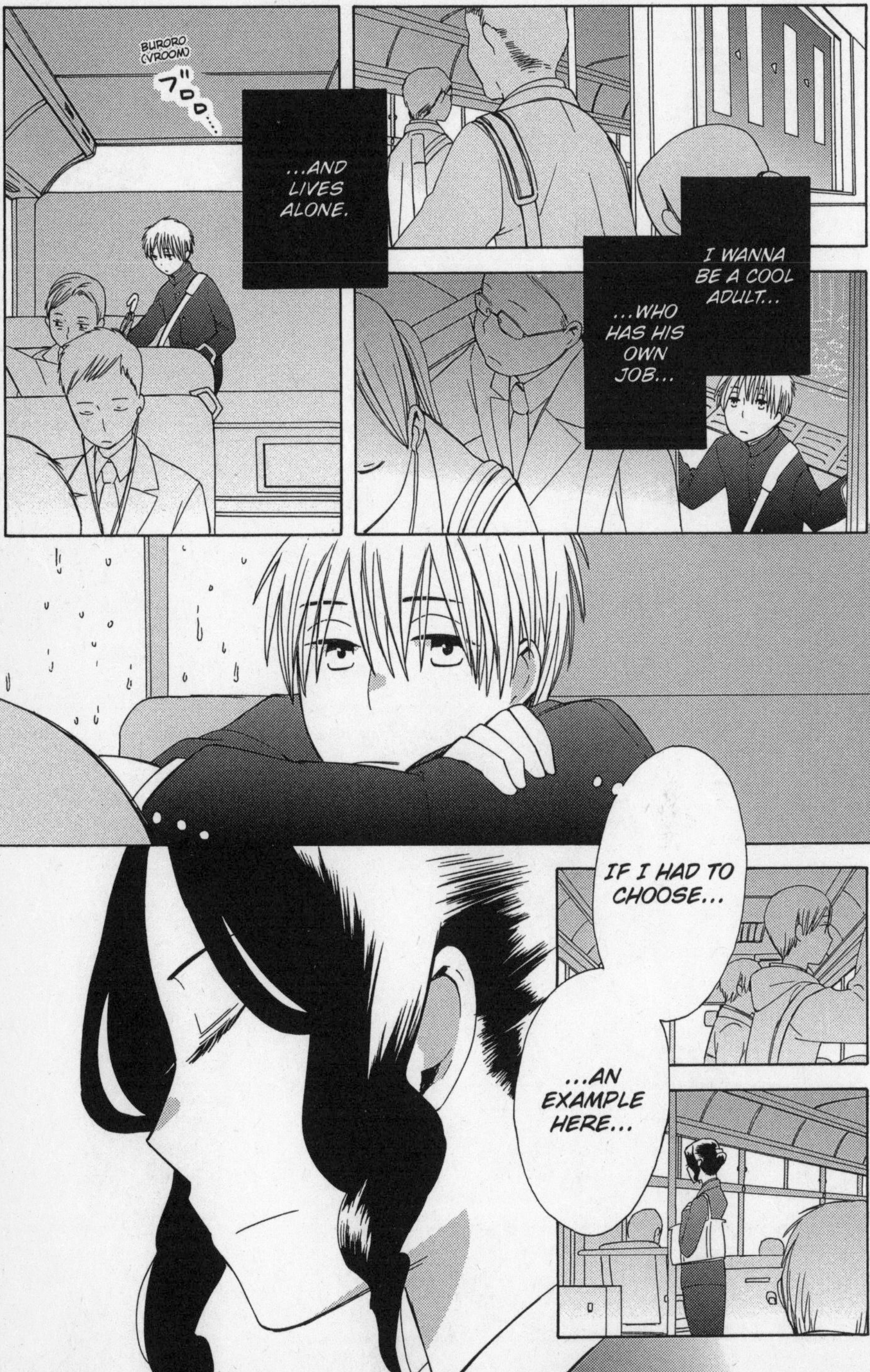
I WANNA BE A COOL ADULT...
...WHO HAS HIS OWN JOB...
...AND LIVES ALONE.
BURORO (VROOM)
ブロロ...
IF I HAD TO CHOOSE...
...AN EXAMPLE HERE...

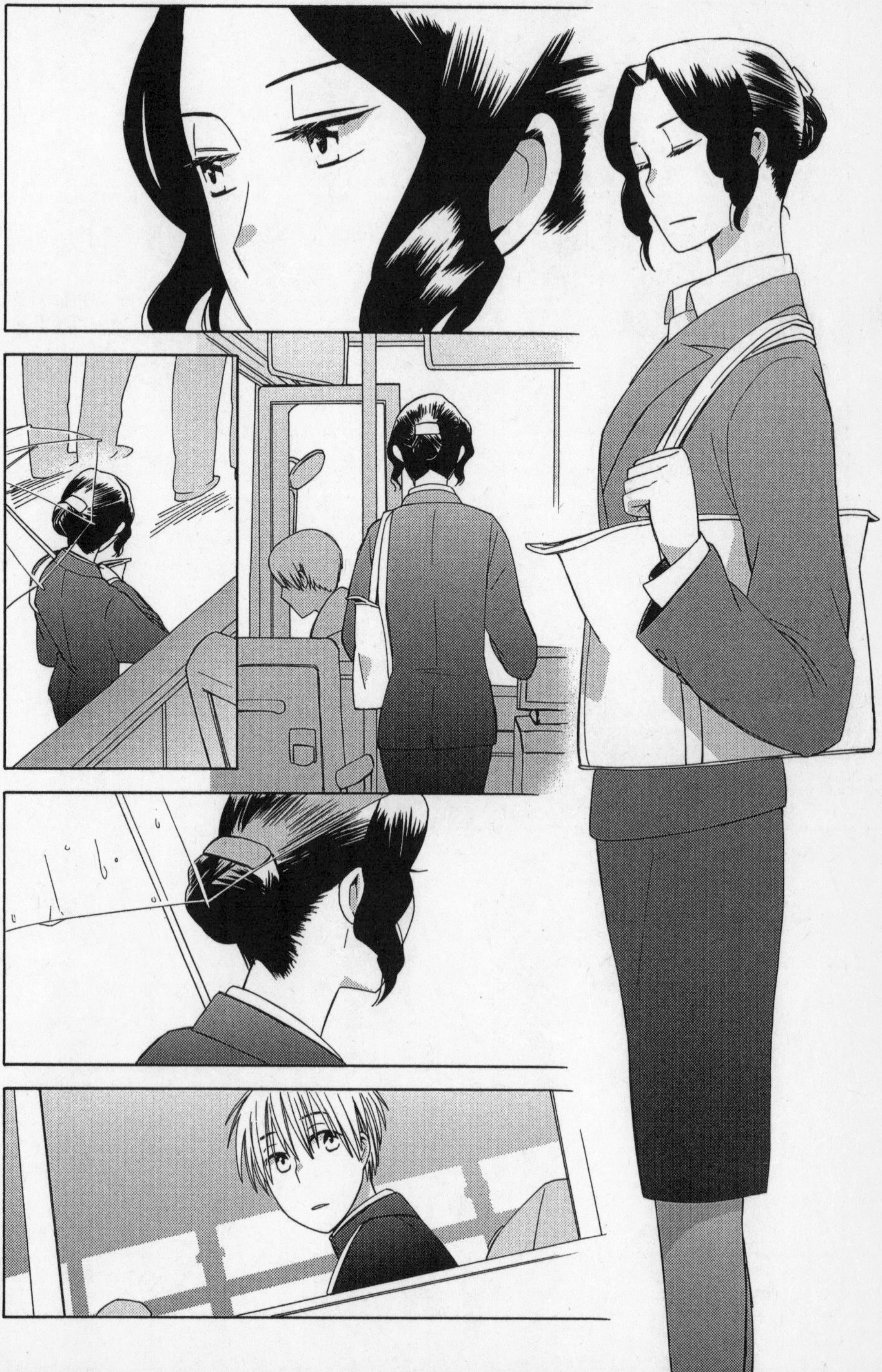

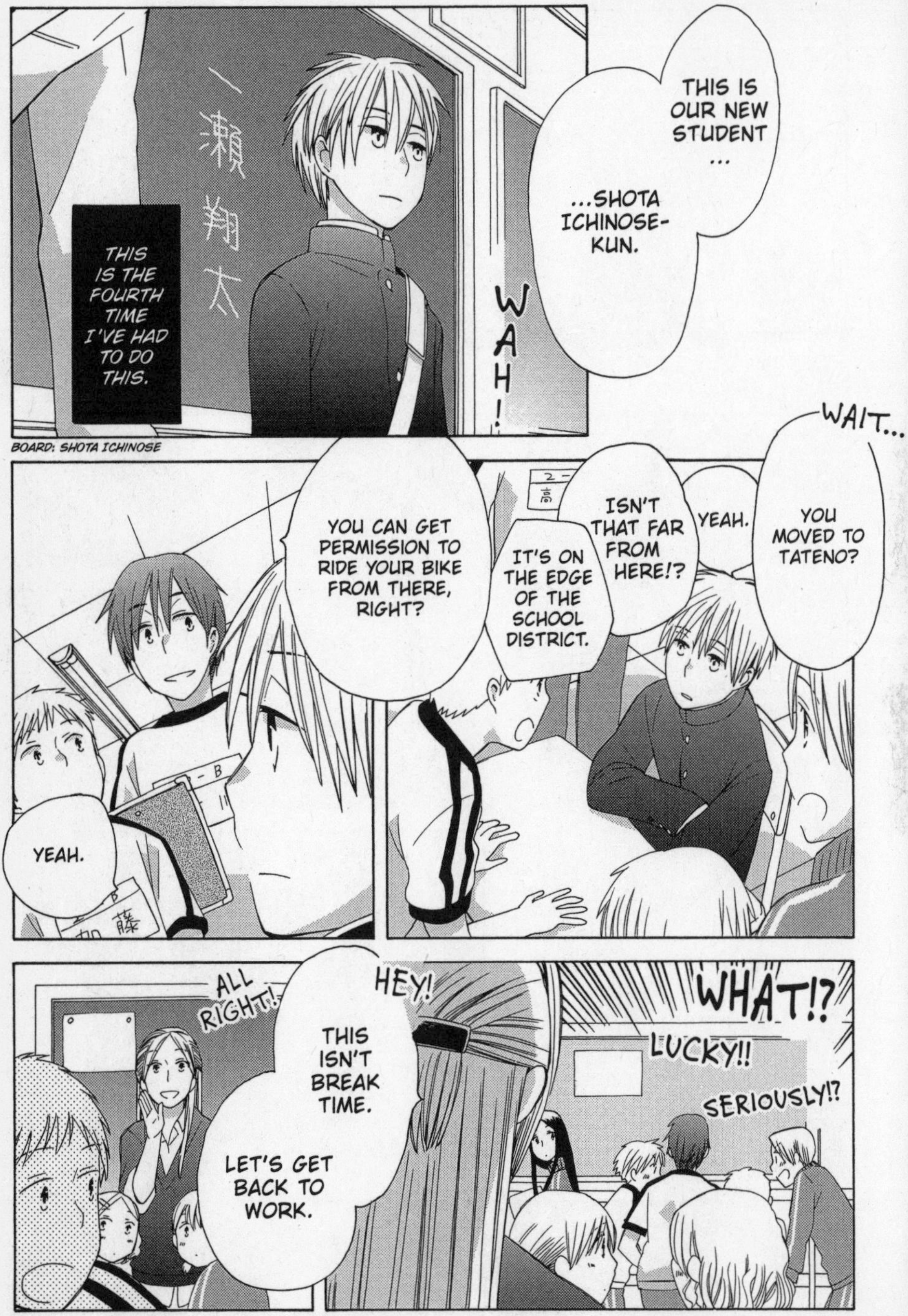
THIS IS OUR NEW STUDENT ...
...SHOTA ICHINOSE-KUN.
WAH!!
THIS IS THE FOURTH TIME I'VE HAD TO DO THIS.
WAIT...
YOU MOVED TO TATENO?
YEAH.
ISN'T THAT FAR FROM HERE!?
IT'S ON THE EDGE OF THE SCHOOL DISTRICT.
YOU CAN GET PERMISSION TO RIDE YOUR BIKE FROM THERE, RIGHT?
YEAH.
WHAT!?
LUCKY!!
SERIOUSLY!?
HEY!
ALL RIGHT!
THIS ISN'T BREAK TIME.
LET'S GET BACK TO WORK.
BOARD: SHOTA ICHINOSE

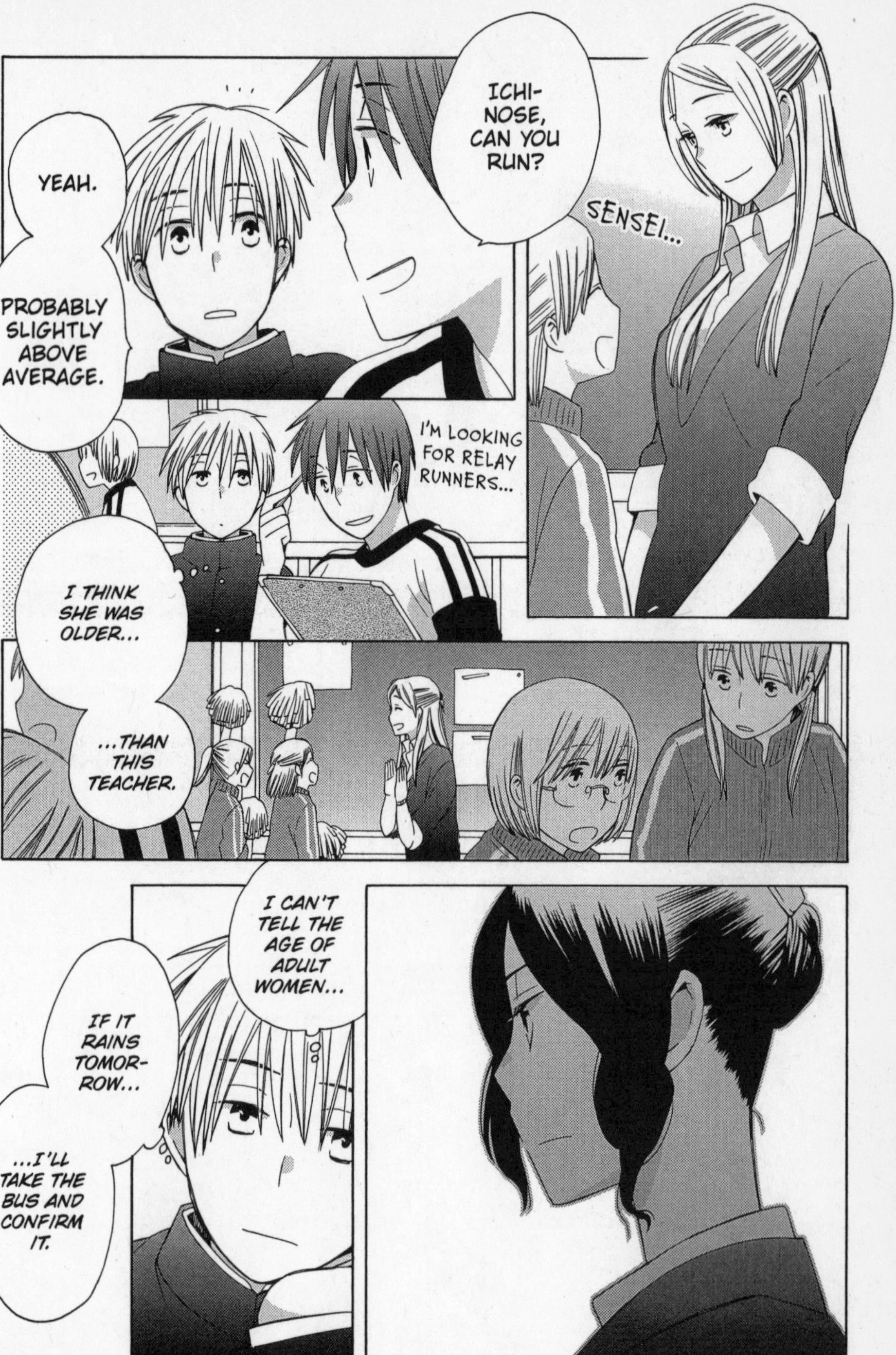
SENSEI...
ICHI-NOSE, CAN YOU RUN?
YEAH.
PROBABLY SLIGHTLY ABOVE AVERAGE.
I'M LOOKING FOR RELAY RUNNERS...
I THINK SHE WAS OLDER...
...THAN THIS TEACHER.
I CAN'T TELL THE AGE OF ADULT WOMEN...
IF IT RAINS TOMORROW...
...I'LL TAKE THE BUS AND CONFIRM IT.

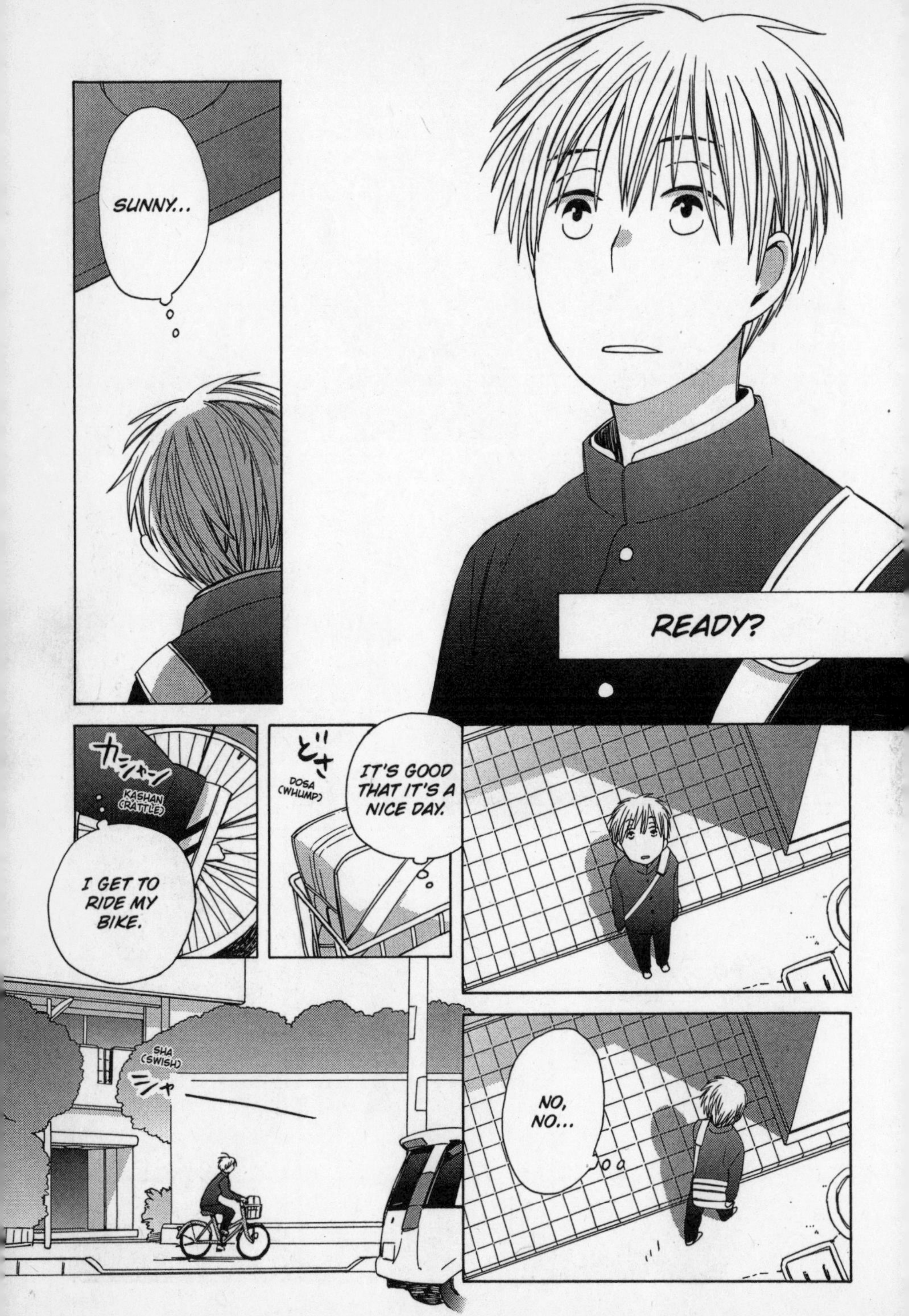
READY?
SUNNY...
...
どさ
DOSA (WHUMP)
IT'S GOOD THAT IT'S A NICE DAY.
カシャン
KASHAN (RATTLE)
I GET TO RIDE MY BIKE.
NO, NO...
SHA (SWISH)
シャ

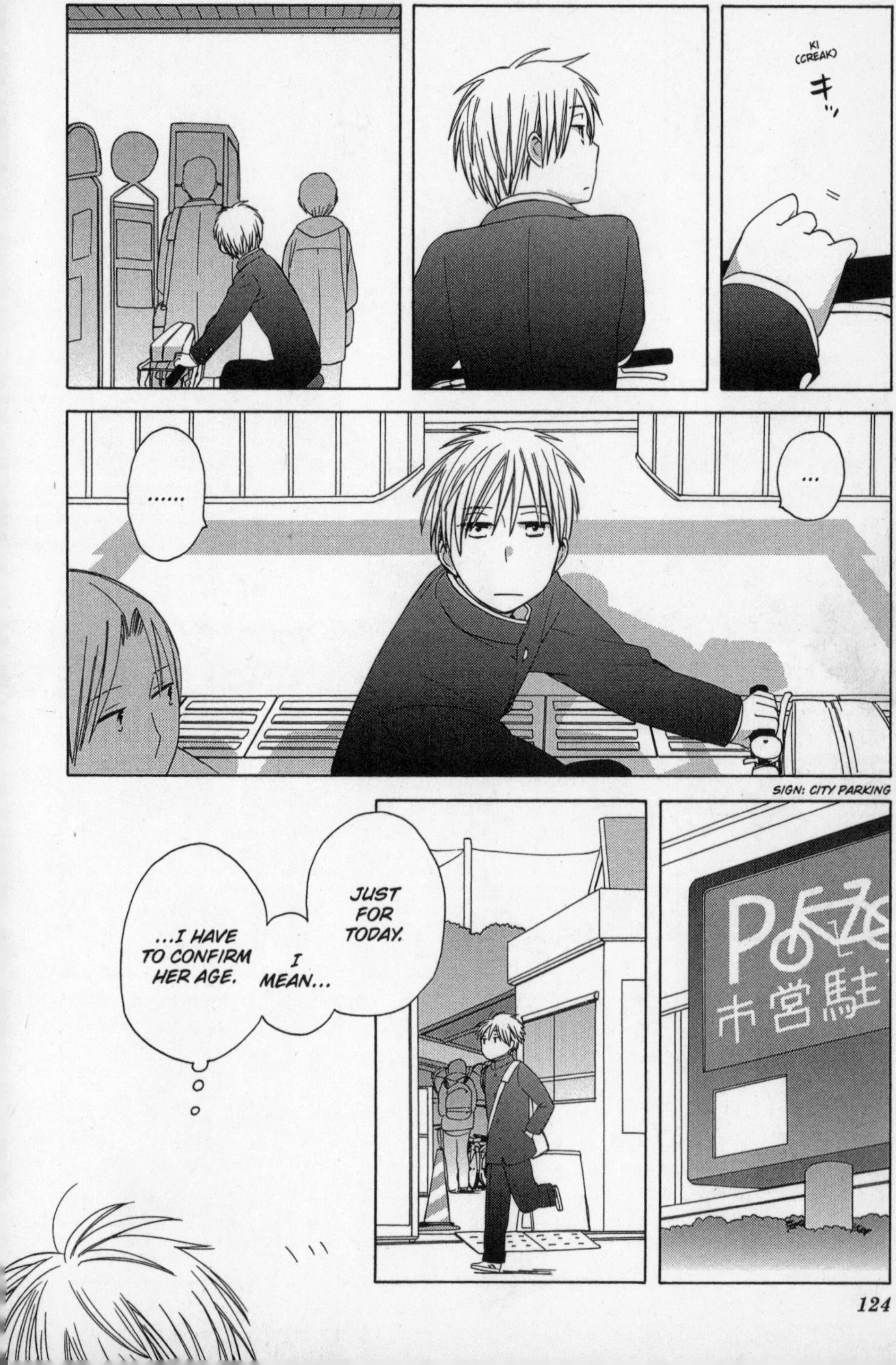
KI (CREAK)
キッ
...
......
SIGN: CITY PARKING
P
市営駐
JUST FOR TODAY.
I MEAN...
...I HAVE TO CONFIRM HER AGE.

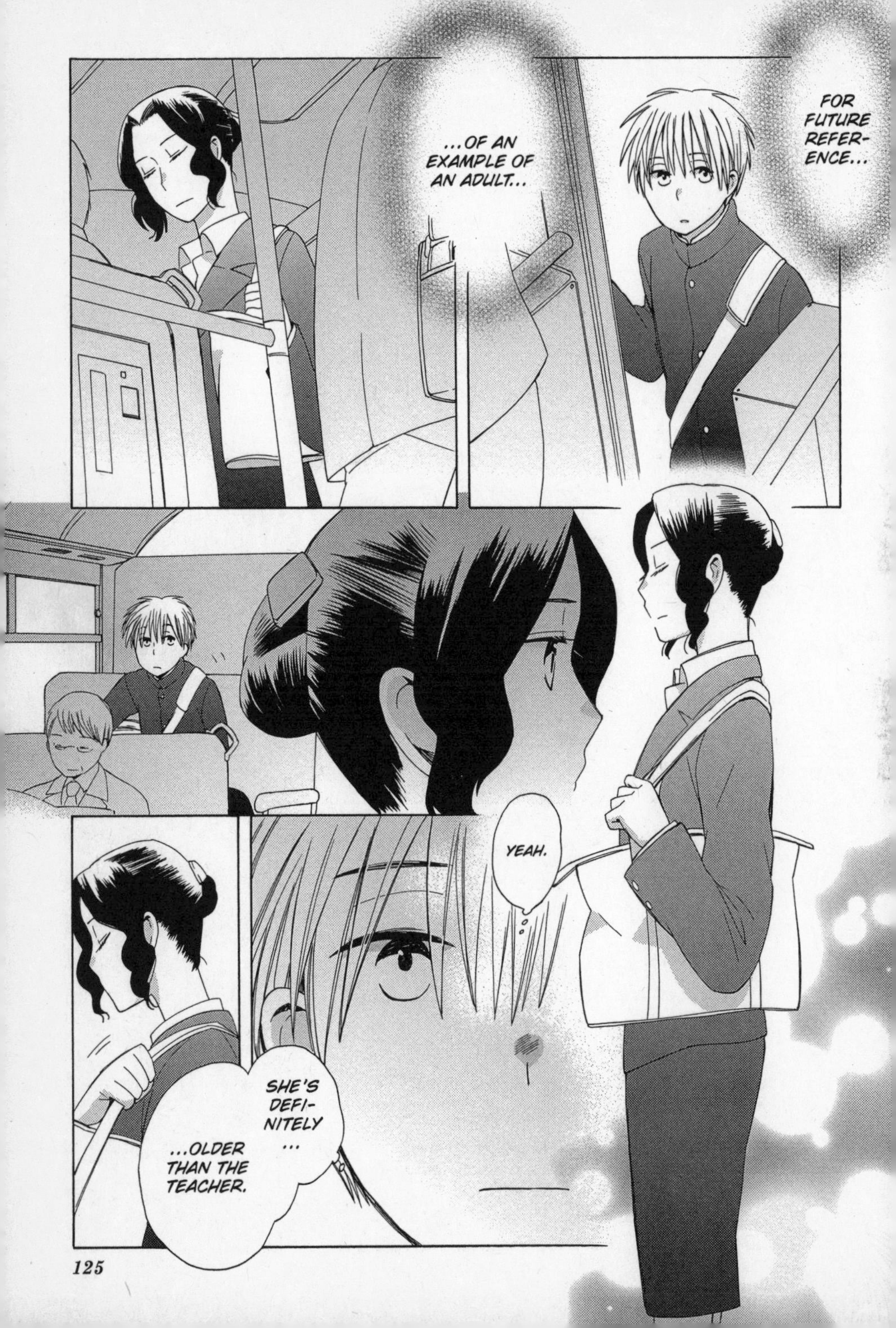
FOR FUTURE REFERENCE...
...OF AN EXAMPLE OF AN ADULT...
YEAH.
SHE'S DEFINITELY...
...OLDER THAN THE TEACHER.

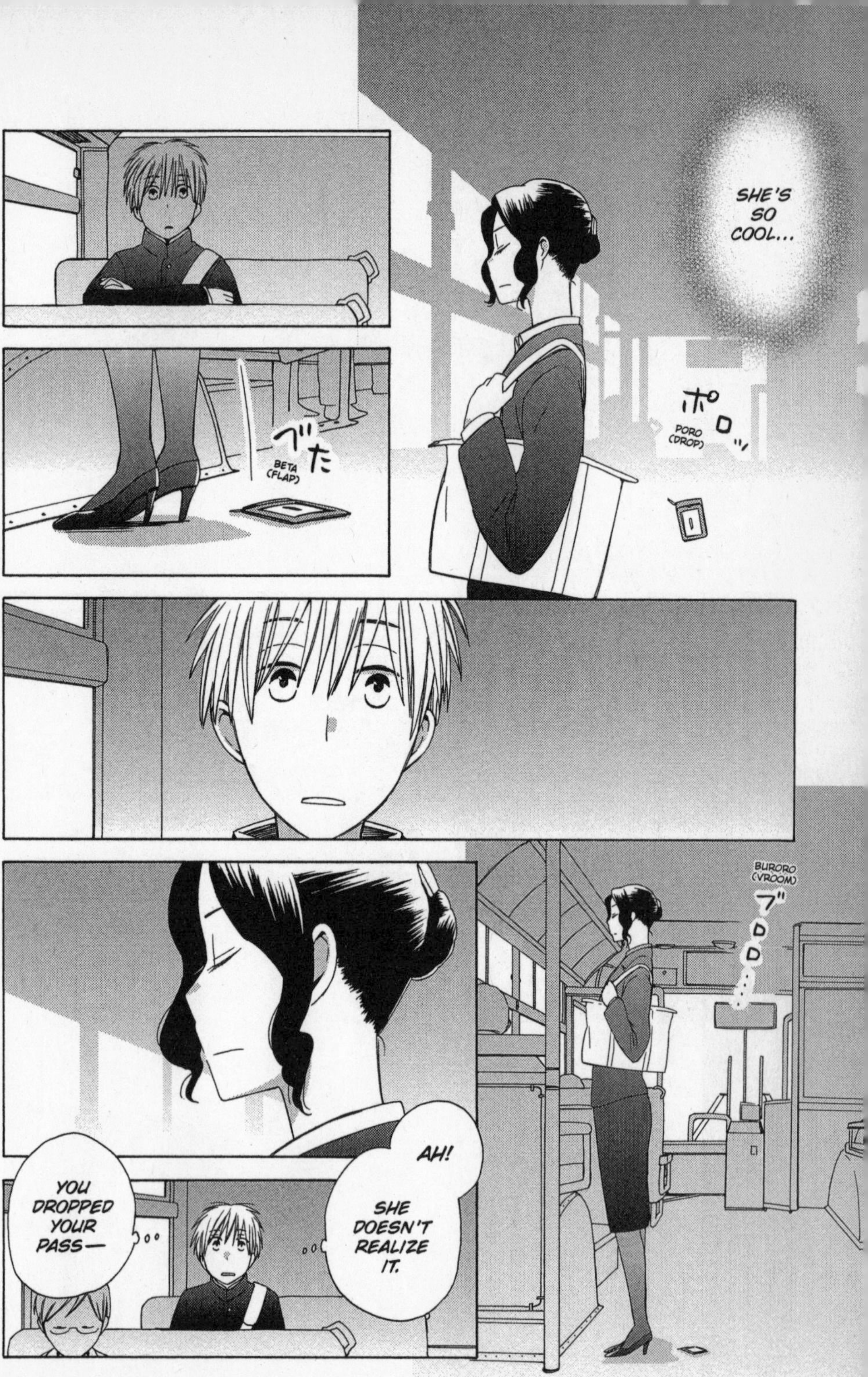
SHE'S SO COOL...
ポロッ
PORO (DROP)
べた
BETA (FLAP)
BURORO (VROOM)
ブロロ…
AH!
SHE DOESN'T REALIZE IT.
YOU DROPPED YOUR PASS—

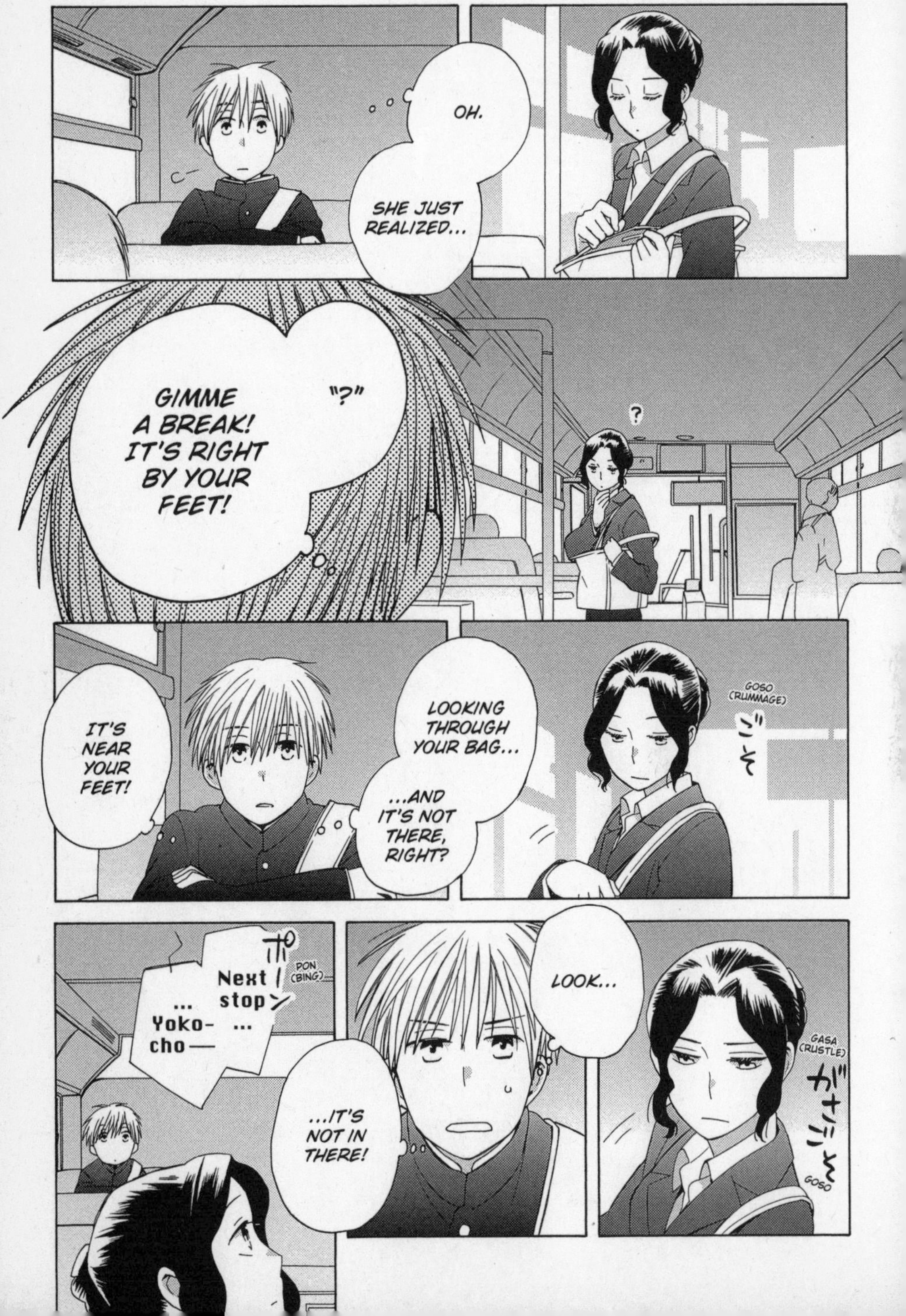
OH.
SHE JUST REALIZED...
?
"?"
GIMME A BREAK! IT'S RIGHT BY YOUR FEET!
GOSO (RUMMAGE)
ごそ
LOOKING THROUGH YOUR BAG...
...AND IT'S NOT THERE, RIGHT?
IT'S NEAR YOUR FEET!
GASA (RUSTLE)
がさごそ
GOSO
LOOK...
...IT'S NOT IN THERE!
ポーン
PON (BING)
Next stop ... Yoko-cho— ...

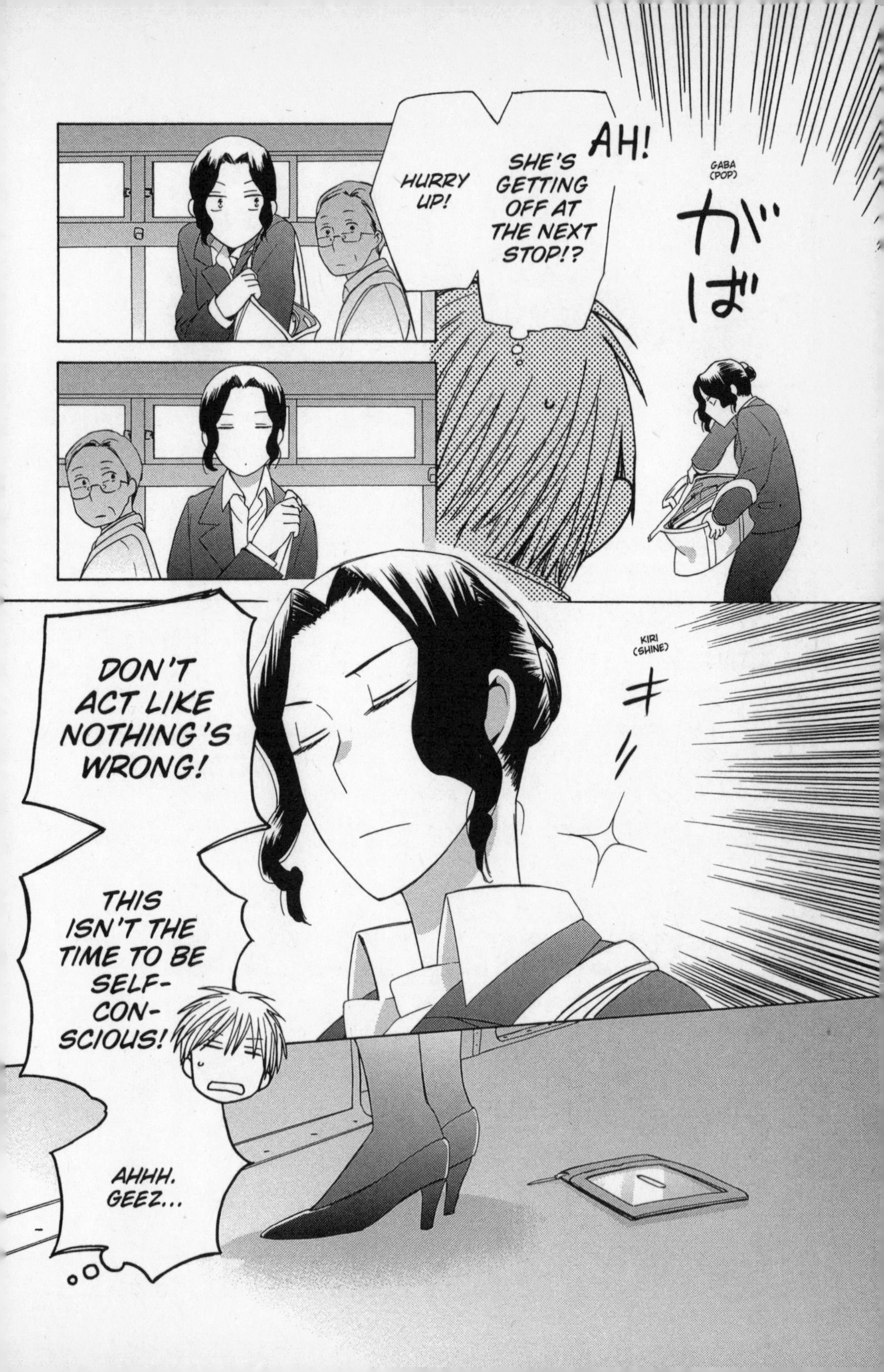
AH!
SHE'S GETTING OFF AT THE NEXT STOP!?
HURRY UP!
GABA (POP)
がば
KIRI (SHINE)
キ
DON'T ACT LIKE NOTHING'S WRONG!
THIS ISN'T THE TIME TO BE SELF-CON-SCIOUS!
AHHH. GEEZ...

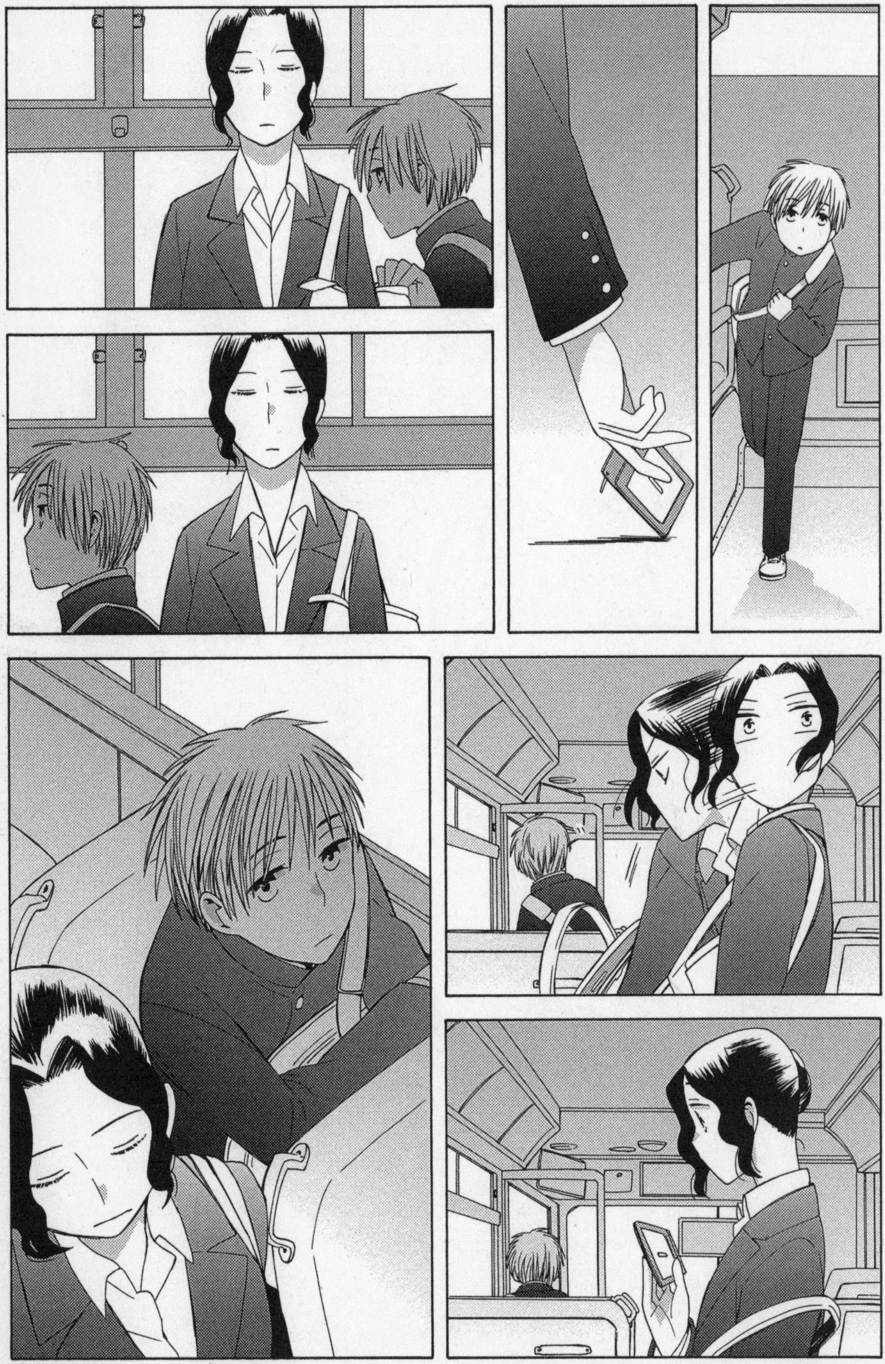

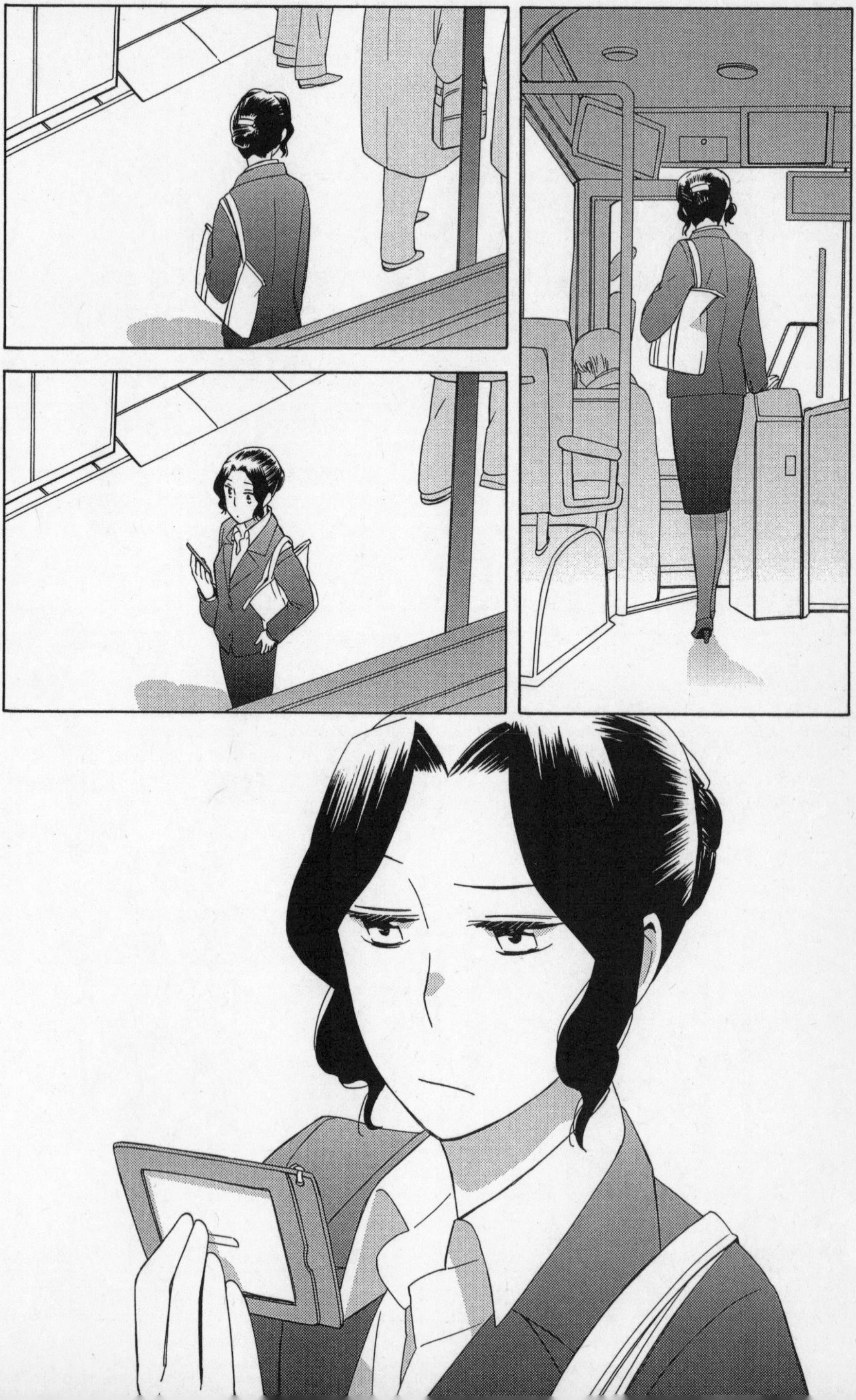

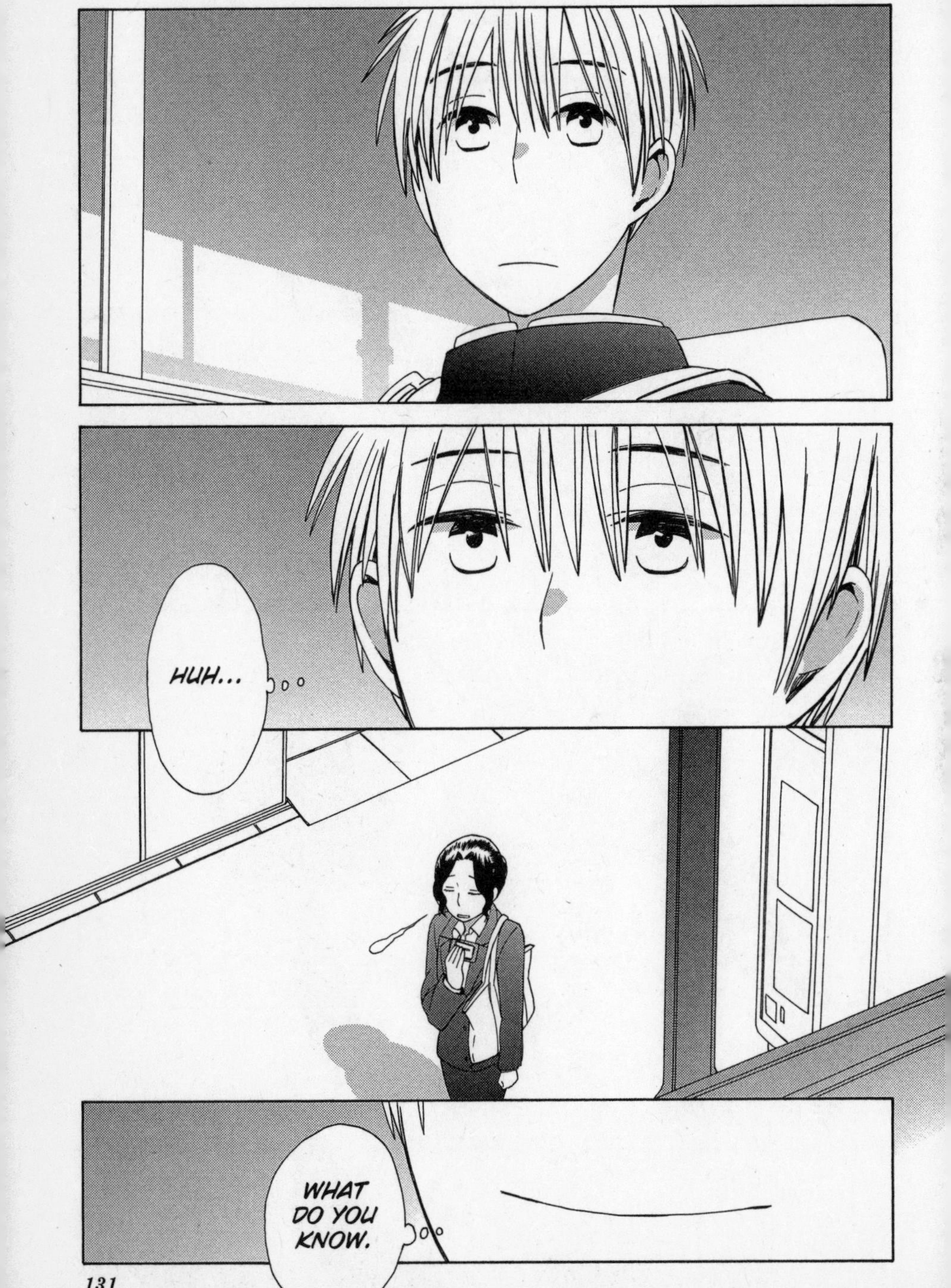
HUH...
WHAT DO YOU KNOW.

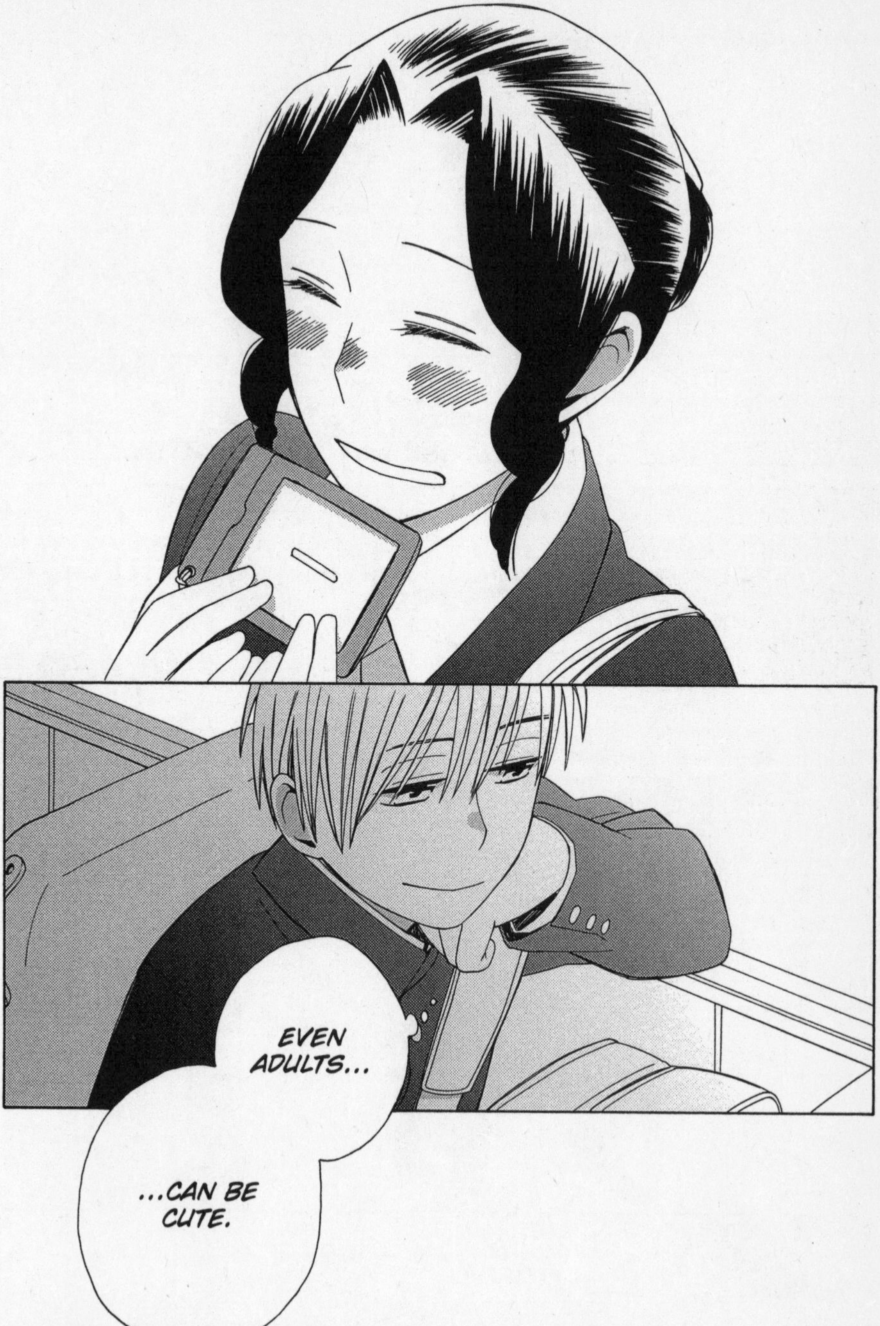
EVEN ADULTS...
...CAN BE CUTE.

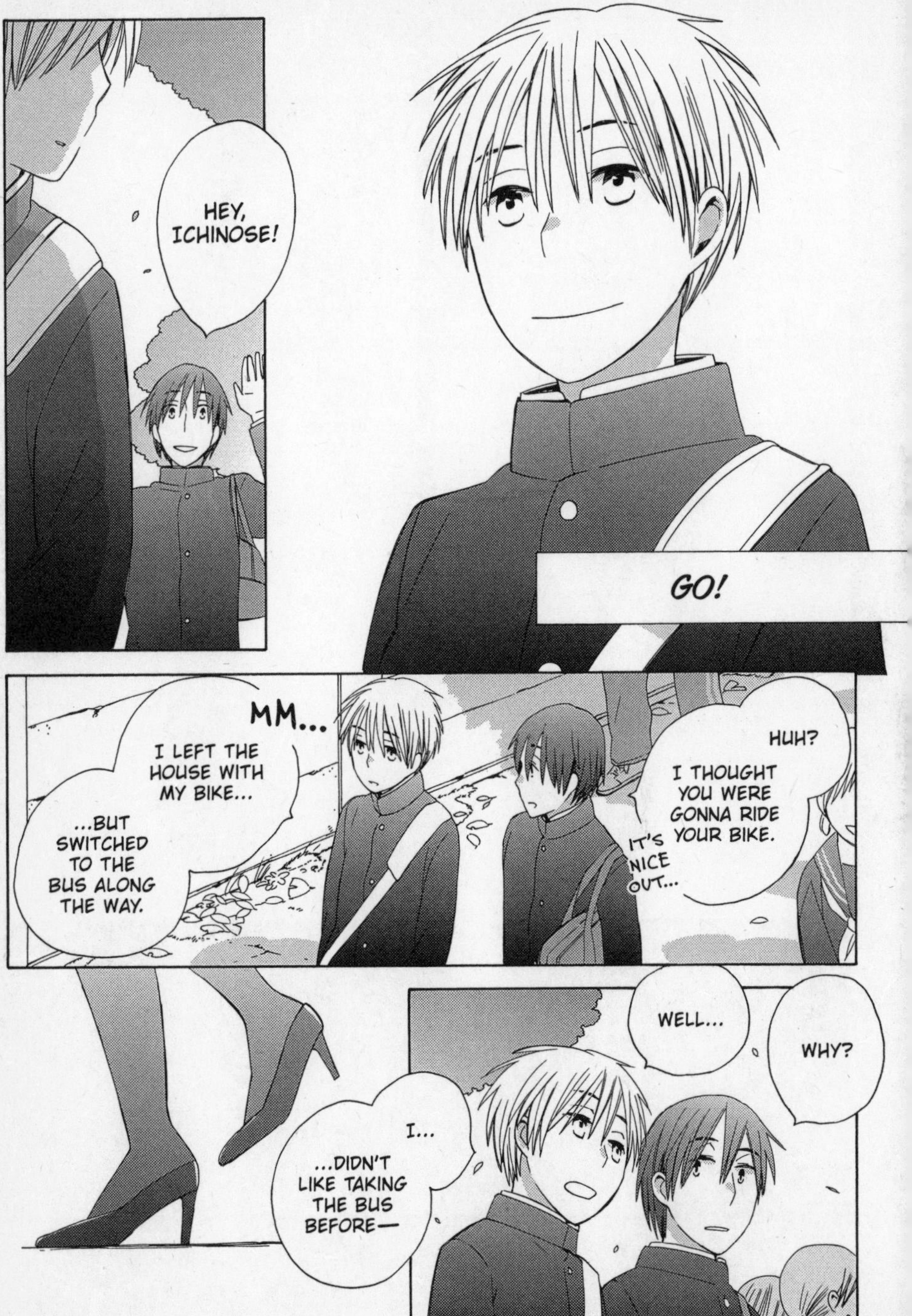
GO!
HEY, ICHINOSE!
HUH?
I THOUGHT YOU WERE GONNA RIDE YOUR BIKE.
IT'S NICE OUT...
MM...
I LEFT THE HOUSE WITH MY BIKE...
...BUT SWITCHED TO THE BUS ALONG THE WAY.
WHY?
WELL...
I...
...DIDN'T LIKE TAKING THE BUS BEFORE—

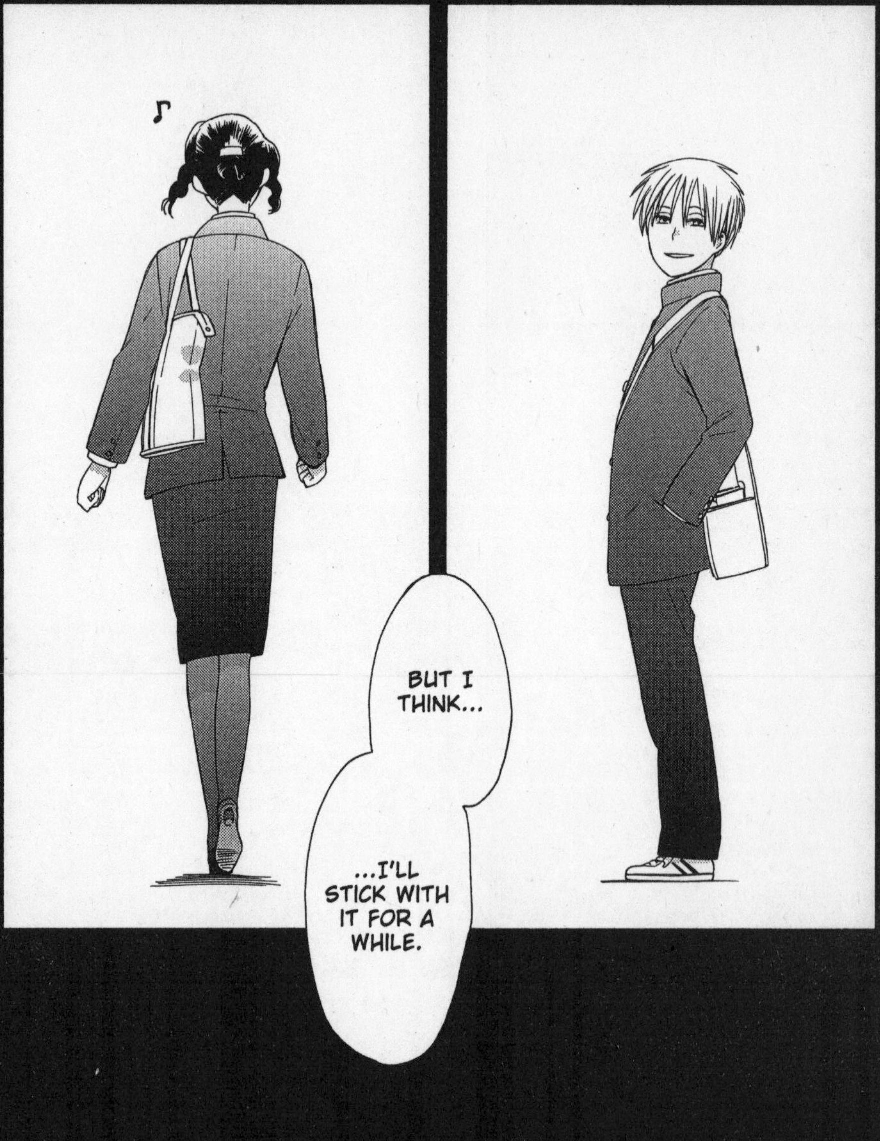
BUT I THINK...
...I'LL STICK WITH IT FOR A WHILE.

Fin

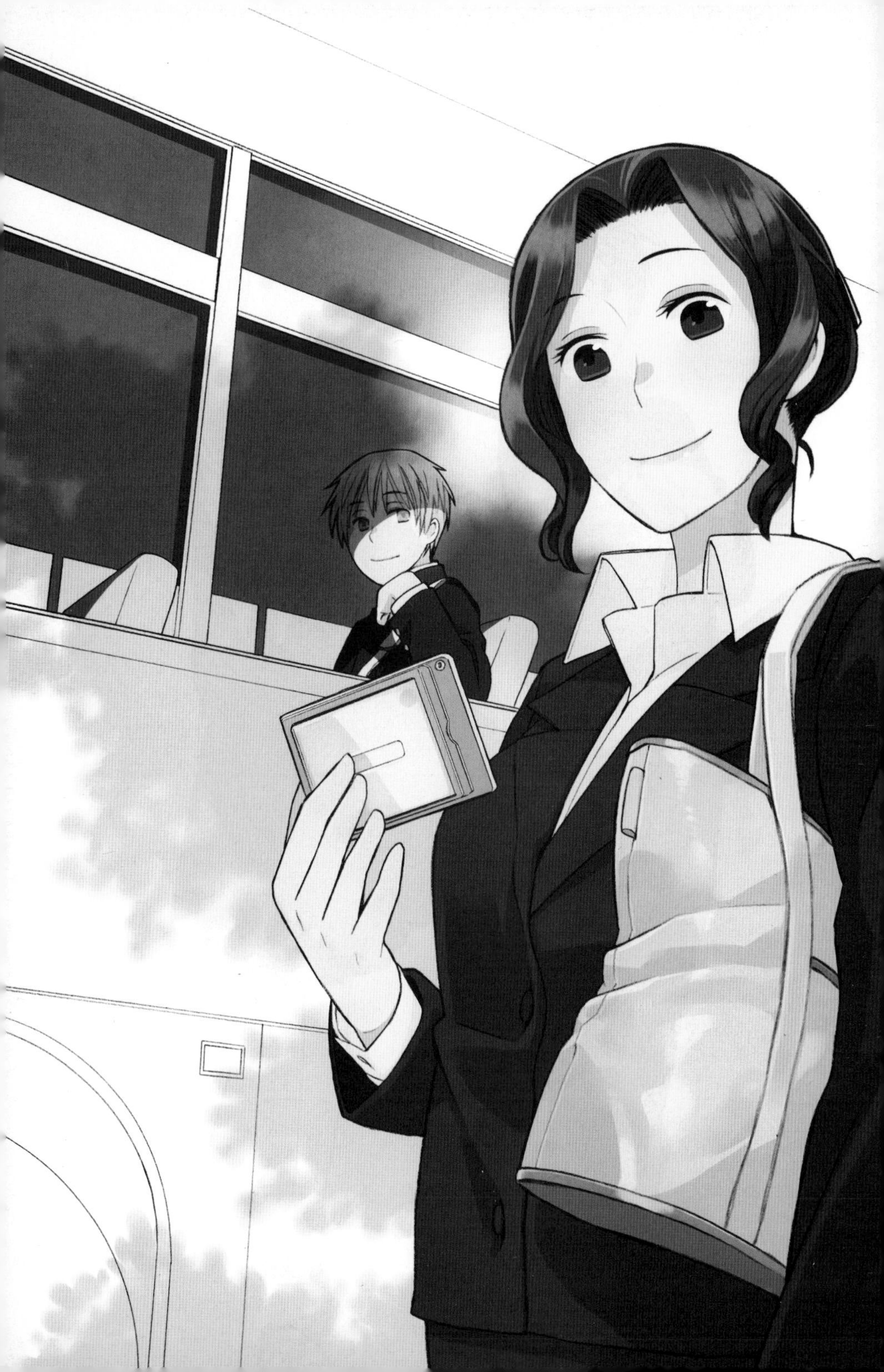

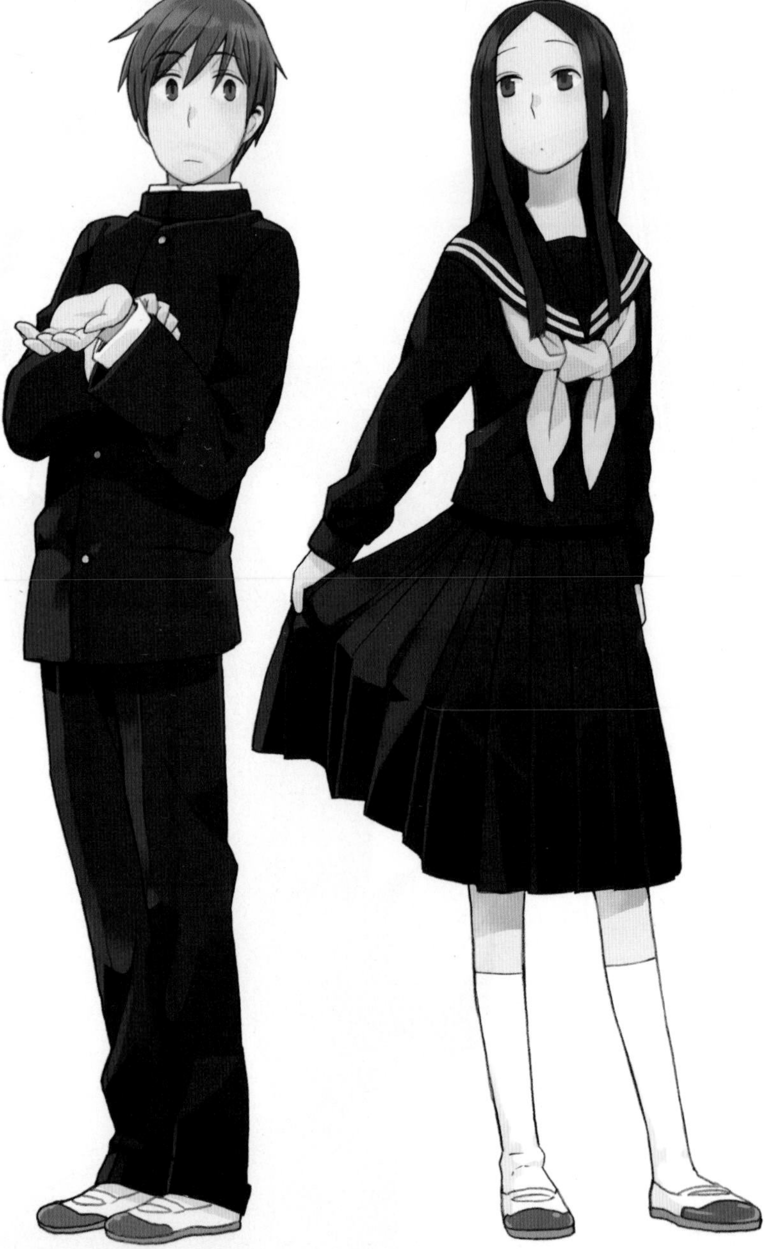

Love at Fourteen

[Chapter 21]

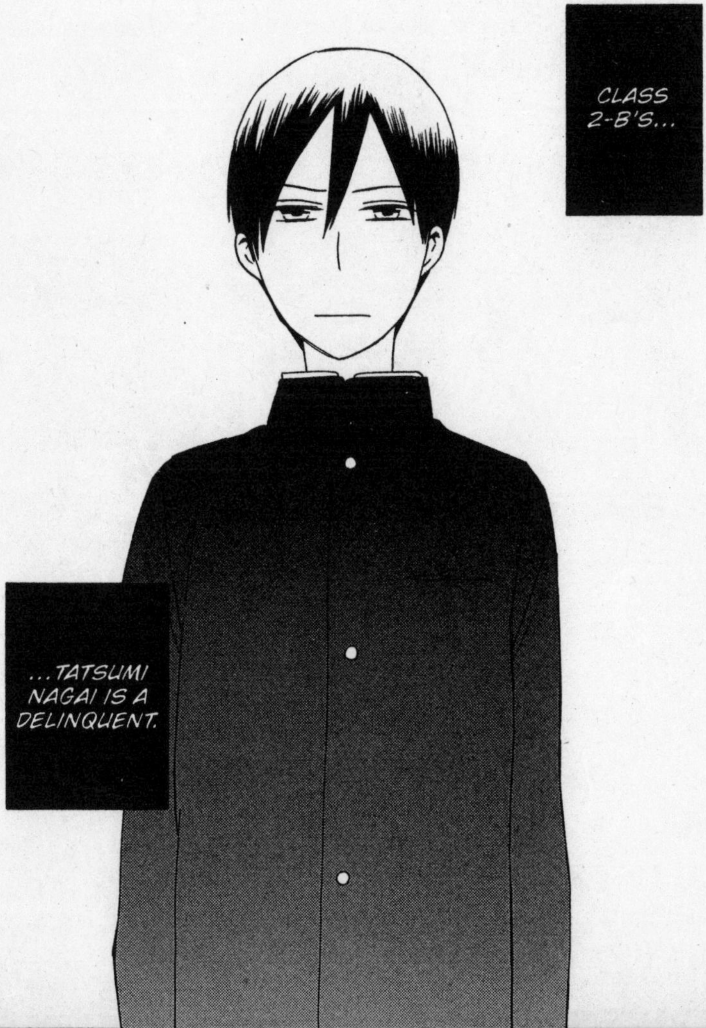
CLASS 2-B'S...
...TATSUMI NAGAI IS A DELINQUENT.

BANNER: 57TH MIDDLE SCHOOL SPORTS FESTIVAL

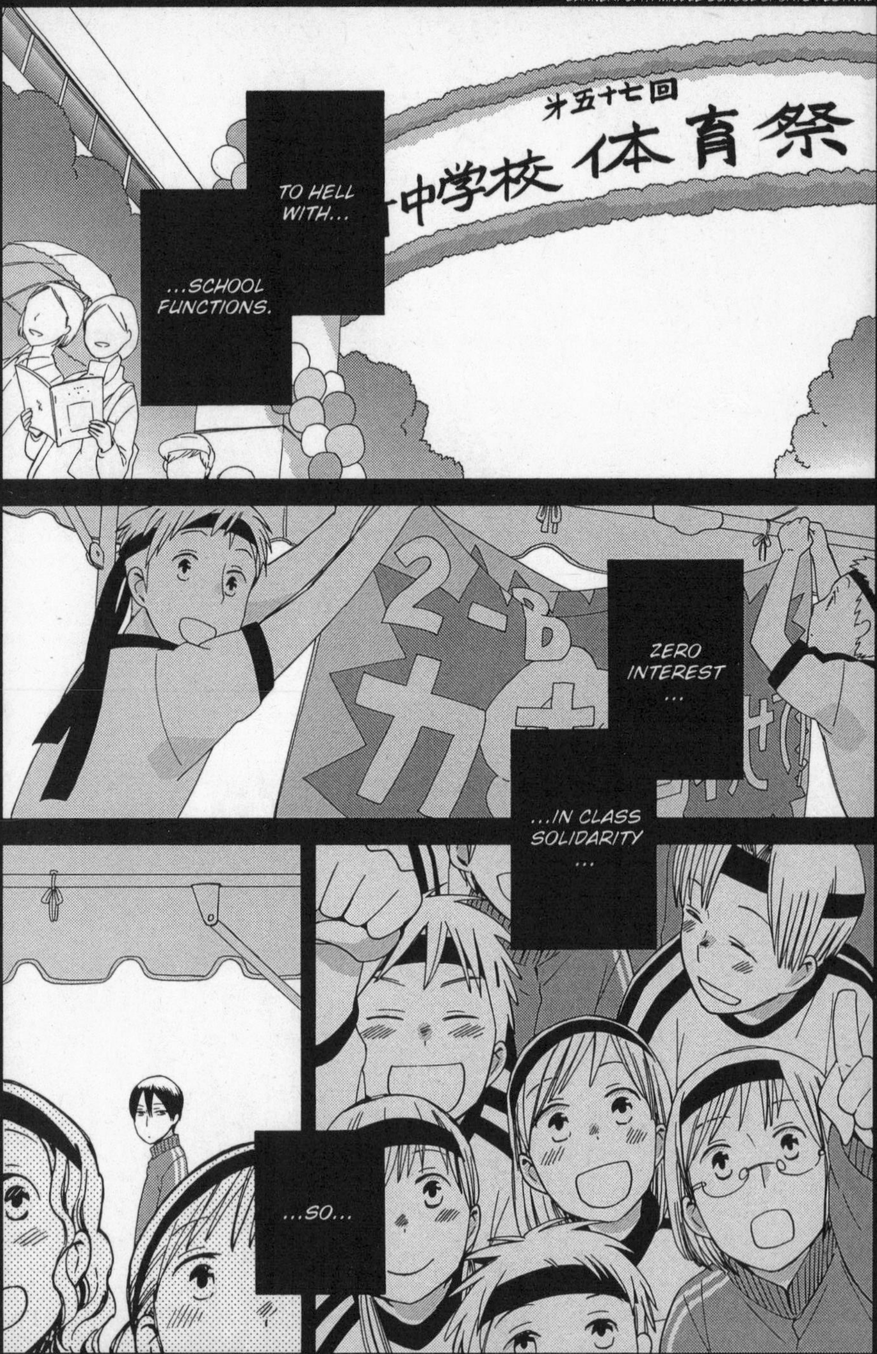
第五十七回
中学校 体育祭
TO HELL WITH...
...SCHOOL FUNCTIONS.
ZERO INTEREST ...
...IN CLASS SOLIDARITY ...
...SO...

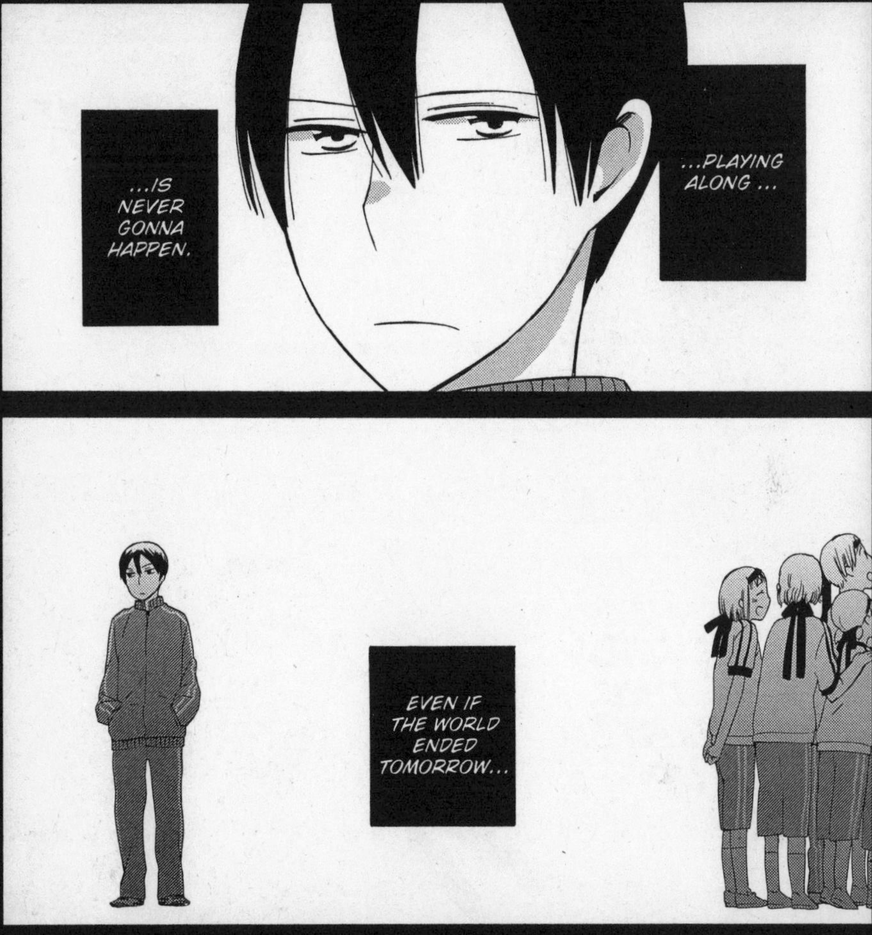
...PLAYING ALONG ...
...IS NEVER GONNA HAPPEN.
EVEN IF THE WORLD ENDED TOMORROW...

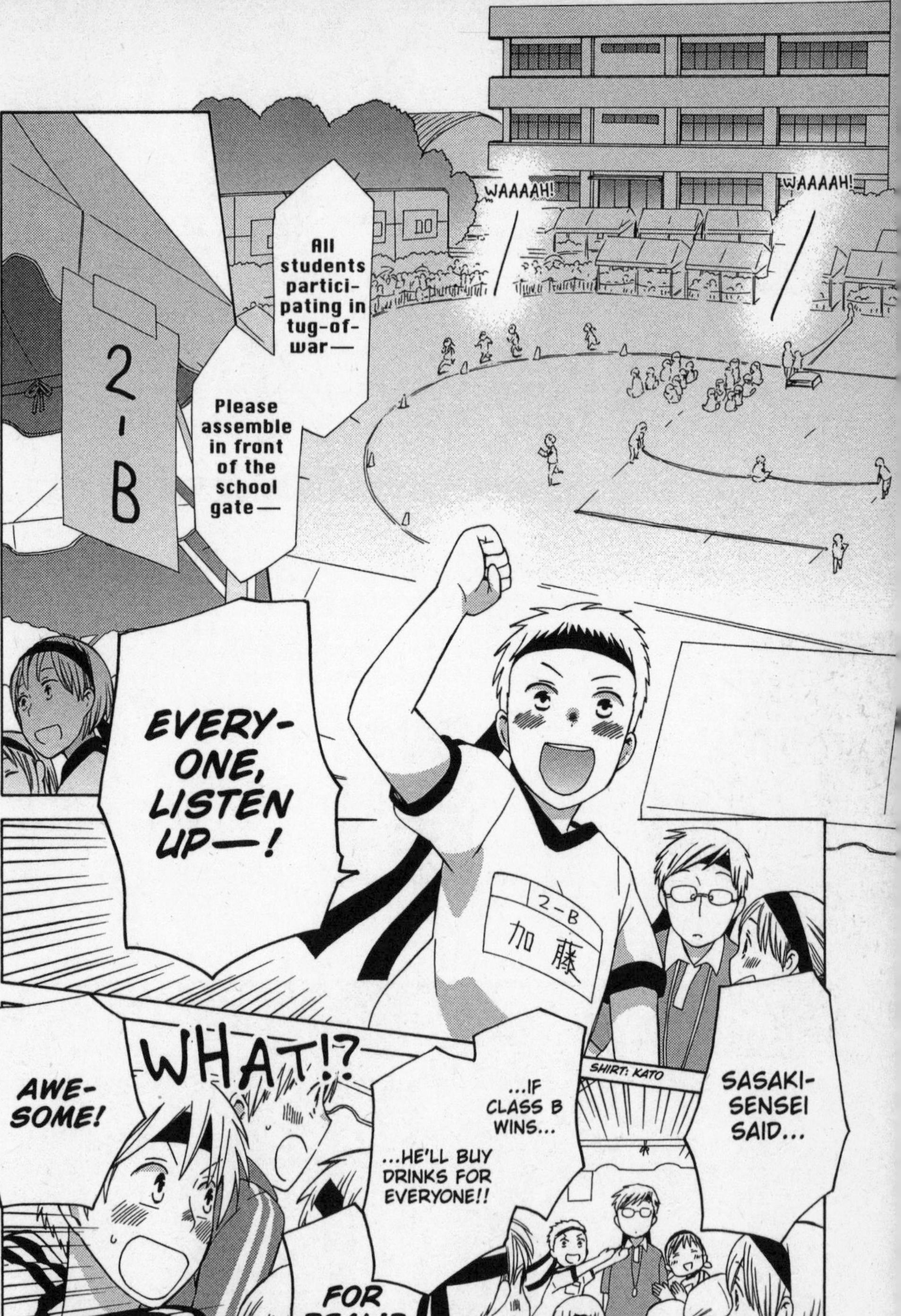
WAAAAH!
WAAAAH!
2-B
All students partici-pating in tug-of-war—
Please assemble in front of the school gate—
EVERY-ONE, LISTEN UP—!
2-B
加藤
SHIRT: KATO
SASAKI-SENSEI SAID...
...IF CLASS B WINS...
...HE'LL BUY DRINKS FOR EVERYONE!!
WHAT!?
AWE-SOME!
FOR REAL!?

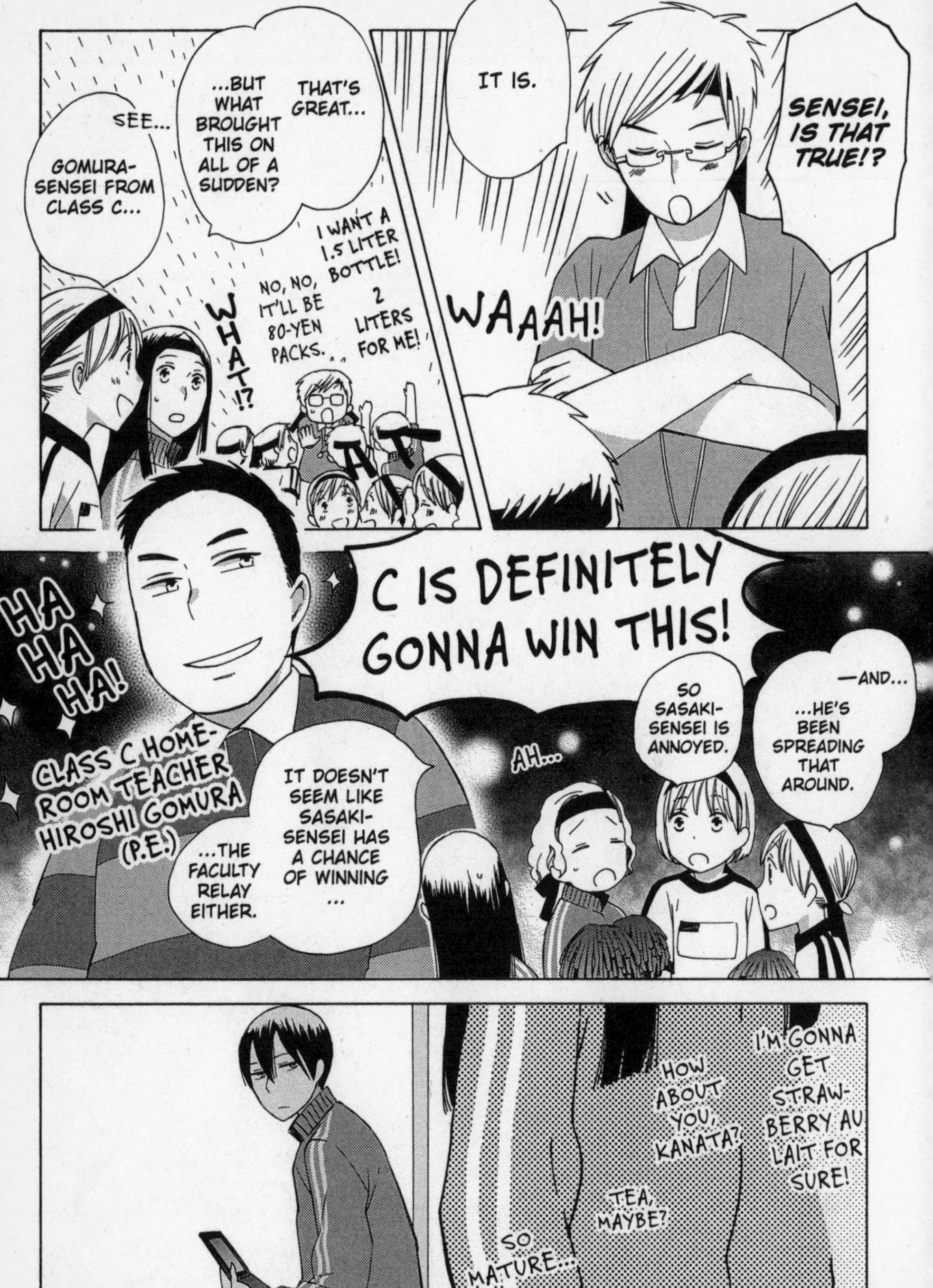
SENSEI, IS THAT TRUE!?
IT IS.
WAAAH!
THAT'S GREAT...
...BUT WHAT BROUGHT THIS ON ALL OF A SUDDEN?
SEE...
GOMURA-SENSEI FROM CLASS C...
I WANT A 1.5 LITER BOTTLE!
2 LITERS FOR ME!
NO, NO, IT'LL BE 80-YEN PACKS.
WHAT!?
C IS DEFINITELY GONNA WIN THIS!
HA HA HA!
CLASS C HOMEROOM TEACHER HIROSHI GOMURA (P.E.)
—AND...
...HE'S BEEN SPREADING THAT AROUND.
SO SASAKI-SENSEI IS ANNOYED.
AH...
IT DOESN'T SEEM LIKE SASAKI-SENSEI HAS A CHANCE OF WINNING...
...THE FACULTY RELAY EITHER.
I'M GONNA GET STRAWBERRY AU LAIT FOR SURE!
HOW ABOUT YOU, KANATA?
TEA, MAYBE?
SO MATURE...

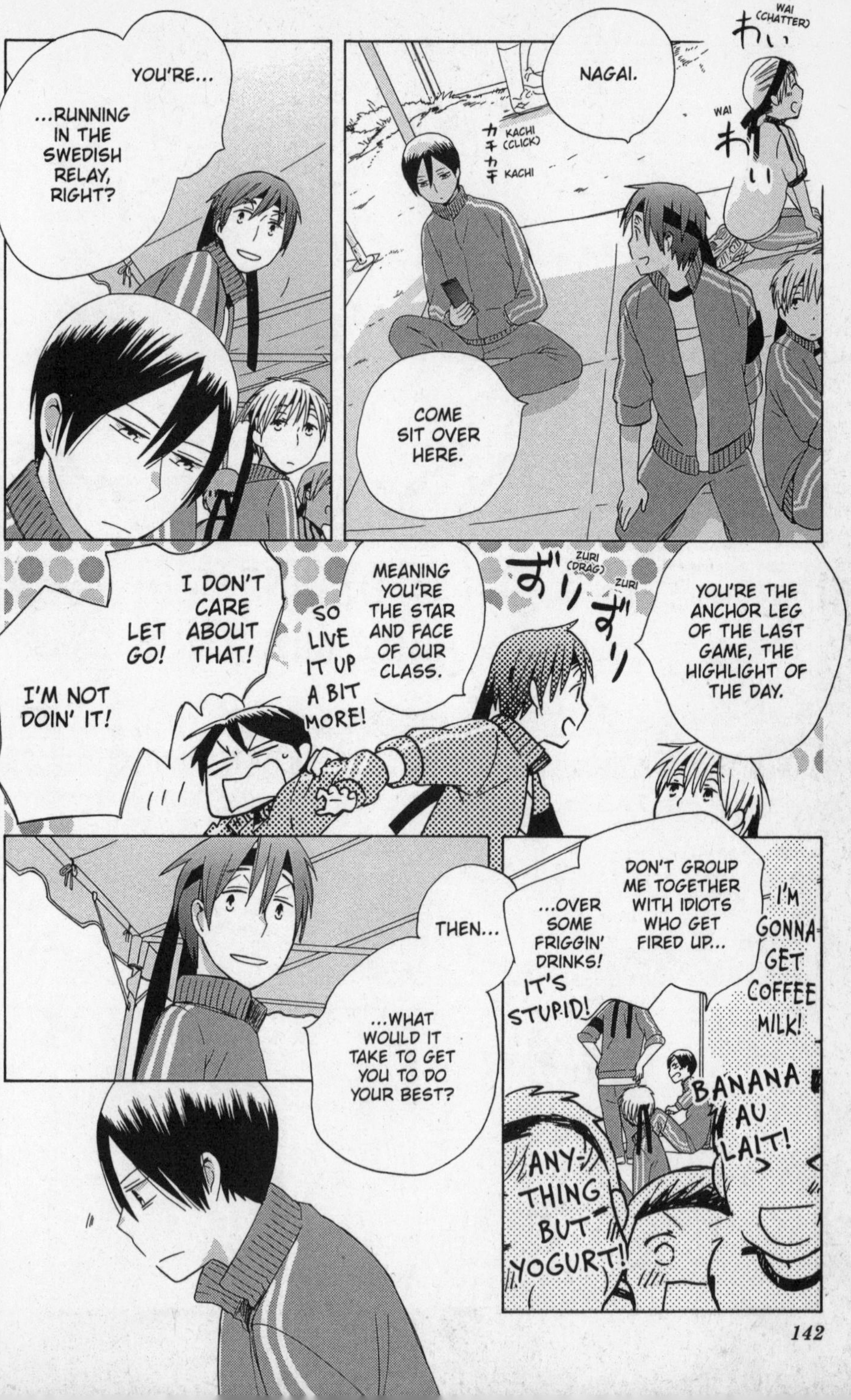
わい
WAI (CHATTER)
わい
WAI
NAGAI.
カチ
KACHI (CLICK)
カチ
KACHI
COME SIT OVER HERE.
YOU'RE...
...RUNNING IN THE SWEDISH RELAY, RIGHT?
YOU'RE THE ANCHOR LEG OF THE LAST GAME, THE HIGHLIGHT OF THE DAY.
ずり
ZURI (DRAG)
ずり
ZURI
MEANING YOU'RE THE STAR AND FACE OF OUR CLASS.
SO LIVE IT UP A BIT MORE!
I DON'T CARE ABOUT THAT!
LET GO!
I'M NOT DOIN' IT!
DON'T GROUP ME TOGETHER WITH IDIOTS WHO GET FIRED UP...
...OVER SOME FRIGGIN' DRINKS!
IT'S STUPID!
I'M GONNA GET COFFEE MILK!
BANANA AU LAIT!
ANY-THING BUT YOGURT!
THEN...
...WHAT WOULD IT TAKE TO GET YOU TO DO YOUR BEST?

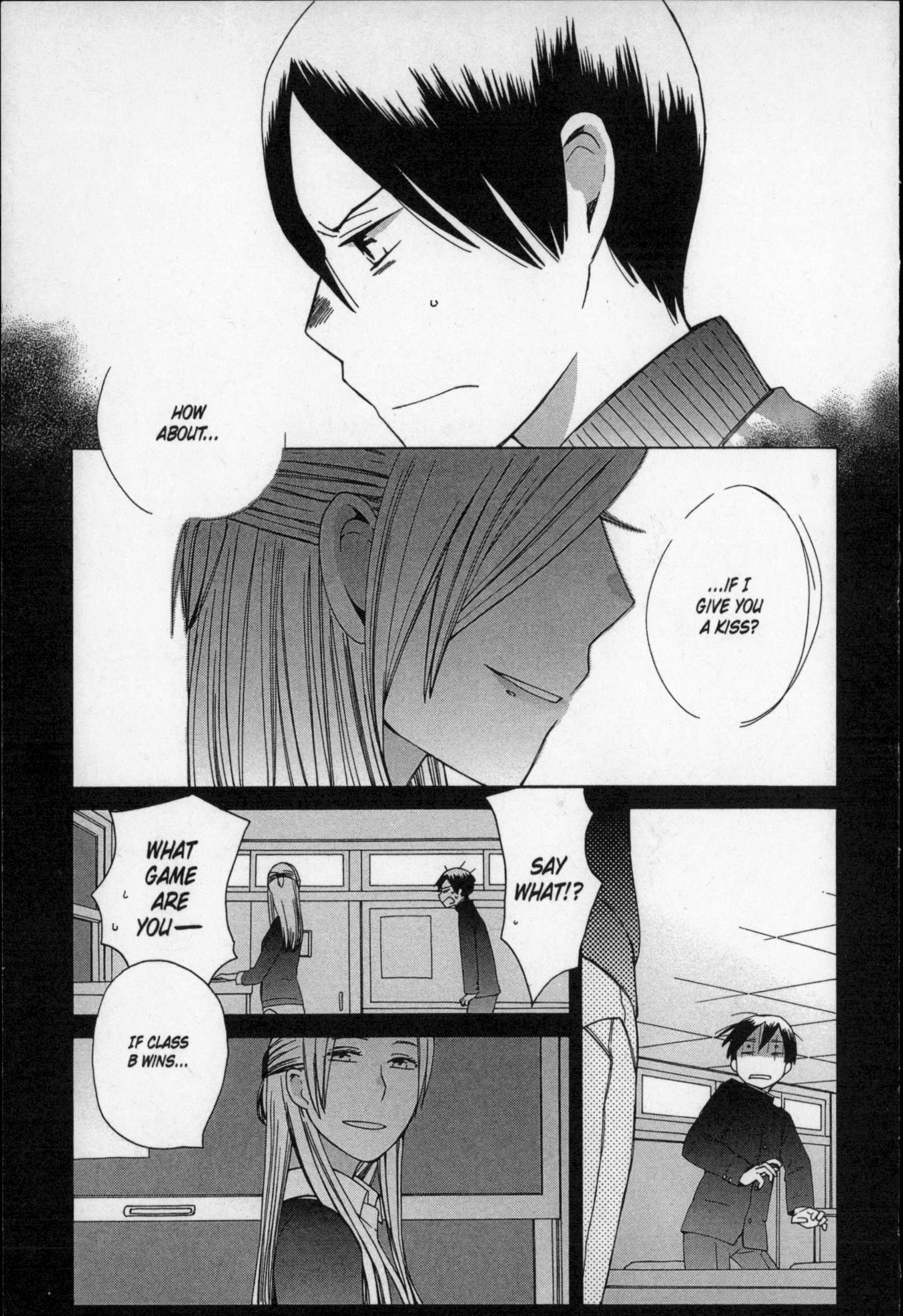
HOW ABOUT...
...IF I GIVE YOU A KISS?
SAY WHAT!?
WHAT GAME ARE YOU—
IF CLASS B WINS...

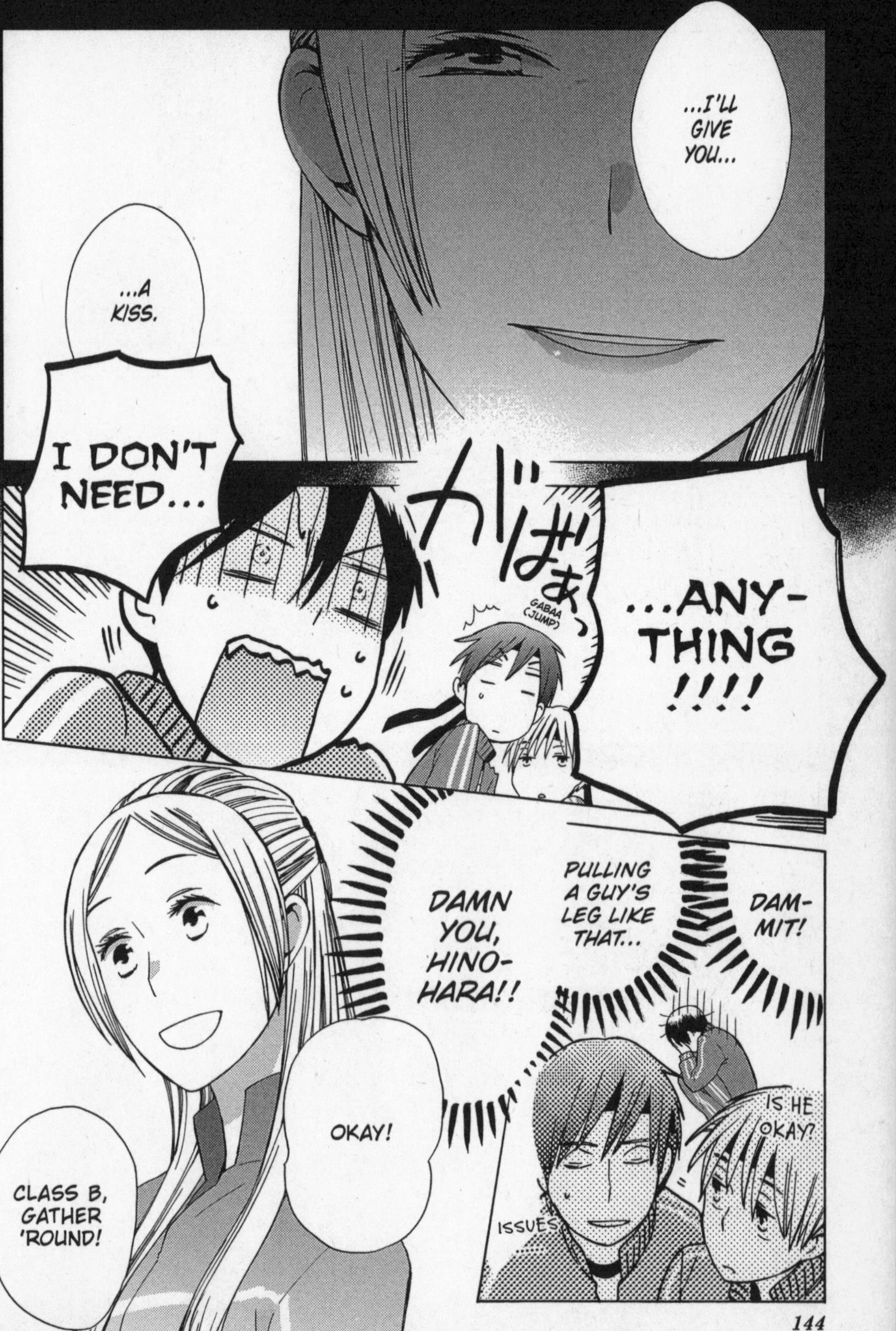
...I'LL GIVE YOU...
...A KISS.
I DON'T NEED...
がばぁ
GABAA (JUMP)
...ANY-THING!!!!
DAM-MIT!
PULLING A GUY'S LEG LIKE THAT...
DAMN YOU, HINO-HARA!!
IS HE OKAY?
ISSUES
OKAY!
CLASS B, GATHER 'ROUND!

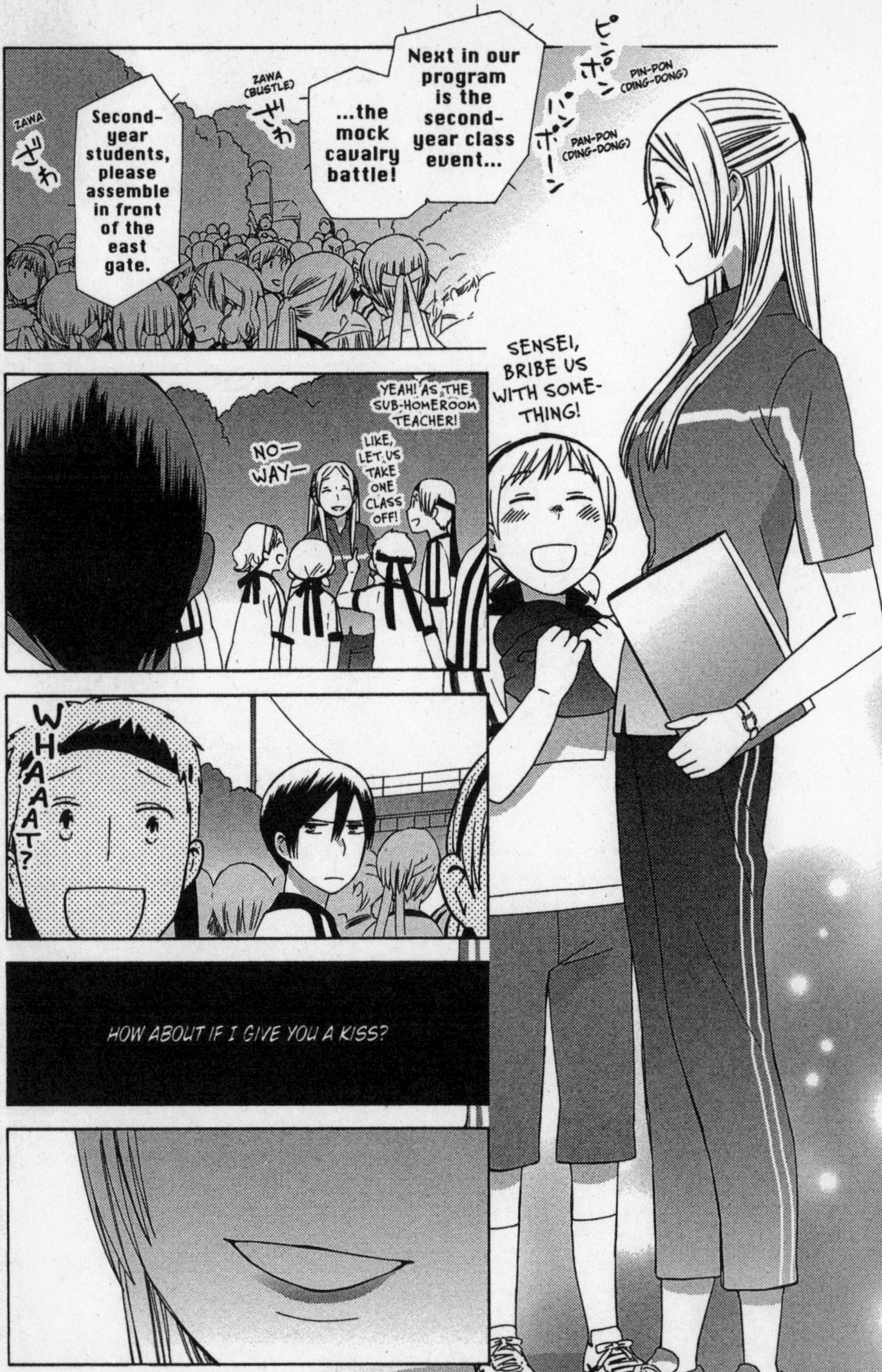
ピンポン
PIN-PON (DING-DONG)
パンポーン
PAN-PON (DING-DONG)
Next in our program is the second-year class event...
...the mock cavalry battle!
ZAWA (BUSTLE)
ざわ
Second-year students, please assemble in front of the east gate.
ZAWA
ざわ
SENSEI, BRIBE US WITH SOMETHING!
YEAH! AS THE SUB-HOMEROOM TEACHER!
LIKE, LET US TAKE ONE CLASS OFF!
NO— WAY—
WHAAAAT?
HOW ABOUT IF I GIVE YOU A KISS?

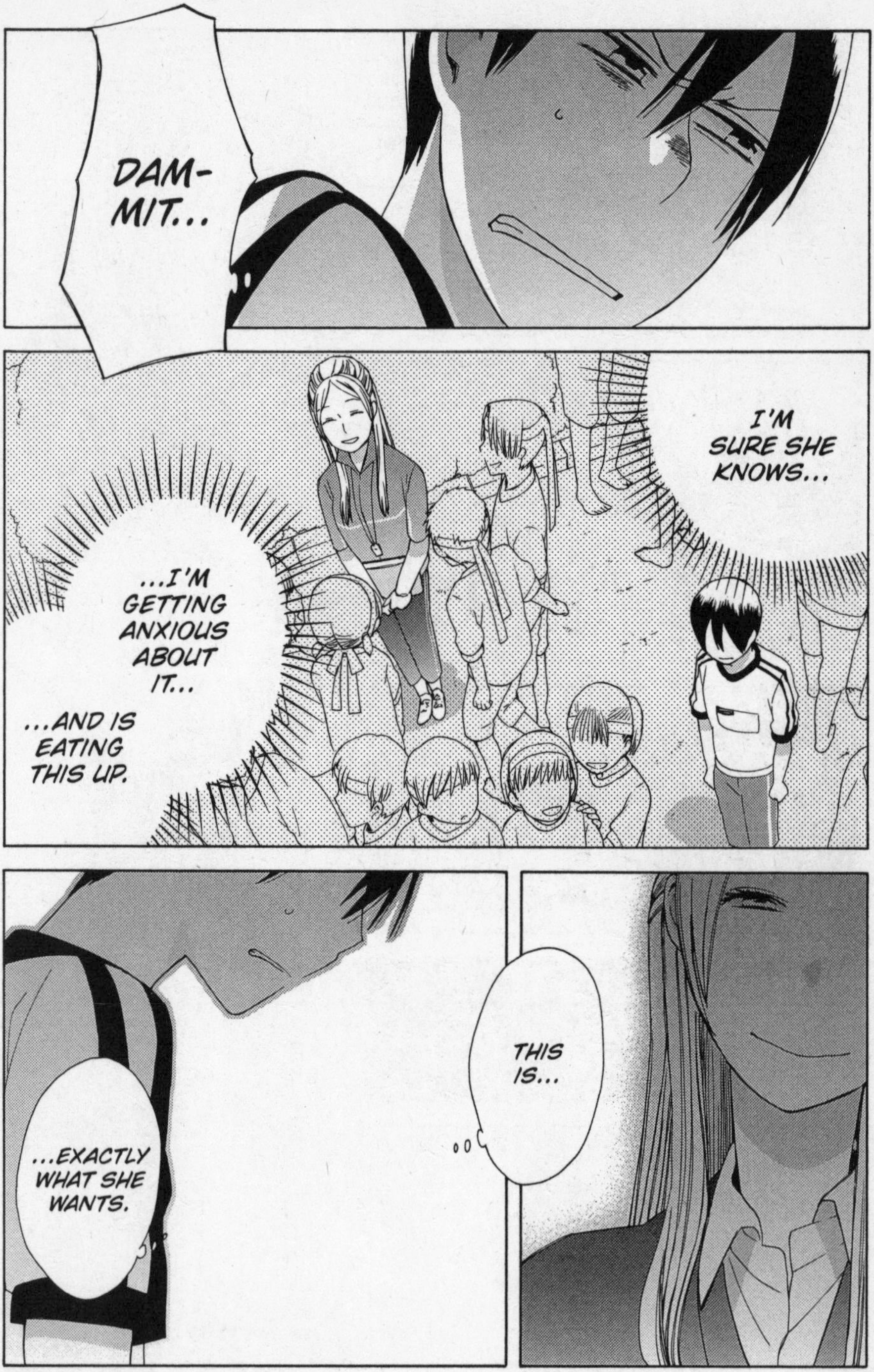
DAM-
MIT...
I'M SURE SHE KNOWS...
...I'M GETTING ANXIOUS ABOUT IT...
...AND IS EATING THIS UP.
THIS IS...
...EXACTLY WHAT SHE WANTS.

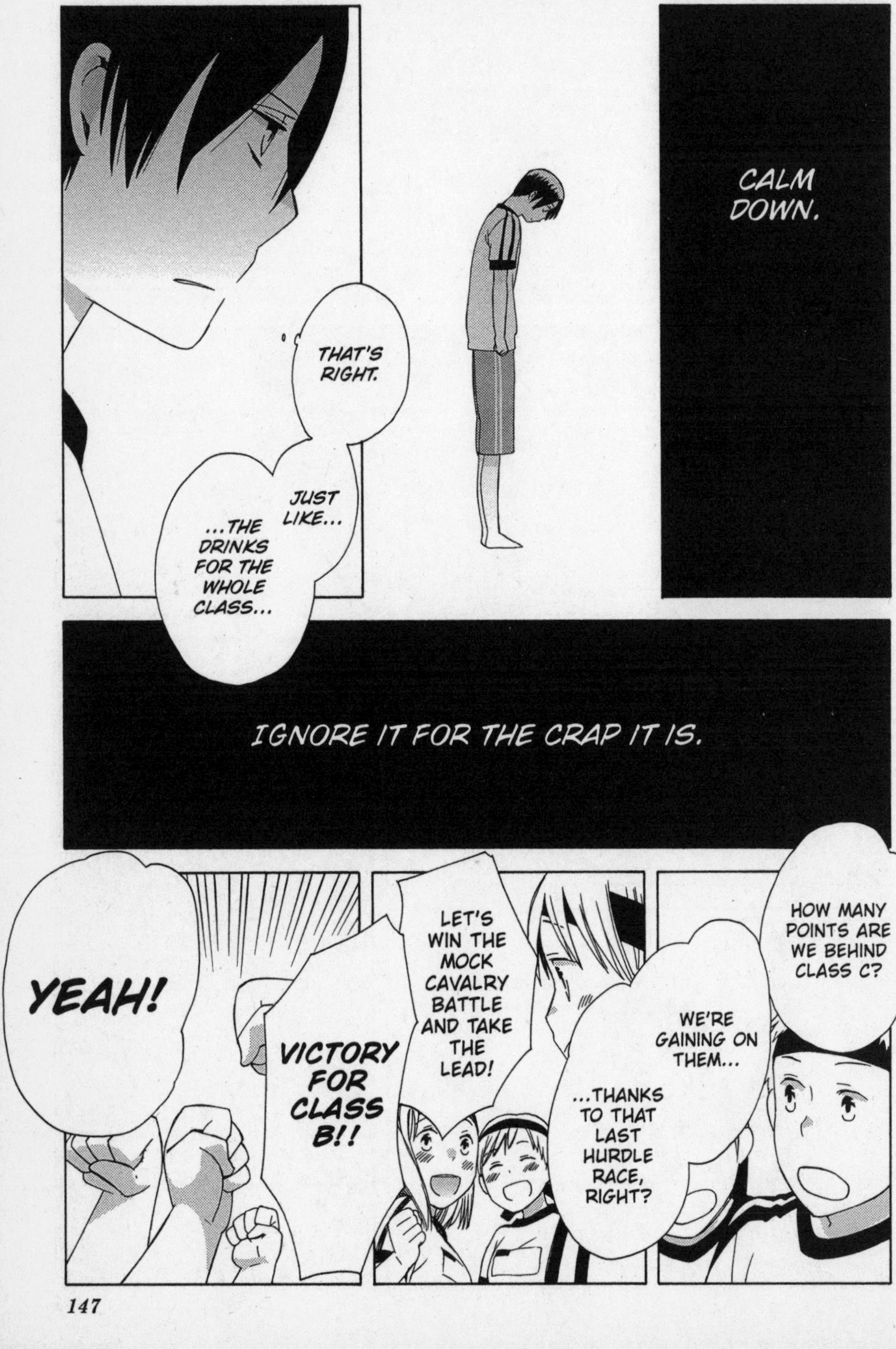
CALM DOWN.
THAT'S RIGHT.
JUST LIKE...
...THE DRINKS FOR THE WHOLE CLASS...
IGNORE IT FOR THE CRAP IT IS.
HOW MANY POINTS ARE WE BEHIND CLASS C?
WE'RE GAINING ON THEM...
...THANKS TO THAT LAST HURDLE RACE, RIGHT?
LET'S WIN THE MOCK CAVALRY BATTLE AND TAKE THE LEAD!
VICTORY FOR CLASS B!!
YEAH!

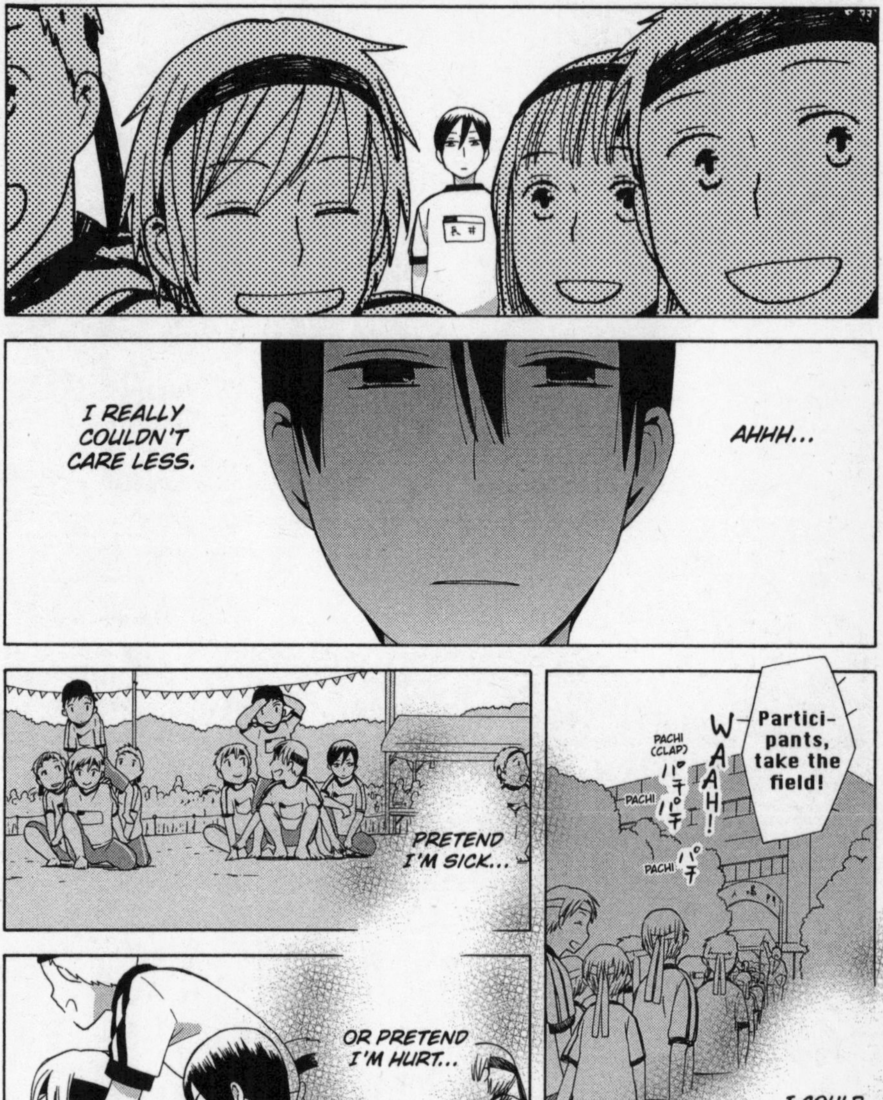

AHHH...
I REALLY COULDN'T CARE LESS.
Partici-pants, take the field!
WAAH!
PACHI (CLAP)
パチパチ
PACHI
PACHI
パチ
I COULD...
...JUST DROP OUT OF THE RELAY.
PRETEND I'M SICK...
OR PRETEND I'M HURT...

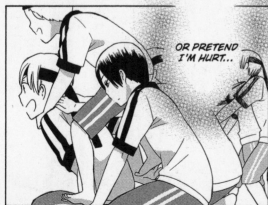

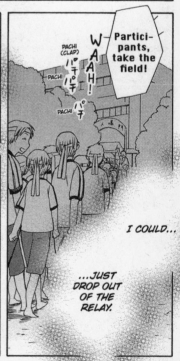

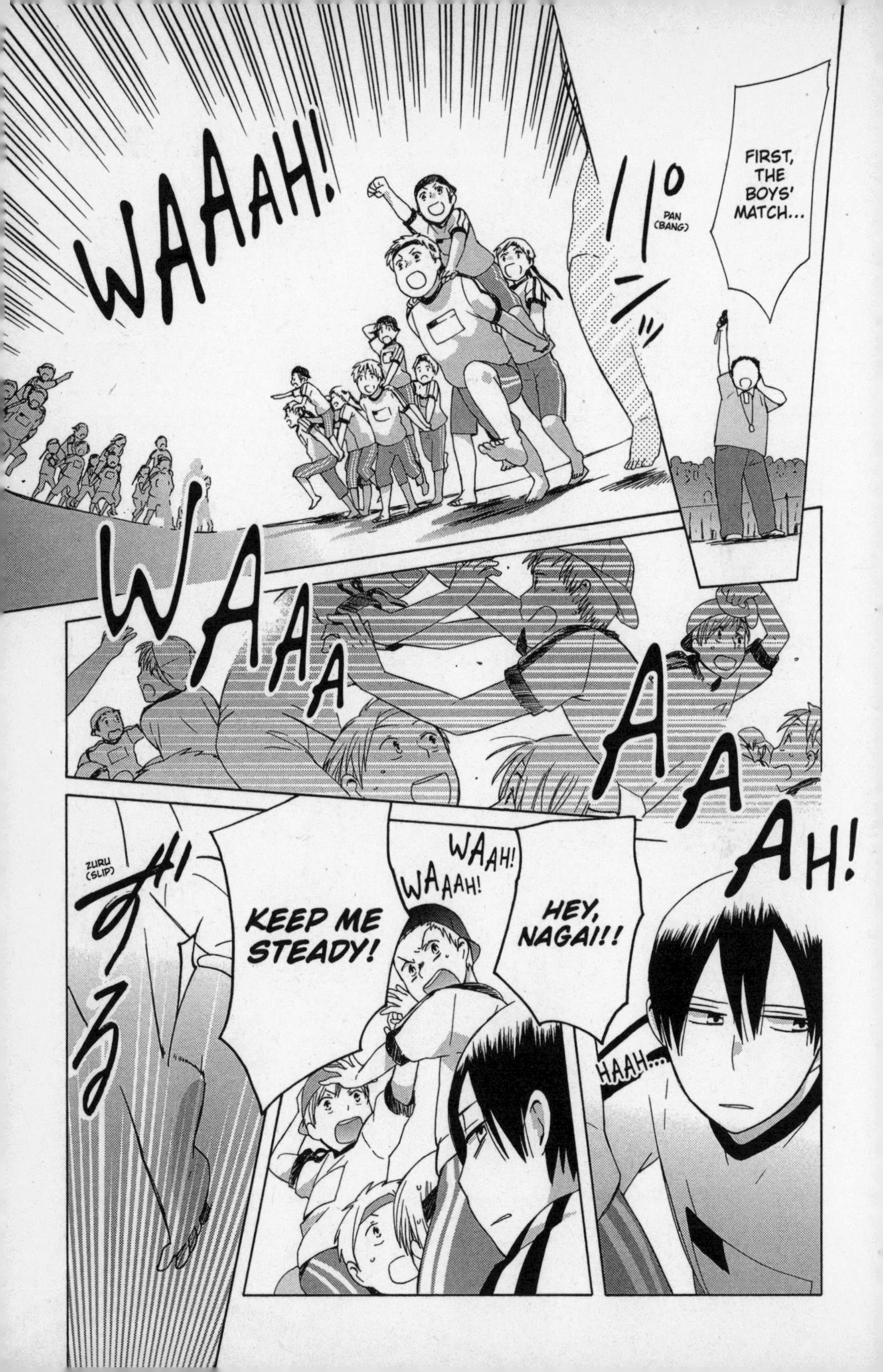
FIRST, THE BOYS' MATCH...
PAN (BANG)
WAAAH!
WAAAA
AAAH!
HAAAH...
HEY, NAGAI!!
WAAAH!
WAAAH!
KEEP ME STEADY!
ZURU (SLIP)

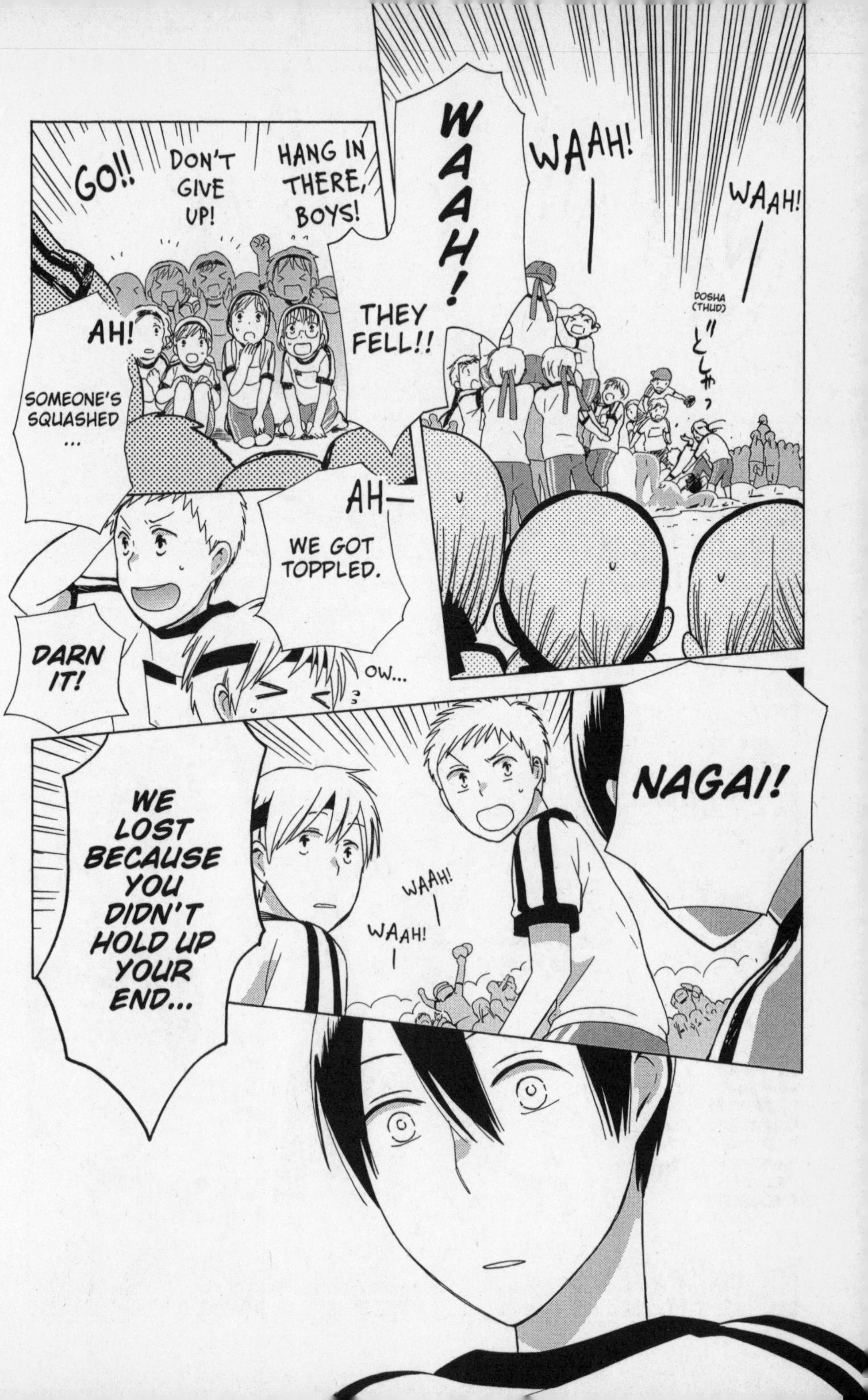
WAAH!
WAAH!
WAAAH!
DOSHA (THUD)
どしゃっ
THEY FELL!!
HANG IN THERE, BOYS!
DON'T GIVE UP!
GO!!
AH!
SOMEONE'S SQUASHED ...
AH—
WE GOT TOPPLED.
DARN IT!
OW...
NAGAI!
WAAH!
WAAH!
WE LOST BECAUSE YOU DIDN'T HOLD UP YOUR END...

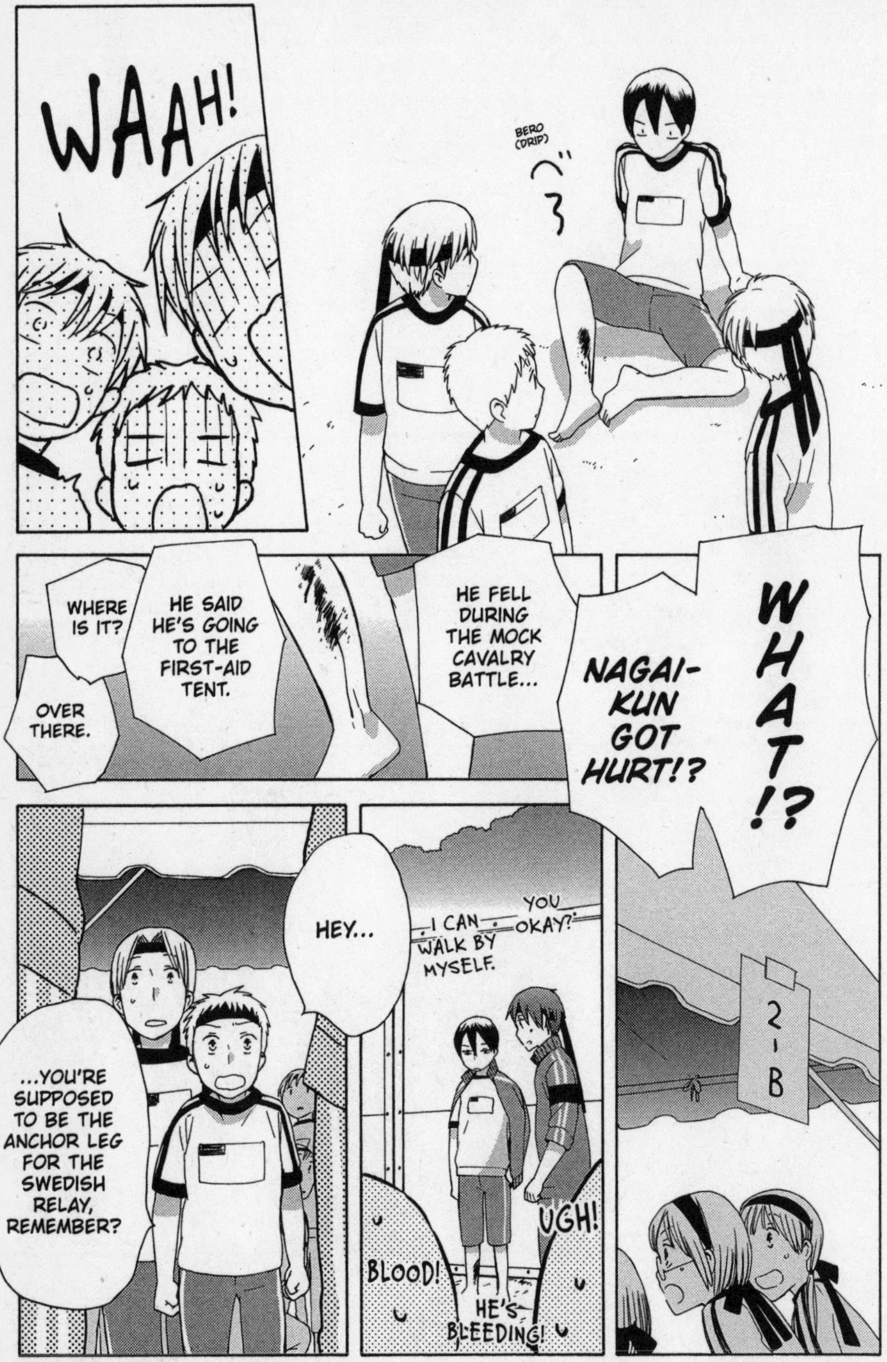
BERO (DRIP)
WAAH!
WHAT!?
NAGAI-KUN GOT HURT!?
2-B
HE FELL DURING THE MOCK CAVALRY BATTLE...
HE SAID HE'S GOING TO THE FIRST-AID TENT.
WHERE IS IT?
OVER THERE.
YOU OKAY?
I CAN WALK BY MYSELF.
UGH!
BLOOD!
HE'S BLEEDING!
HEY...
...YOU'RE SUPPOSED TO BE THE ANCHOR LEG FOR THE SWEDISH RELAY, REMEMBER?

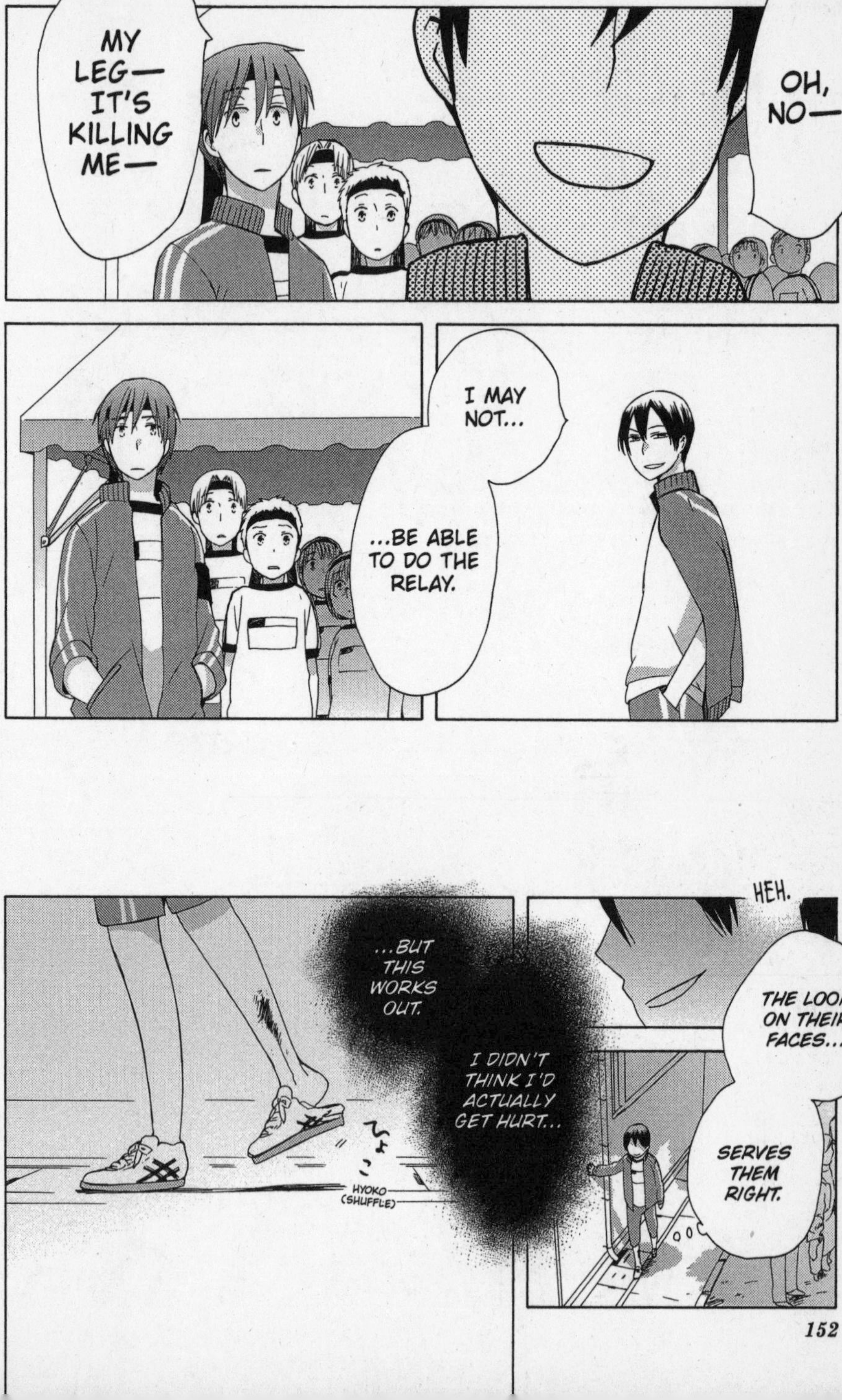
OH, NO—
MY LEG— IT'S KILLING ME—
I MAY NOT...
...BE ABLE TO DO THE RELAY.
HEH.
THE LOOK ON THEIR FACES...
SERVES THEM RIGHT.
...BUT THIS WORKS OUT.
I DIDN'T THINK I'D ACTUALLY GET HURT...
ひょこ
HYOKO (SHUFFLE)

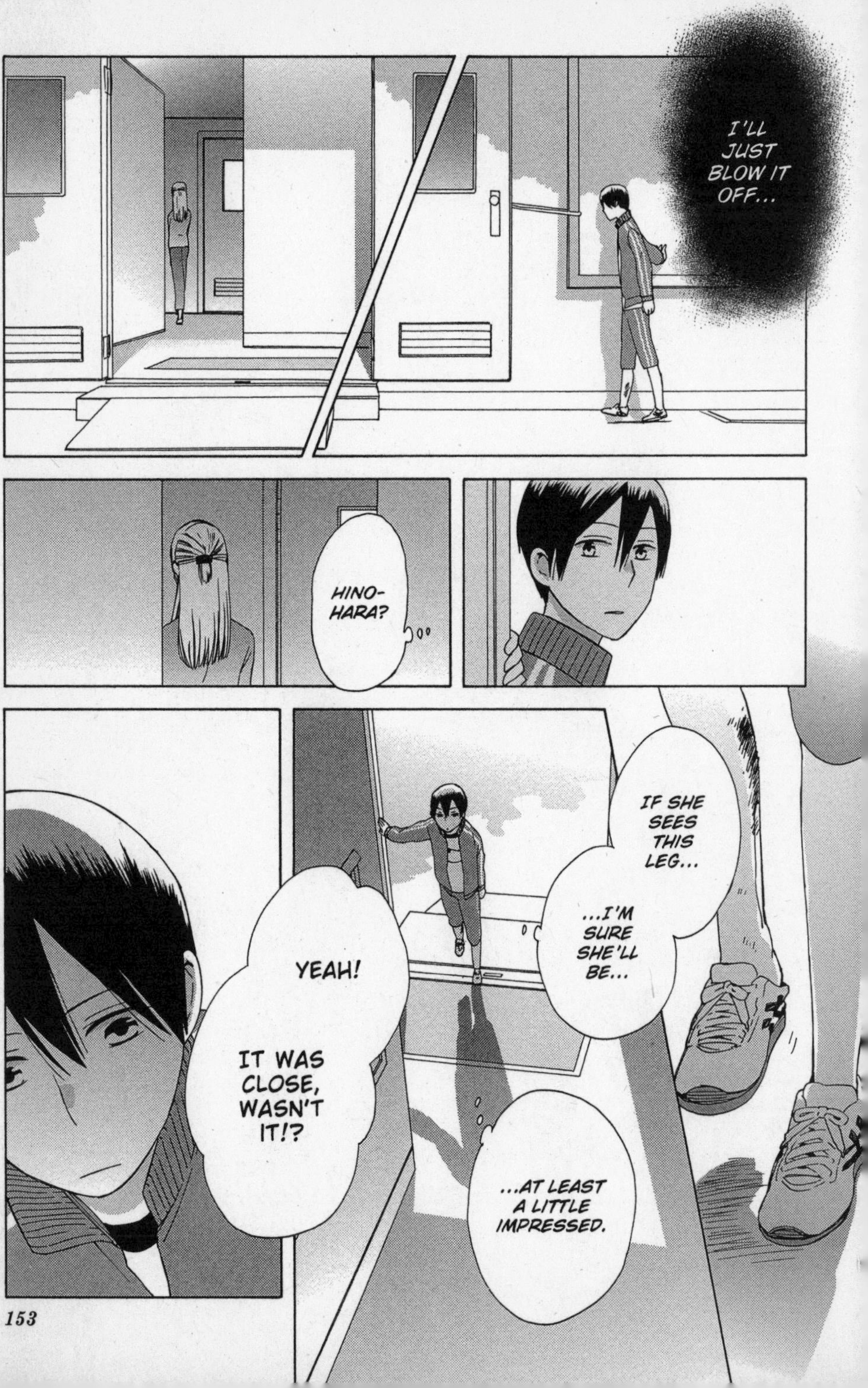
I'LL JUST BLOW IT OFF...
HINO-HARA?
IF SHE SEES THIS LEG...
...I'M SURE SHE'LL BE...
...AT LEAST A LITTLE IMPRESSED.
YEAH!
IT WAS CLOSE, WASN'T IT!?

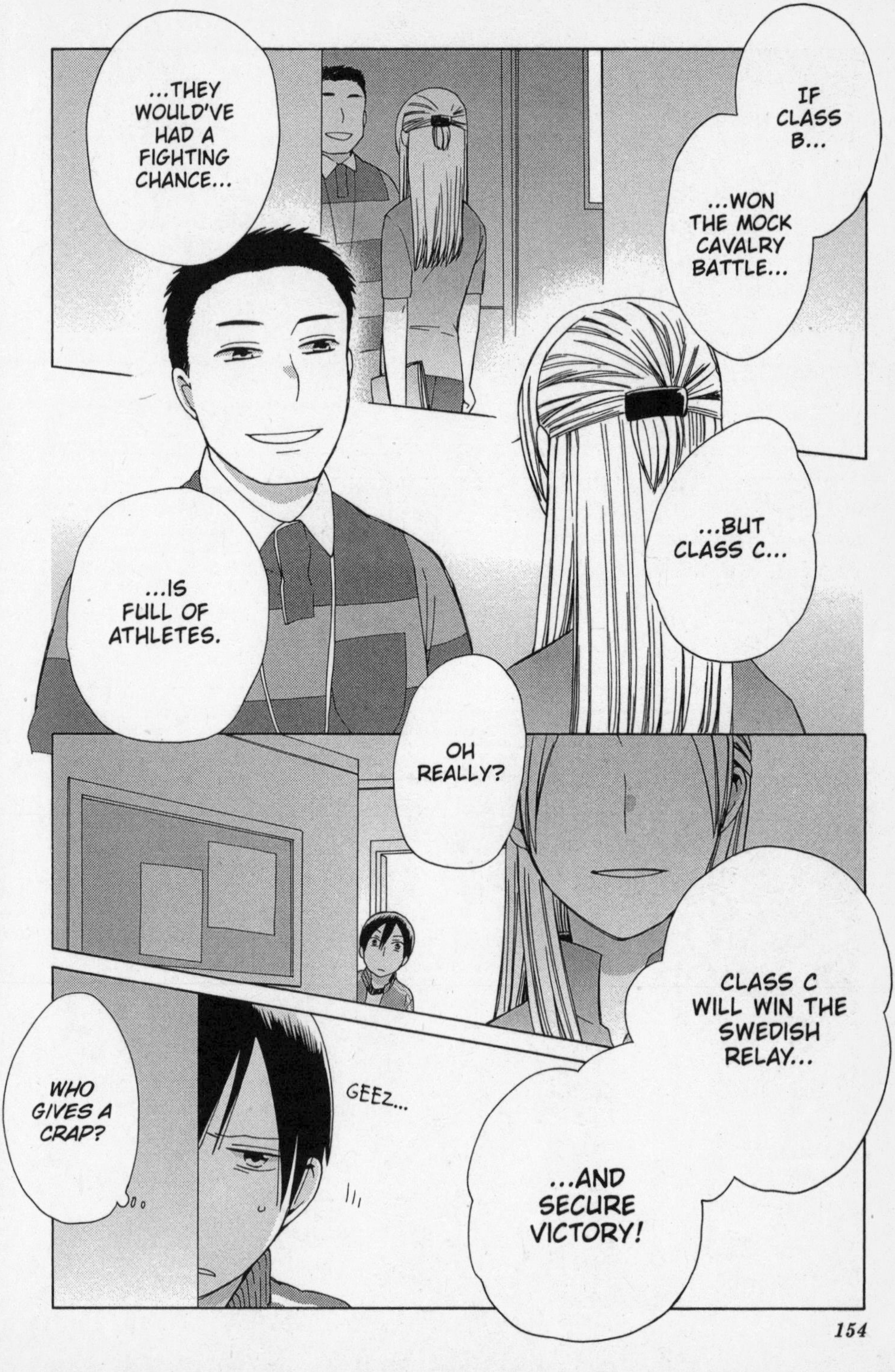
IF CLASS B...
...WON THE MOCK CAVALRY BATTLE...
...THEY WOULD'VE HAD A FIGHTING CHANCE...
...BUT CLASS C...
...IS FULL OF ATHLETES.
OH REALLY?
CLASS C WILL WIN THE SWEDISH RELAY...
...AND SECURE VICTORY!
GEEZ...
WHO GIVES A CRAP?

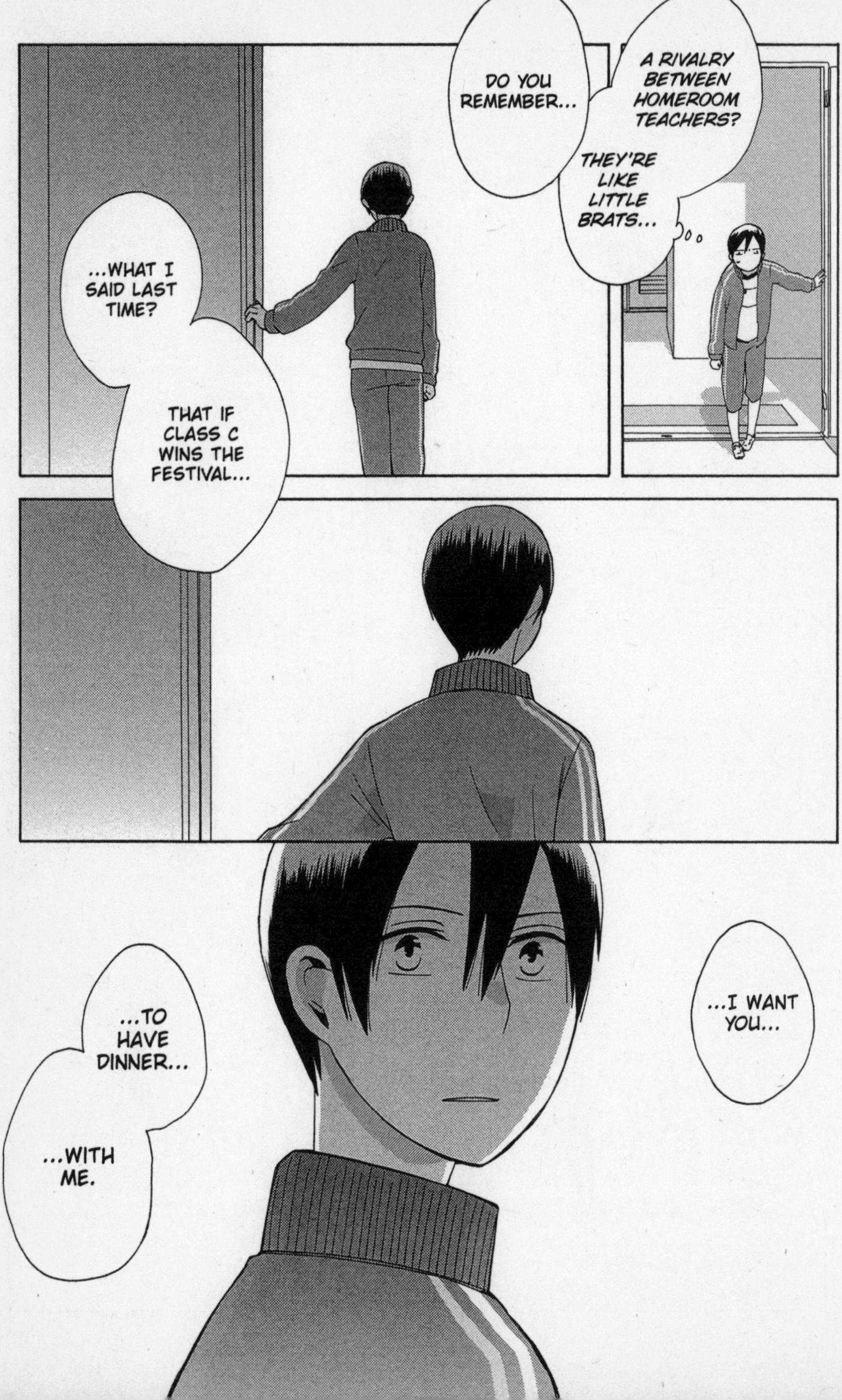
A RIVALRY BETWEEN HOMEROOM TEACHERS?
THEY'RE LIKE LITTLE BRATS...
DO YOU REMEMBER...
...WHAT I SAID LAST TIME?
THAT IF CLASS C WINS THE FESTIVAL...
...I WANT YOU...
...TO HAVE DINNER...
...WITH ME.

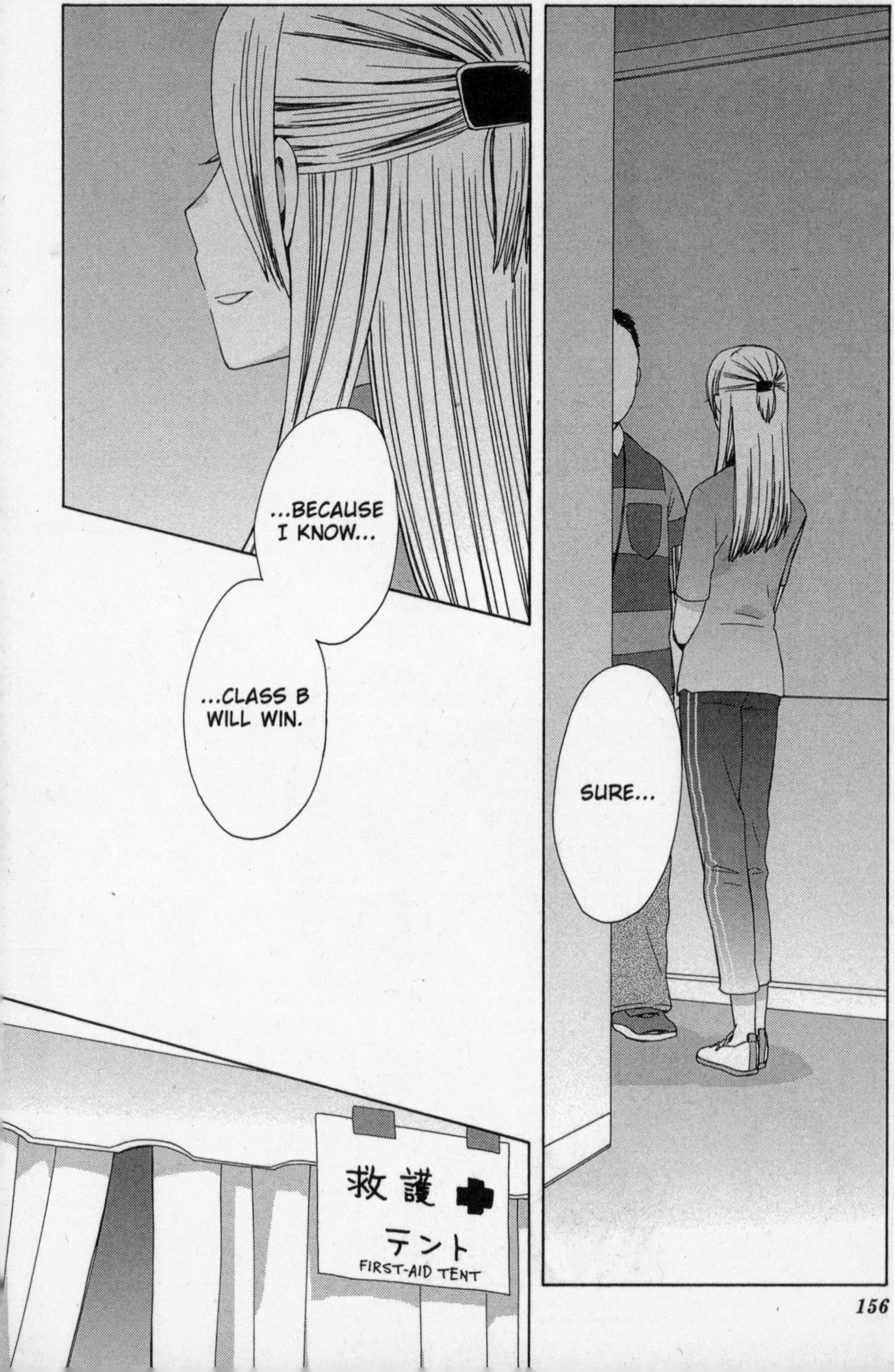
SURE...
...BECAUSE I KNOW...
...CLASS B WILL WIN.
救護
テント
FIRST-AID TENT

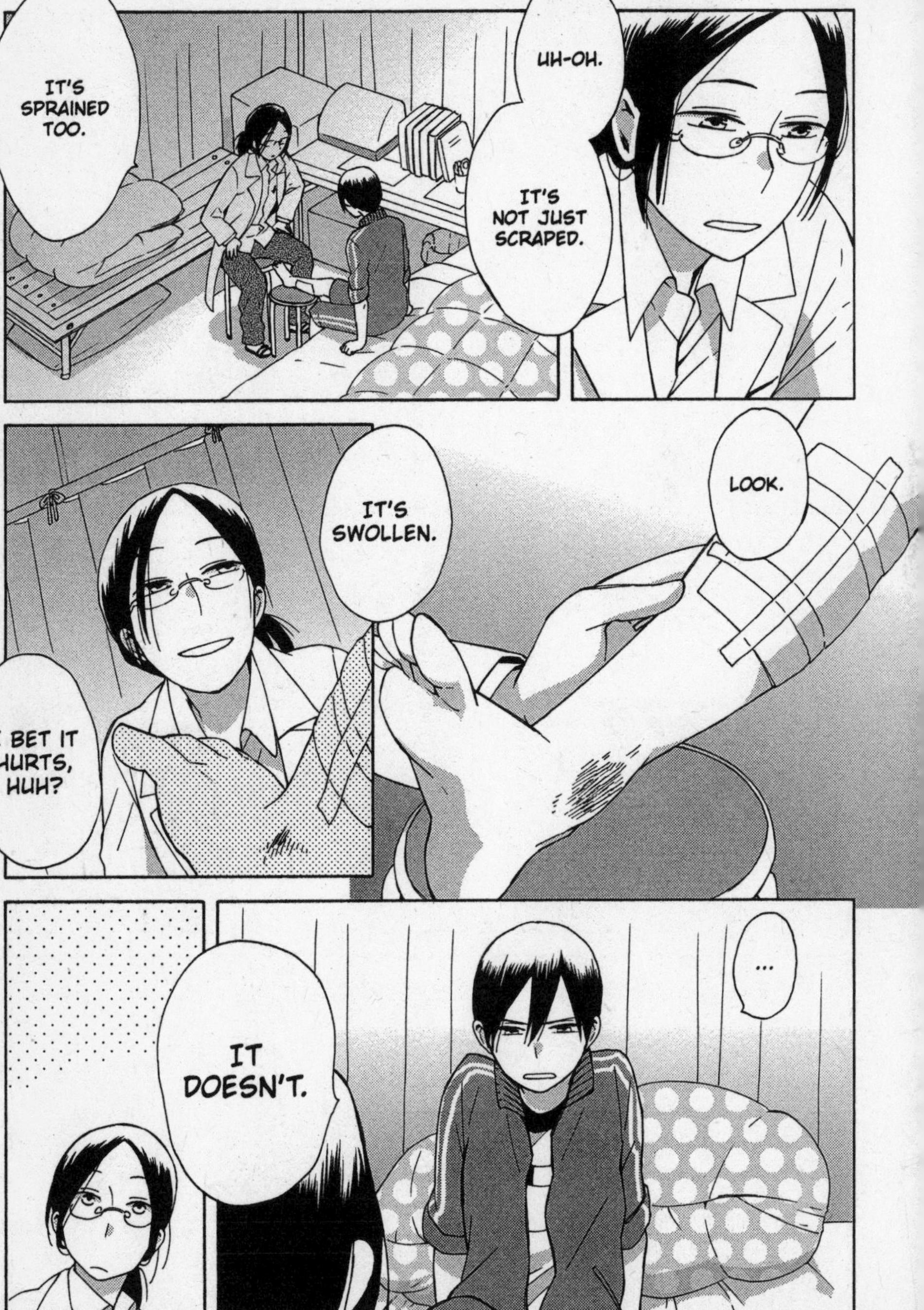
UH-OH.
IT'S NOT JUST SCRAPED.
IT'S SPRAINED TOO.
LOOK.
IT'S SWOLLEN.
I BET IT HURTS, HUH?
...
IT DOESN'T.

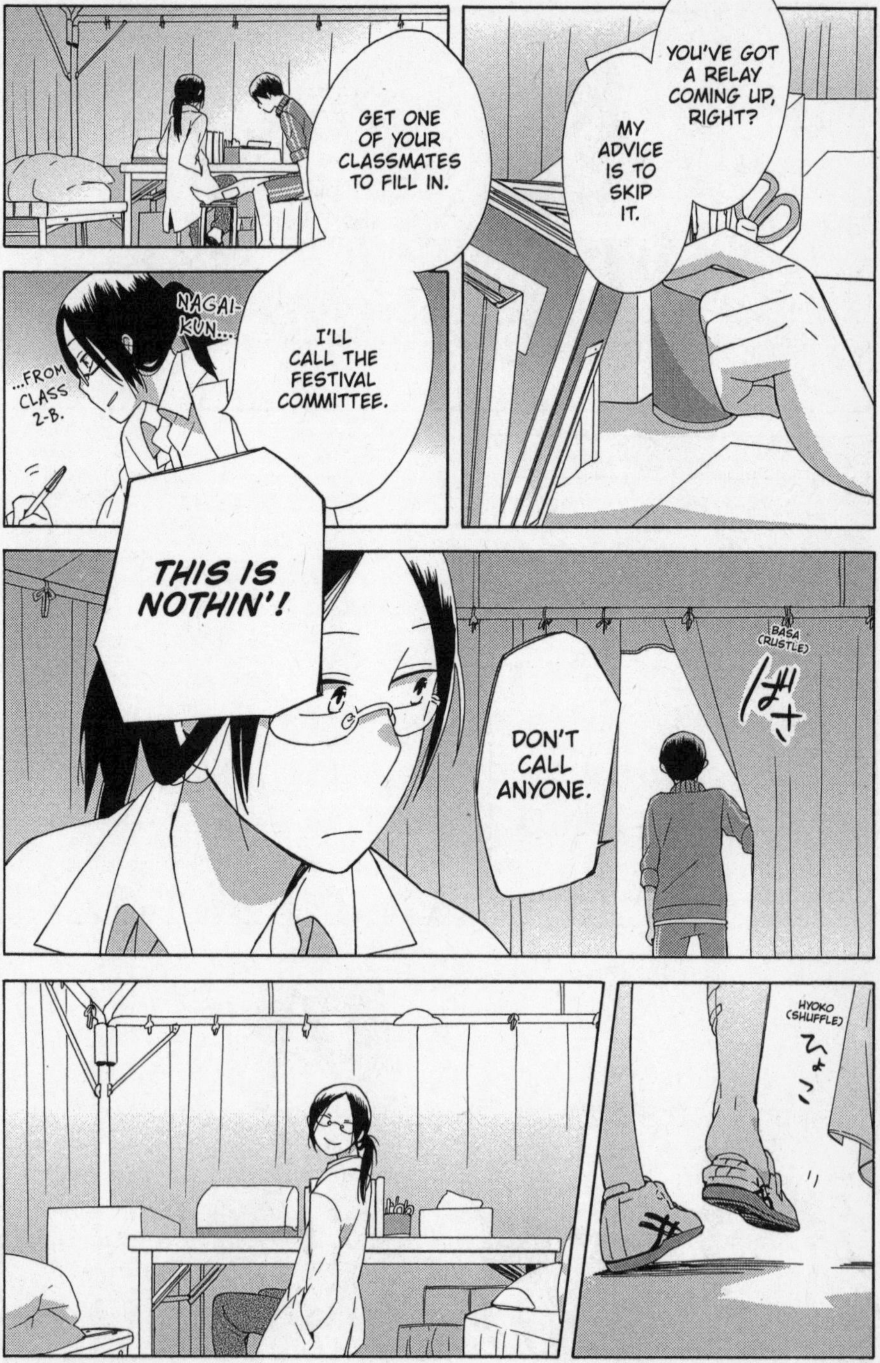
YOU'VE GOT A RELAY COMING UP, RIGHT?
MY ADVICE IS TO SKIP IT.
GET ONE OF YOUR CLASSMATES TO FILL IN.
I'LL CALL THE FESTIVAL COMMITTEE.
NAGAI-KUN...
...FROM CLASS 2-B.
BASA (RUSTLE)
ばさ
DON'T CALL ANYONE.
THIS IS NOTHIN'!
HYOKO (SHUFFLE)
ひょこ

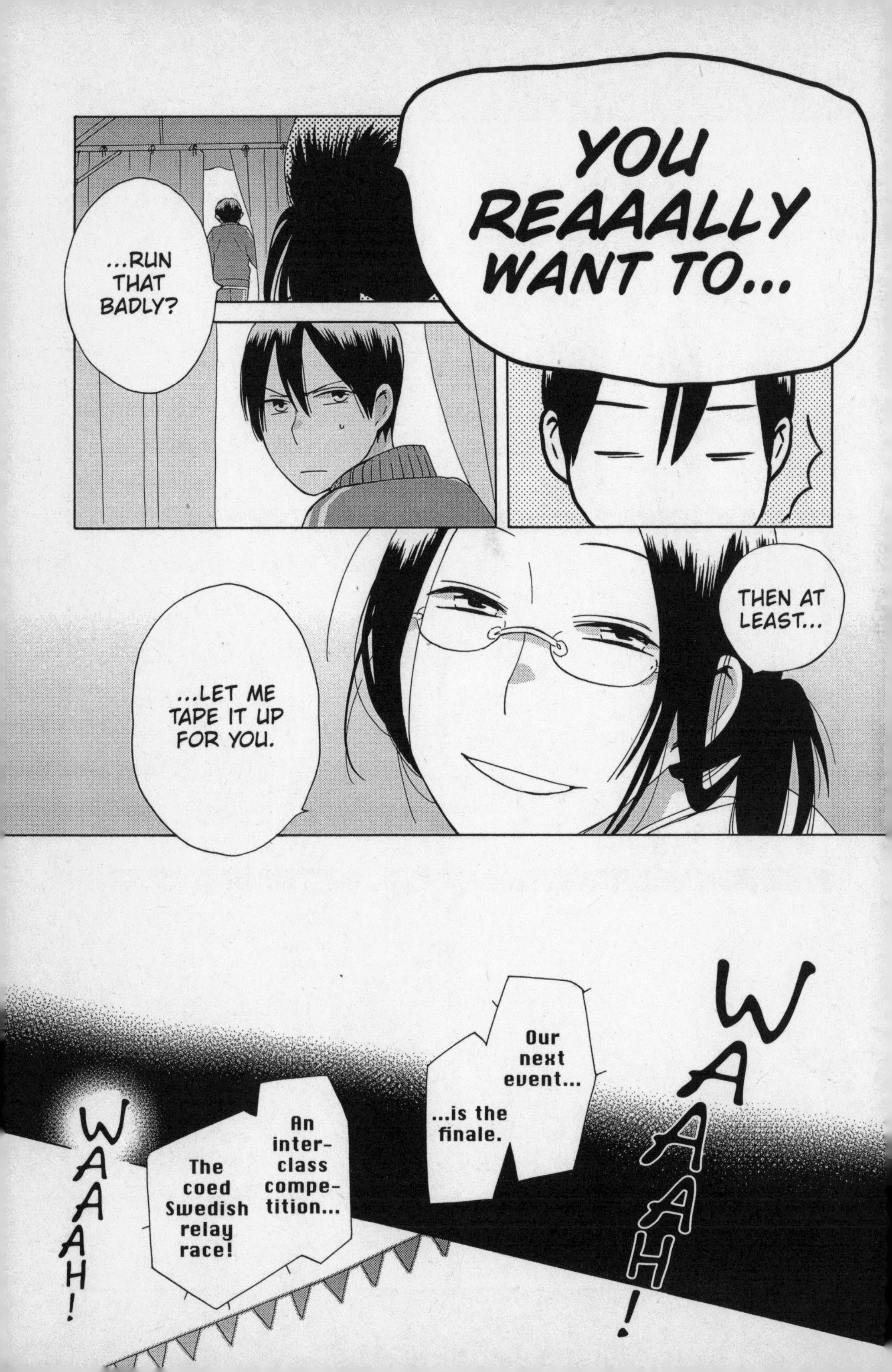
YOU REAAALLY WANT TO...
...RUN THAT BADLY?
THEN AT LEAST...
...LET ME TAPE IT UP FOR YOU.
WAAAAH!
Our next event...
...is the finale.
An inter-class compe-tition...
The coed Swedish relay race!
WAAAH!

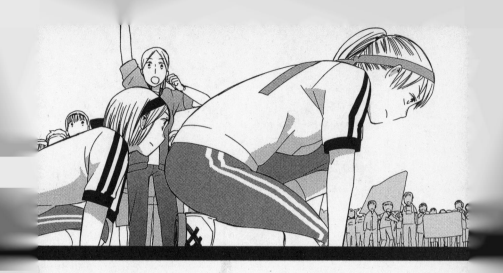

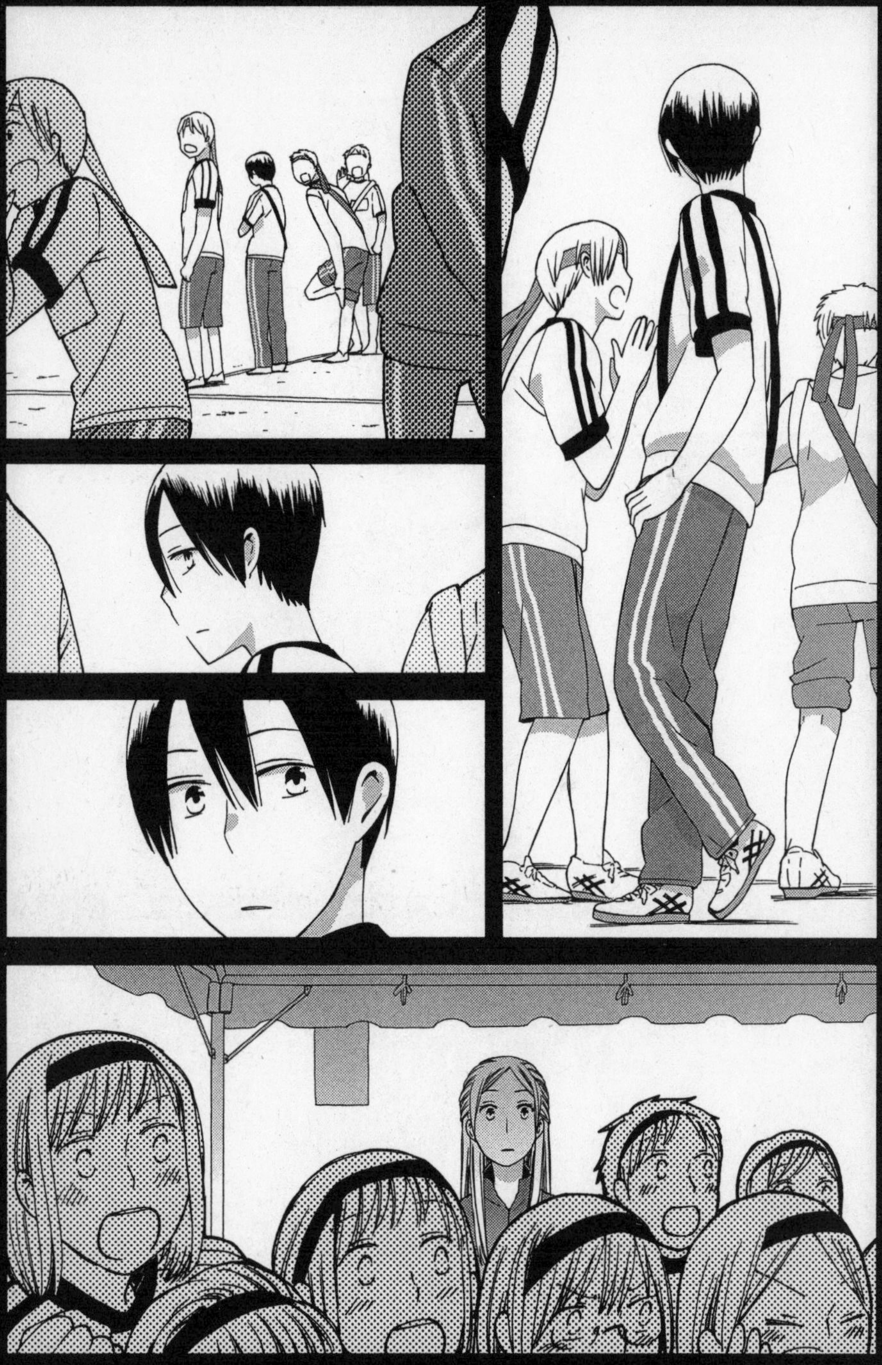

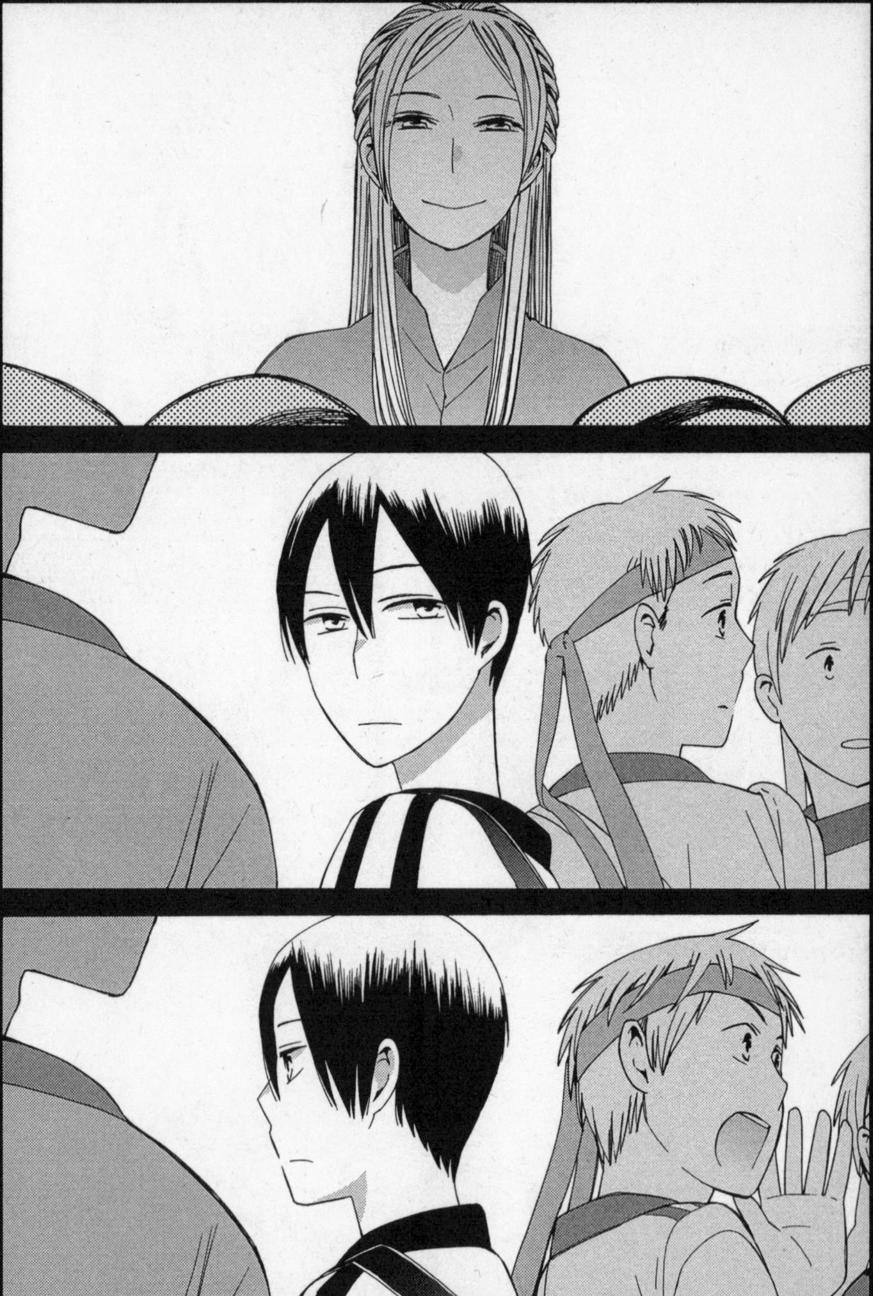

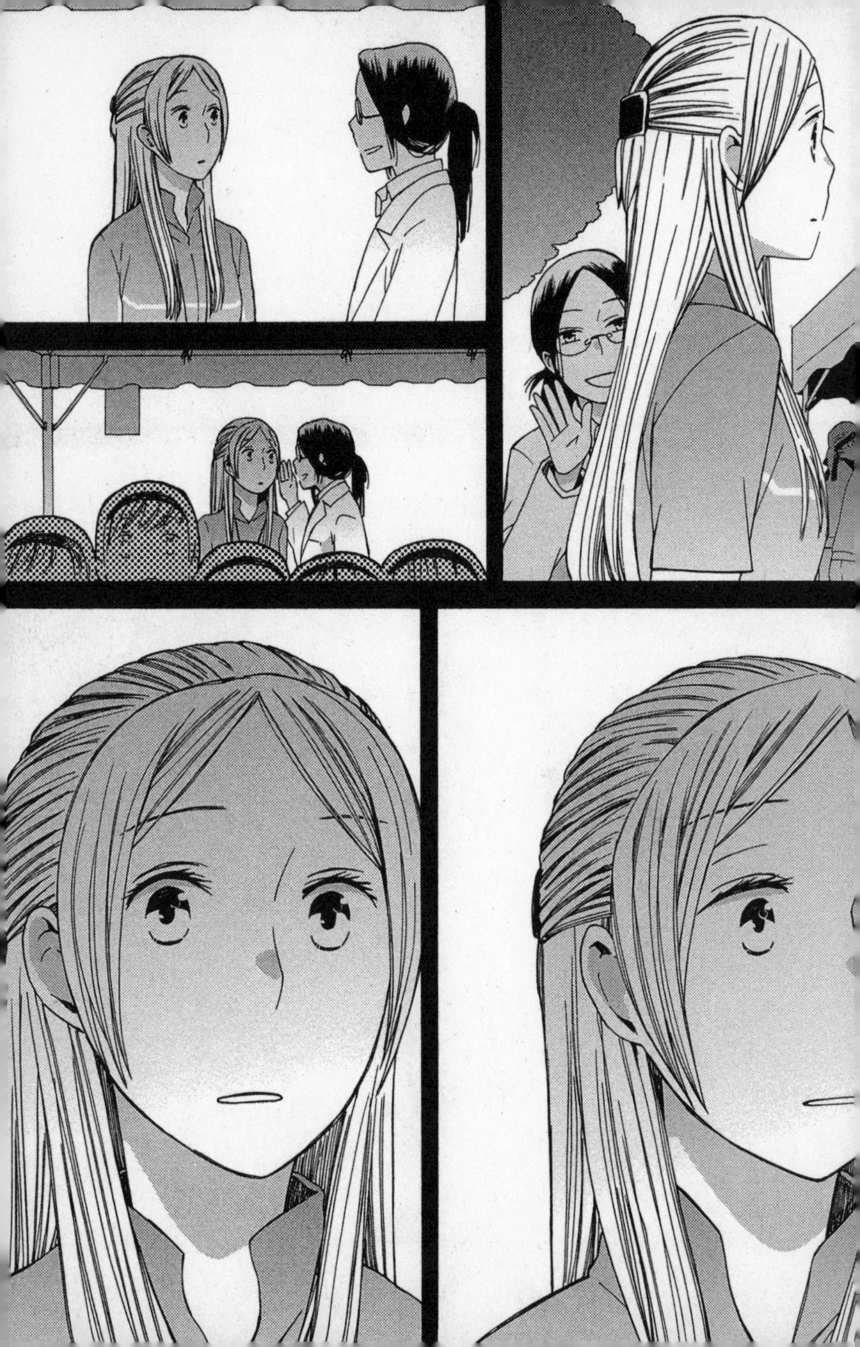

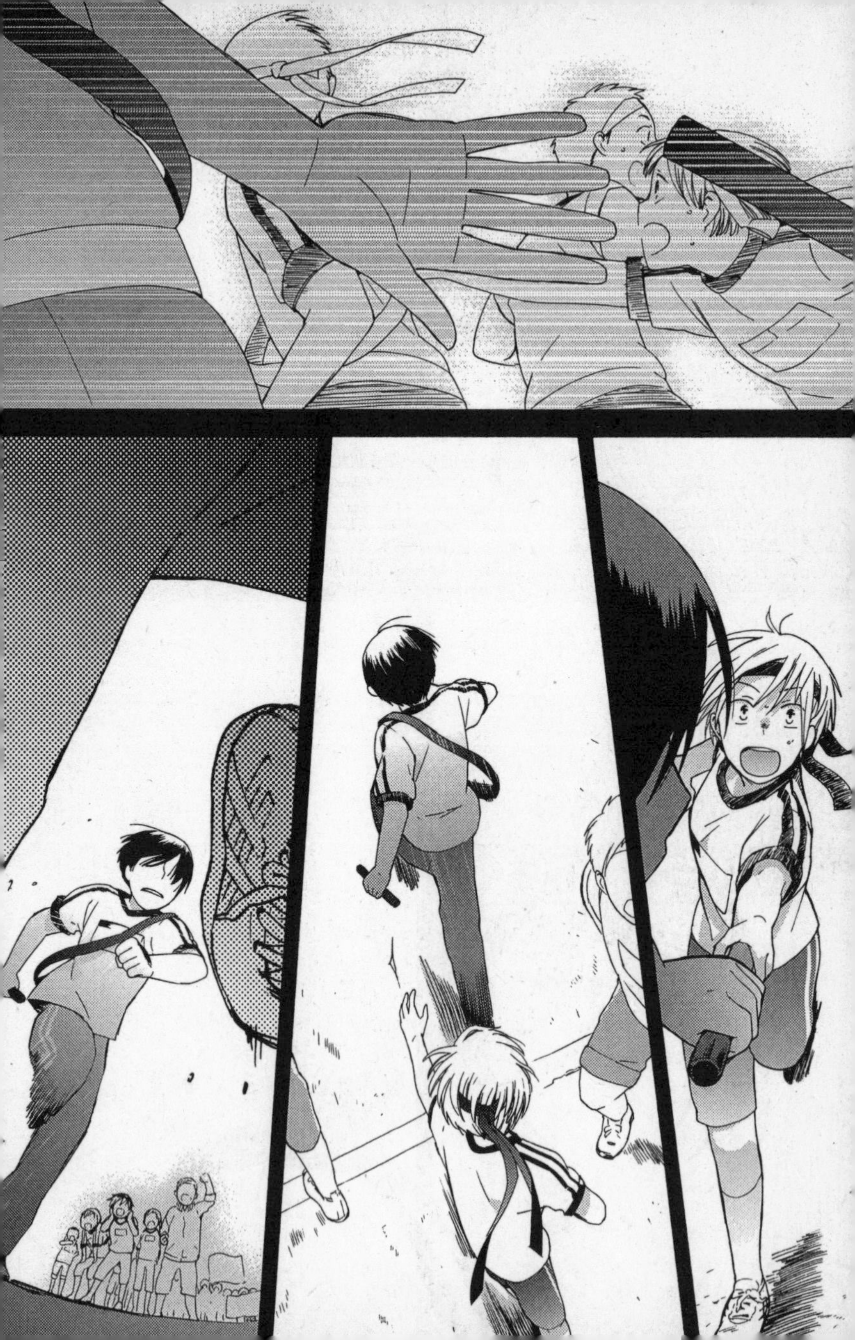

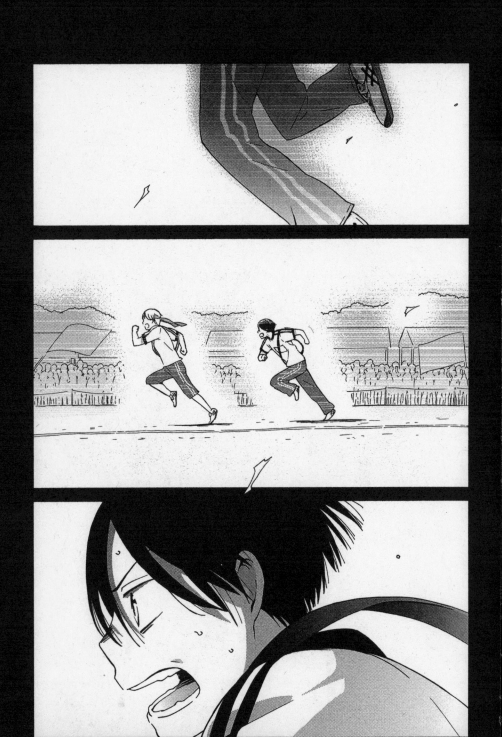

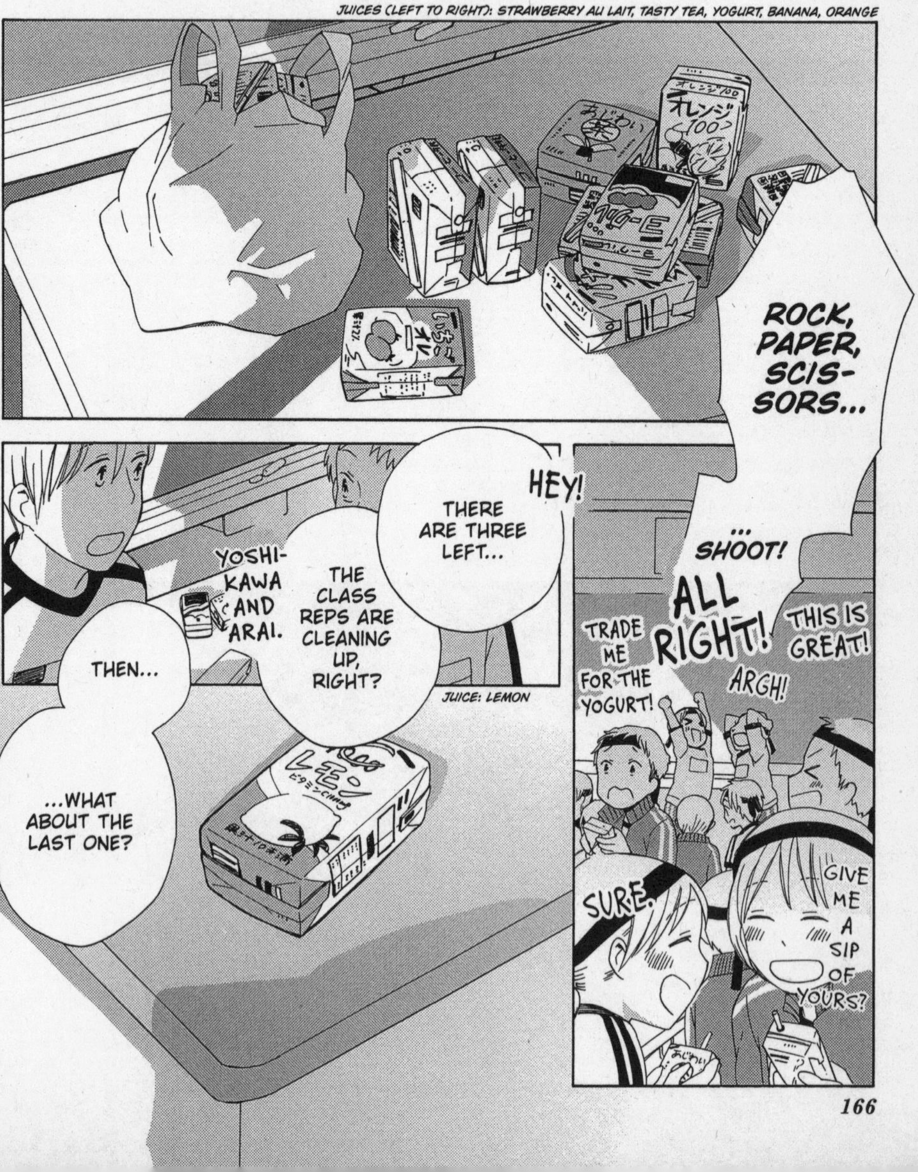
JUICES (LEFT TO RIGHT): STRAWBERRY AU LAIT, TASTY TEA, YOGURT, BANANA, ORANGE
ROCK, PAPER, SCIS-SORS...
...SHOOT!
ALL RIGHT!
THIS IS GREAT!
TRADE ME FOR THE YOGURT!
ARGH!
SURE.
GIVE ME A SIP OF YOURS?
HEY!
THERE ARE THREE LEFT...
THE CLASS REPS ARE CLEANING UP, RIGHT?
YOSHI-KAWA AND ARAI.
JUICE: LEMON
THEN...
...WHAT ABOUT THE LAST ONE?

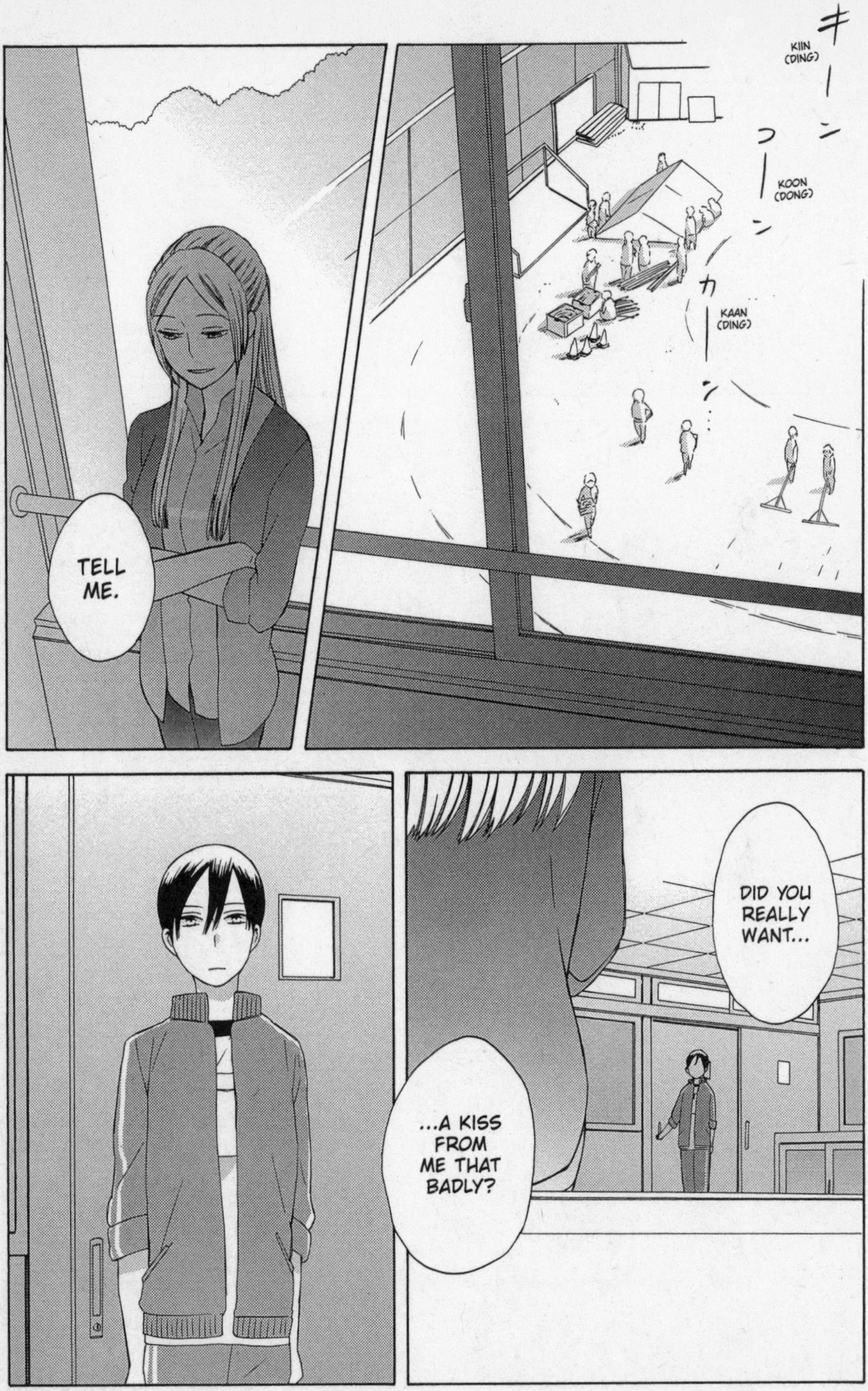
キーン
KIIN (DING)
コーン
KOON (DONG)
カーン…
KAAN (DING)
TELL ME.
DID YOU REALLY WANT...
...A KISS FROM ME THAT BADLY?

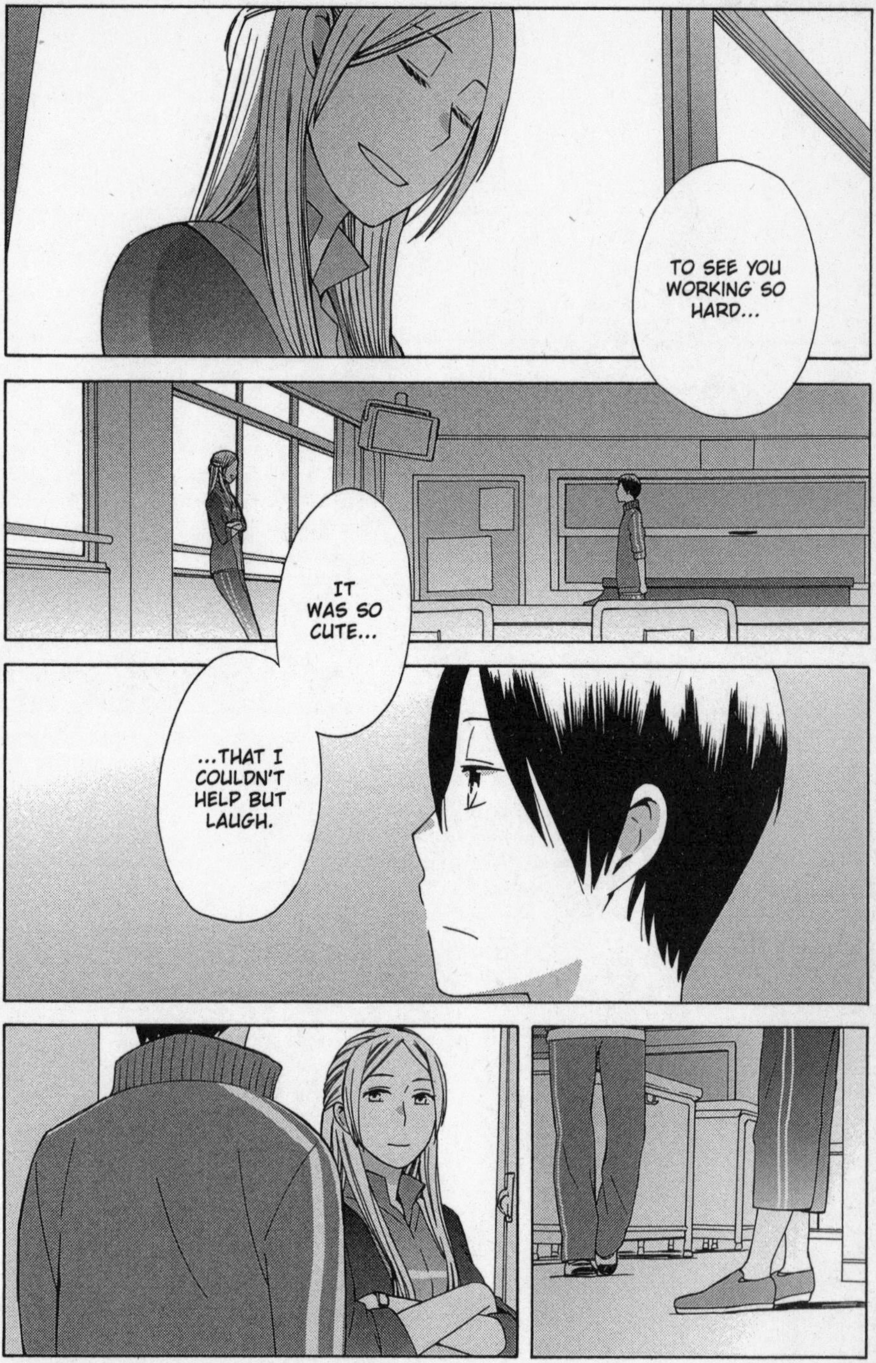
TO SEE YOU WORKING SO HARD...
IT WAS SO CUTE...
...THAT I COULDN'T HELP BUT LAUGH.

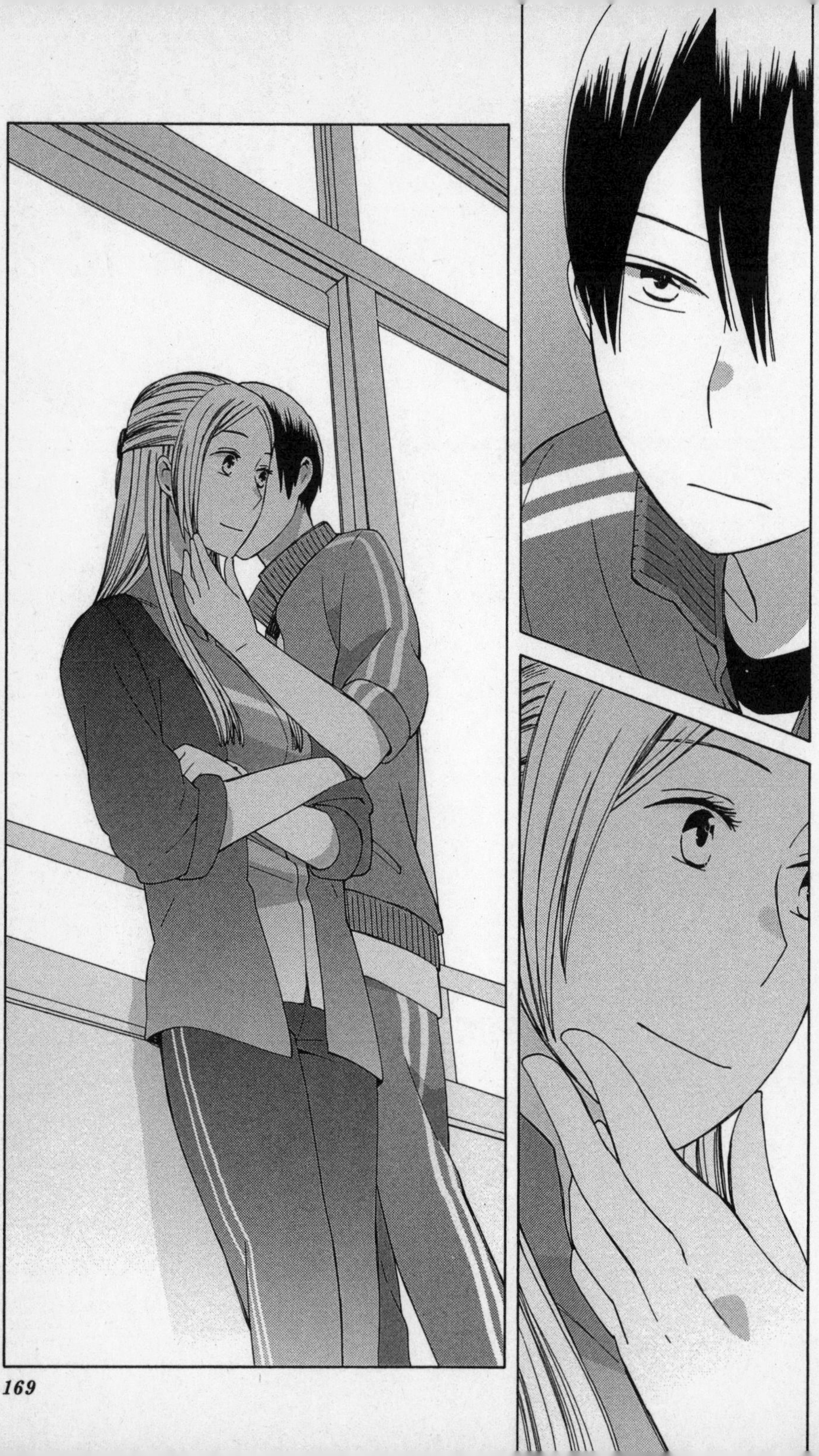

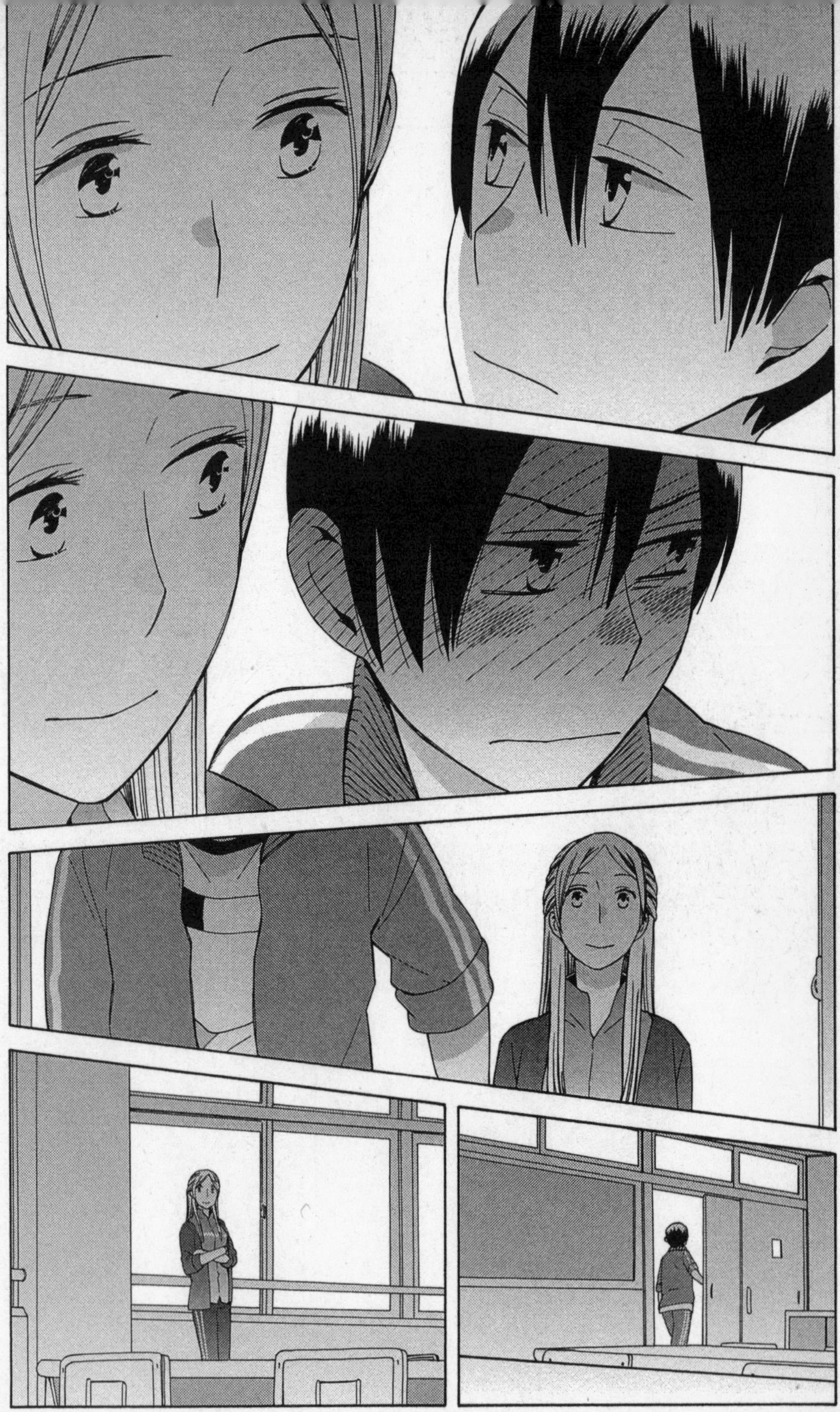

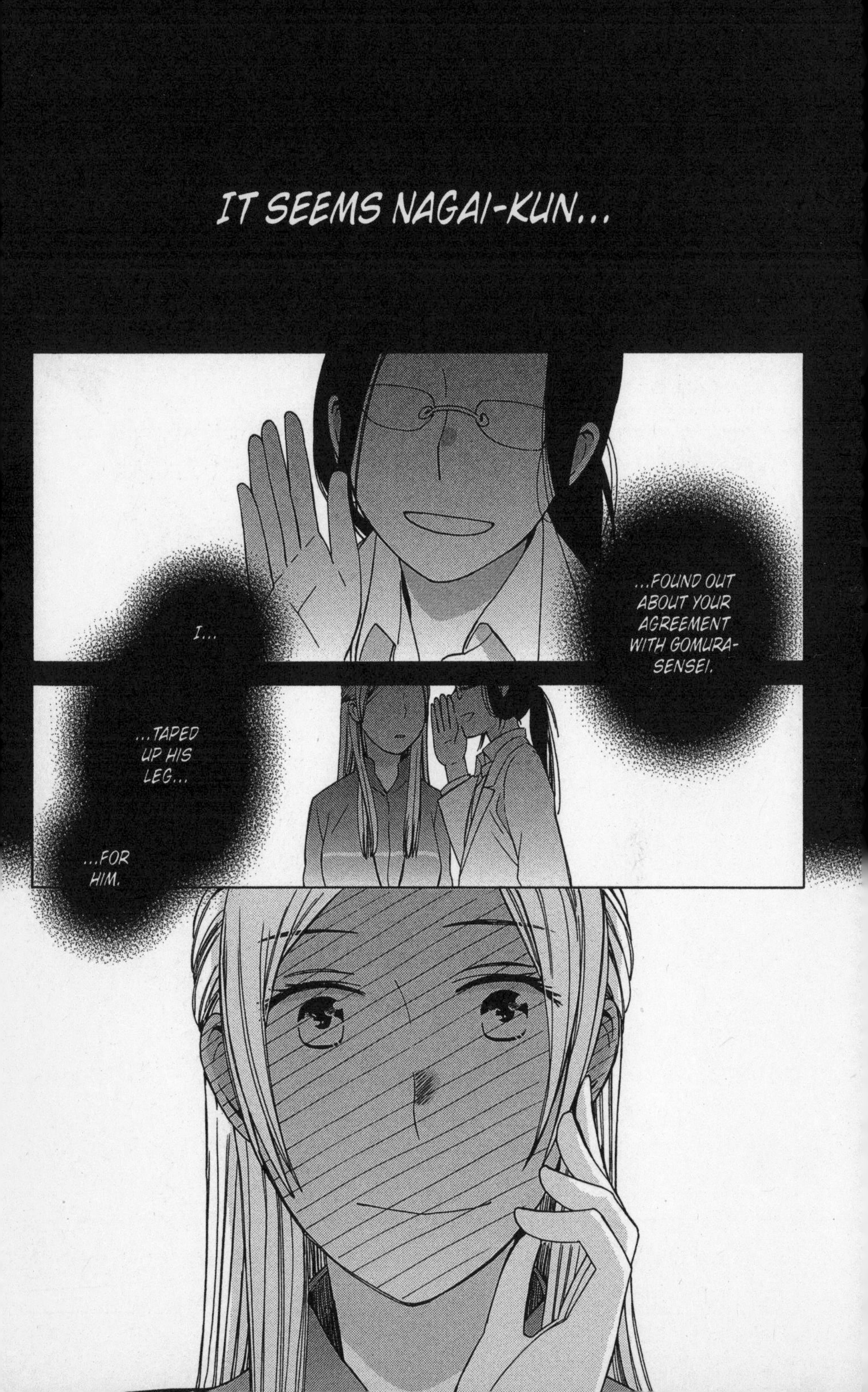
IT SEEMS NAGAI-KUN...
...FOUND OUT ABOUT YOUR AGREEMENT WITH GOMURA-SENSEI.
I...
...TAPED UP HIS LEG...
...FOR HIM.

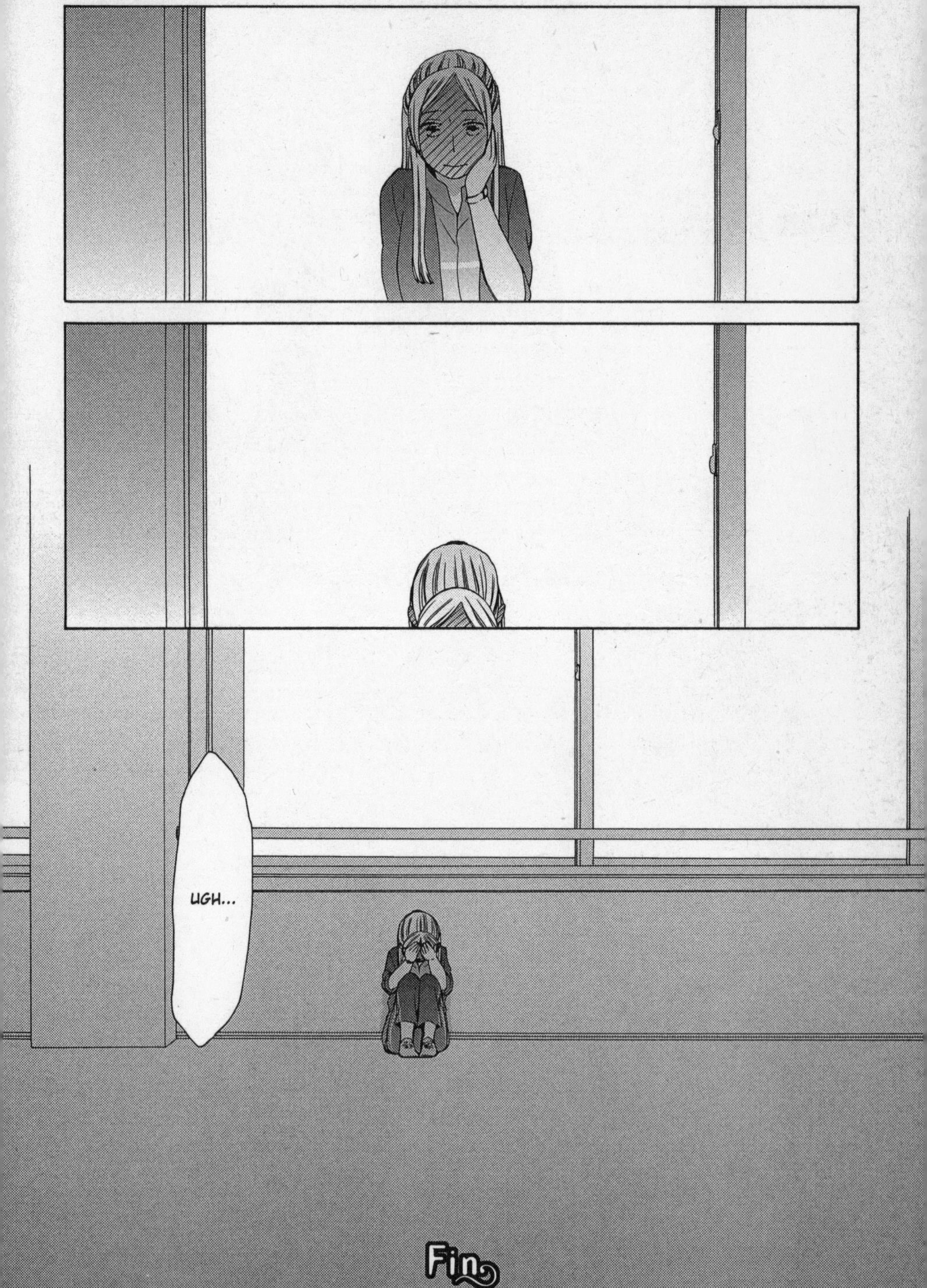
UGH...
Fin

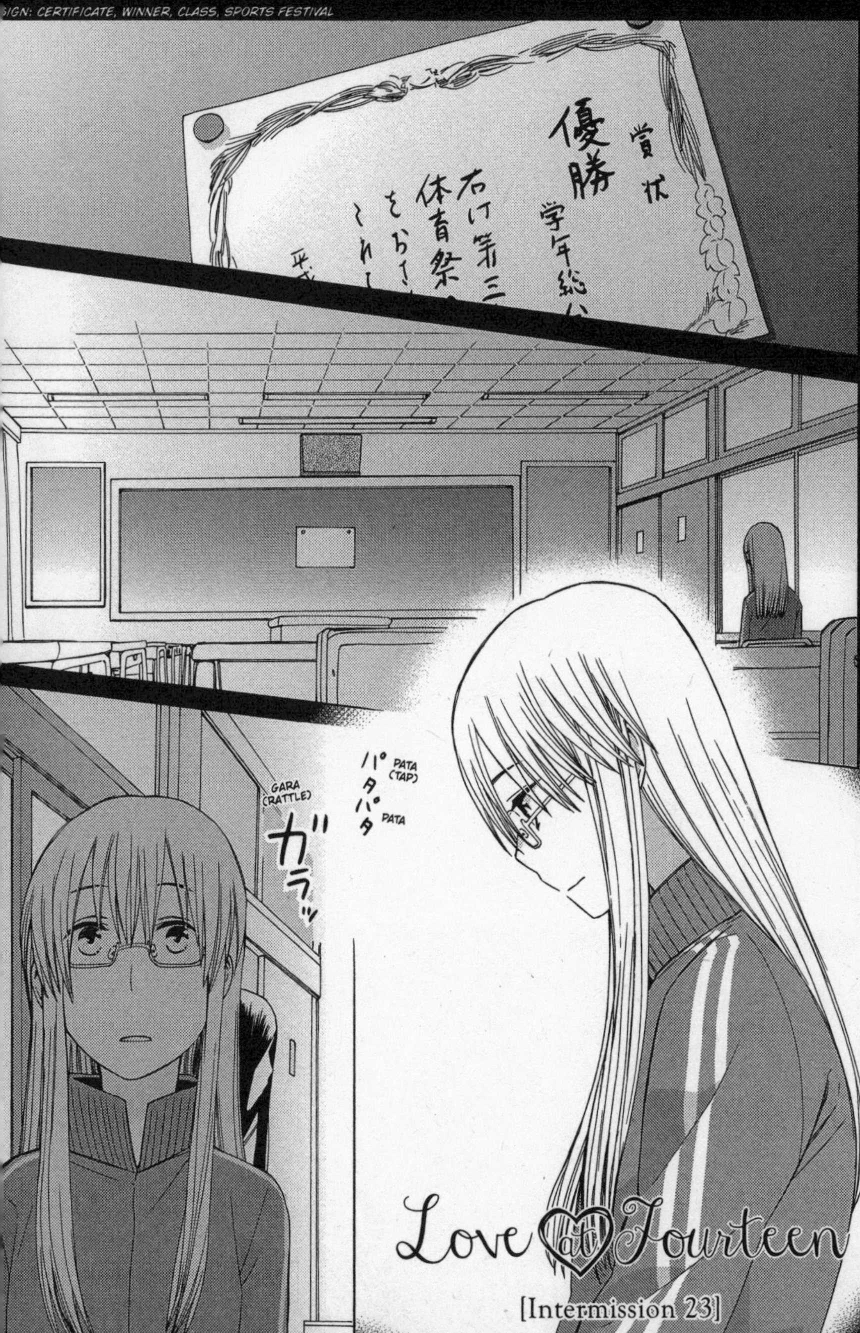
SIGN: CERTIFICATE, WINNER, CLASS, SPORTS FESTIVAL
賞状
優勝
パタパタ
PATA (TAP) PATA
ガラッ
GARA (RATTLE)
Love at Fourteen
[Intermission 23]

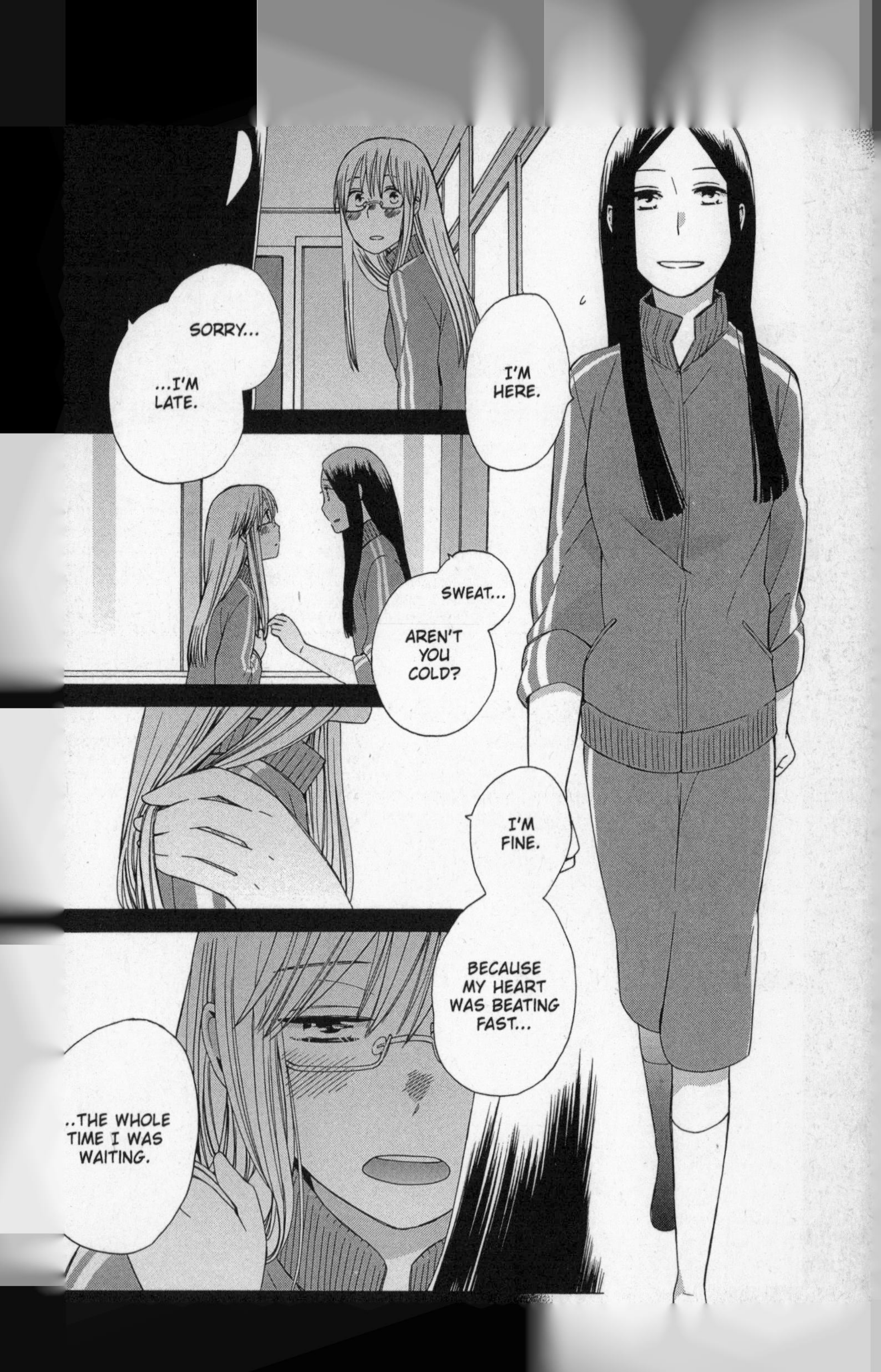
SORRY...
...I'M LATE.
I'M HERE.
SWEAT...
AREN'T YOU COLD?
I'M FINE.
BECAUSE MY HEART WAS BEATING FAST...
..THE WHOLE TIME I WAS WAITING.

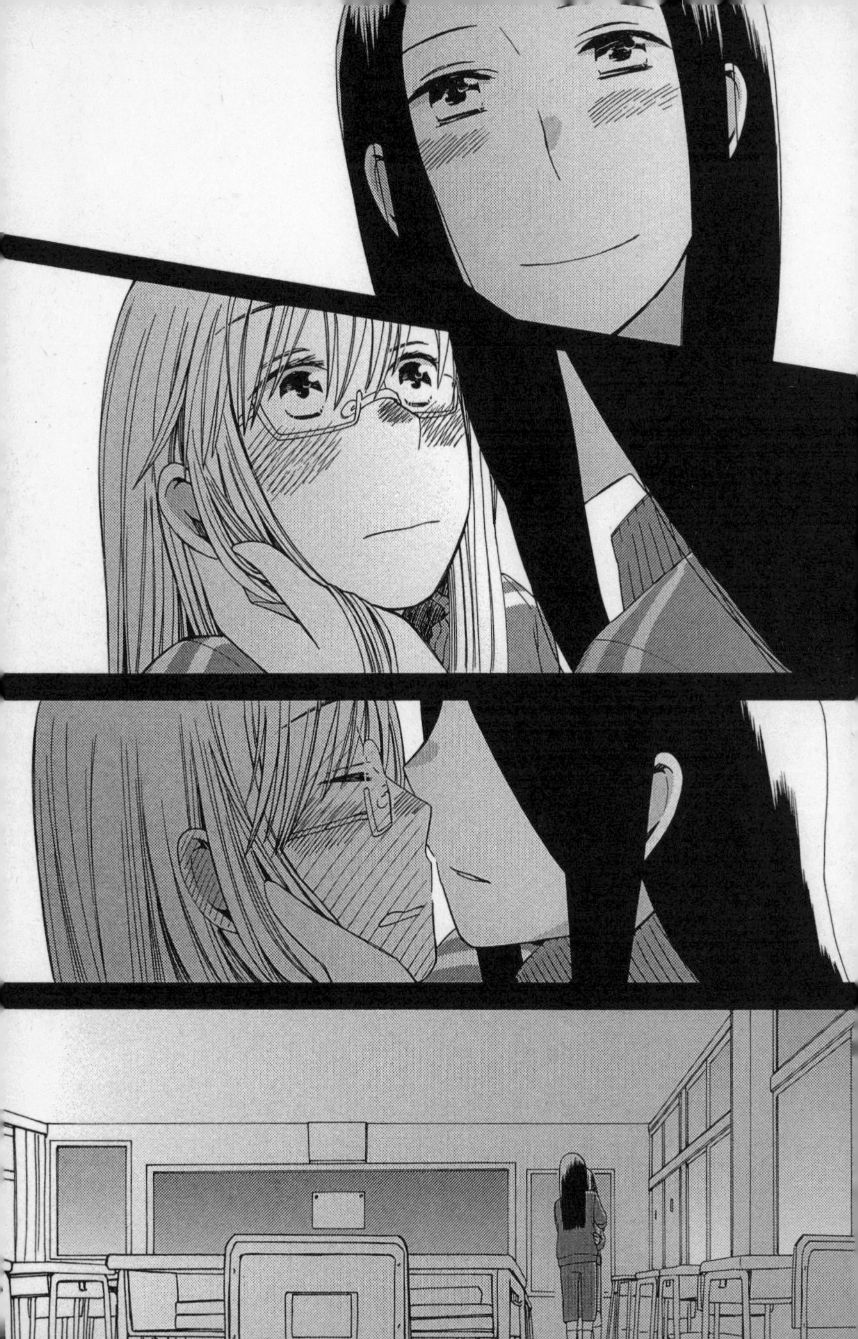

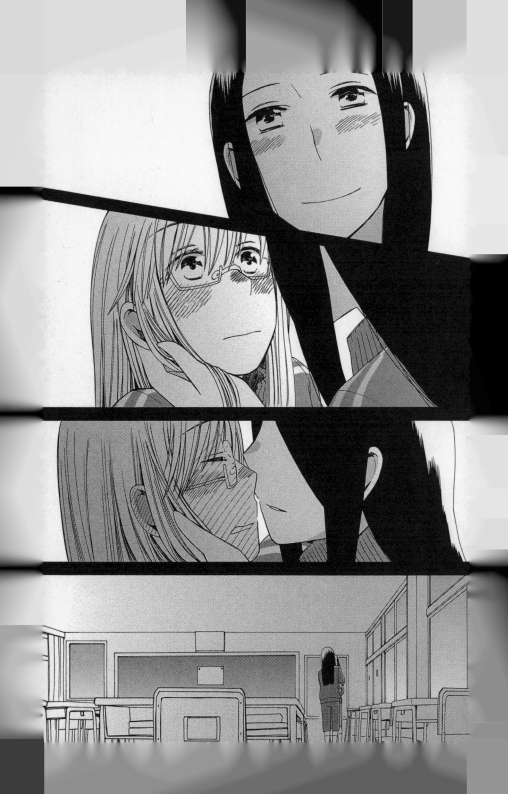

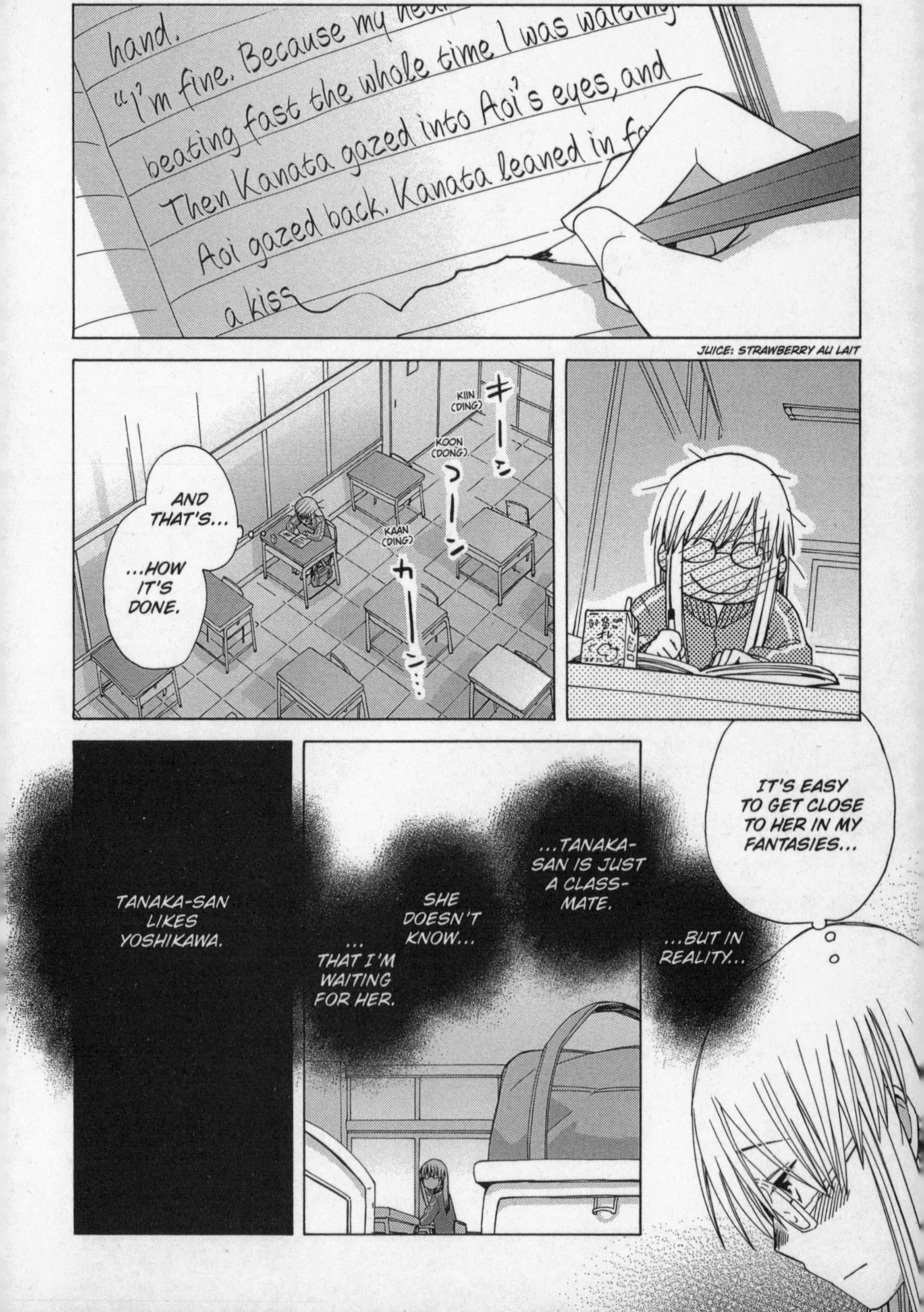
hand.
“I'm fine. Because my
beating fast the whole time I was waiting
Then Kanata gazed into Aoi's eyes, and
Aoi gazed back. Kanata leaned in
a kiss
JUICE: STRAWBERRY AU LAIT
KIIN (DING)
KOON (DONG)
KAAN (DING)
AND THAT'S...
...HOW IT'S DONE.
IT'S EASY TO GET CLOSE TO HER IN MY FANTASIES...
...BUT IN REALITY...
...TANAKA-SAN IS JUST A CLASSMATE.
SHE DOESN'T KNOW...
...THAT I'M WAITING FOR HER.
TANAKA-SAN LIKES YOSHIKAWA.

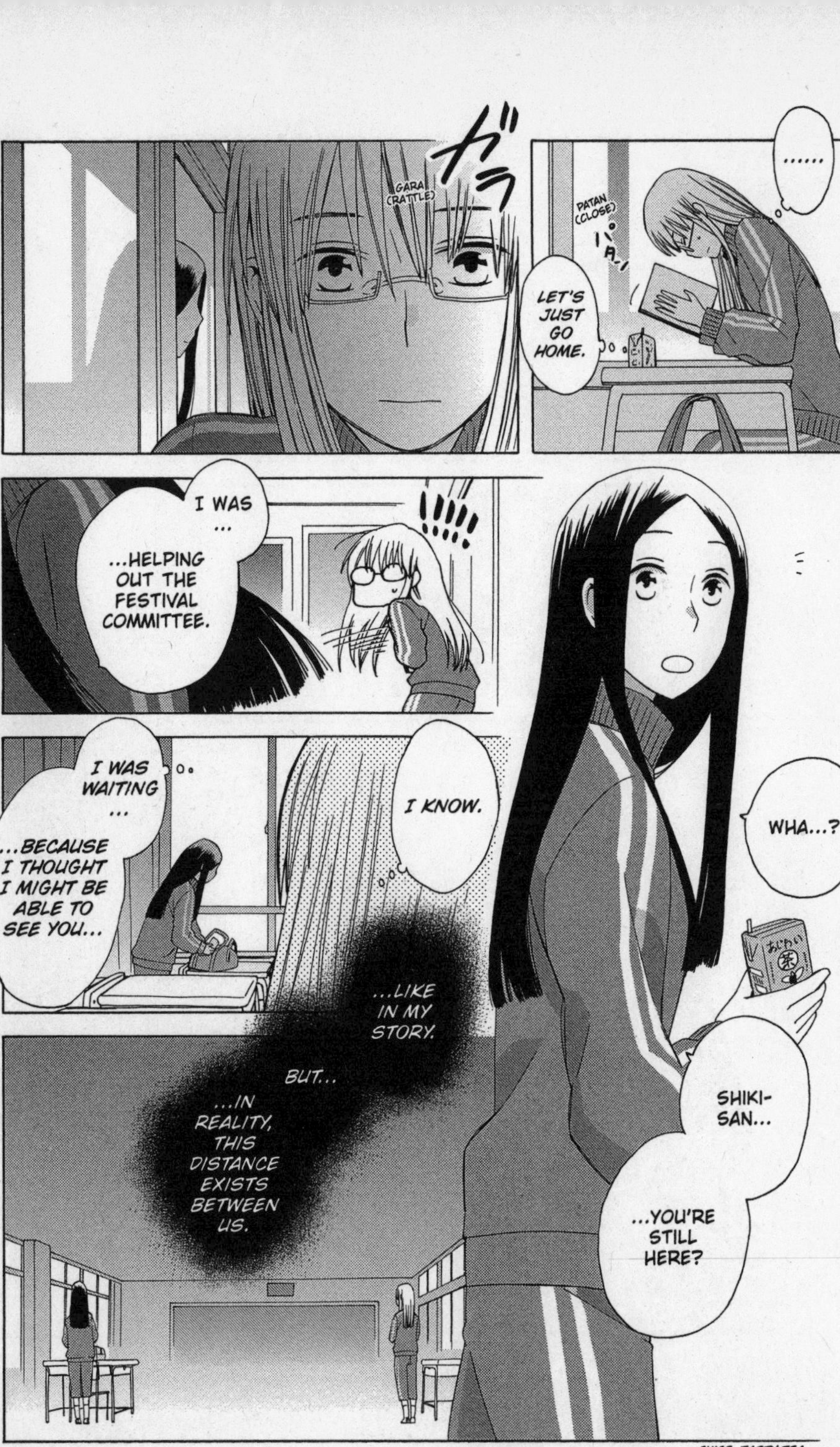
......
PATAN (CLOSE)
LET'S JUST GO HOME.
GARA (RATTLE)
WHA...?
SHIKI-SAN...
...YOU'RE STILL HERE?
I WAS ...
...HELPING OUT THE FESTIVAL COMMITTEE.
I KNOW.
I WAS WAITING ...
...BECAUSE I THOUGHT I MIGHT BE ABLE TO SEE YOU...
...LIKE IN MY STORY.
BUT...
...IN REALITY, THIS DISTANCE EXISTS BETWEEN US.

JUICE: TASTY TEA

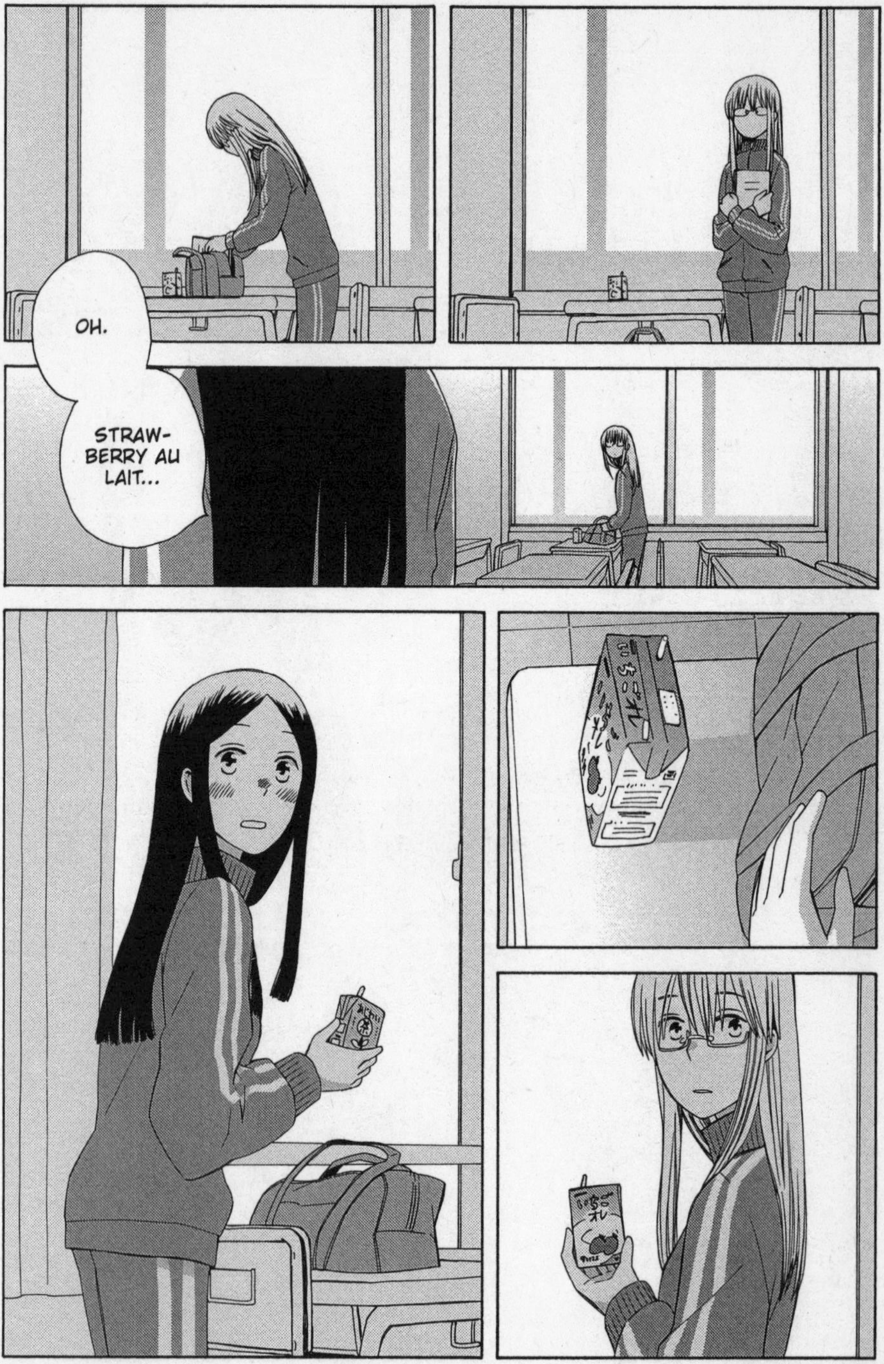
OH.
STRAW-BERRY AU LAIT...

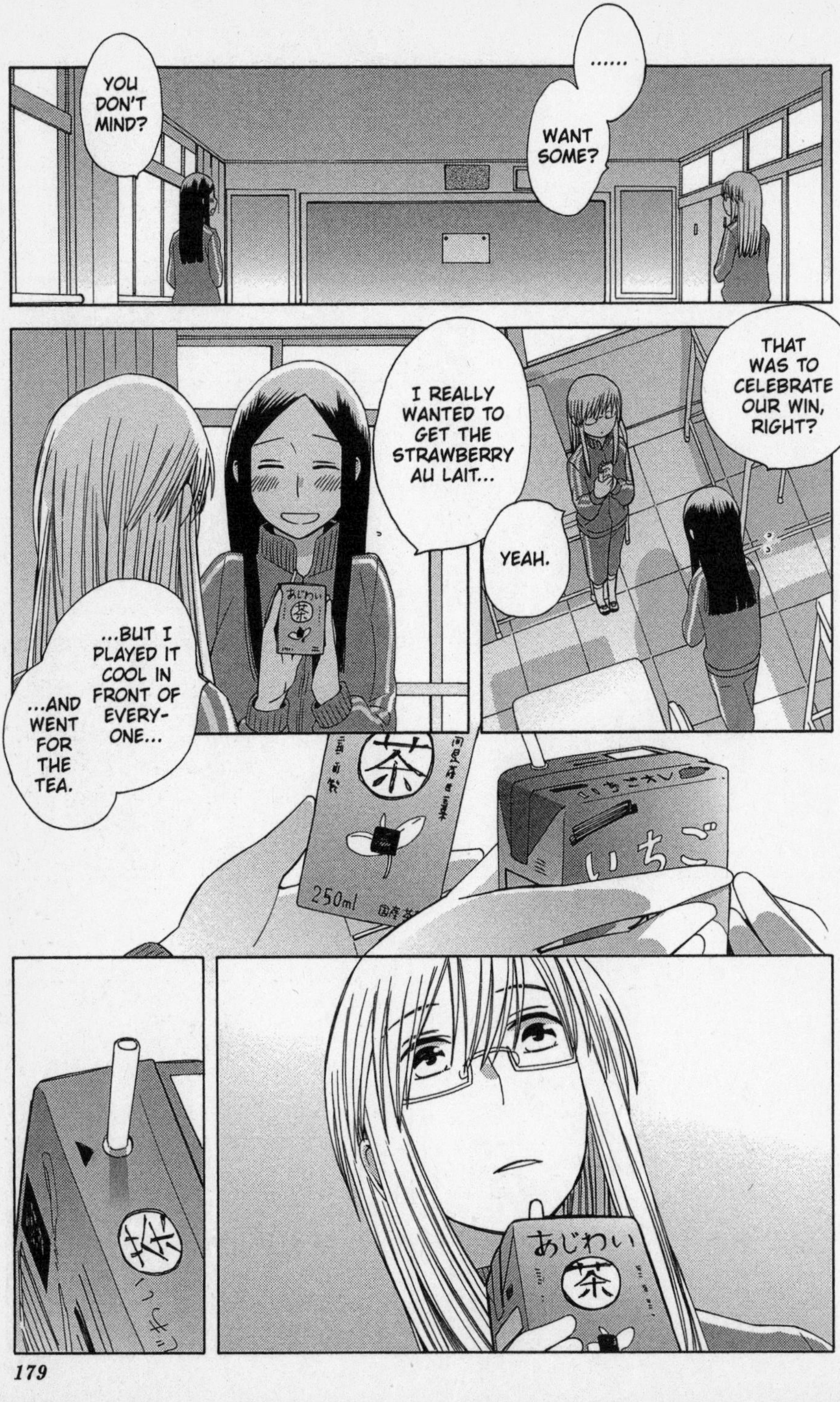
......
WANT SOME?
YOU DON'T MIND?
THAT WAS TO CELEBRATE OUR WIN, RIGHT?
YEAH.
I REALLY WANTED TO GET THE STRAWBERRY AU LAIT...
...BUT I PLAYED IT COOL IN FRONT OF EVERY-ONE...
...AND WENT FOR THE TEA.
いちご
茶
250ml
あじわい
茶

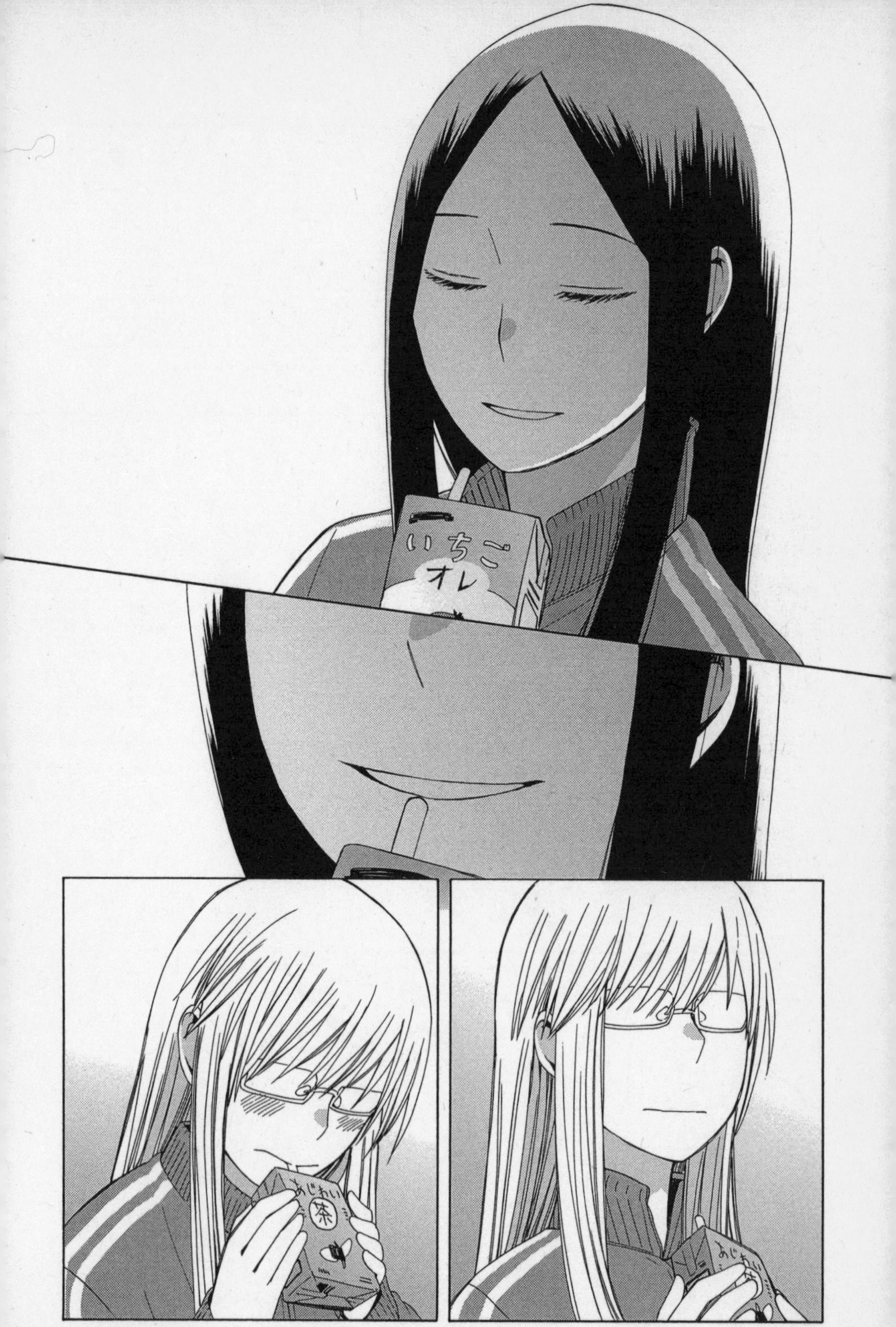
いちご
オレ
あじわい
あじわい
茶

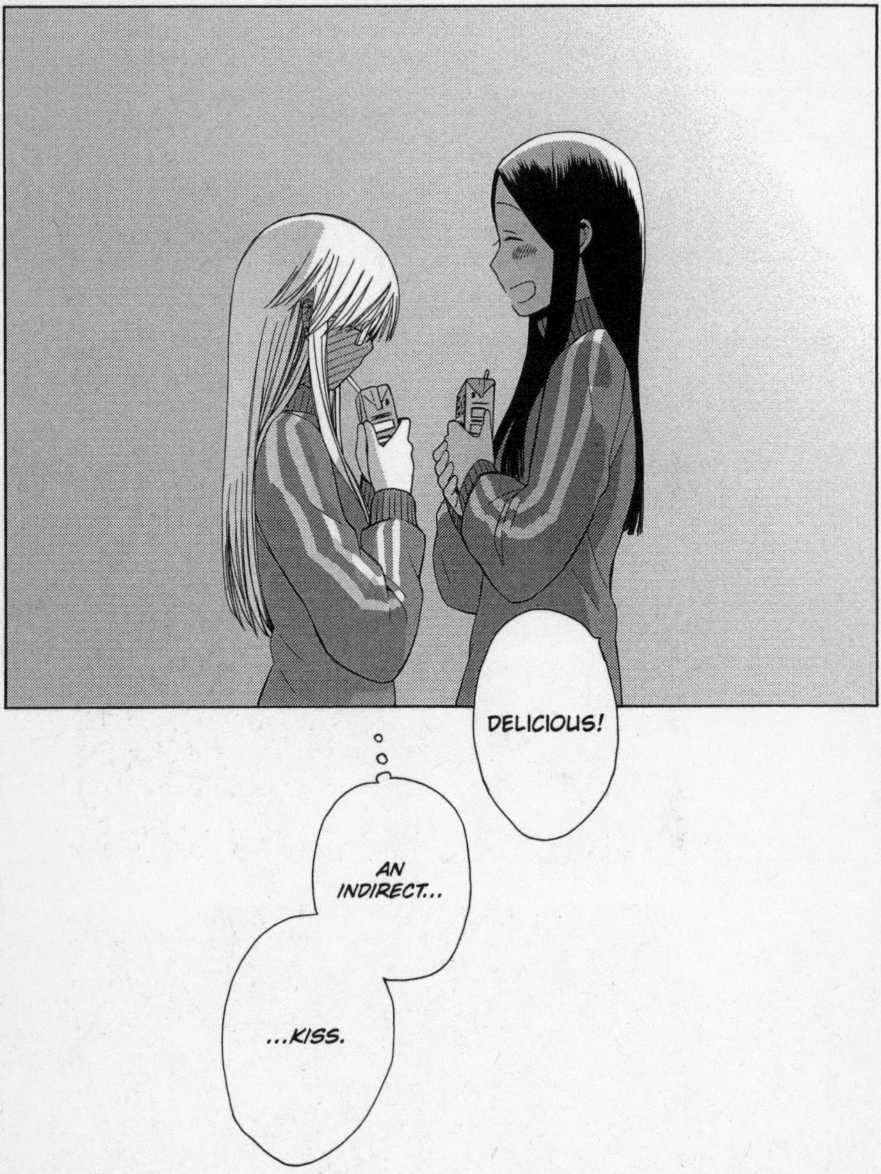
DELICIOUS!
AN INDIRECT...
...KISS.

Fin

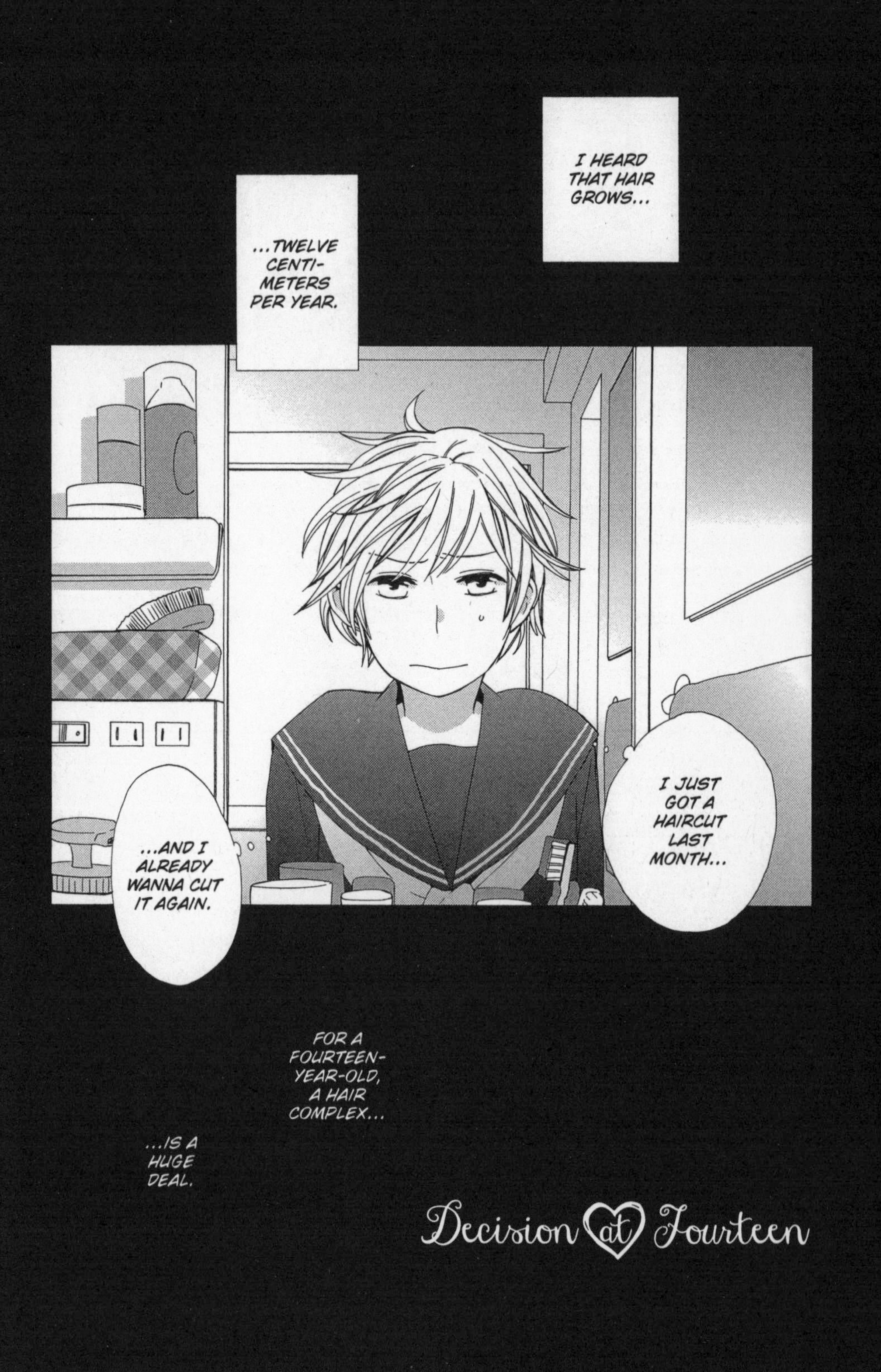
I HEARD THAT HAIR GROWS...
...TWELVE CENTIMETERS PER YEAR.
I JUST GOT A HAIRCUT LAST MONTH...
...AND I ALREADY WANNA CUT IT AGAIN.
FOR A FOURTEEN-YEAR-OLD, A HAIR COMPLEX...
...IS A HUGE DEAL.
Decision at Fourteen

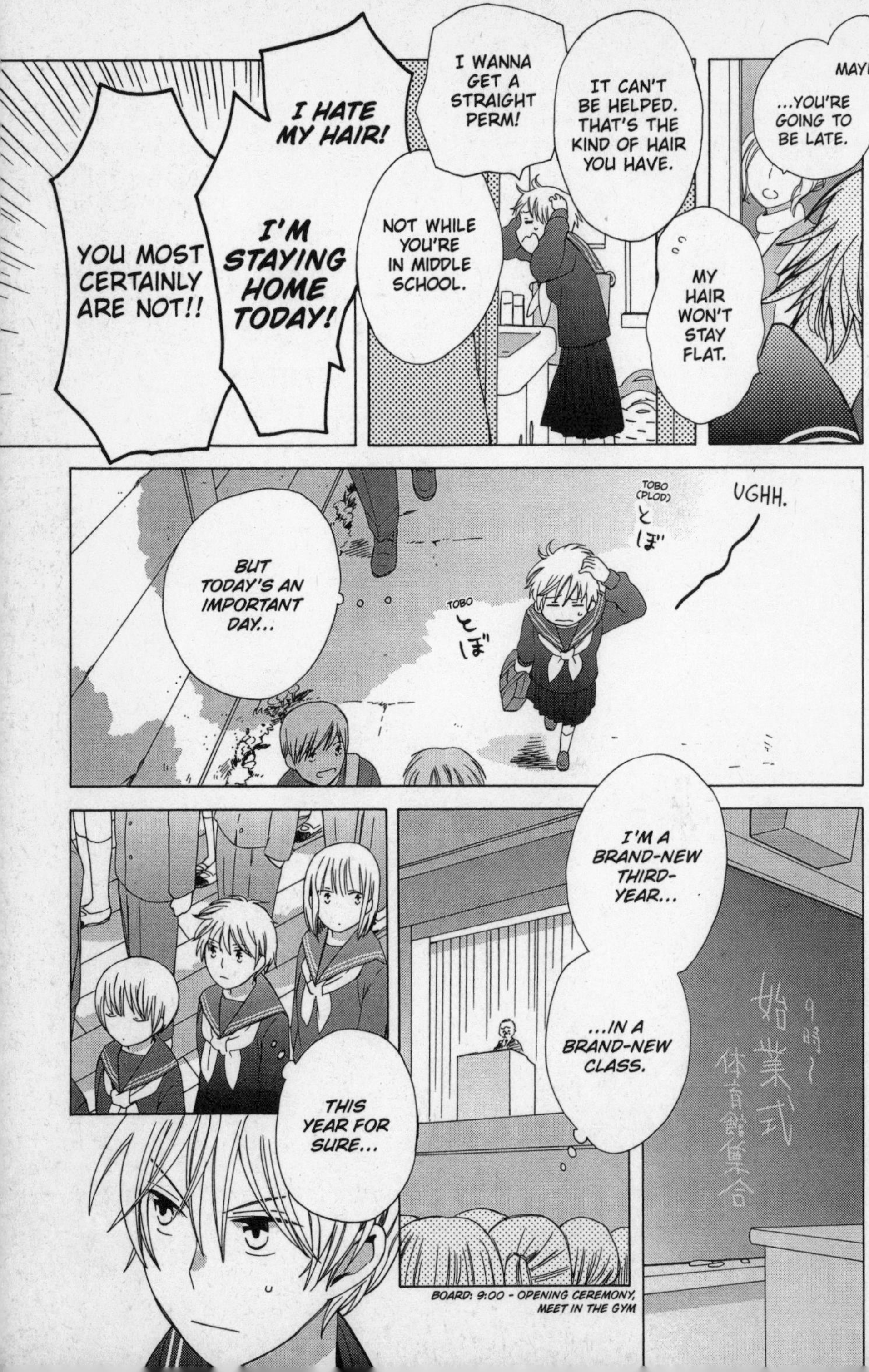
MAYU...
...YOU'RE GOING TO BE LATE.
MY HAIR WON'T STAY FLAT.
IT CAN'T BE HELPED. THAT'S THE KIND OF HAIR YOU HAVE.
I WANNA GET A STRAIGHT PERM!
NOT WHILE YOU'RE IN MIDDLE SCHOOL.
I HATE MY HAIR!
I'M STAYING HOME TODAY!
YOU MOST CERTAINLY ARE NOT!!
UGHH.
TOBO (PLOD)
とぼ
TOBO
とぼ
BUT TODAY'S AN IMPORTANT DAY...
I'M A BRAND-NEW THIRD-YEAR...
...IN A BRAND-NEW CLASS.
9時〜
始業式
体育館集合
BOARD: 9:00 - OPENING CEREMONY, MEET IN THE GYM
THIS YEAR FOR SURE...

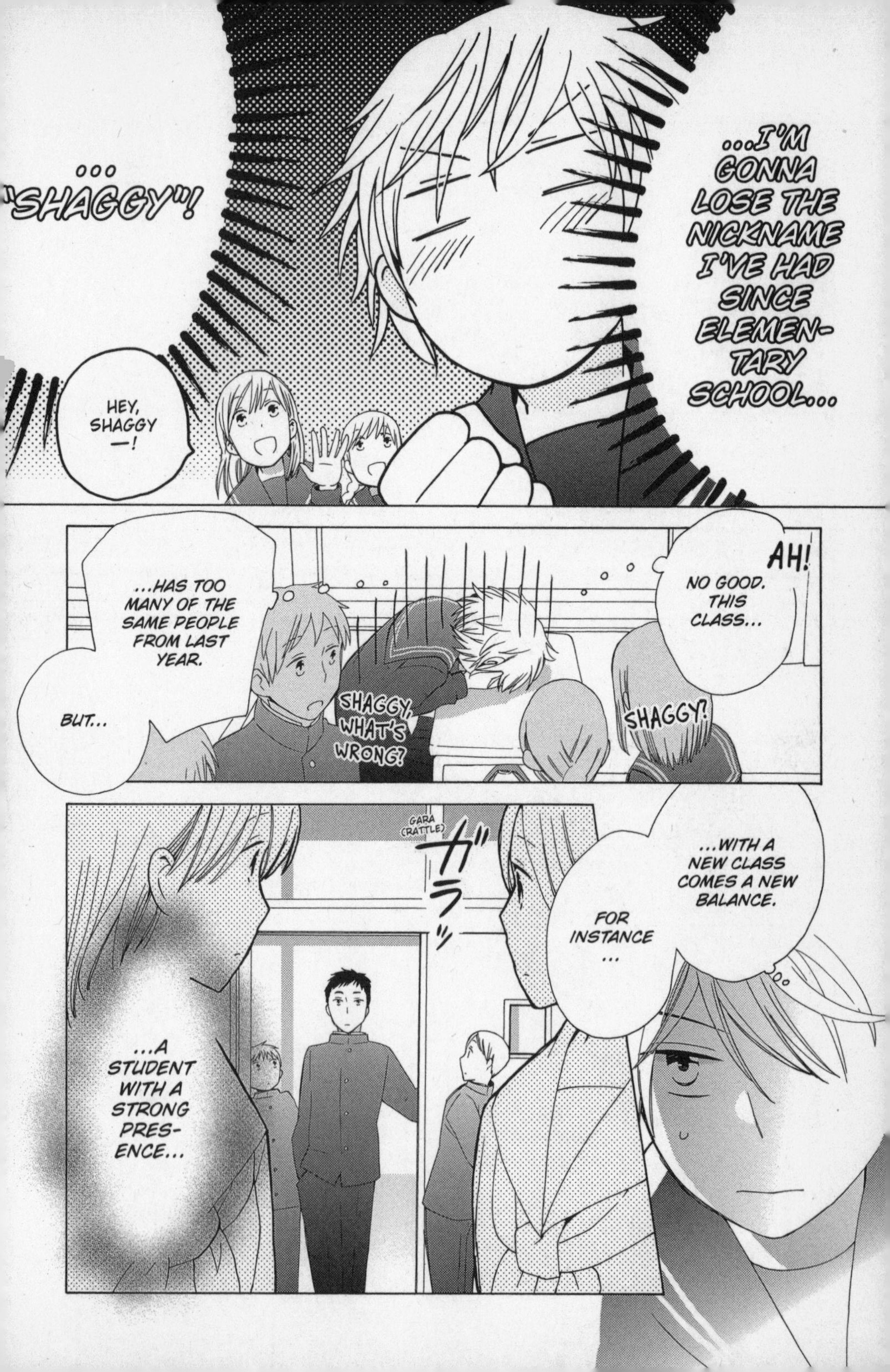
...I'M GONNA LOSE THE NICKNAME I'VE HAD SINCE ELEMENTARY SCHOOL...
... "SHAGGY"!
HEY, SHAGGY—!
AH!
NO GOOD. THIS CLASS...
SHAGGY?
SHAGGY, WHAT'S WRONG?
...HAS TOO MANY OF THE SAME PEOPLE FROM LAST YEAR.
BUT...
...WITH A NEW CLASS COMES A NEW BALANCE.
FOR INSTANCE...
GARA (RATTLE)
ガラッ
...A STUDENT WITH A STRONG PRESENCE...

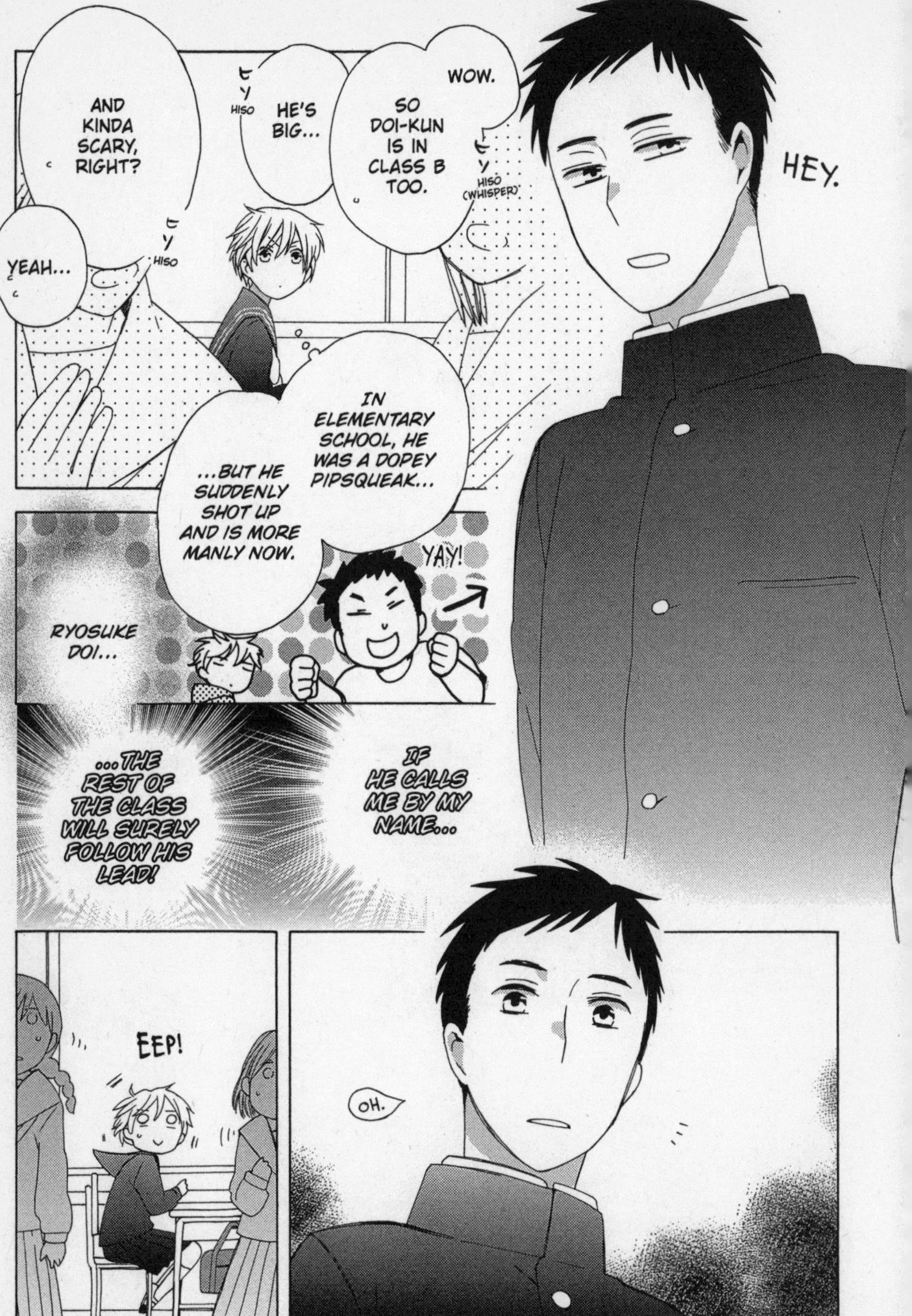
HEY.
WOW.
SO DOI-KUN IS IN CLASS B TOO.
HISO (WHISPER)
HE'S BIG...
HISO
AND KINDA SCARY, RIGHT?
YEAH...
HISO
IN ELEMENTARY SCHOOL, HE WAS A DOPEY PIPSQUEAK...
...BUT HE SUDDENLY SHOT UP AND IS MORE MANLY NOW.
YAY!
RYOSUKE DOI...
IF HE CALLS ME BY MY NAME...
...THE REST OF THE CLASS WILL SURELY FOLLOW HIS LEAD!
OH.
EEP!

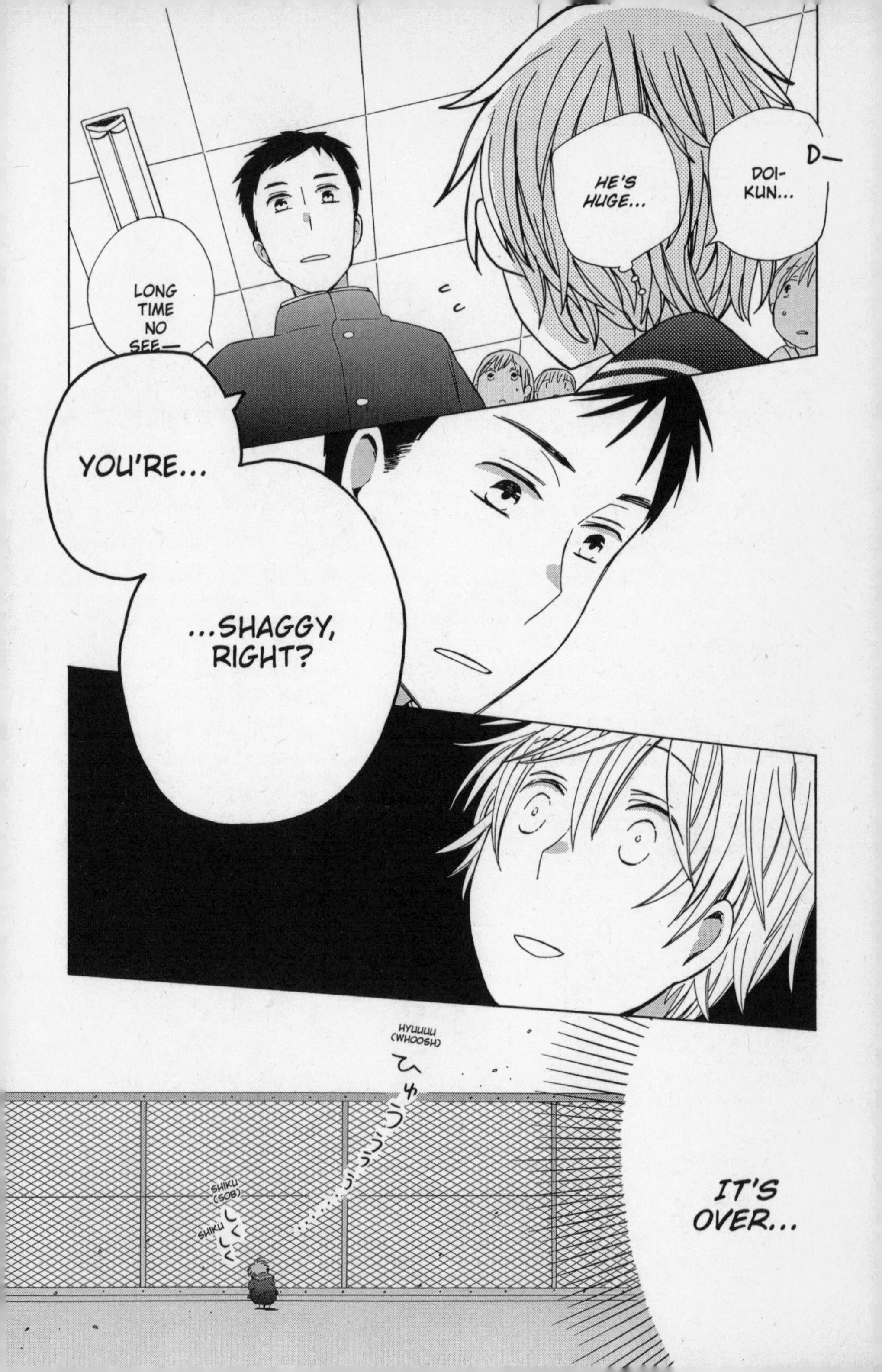
D—
DOI-KUN...
HE'S HUGE...
LONG TIME NO SEE—
YOU'RE...
...SHAGGY, RIGHT?
HYUUUU (WHOOSH)
IT'S OVER...
SHIKU (SOB) SHIKU

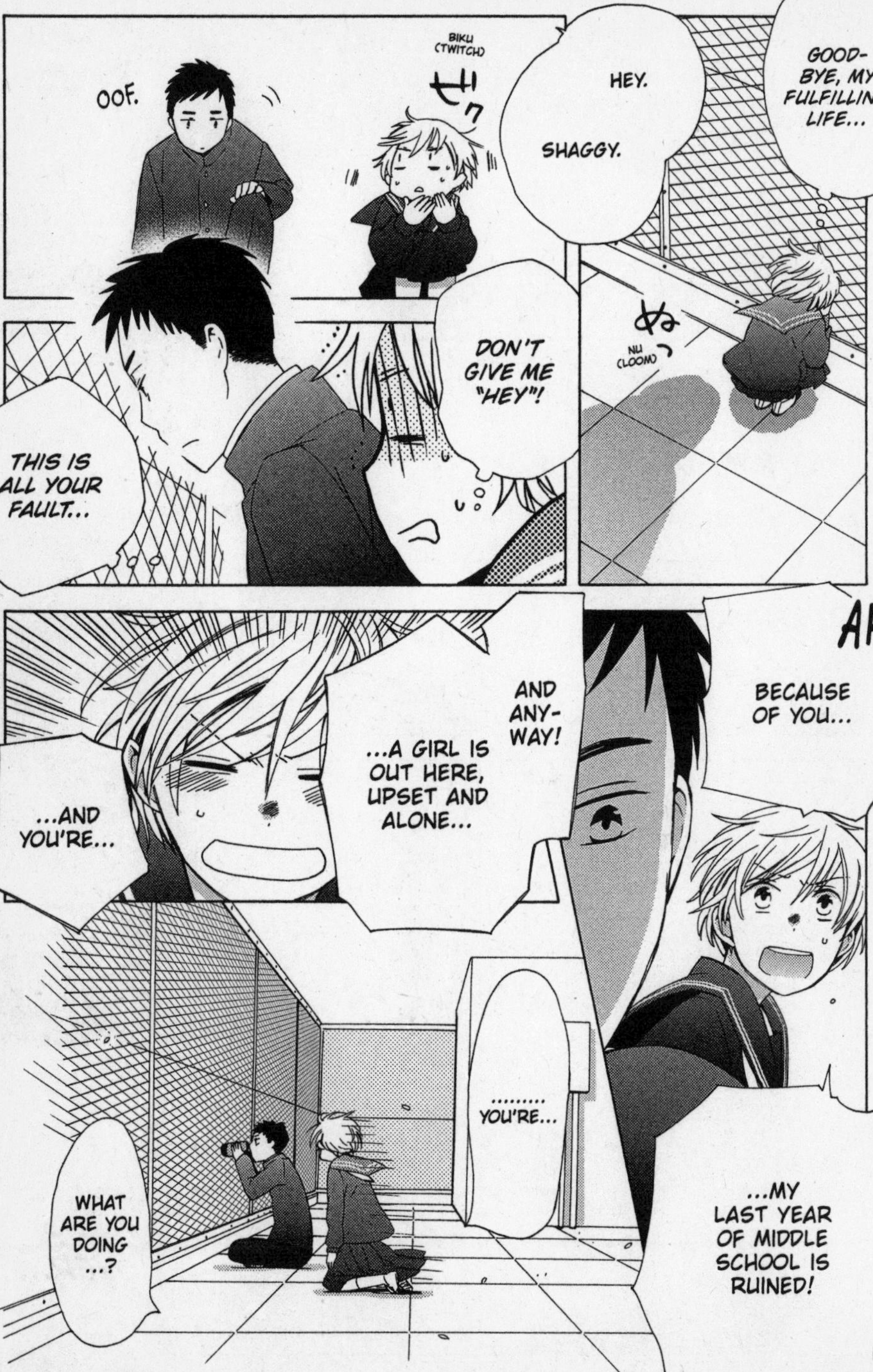
GOOD-BYE, MY FULFILLING LIFE...
NU (LOOM)
HEY.
SHAGGY.
BIKU (TWITCH)
OOF.
DON'T GIVE ME "HEY"!
THIS IS ALL YOUR FAULT...
AH!
BECAUSE OF YOU...
...MY LAST YEAR OF MIDDLE SCHOOL IS RUINED!
AND ANY-WAY!
...A GIRL IS OUT HERE, UPSET AND ALONE...
...AND YOU'RE...
.... YOU'RE...
WHAT ARE YOU DOING ...?

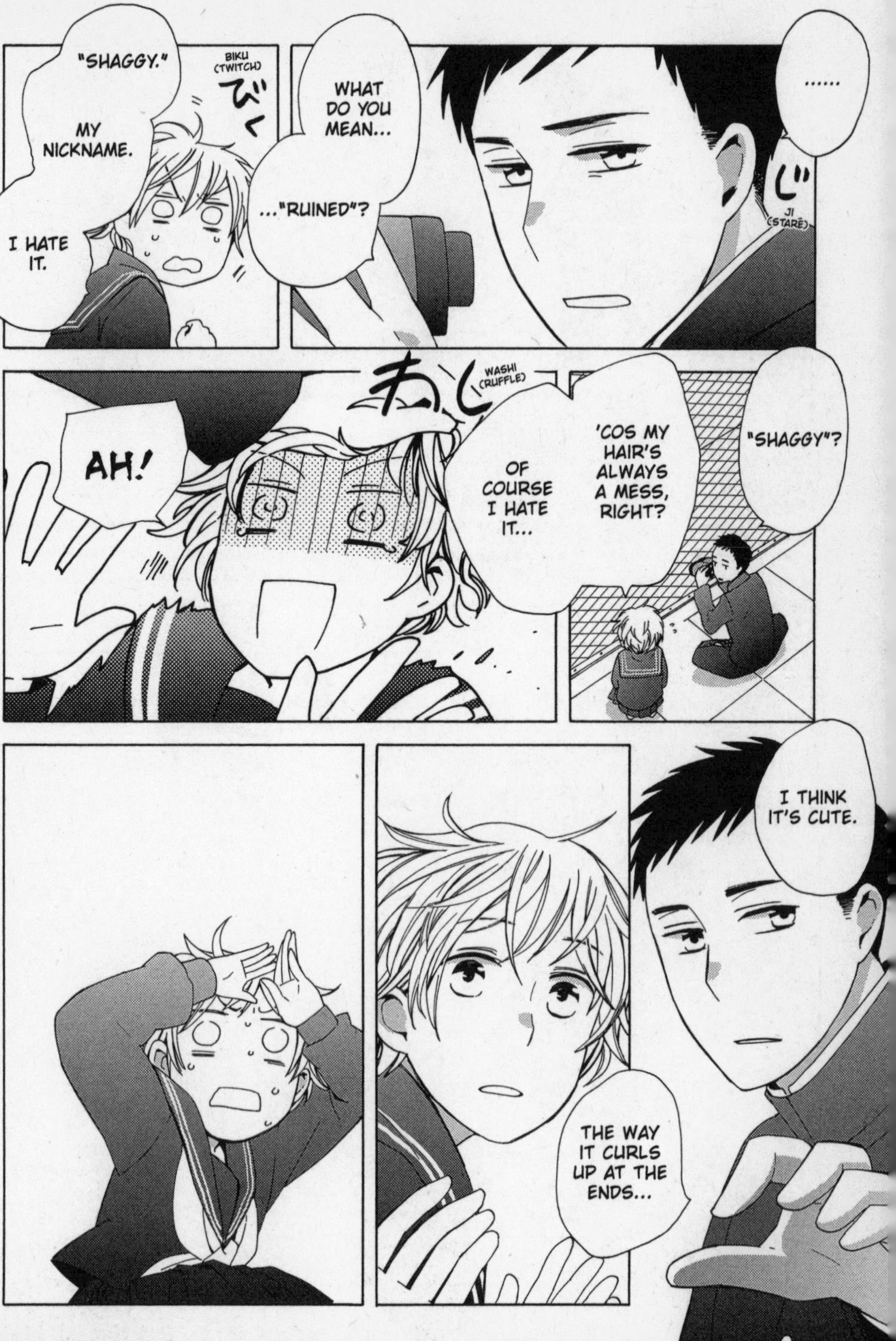
......
じ
JI (STARE)
WHAT DO YOU MEAN...
..."RUINED"?
びく
BIKU (TWITCH)
"SHAGGY."
MY NICKNAME.
I HATE IT.
"SHAGGY"?
'COS MY HAIR'S ALWAYS A MESS, RIGHT?
OF COURSE I HATE IT...
わし
WASHI (RUFFLE)
AH!
I THINK IT'S CUTE.
THE WAY IT CURLS UP AT THE ENDS...

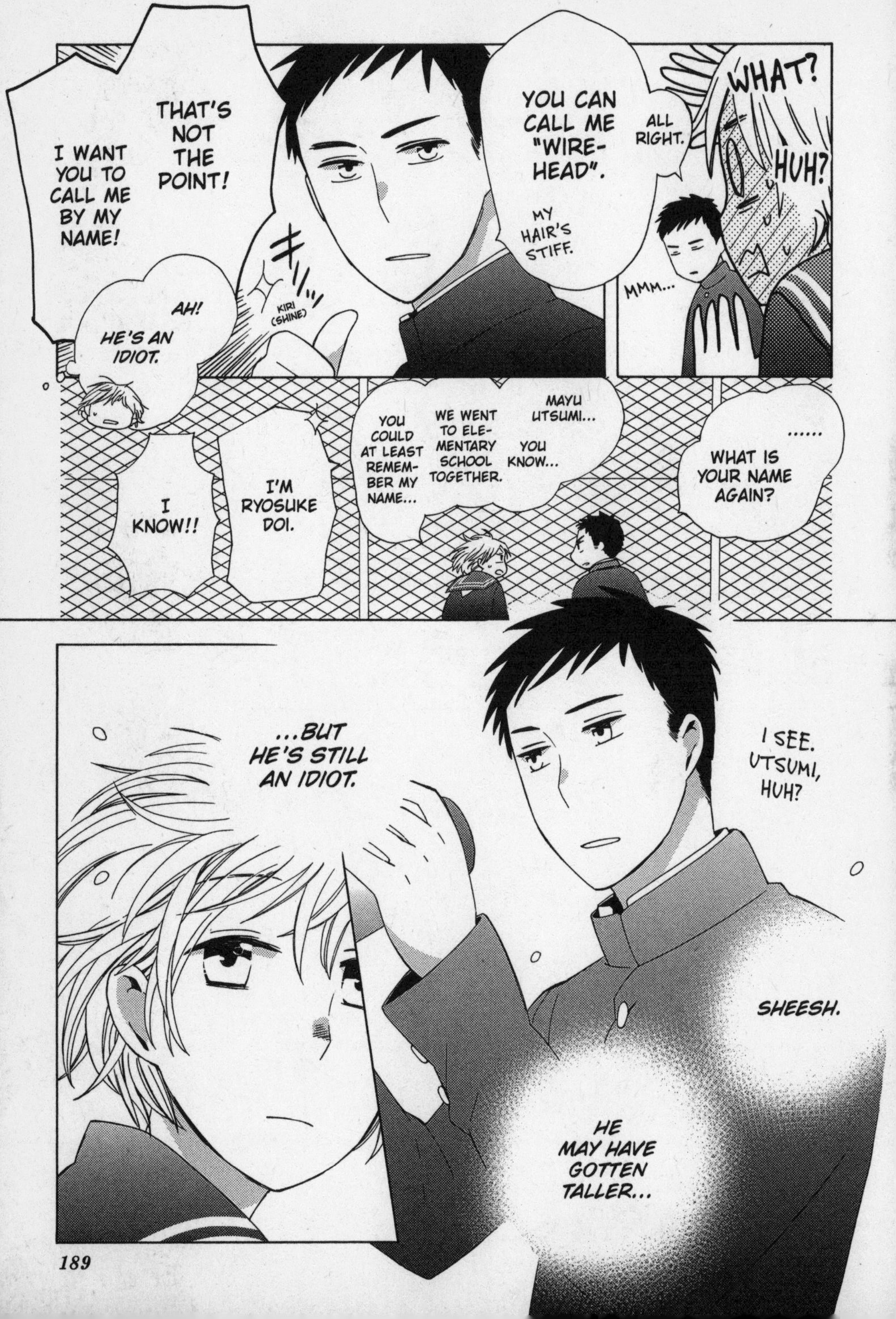
WHAT?
HUH?
ALL RIGHT.
MMM...
YOU CAN CALL ME "WIRE-HEAD".
MY HAIR'S STIFF.
THAT'S NOT THE POINT!
I WANT YOU TO CALL ME BY MY NAME!
KIRI (SHINE)
AH!
HE'S AN IDIOT.
......
WHAT IS YOUR NAME AGAIN?
MAYU UTSUMI...
YOU KNOW...
WE WENT TO ELEMENTARY SCHOOL TOGETHER.
YOU COULD AT LEAST REMEMBER MY NAME...
I'M RYOSUKE DOI.
I KNOW!!
I SEE. UTSUMI, HUH?
SHEESH.
HE MAY HAVE GOTTEN TALLER...
...BUT HE'S STILL AN IDIOT.

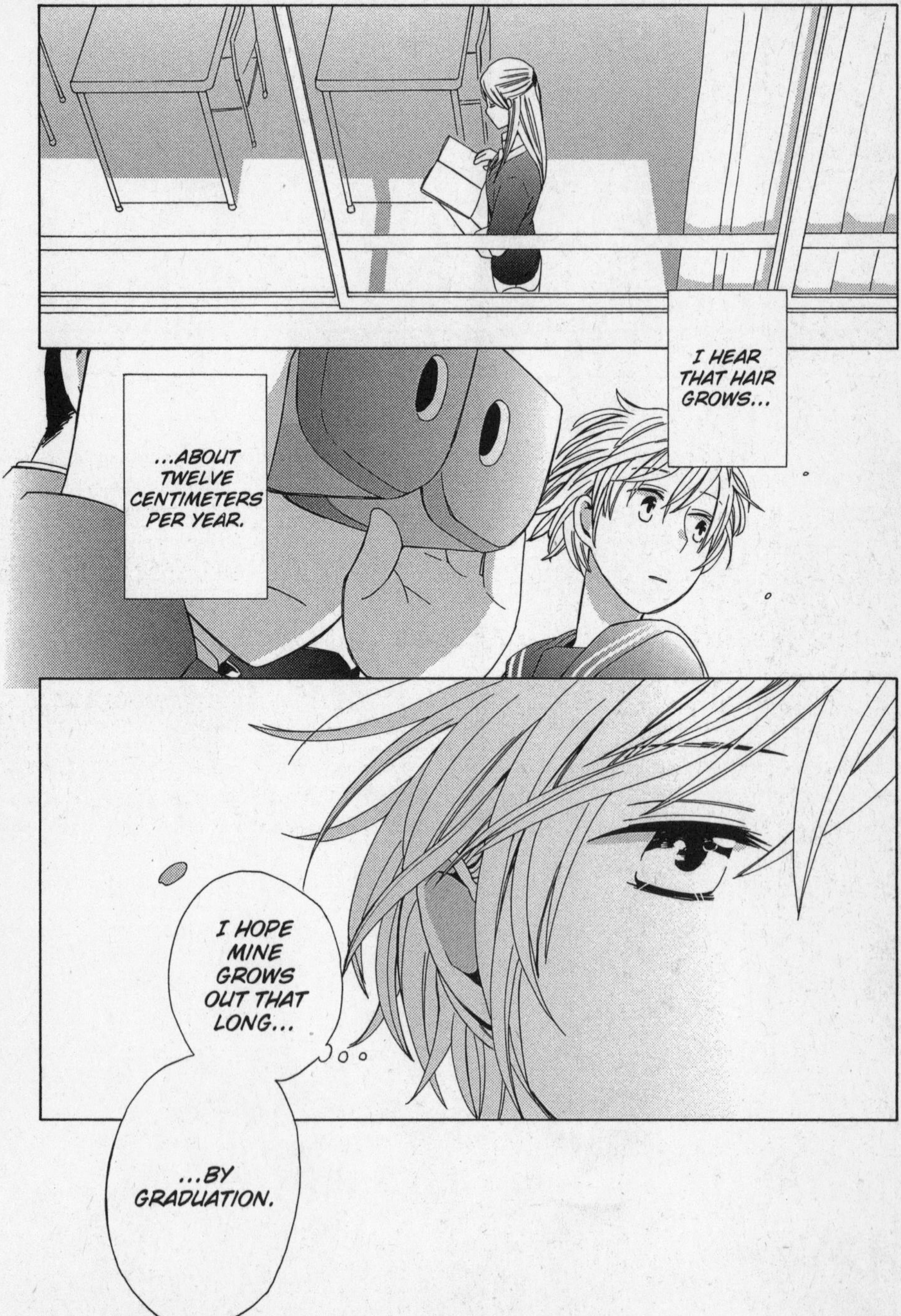
I HEAR THAT HAIR GROWS...
...ABOUT TWELVE CENTIMETERS PER YEAR.
I HOPE MINE GROWS OUT THAT LONG...
...BY GRADUATION.

Fin

Special Thanks

Iida-sama of Hakusensha

Kohei Nawata Design

My family   My great friends

Sayo Murata-chan

And all of you who are reading this now.

I hope we can meet again in the pages of Volume 5.
Thank you for reading this far!

I bought school uniforms.

Spring 2014

水谷 フーカ
Fuka Mizutani

TRANSLATION NOTES

COMMON HONORIFICS:

no honorific: Indicates familiarity or closeness; if used without permission or reason, addressing someone in this manner would constitute an insult.

-san: The Japanese equivalent of Mr./Mrs./Miss. If a situation calls for politeness, this is the fail-safe honorific.

-sama: Conveys great respect; may also indicate that the social status of the speaker is lower than that of the addressee.

-kun: Used most often when referring to boys, this indicates affection or familiarity. Occasionally used by older men among their peers, but it may also be used by anyone referring to a person of lower standing.

-chan: An affectionate honorific indicating familiarity used mostly in reference to girls; also used in reference to cute persons or animals of either gender.

-senpai: A suffix used to address upperclassmen or more experienced coworkers.

-sensei: A respectful term for teachers, artists, or high-level professionals.

Love ♡ at Fourteen

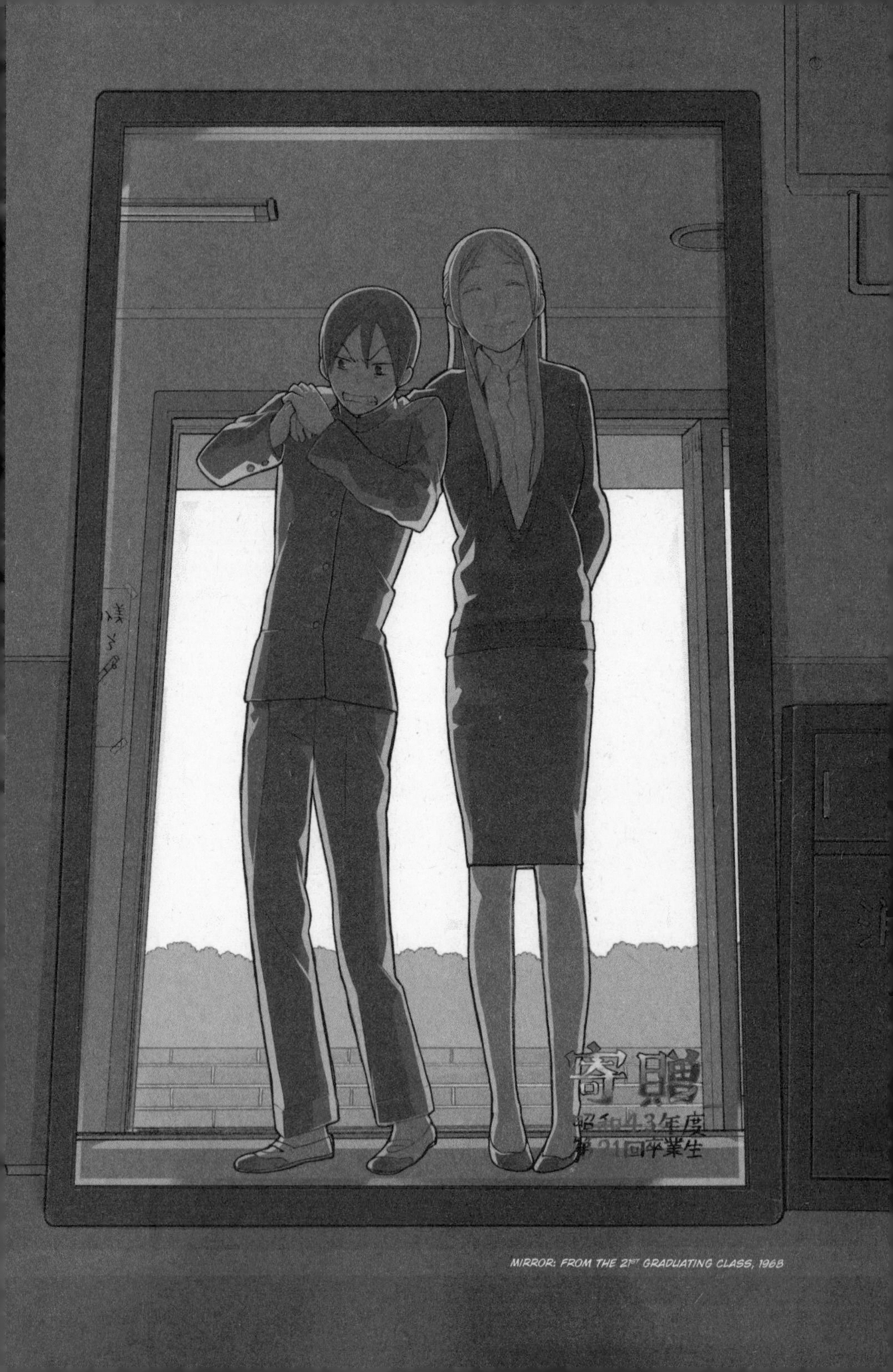
寄贈
昭和43年度
第21回卒業生
MIRROR: FROM THE 21ST GRADUATING CLASS, 1968

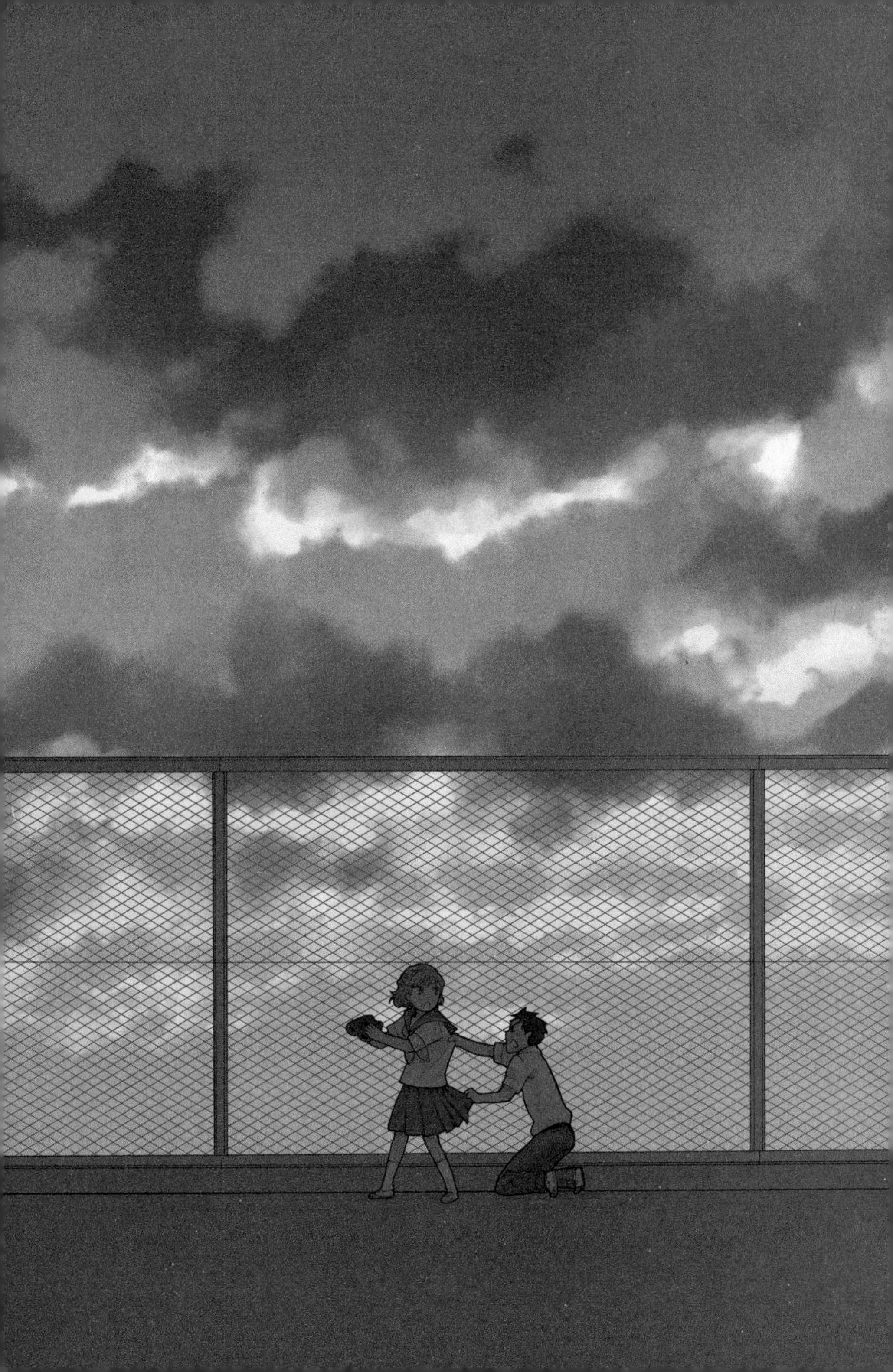

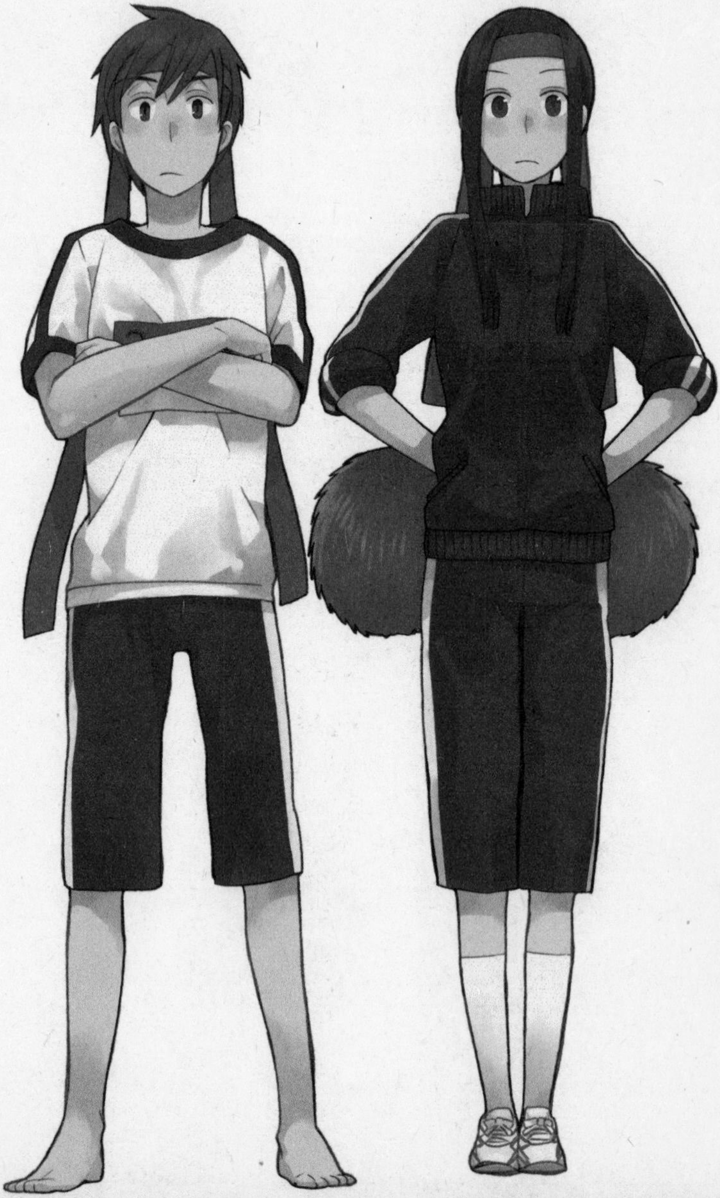

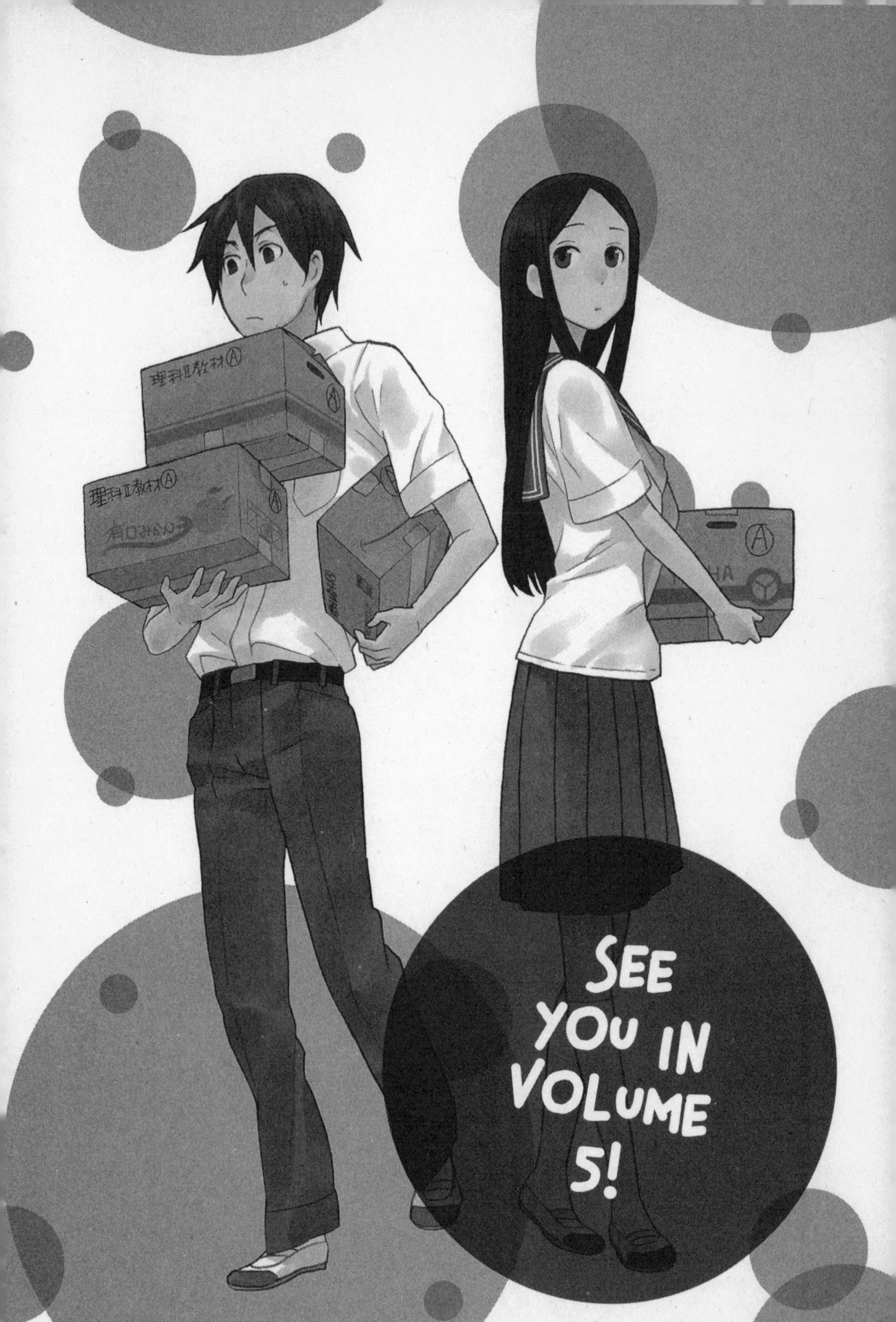
SEE YOU IN VOLUME 5!
理科Ⅱ教材
BOXES: MATERIALS